T

A Werewolf in Manhattan

"Enough heated sex scenes to satisfy any werewolf romance fan."
—*Publishers Weekly*

"Another keeper. This is not just another werewolf romance.... If you're looking for a fun, lighthearted romance with plenty of sizzle to turn up the heat on these cold winter nights, this one's for you."
—The Romance Dish

"Readers will enjoy Vicki Lewis Thompson taking a bite ... out of the Big Apple."
—Genre Go Round Reviews

"I loved this book and I can't wait for the next one ... a definite keeper and will be on my shelf for a lifetime."
—Night Owl Reviews (top pick)

"Characters that pop right off the pages."
—Romance Junkies

The *Babes on Brooms* Novels

Chick with a Charm

"Thompson again gives readers a charming, warm, humorous, sexually charged romance with likable characters, a magical dog, and a feel-good ending." —*Booklist*

Blonde with a Wand

"Extremely readable ... terrific writing and great character development.... Readers will fully enjoy this confection."
—*Romantic Times* (4 stars)

continued ...

The *Hexy* Romances

Casual Hex

"A romantic tale that's sprinkled with magic and reinforced by love . . . a fast-paced read." —Darque Reviews

"An enjoyable, lighthearted story . . . Fans will enjoy this jocular jaunt." —*Midwest Book Review*

Wild & Hexy

"Will have you laughing from the start . . . simply delightful." —Darque Reviews

"A must read!" —Fallen Angel Reviews

"A keeper for sure!" —Fresh Fiction

"Brewing with lots of magical fun." —Romance Reader at Heart

"Pure FUN from first page to last!" —The Romance Readers Connection

Over Hexed

"A snappy, funny, romantic novel." —*New York Times* bestselling author Carly Phillips

"Filled with laughs, this is a charmer of a book." —The Eternal Night

"[A] trademark blend of comedy and heart." —*Publishers Weekly*

"Thompson mixes magic, small-town quirkiness, and passionate sex." —*Booklist*

"An enchanting tale . . . and enough passion to scorch the pages." —Darque Reviews

Further Praise for
Vicki Lewis Thompson and Her Novels

"Count on Vicki Lewis Thompson for a sharp, sassy, sexy read. Stranded on a desert island? I hope you've got this book in your beach bag."   —Jayne Ann Krentz

"Wildly sexy . . . a full complement of oddball characters and sparkles with sassy humor."   —*Library Journal*

"A riotous cast of colorful characters . . . fills the pages with hilarious situations and hot, creative sex."
—*Booklist*

"Smart, spunky, and delightfully over-the-top."
—*Publishers Weekly*

"[A] lighthearted and frisky tale of discovery between two engaging people."   —*The Oakland Press* (MI)

"Delightfully eccentric . . . humor, mystical ingredients, and plenty of fun . . . a winning tale."
—The Best Reviews

"A funny and thrilling ride!"
—Romance Reviews Today

"A hilarious romp."   —Romance Junkies

"Extremely sexy . . . over-the-top . . . sparkling."
—*Rendezvous*

"A whole new dimension in laughter. A big . . . BRAVO!"
—A Romance Review

A Werewolf in Seattle

A WILD ABOUT YOU NOVEL

Vicki Lewis Thompson

A SIGNET ECLIPSE BOOK

SIGNET ECLIPSE
Published by New American Library, a division of
Penguin Group (USA) Inc., 375 Hudson Street,
New York, New York 10014, USA
Penguin Group (Canada), 90 Eglinton Avenue East, Suite 700, Toronto,
Ontario M4P 2Y3, Canada (a division of Pearson Penguin Canada Inc.)
Penguin Books Ltd., 80 Strand, London WC2R 0RL, England
Penguin Ireland, 25 St. Stephen's Green, Dublin 2,
Ireland (a division of Penguin Books Ltd.)
Penguin Group (Australia), 250 Camberwell Road, Camberwell, Victoria 3124,
Australia (a division of Pearson Australia Group Pty. Ltd.)
Penguin Books India Pvt. Ltd., 11 Community Centre, Panchsheel Park,
New Delhi - 110 017, India
Penguin Group (NZ), 67 Apollo Drive, Rosedale, Auckland 0632,
New Zealand (a division of Pearson New Zealand Ltd.)
Penguin Books (South Africa) (Pty.) Ltd., 24 Sturdee Avenue,
Rosebank, Johannesburg 2196, South Africa

Penguin Books Ltd., Registered Offices:
80 Strand, London WC2R 0RL, England

First published by Signet Eclipse, an imprint of New American Library,
a division of Penguin Group (USA) Inc.

First Printing, April 2012
10 9 8 7 6 5 4 3 2 1

To Romance Writers of America and the three authors who welcomed me into the organization many years ago—Mary Tate Engels, Rita Clay Estrada, and Parris Afton Bonds. You opened a whole world new to me. Thank you!

ACKNOWLEDGMENTS

Writing a book can be a lonely proposition, but I'm blessed with many people who make it less lonely. That includes my supportive group of writing buddies; my editor, Claire Zion; my agent, Robert Gottlieb; and my assistant, Audrey Sharpe. I acknowledge them with every book and will continue to do so, because they're awesome.

Chapter 1

Colin MacDowell was one jet-lagged werewolf. The trip from Scotland to Aunt Geraldine's private island off the coast of Washington State hadn't seemed this arduous the last time he'd made it. Apparently a seventeen-year-old pup could take more travel abuse than a thirty-two-year-old Were.

A dark-haired werewolf in human form named Knox Trevelyan had greeted Colin at SeaTac International on this balmy June afternoon and had escorted him to a private helipad. Knox operated an air taxi service, one of many businesses owned by the powerful Trevelyan pack in the Seattle-Tacoma area.

"I'm really sorry about your aunt," Knox said as he loaded Colin's suitcase and carry-on into the helicopter.

"Thank you. It was a shock." Colin was touched by the sincerity in Knox's voice.

Colin's Scottish aunt and her Vancouver-born mate, Henry Whittier, had avoided Trevelyan pack politics in favor of a quiet existence on their little island. Henry's death a few years ago hadn't made much of a stir in the local Were community, which was how Geraldine had wanted it. Colin hadn't expected anyone to mourn Geraldine's passing, either.

"I was there when she died," Knox said.

"Really!"

"Yeah. Her personal assistant, Luna Reynaud, called me in the middle of the night. I flew over to the island with the best Were medical team in Seattle. They tried, but they couldn't save her. Her heart just gave out."

"So it was you who made that emergency run?" Colin held out his hand to the pilot. "I can't tell you how grateful I am for that."

Knox returned his handshake firmly. "I wish we'd been in time."

"From what her lawyer said, nobody could have made it in time. But considering how they'd avoided being part of the community, you went beyond what could be expected."

"They didn't have much of a pack mentality, but they donated generously to our environmental work."

Colin nodded. "I did know about that."

"Besides, Geraldine was a hoot. I'd pick her up every month or so for her recreational shopping trips in Seattle. Even after Henry passed away, she still loved hitting the resale shops for designer clothes and shoes."

"I'm sure she did." The thought was bittersweet. Geraldine had specified that the contents of her closet be donated to charity, so he'd see to that while he was there. She'd willed a few pieces of jewelry to her household staff, and he'd distribute that, too.

Knox sighed. "Damn shame. Well, might as well get you over there."

"Right." Colin climbed into the small chopper. Once he was settled in, his jet-lagged brain nudged him to do the polite thing and ask how the Trevelyan pack was faring.

"Quite well," Knox replied. "My father runs a tight

ship, and all the various concerns, including my air taxi service, are showing healthy profits."

"Excellent." Colin remembered another bit of disturbing Were news that he wanted to check out while he was in America. "We got word over in Scotland about the Wallace pack—two brothers each taking human mates. Is any of that happening in your pack?"

"Not that I've heard. But I met Aidan and Roarke Wallace last year, and they both seem happy with their choices. Maybe taking a human mate can work in some cases."

"It seems bloody reckless to me." Colin had used those very words the last time he'd had an argument with his younger brother, Duncan, about human-Were mating.

Knox shrugged. "Time will tell."

"It's a colossal mistake." Colin shuddered at the possibility of humans breaching the security of the Were world. Through the ages, werewolves had suffered horribly whenever humans had uncovered their existence, so secrecy was the only protection they had.

Humans could be business associates, perhaps friends, and occasionally even lovers. But they couldn't be trusted with the knowledge that Were packs controlled much of the wealth in major cities all over the world. One Were mating with one human risked all Weres losing everything, not to mention how it would dilute the werewolf gene pool.

Then there was the issue of whether the half-breed offspring would be Were or human, something the parents wouldn't know until their child reached puberty. Colin couldn't imagine waiting until then to discover if he'd sired a Were or a human. He shuddered at the thought.

Knox reached for his headset. "You could be right,

but at this point it's not a problem we're dealing with in Seattle." He turned to Colin. "Ready to go?"

"Yes." Or as ready as he'd ever be. The sound of the rotor sabotaged any further conversation, and he was happy to slip back into his jet-lagged stupor. Exhaustion coupled with guilt sapped his desire for small talk.

Although he'd spent five summers on the island—from the age of twelve until he turned seventeen—he hadn't been back since. What was done was done and he couldn't change anything now, but regret weighed on his soul.

He could come up with a million excuses for why he hadn't visited. He'd been busy earning an economics degree. Then he'd dealt with his father's poor health, and eventually he'd taken over as laird of Glenbarra. But surely in the past fifteen years he could have spared a week or two?

Nostalgia gripped him as the chopper approached Seattle. The Space Needle rose like an exclamation mark that would forever identify the city, and would forever remind him of the day he'd spent playing tourist with Geraldine. She'd treated him to dinner in the Needle's revolving restaurant where he'd gazed endlessly at the lights that sparkled below them like the Milky Way.

Closing his eyes, Colin leaned back against the headrest and dozed. He roused himself as the chopper veered northwest and skimmed over Puget Sound headed for the San Juans, an archipelago that included dozens of islands large and small. They all had official names on the map, but Colin had forgotten what his aunt's island was called. Now he just thought of it as Le Floret.

On his first visit, he'd told Geraldine that the island looked like a giant clump of broccoli rising from the sea. She'd promptly declared they would call it Le Floret from now on instead of whatever boring name the map showed. She'd laughed whenever she'd told that story. She'd had a great laugh.

As Knox began the descent, wind from the spinning blades ruffled water bright as polished chrome. Colin blamed the glare for making his eyes water. Taking off his Wayfarers, he wiped away the moisture before settling the sunglasses back in place. Soon he'd walk into Whittier House, and Aunt Geraldine wouldn't be there. That was going to be very tough.

A maverick to the end, she'd nixed the idea of a funeral. Her lawyer had read Colin her final instructions over the phone, and they were typical Geraldine. *Just dump my ass—I mean ashes—in with Henry's and sprinkle them on Happy Hour Beach while you toast us with a very dry martini. Make sure we're shaken, not stirred.*

Then the lawyer had dropped the bombshell. Geraldine had left all her worldly possessions—the island, the turreted, Scottish-style mansion Henry had built for her, and every valuable antique in that mansion—to Colin. It was an incredibly wonderful gesture, but he wished to hell she hadn't done it.

Much as he'd loved his irreverent aunt, he had no use for an island and an estate halfway around the world from Glenbarra. Sure, he had some fond memories of Le Floret and Whittier House, but keeping the property would be sentimental and impractical. As the new laird, he couldn't afford to be either.

Geraldine's lawyer had provided the name of a reputable Were real estate agent from Seattle, and Colin had contacted him before leaving Scotland. The agent would arrive the following afternoon, which would give Colin a chance to scatter the ashes and get some sleep.

That left the matter of the staff at Aunt Geraldine's estate. That old codger Hector was still the groundskeeper, but the others had been hired since Colin had last visited. Perhaps the new owner would need them, but if not, Colin would hand the more recent hires a generous severance check and a letter of recommendation. He'd set up some sort of pension for Hector in recognition of his many years of service.

Selling a place that had meant so much to his aunt didn't make him particularly happy. Geraldine had probably hoped that he'd cherish the estate as she had. But he couldn't imagine flying more than twelve hours each way and dealing with an eight-hour time difference on a regular basis.

Logically, he had no choice but to unload what could become an albatross around his neck. The proceeds would bolster the MacDowell coffers, and after years of his father's financial neglect and Duncan's carefree lifestyle, the coffers could use some bolstering.

The rapid beat of helicopter blades vibrated the crystal chandelier over Luna Reynaud's head and sent music and rainbows dancing through the entry hall. Tension coiled in her stomach. This Scottish laird had the power to ruin everything for her and the rest of the staff if he refused to consider her plan.

But he would consider it. He *had* to. She'd finally found a place where she belonged. Not only was she living among Weres for the first time in her life, but she was part of a close-knit community. She wasn't about to give that up without a fight. The loss of Geraldine had been a cruel blow, and she grieved along with the rest of the staff. If, on top of that, she lost this precious haven, too . . .

Well, she wouldn't. No doubt Colin would arrive planning to sell the island. Although Geraldine had lovingly recounted tales from the five summers he'd spent here, he hadn't been back since, so how much did he really care about it?

It was impractical as a second home, or in his case, second castle. Geraldine had called it a house, but no mere house had four towers, sixteen turrets, fourteen bedrooms, ten fireplaces, and twenty giant tapestries.

But if Luna could convince Colin that this old pile, as Geraldine used to call it, would make a fabulous Were vacation spot, half the battle was won. If he'd trust her to manage it for him, then *voila*, an income stream for him and jobs for her and the staff. Most important of all, she wouldn't have to leave a place that felt like home and people who had become her family.

She planned to appeal to his business sense, but she hoped he had a sentimental streak, too. Repeating the stories Geraldine had told her might stir his nostalgic memories and make him reluctant to sell.

She wouldn't start her campaign right away, though. First she'd let him settle in and recover from his long journey. To help him do that, she'd provide him with every comfort Whittier House had to offer.

Preparations for his stay had begun the moment she'd been told of his arrival. When Geraldine was alive, Luna had managed the household while Dulcie and Sybil cleaned, Janet cooked, and Hector took care of the grounds with the help of some local teenaged Weres. But so much hinged on Colin's visit that Luna had spent the past few days working side by side with Dulcie and Sybil.

She'd oiled woodwork, polished silver, and scrubbed the pink marble floor in the entry hall until she could see her face in it. This morning she'd wielded a duster on an extension pole to clean the magnificent chandelier that greeted visitors when they first walked through the carved front door. Then she'd switched it on to make sure that every facet sparkled.

But now late-afternoon sunlight streamed through a window set above the massive door, a window placed there specifically to fill the entry hall with rainbows on sunny days. Luna turned off the artificial light. No point in letting Colin think she wasted resources. He was a Scot, after all, and they were supposed to be frugal.

Although she'd spent the first twelve years of her life in New Orleans, the city that proudly suggested "Let the good times roll," she could be frugal, too. Thriftiness was one of the virtues that she intended to mention when she proposed her concept. Self-reliance was another.

She'd never known her father, and her mother had died when she was eight. She'd fled her grandmother's house at fourteen and had been on her own ever since. She'd survived just fine.

Pulling her phone from the pocket of her tailored slacks, she called Dulcie. "Time for y'all to line up."

"I heard the helicopter. I'll get Sybil." Dulcie's voice was breathless. No doubt she was anxious about this moment, too, because she knew that they had to impress their visitor or risk leaving the island forever.

"Get Janet, too."

"She'll be watching her soap."

"I know." Janet's skills rivaled those of Emeril, but she was also addicted to soap operas and had a flat screen in the kitchen. "Tell her to TiVo it and march herself out here. We want him to fall in love with Whittier House all over again, so fawning is in order."

"I'll get her."

"Thanks. I estimate we have less than five minutes before Hector meets him at the helipad and brings him in." She mentally crossed her fingers. She didn't worry so much about the behavior of the two housekeepers and the cook, who all understood the gravity of the situation.

Hector was a different story. He'd been working for Geraldine and Henry ever since their marriage forty-five years ago. He considered himself part of the family rather than an employee. At sixty-eight, he was probably ready to retire now that they were both gone. He had nothing to lose and didn't take kindly to direction.

When she'd suggested using the electric cart to transport Colin and his luggage to the house, Hector had rolled his eyes. "It's just Colin, for crying out loud. He knows the place backward and forward. He doesn't expect that kind of mollycoddling."

"He might now that he's a laird." Luna wasn't clear on exactly what being a laird entailed, but the title sounded elegant to her. Certainly worthy of being met with an electric cart.

"It's no more than a hundred yards," Hector had said. "Ferrying a perfectly healthy Were from the helipad to the front door is plain ridiculous, and Colin would think I'd gone senile if I tried it. Most folks have wheels on their suitcases. If he doesn't, I'll help carry. That's plenty hospitable, if you ask me."

Luna had known better than to argue with Hector. Short of driving the cart herself, which she didn't intend to do because she wanted to be waiting in the entry hall with the staff lined up like they did in the movies, she was stuck with letting Colin walk and drag his suitcase along the curved and somewhat bumpy path from the helipad to the front door.

Sybil, who was in her mid-forties, arrived in the entry hall ahead of Dulcie and Janet. Short, dark-haired, and plump, Sybil had given up on finding a mate and now spent her free time making decorative items from driftwood. Dulcie, a curvaceous, fiftyish redhead with traces of gray in her curly hair, showed up next. She'd been widowed young and still dreamed of finding someone to share her golden years.

That wasn't the case with Janet, a buxom blonde in her late forties who had no interest in another mate.

She'd adored her late husband and couldn't imagine anyone else measuring up. Janet entered the hallway last.
She wore a bib apron over her T-shirt and jeans.

Luna recognized the cook's shirt because it was one
of Janet's favorites. It spelled out YOU CAN'T TOUCH THIS!
in bright red letters across her ample chest. Fortunately
the apron covered most of the message. Geraldine had
never required uniforms of her staff, so they all dressed
for comfort and as an expression of their personal style.

Sybil favored sweats and loose cotton blouses that
disguised her ample figure, while Dulcie liked capris and
sparkly T-shirts that highlighted her shape. Luna wondered now if Colin would be expecting uniforms. The
three female Weres looked more like girlfriends who'd
met for coffee than a trained staff of professionals. But it
was too late to do anything about it now.

Besides, with Geraldine gone, Luna wasn't sure how
much authority she had to make changes. Probably none,
and besides, she didn't want to alienate anyone by imply-
ing that their clothing wasn't appropriate. They'd approved of her plan for saving their jobs, but that didn't
mean she was in charge of the entire operation. At least
not yet.

In fact, she was technically the junior member of the
group since she was the last one hired. Nobody deferred
to her. In fact, all three affectionately teased her about her
Southern accent and her celibate existence, which was admittedly unusual for a female Were of twenty-seven.

Luna didn't mind the teasing, but she wasn't ready to
explain that she was a virgin who'd never dared to have
a relationship with a Were or a human. Her human mother
had died without telling her that she'd been fathered by
a Were. On a stormy night soon after her fourteenth
birthday, she'd had her first period, which she'd expected,
followed by her first shift, which she hadn't.

She'd run away, convinced that she was a monster who would be hunted and killed. Although she eventually figured out she wasn't the only Were in the world, she also knew that she was a half-breed. She assumed that wasn't a good thing and could mean rejection if any Were found out.

She'd buried that secret deep and kept on the move, trusting neither humans nor Weres. She hadn't felt safe until she'd set foot on Le Floret and had met Geraldine. For the first time, she'd remained in one place long enough to bond with Were females. Maybe someday she'd work up the courage to confide her half-breed ancestry to her new friends, if they all managed to stay here under Colin's ownership.

She'd lived on the island less than a year, replacing a Were who'd made the mistake of patronizing Geraldine as if age had left her mentally incapable. Luna was grateful for that departed Were's tactless behavior, because it had allowed Luna to live in a place that had felt like home from the moment she'd arrived.

Janet took off her apron and glanced around, as if searching for a place to put it. Now, every word on her shirt stood out as if written in flashing neon.

"I think wearing the apron is better," Luna said. "That way he knows immediately that you're the chef. He'll be tired from all that traveling, and he's dealing with grief just like the rest of us. He might have trouble remembering who we are and what each of us does."

Sybil grinned. "Personally, I think he'll remember that T-shirt, no problem."

"My T-shirt?" Janet glanced down at her chest and groaned. "I completely forgot I was wearing this one." She quickly donned the apron again. "I'm not used to having a male around."

"Hector's a male," Dulcie pointed out.

"I mean a *male*, as in broad shoulders, narrow hips, nice tush. In other words, not Hector."

"I hadn't even thought about whether he'd be good-looking or not," Sybil said. "Does anybody know?"

"Geraldine showed me a picture of him when he was seventeen," Luna said. "He was tall and skinny, with big hands and feet." And a beautiful smile, but she decided not to mention that. They'd accuse her of being interested, which she wasn't.

Dulcie threw back her shoulders and tugged down the hem of her rhinestone-studded shirt. "You know what they say about big hands and big feet. And he'll probably sound like Sean Connery. I'd love me some Scottish brogue."

"Geraldine said he was privately tutored to minimize his accent," Luna said.

"Even better." Dulcie smiled. "A cultured Scottish brogue."

Janet elbowed her. "Cool it, Dulcie. He's thirty-two, so he's young enough to be your kid."

"Just barely! I may be a wolf, but that doesn't mean I can't be a cougar, too."

"Plus he's probably pledged to some high-placed Were back in Scotland," Sybil added. "Someone to fill the slot as the next lairdess."

"*Lairdess*?" Janet frowned. "I don't know beans about Scottish titles, but that can't be right."

Sybil started to giggle. "Yeah, that has to be wrong. Can you imagine being called *Your Lairdess*?"

"Especially if she has some junk in the trunk." Dulcie got the giggles, too.

Janet began prancing around with her fanny sticking out. "Make way for Her Royal Lairdess! Her Royal Lairdess is coming through!" She was in midprance, with everyone laughing, including Luna, when the front door opened.

She swung around to face the door. So much for the dignified greeting she'd planned. Then she looked into the bluest eyes she'd ever seen, and forgot every blessed preparation she'd made for this moment.

Colin MacDowell was, hands down, the most beautiful creature in the universe.

Chapter 2

Apparently Luna had expected someone who looked like the seventeen-year-old in the picture she'd seen. But that gangly teenager had been replaced by an adult Were who took her breath away.

His features had matured into crisp, classic lines — strong nose, deep-set eyes, chiseled jaw. If pressed to name the color of his collar-length hair, she'd call it brown. But that wouldn't begin to explain the strands of gold, bronze, and caramel highlighted by the sunlight pouring through the front door.

He wore slacks, a dress shirt unbuttoned at the neck, and a sport coat. On anyone else, the clothes would be ordinary, but Colin, backlit as he was, looked like a god, or perhaps an angel. And not one of those gauzy, delicate angels, either. Colin radiated power.

She drew in a breath and the sweet scent of him filled her with a kind of hunger she'd never felt before. His scent was familiar, as if she knew him from somewhere, and yet that was impossible.

Tucking his sunglasses into the breast pocket of his jacket, he released the handle of his rolling bag and stepped toward her. His smile was a ghost of the one she'd seen in his teenaged picture. Carefree innocence had been replaced with a polite gesture tinged by weariness. She wanted to wrap her arms around him and give whatever comfort she could.

"Hello." He held out a large hand to her. "I'm Colin MacDowell, Geraldine's nephew." A slight accent that sounded almost British flavored his speech.

"I know." Her words were more an expression of awe than a comment. That rich baritone of his would charm a female regardless of the accent. She took his very warm hand and held on as she gazed at him with rapture.

His eyebrows lifted in a subtle but unspoken question.

That silent signal brought her back to reality and her plan. She let go of his hand and cleared her throat. "We are so pleased to welcome y'all to Whittier House."

"*Y'all*?" He looked puzzled. "You're not from the Trevelyan pack, are you?"

"I'm not from Seattle, Your . . ." Grace? Highness? Lairdness? She should have researched his title and figured out what to call him. She'd been so busy scrubbing and polishing that she hadn't thought of it. "Your, um, Sirness." She winced. That wasn't right, either. Behind her she heard a snort from someone, probably Janet.

Colin ducked his head, obviously hiding a smile. Great. Now he was laughing at her.

When he looked up again, his face was composed but some of the weariness had left his expression. "Colin's fine. Where are you from?"

"New Orleans, Louisiana, sir."

"Colin," he prompted again.

"Colin." Saying his name felt like a privilege. She'd have to get over this hero-worship, though, if she expected to convince him that he could leave Whittier House in her capable hands.

"I didn't know any Weres lived that far south."

She gave him the story she'd used with everyone. "My parents were loners, and after they died, I came up here to be with other Weres." It was a partial truth. She'd come in search of her father, not knowing he'd died before she was born.

"And your name is . . . ?"

"Oh!" Her face grew hot. She couldn't believe she hadn't introduced herself. "I'm Luna Reynaud. I was your aunt's personal assistant for about ten months, and I managed the household for her."

"I'll bet she also taught you to mix a very dry martini, shaken, not stirred."

"As a matter of fact, she did." She paused, thinking that might be a subtle hint that he could use a drink. "I can fix one in about two minutes if you'd like a—"

"I don't need it yet. But her instructions for scattering her, uh . . . ashes . . ." He looked down and swallowed. "Hers and Henry's, that is. She wants me to toast the . . . the *occasion* with her favorite beverage."

His barely disguised grief tugged at her heart. "On Happy Hour Beach."

He raised his head and sorrow clouded his blue eyes. "Yes."

"Bless your heart." Luna's throat tightened. She might have guessed that Geraldine would want her ashes scattered there along with her husband's. The two urns sat waiting on the mantel of Geraldine's sitting room fireplace, but as Luna wasn't next of kin, the lawyer hadn't revealed Geraldine's instructions for those ashes.

Behind her someone sniffed. Luna suspected it was Sybil, the most tenderhearted of the staff. Another couple of seconds spent on the topic, and everyone would be crying, which wouldn't help Colin get through this.

Luna injected brisk efficiency into her voice. "I'll help with that, then."

"The martini or the scattering?"

"Whatever you want."

"Then I'd like help with both."

"Absolutely." The urge to wrap her arms around him swamped her again and she tamped it down. "Now, let me introduce the rest of the staff." She turned to discover that Janet, Dulcie, and Sybil had lined up as they'd originally practiced. Each of them seemed to be working hard to hold it together, which she appreciated.

A warm rush of loyalty and sense of family made her more determined than ever to save everyone's job. She gestured to each one in turn. "Janet is our chef, and she's amazing. She can make most anything in the world."

He stepped forward and shook Janet's hand. "Can you make haggis, then?"

To Janet's credit, she didn't blink. "Maybe not on short notice, but given a little time to research, I can."

"Not necessary. I think haggis is dreadful stuff. If you can make salmon the way I remember, then I'll be overjoyed. I think there was a plank involved."

"I know exactly what you mean, and I can do that."

"Thank you. I'll look forward to it."

The soft burr in his voice nearly put Luna into a trance again. She forced herself to concentrate as she introduced Dulcie and Sybil. "These two are the housemaids, and you'll never find more dedicated and professional workers. If you need anything, buzz them on the intercom."

"I'll come running," Dulcie said as she shook his hand.

"And I'll come walking," Sybil said. "I don't do that running thing, but I know all the hallway shortcuts, so I'm almost as speedy as Dulcie."

Colin smiled at her. "Don't rush on my account. All I need right now is a hot shower."

Luna thought of him standing in that hot shower and was gripped by a yearning she'd worked to subdue ever since puberty. Whenever she'd felt desire for a male in the past, she'd been able to block it. Giving in to her sexuality would have been reckless when she had no idea how lovemaking affected Weres, or in her case, half-breeds. And she certainly wasn't going to ask anyone and reveal her ignorance or her half-breed status.

But Colin's potent appeal broke through every defense she'd constructed. Her body grew moist, and she ached in places she'd managed to ignore for years. She hadn't counted on this complication, but she couldn't allow it to distract her from her goal.

Hector's voice boomed out from the doorway. "Are you going to keep the poor boy standing in the hall forever, or can I take him up to his room?"

Luna glanced at the lanky Were holding Colin's leather carry-on bag. Impatience flattened his mouth into a thin line and his shock of white hair stood on end where he'd run his fingers through it. Logically he'd feel Geraldine's loss more than anyone here because of his long association with her, so Luna cut him some slack. Perhaps grief made him more cantankerous than usual.

She hadn't discussed her plan with him because she was afraid he'd be against it. He'd often told her he liked the peace and quiet of this isolated island. If her plan succeeded, it would bring a constant flood of guests.

"I thought Colin would like to meet everyone," she said. "But perhaps that wasn't—"

"I did want that." Colin leveled his blue gaze on her again. "Thank you all for coming out to greet me. I would have hated walking into an empty hallway."

A hallway without Geraldine in it, Luna realized.

"That wouldn't have been right," she said. Although she'd had more than a week to adjust to Geraldine being gone, Colin had never stayed in this house without his aunt being here, too. "But we're done with the introductions, so Hector can take you upstairs."

"If it's the same room, I know the way."

"It's the same room," Hector said. "I made sure of that. But I'll go with you and see that everything's the way you like it."

Dulcie and Sybil both stiffened as if ready to take offense at the suggestion that they hadn't prepared Colin's room well enough.

Luna sent them a warning glance, and they kept quiet. In Luna's opinion, Hector had a right to be a little protective of Colin. They would have shared memories of Geraldine that the rest of them did not. "Thanks, Hector. Colin, let me know when to mix up that martini."

He looked out the front door, which was still open. "It's nearly happy hour, although I suppose if the sun doesn't set until after nine these days, happy hour could be anytime from now until then."

"Janet could fix us some food to take along if you're getting hungry." That would be a good idea, regardless. She didn't want a tipsy Were on her hands.

"Food would be nice," he said. "Just sandwiches, something simple."

"I'll pack a light dinner," Janet said. "How soon do you want it to be ready?"

Colin glanced at his watch. "An hour?"

"That's fine." Janet nodded. "I'll bring a basket to Geraldine's sitting room. The wet bar's there."

"I remember." A smile flitted across his face. Then he glanced at Luna. "Does that work for you?"

"Of course. I'll be in Geraldine's sitting room in an hour with a martini shaker and a basket of food."

"Make sure to bring two glasses. I hate to drink alone."

"All right."

Colin turned to Hector. "Ready?"

"Been ready." Hector started toward the curving marble staircase, and Colin followed.

Luna stayed in the hallway with Dulcie, Sybil, and Janet as Colin carried his suitcase up the stairs. He looked about as wonderful from the back as he did from the front.

After they disappeared down the corridor, Dulcie was the first to break the silence. "Oh, baby." She packed a wealth of appreciation into those two words.

Luna couldn't agree more, but she wasn't about to say so. "Thanks for not responding to Hector's remark about the condition of the room. Colin may be the closest thing to family he has left."

"That's true," Janet said. "Whittier House has been Hector's whole life."

"He's still a pain in the rear, but I'll lay off for now." Dulcie put her hand on her heart and sighed dramatically. "Because any friend of Colin's is a friend of mine."

"You might as well give up that project, Dulcie," Sybil said. "He only has eyes for our Southern belle here."

Heat swept through Luna. "That's not true!"

"Yeah, it is." Janet gave her a knowing look.

"Don't count me out yet," Dulcie said.

Janet slung an arm around Dulcie's shoulders. "Sorry, old girl. Luna has the inside track on this one. And it's about time our little magnolia blossom had some romance in her life."

Luna's pulse skyrocketed at Janet's implication, but she shook her head and adopted a businesslike tone. "Not happening. Too much at stake."

"But, sweetie," Janet said. "That's exactly why you

should seduce that beautiful Were. The male of the species tends to mellow out after good sex. A roll in the hay might tip the scales in your favor."

Both the subject and her lack of experience caused her face to flame. "I don't think so. I'm not ... great at that kind of thing."

Dulcie grinned at her. "I wouldn't worry about it, toots. Something tells me he is."

Colin had dreaded walking into Whittier House now that Geraldine was gone, but it hadn't been too bad thanks to Luna Reynaud. Yes, her wavy dark hair, fair skin, and wide green eyes would capture any male's attention, but it wasn't her beauty that had lifted his heavy heart. It was her endearing lack of sophistication.

He could see immediately why Geraldine had hired her. Earnest sincerity was a quality his aunt had prized, and Luna had that, plus a subtle vulnerability that inspired his protective instincts. He had no doubt Luna had taken excellent care of Geraldine, but Geraldine had probably mothered Luna more than a little bit.

It was obviously a happy household, even in grief. He'd felt better the minute he'd heard laughter coming from behind the closed door. He'd known from Hector's scowl that the groundskeeper disapproved of laughter at a time like this. But Colin had been pathetically grateful for that first glimpse of Luna's smiling face when he'd opened the door. She'd banished the shadows he'd expected to find and had replaced them with sunshine.

Next time he saw her, he'd ask what they'd been laughing about. He liked knowing that Geraldine had continued to surround herself with cheerful people. The one exception was Hector, who had always been on the grumpy side, even fifteen years ago.

"So everyone's new except you, then," he said as they headed toward the room at the end of the corridor, the same one Colin had been given as a teenager.

"Luna's new. The others have all been here about ten years, I guess."

"And she's been here less than a year? She seems to fit right in, and to be a good sort."

Hector didn't respond.

Colin glanced at him. "You don't like her?"

"It's not a matter of like or don't like. She's hiding something. I'd take bets on it."

"Such as?"

"Not sure."

"Apparently my aunt trusted her."

"Yeah."

Colin had a sudden thought. Hector's nose could be out of joint if he'd expected to be part of scattering the ashes. "Listen, Hector, would you like to go with me down to Happy Hour Beach? I can tell Luna to skip it— "

"Hell, no. I'm glad to have you two take care of it. Not my thing. Anyway, we're here." He gestured for Colin to go ahead of him into the bedroom at the end of the hall. "Let's get you settled."

Tabling the subject of Luna for now, Colin walked into the room Geraldine had chosen for him on his first visit. In the far right corner, a spiral metal staircase led to a trapdoor that opened onto the crenellated tower above. No teenager could resist a feature like that, and somehow she'd known, despite having no children herself.

The room was achingly familiar, with tattered paperbacks in the bookshelf along with a stack of board games. Two sports pennants, one for the Seahawks and one for the Mariners, were tacked to the wall over the bookcase.

Grief lodged in his throat as he was swept back to his first summer, the summer after he'd reached puberty.

He'd known puberty would bring the ability to shift. All Were children were carefully instructed in how to deal with that change. But being told what to expect was a far cry from actually experiencing it.

A few times over the years he'd heard humans complain about those miserable years when they were neither child nor adult. He'd had to laugh. Sure, human kids had hormonal issues and zits, but they didn't periodically shift into a creature with fangs and fur. Try dealing with that on a first date.

Until he'd learned to control that ability, he couldn't go to a movie or an arcade frequented by human teens without worrying that the urge would suddenly come upon him. All a teenage boy had to fear was an unexpected erection. Weres risked an unexpected transformation that could get them killed.

Now he wouldn't trade his Were status for anything, but those teenage years had been hell. Aunt Geraldine and Uncle Henry had offered this island as a refuge while he was learning to adapt to a confusing new reality. Colin had liked Henry okay, but he'd adored Geraldine, who had seemed to understand his youthful insecurities.

Damn it, he should have come to see her when Henry had died several years ago. He should have flown over to offer whatever comfort he could. But he hadn't, and that failure would haunt him for a long time.

"Far as I know, nothing's been changed in here," Hector said. "Aired and cleaned, of course, but not changed."

"I'm glad it hasn't changed." That first summer, his aunt had been anxious about whether he'd like the drapes and bed linens she'd chosen for him, which depicted the night sky in silver against a dark blue background.

He'd thought the pattern was beautiful, and it had sparked an interest he still had. When she'd realized the astronomy decor suited him, she'd bought him a telescope. Winters were rainy here, but summers were generally clear, and he'd spent hours on the flat roof of the tower studying the heavens.

Colin set down his suitcase and turned to Hector. "Do you know if the telescope's still around?"

"Probably in the closet. She wouldn't have gotten rid of it."

No, she wouldn't have, because she'd probably thought he might come back and use it again. Walking over to the closet, he opened the door. The telescope box sat on a shelf over the clothes rod. All the wooden hangers were empty except one.

He turned on the light and his heart squeezed. She'd kept the Seattle Space Needle hooded sweatshirt he'd bought and left here to wear on cool summer nights. Taking off his sport coat, he hung it up, unzipped the sweatshirt, and slipped it from the hanger.

Maybe it smelled a little musty, but he didn't care. Maybe it was a little tight through the shoulders. Didn't matter. He tugged it on and zipped it partway up.

Then he glanced toward the doorway where Hector stood. "I miss her like the devil, Hector."

The groundskeeper nodded.

Chapter 3

Luna changed into jeans, a forest green sweater, and canvas slip-ons before heading to Geraldine's sitting room. Janet had been there ahead of her, and a wicker picnic basket sat on the wet bar's counter. Luna smelled roast beef sandwiches and tried to remember when she'd last eaten. She'd been too involved in preparations for Colin to think about it.

With an ease born of practice, she opened the liquor cabinet under the counter, took out the gin and vermouth, and began mixing a shaker of martinis. The stainless-steel container held five servings, and she filled it to capacity out of habit. She hadn't performed this ritual in more than a week, and doing it now, without Geraldine kibitzing from a bar stool on the other side of the counter, felt strange.

Luna had learned how to make the drink exactly as her employer had liked it, with only a whisper of Vermouth to flavor the gin and a dash of bitters. Geraldine had encouraged Luna to share in the happy hour tradition, and she'd eventually become used to the strong taste. But Geraldine usually consumed the lion's share of the shaker's contents.

Happy Hour Beach was Geraldine's favorite place to enjoy drinks in the early evening, but the sitting room with its cozy fireplace and shelves of books had run a close second. Geraldine had mentioned that she and Henry had often enjoyed their drinks here when the weather was too ugly to be outside.

Luna wished that she'd had a chance to meet Henry, too, but that would have been impossible. Geraldine hadn't needed to hire a personal assistant until after Henry died. And now they were both gone.

Although Luna didn't feel exactly right participating in this informal ceremony to scatter the ashes, Colin had asked, and as Geraldine's heir, he called the shots. She hoped her presence would help. She'd never scattered anyone's ashes before.

As she poured gin into the martini shaker, she thought about the above-ground tombs in New Orleans and the noisy parades for the deceased. This Happy Hour Beach plan wasn't quite the same, but Luna felt sure that Geraldine had meant for it to be a celebration of life, not a mournful acknowledgment of death.

"It's amazing how well I remember my way around this place." Colin walked into the sitting room, his hair still a little damp from his shower, his amazing scent now mixed with that of shampoo and soap. He'd changed into jeans, running shoes, and a black T-shirt.

But it was the zip-up hoodie he wore over the T-shirt that caught Luna's attention. An obvious souvenir from the Space Needle, it was at least a size too small for him. She suspected it had sentimental value, and the tight fit emphasized the breadth of his shoulders, so she wasn't complaining.

She couldn't imagine any female would complain about sharing space with Colin MacDowell, who could look good no matter what clothes he wore. Or didn't wear. She took a shaky breath and routed her thoughts away from that dangerous subject.

Janet might think sex was a good tactic, but Luna wasn't going there, no matter how much her body wanted to. "I like your sweatshirt," she said.

"Me, too. It doesn't fit the way it did when I was seventeen, but it was hanging in my closet upstairs, so I put it on." His gaze went to the pair of urns on the mantel and slid away again.

"Sounds like the right move to me." She screwed the lid on the cocktail shaker and tucked it into an insulated carrier Geraldine had bought expressly for trips to Happy Hour Beach. Besides a thermos for ice, the carrier had a divided section for two stemmed glasses, a place for a small jar of olives, and another compartment for toothpicks.

"That carrier's new," Colin said. "When I was here, they used a canvas bag."

Luna lifted the carrier by its strap. "Progress. Do you want to take folding chairs? When I'd have happy hour with Geraldine, we took two camp chairs."

"There used to be big pieces of driftwood on that beach."

"There still are, but Geraldine didn't like to perch on them, especially after a couple of martinis."

Colin smiled. "I can understand that. But I plan to have only one drink, so the driftwood should work for me."

"For me, too." She'd probably overdone it on the martinis, but she'd heard that Scotsmen liked their liquor. Maybe he'd change his mind and have more than one.

"Then let's forget the chairs and just go."

"Okay." She started to pick up the wicker basket by its handle.

Colin moved toward her. "I can get that. In fact, let me carry the drinks and the food."

"I'd rather you took the urns."

He hesitated for a fraction of a second. "Right." Shoulders back, jaw set, he walked straight to the mantel and gripped an urn in each of his large hands. "Let's go."

Luna led the way back out into the entry hall and through the front door. The sun had drawn closer to the horizon, but darkness wouldn't come for another two hours, at least.

A wind whipped Luna's hair back from her face as she gazed out at the island-dotted expanse of blue-gray water. "Geraldine would have loved this sunny weather," she said.

"Yes." Colin sounded subdued.

Luna turned to him. "It's not really my place to say, but I think she would have wanted us to make this a joyful occasion."

"Yes, you're right." He took a deep breath. "So we'll do that. Lead on."

"That's the spirit." She gave him a quick smile of encouragement. Then she took a path to her left, which bordered a grassy area where Geraldine had often set up a croquet game. If Colin approved Luna's plan, she wanted to offer guests a chance to play here. It would be a shame not to.

Once past the croquet lawn, she started down narrow stone steps that descended about ten feet to a small crescent beach that faced west. Colin followed, his footsteps sure, his breathing steady.

Because Luna had spent years minimizing close encounters with eligible males, being alone with a virile Were like Colin gave her the jitters. She reminded herself he was Geraldine's cherished nephew, not someone to be avoided. In fact, if she ever wanted to have a sexual experience, Colin would be a safe candidate, given how much Geraldine had trusted him.

But he also had the power to decide whether she'd be staying on the island. She couldn't risk doing anything that would adversely affect his decision to let her open an inn.

When they reached the sand, Colin let out a sigh. "Just the same as I remembered. That's comforting, in a way. Geraldine is gone, but the beach remains the way it's always been."

"It does." The water was calm, and the waves lapped at the shoreline in a lazy rhythm. Luna wanted this to be a celebratory occasion, but the beauty of the little cove seemed to emphasize that the former owner would never enjoy it again.

About two weeks ago, Luna had sat on the beach with Geraldine, and she remembered that last evening with fondness. They'd watched a spectacular sunset while drinking martinis and eating finger sandwiches.

Memories of Geraldine swirled through Luna's mind as she set the picnic basket and the insulated carrier next to a huge piece of gray driftwood, its trunk as big around as she was. It would make a good seat for both her and Colin, provided they didn't drink too much gin. At the moment, drinking too much gin to fill the void Geraldine had left was an appealing thought.

"Luna, look!"

The urgency in Colin's voice shattered her melancholy. Glancing up, she gasped in delight as a pair of orcas arched out of the water about twenty yards offshore. Their black-and-white, tuxedolike markings glistened as they undulated in tandem through the calm water.

"I'd forgotten." Still clutching a funerary urn in each hand, Colin watched the whales make their way past the island until they became indistinguishable from the movement of the gentle waves. He set the urns in the sand and turned to Luna. "How could I forget about the orcas?

They were one of my favorite things about the summers I spent on this island."

"Fifteen years is a long time."

"Too long." His expression was bleak. "I loved it here. I should have made it a priority to come back for a visit."

"She knew you were busy." Luna hated to see him in pain, but maybe this meant her plan had a chance of succeeding. "She was proud of your accomplishments."

"She talked about me?"

"All the time. Considering she left everything to you, it's safe to say you were the son she never had."

Feet braced apart, hands bracketing his hips, Colin stared at the sand beneath his feet. "And a bloody inattentive one, at that." He shifted his focus to the horizon. "At first I thought it was my duty to step aside and allow my younger brother to have his turn over here, but he wasn't interested."

"Geraldine mentioned your brother. I gather he's a handful."

"Aye. Duncan's what you'd call a party animal. He thought spending the summer over here sounded as exciting as watching a sheep grow wool."

"He must be very different from y'all."

He glanced over at her. "You mean different from my whole family, or just me?"

"Just, uh, you." She flushed. "Sorry. It's just the way I talk. It's confusing enough for someone who's not Southern, let alone someone who's not even from this country."

His blue gaze gentled. "Please don't worry about it. I enjoy the way you talk."

"I enjoy the way you talk, too. Your voice reminds me of Geraldine's."

His eyebrows lifted. "Then maybe I need to pitch it somewhat lower."

That surprised a laugh out of her. "I didn't mean you sounded feminine. I just—"

"I know." He flashed a grin. "Just teasing."

Her breath caught. He really was gorgeous with the sun picking out the gold in his hair and bronzing his skin. She could get lost in those blue eyes and that warm smile. No wonder Geraldine had loved him. He'd be easy to love.

"I'm not sure what I did to put that look on your face," he said, "but it's very becoming."

Oh, dear. Once again she was staring at him as if she had a schoolgirl crush. She cleared her throat. "I was thinking that we need to get started."

He gave her a half smile, as if he didn't believe a word of that. "Drinking or scattering?"

"Your choice."

He nodded. "I suppose it is, so I choose drinking first, scattering second. I think I'll handle this better with a little alcohol in my system."

"Me, too." She knelt beside the insulated carrier and unzipped the lid.

"Can I help?" His voice was very close.

She turned to find him crouched right beside her. His scent and body heat were unbelievably distracting. But asking him to move away would be rude, and he wouldn't understand why. Most Were females would be thrilled to have him nearby, and they wouldn't be skittish about it, either.

Forcing herself to concentrate, she pulled the martini shaker out of the carrier, opened it, and added ice from the thermos. Then she screwed on the lid and handed it to him. "You can do the shaking and the pouring."

"How many does this thing hold?"

"Five, but we certainly don't have to drink them all. Geraldine thought it was better to be oversupplied than undersupplied for a trip to Happy Hour Beach."

"I remember that. She wouldn't let me drink martinis with her and Henry, but I was welcome to join them with a six-pack of soda." He stood and began rattling the ice in the stainless-steel container. "Every time I hear a bartender doing this I think, *Shaken, not stirred.*"

"Was Geraldine a double-oh-seven fan back then, too?" Luna set the stemmed glasses upright in the carrier and added the olives.

"Rabid. It's a wonder Henry wasn't jealous, the way she carried on about Sean Connery. But Henry was a good sport about it. He was daft about her."

"From things she said to me, I think she was daft about him, too." Luna didn't normally use the word *daft*, but she liked the idea of employing a word Colin used. It sounded more cultured than *crazy*. She picked up both glasses and carefully stood so she wouldn't dump the olives.

"She must have been deeply in love," Colin said. "The story was that she came over to Vancouver on vacation, met Henry, and never returned to Scotland. The Whittier pack in Vancouver wasn't happy because Henry was supposed to mate with someone else, and the MacDowell pack wasn't happy because she'd abandoned them for some Canadian Were."

"No wonder they decided to buy an island and live by themselves." She held out the glasses. "Fill 'em up. We need to toast Geraldine and Henry, who valued their own happiness over the opinions of others."

"That they did." Colin poured the clear liquid into each glass. "They marched to their own drummer, which isn't common in our world."

"No." She felt a prick of unease. It might be Colin's world, but she still wasn't convinced it was hers. Sometimes she thought it could be, and other times she felt like a half-breed fraud who didn't belong with either humans or Weres.

Keeping his glass level, he leaned down, settled the shaker in the carrier, and flipped the lid over it. Then he straightened and touched the rim of his glass to hers. "To Henry and Geraldine, who created the life they wanted."

"To Henry and Geraldine." She met his gaze and added a fervent wish that he'd allow her to create the life she wanted here on Le Floret. As she took a sip of her drink, she watched him from beneath her lashes.

His mouth fascinated her. She'd had one kiss in her life, a hard, demanding, and disgusting kiss forced on her by a guest at one of the hotels where she'd worked as a maid. If that was kissing, she wanted no part of it. But she couldn't imagine Colin behaving with such aggression and lack of finesse.

He took a long swallow and glanced up. "Nicely done, Luna. James Bond would approve of this martini."

"Thank you."

"Shall we sit?" He gestured toward the giant piece of driftwood.

"Okay." She picked out a level spot and settled down on the water-polished wood.

Colin surveyed the driftwood and chose a section about two feet away from her. Balancing on the driftwood, he nudged off his shoes. "Ah, that's better. Geraldine didn't think anyone should wear shoes on the beach."

"That's right." Luna had thought about that, but she hadn't wanted to appear overly casual. Now that Colin was going barefoot, she could, too.

Toeing off her shoes, she nudged them aside and wiggled her toes in the warm sand. The familiar sensation soothed her. "Geraldine believed in enjoying life to the fullest, whatever that meant to someone."

"That she did." Colin took another swallow of his martini and gazed out at the water. "And she encouraged others to do the same. I wonder . . ."

"What?" She glanced over at him.

His attention remained fixed on the horizon, as if he were looking for answers. "Maybe I hesitated to come back here because I knew I wasn't following her advice."

"How is that?"

He sipped his martini. "If I stop to evaluate my choices since my seventeenth summer, they've all been based on what my family wanted, what my pack needed. Never on what I needed."

She went very still, afraid to do the wrong thing, say the wrong thing, and ruin this moment. She doubted he confided that sort of insight very often, if ever. Perhaps he was lulled into this reflective mood by the private beach, the martini, and the reminder that life could end at any time.

He glanced over at her. "Did she give you the same advice?"

"Yes." Geraldine had been the first person in years who Luna had allowed close enough to give her advice.

He drank more of his martini. "And what do you want, Luna Reynaud?"

She could tell him, but it seemed too soon, and a business discussion wasn't appropriate tonight. She drew circles in the sand with her toes. "What everyone wants, I suppose. Fulfillment, joy, a feeling of security." She looked up. "How about you?"

"The same, perhaps, although a need for security can end up weighing a person down." He studied her as he sipped his martini. "You do realize I'm planning to sell this place?"

"I assumed so."

"If you have to leave Le Floret as a result, what will you do?"

She met his gaze. "I'll be fine." She didn't want him to think she had no alternative to staying on here. That would look as if her idea had been inspired by desperation, rather than a solid business plan.

"Financially you'll be fine, because I'll give you a great recommendation and a generous severance package. But you seem to be without strong pack ties, and so I can see how the island . . ."

"Works for me the way it worked for Henry and Geraldine?"

"Essentially, yes. Those who choose to stay here don't want to be closely involved with a pack. That's not a common Were profile."

"No, it isn't." She held his gaze. "I'm a little different." Another half-truth that she hoped would satisfy him.

"And that's why you fit in with Geraldine and the others," he said, his voice gentle. "But they may be able to keep their jobs under new ownership, because Whittier House needs a staff. Chances are slim there will be a place here for you. A personal assistant is a more specialized position." He sounded genuinely worried about her future plans.

Unexpectedly, her eyes misted and a lump rose to her throat. Damn. This was no time to get emotional just because he was being considerate. For years she'd kept a sturdy wall around herself that had prevented anyone from getting close enough to worry about her.

Geraldine had partially penetrated that wall, leaving Luna more vulnerable than she'd been since losing her mother nineteen years ago. But she couldn't expect Colin to trust her with his legacy if she got teary at the slightest hint of kindness. She needed to project an air of calm control and competency.

Clearing her throat, she looked him straight in the eye. "I appreciate your concern, but I've been on my own for most of my life. I can take care of myself."

Chapter 4

Taken aback by her sudden switch in mood, Colin stared at Luna. A second ago she'd been leaning toward him, her expression soft and vulnerable, her eyes damp. She'd looked in need of comfort, and he'd considered putting down his drink and drawing her into his arms.

But this new Luna wouldn't welcome that gesture. She sat ramrod straight on the driftwood, her chin firm and her eyes clear. For some reason he couldn't fathom, she'd armored herself against him.

Far be it for him to force unwanted concern on anyone. "I didn't mean to imply you couldn't take care of yourself," he said in his best laird of Glenbarra manner.

She gasped. "I was rude, wasn't I? I'm sorry. You were only trying to be nice."

"And apparently I insulted you in the process." He drained the rest of his martini.

"Not at all." She sighed. "I just don't want to appear helpless and . . . without resources."

"I'm sure you're not." He must have hit one of her sore points, and if she'd been on her own for a long time, her ability to take care of herself would be a source of pride. Yet she'd allowed him a glimpse of her vulnerability, and she probably regretted that.

Colin thought of Duncan's favorite slogan: When in doubt, have another round. He raised his martini glass. "I'm going to have another one of these, after all." Flipping back the soft lid of the carrier, he pulled out the shaker. "Can I top off yours?"

"Um, yes, please." She held out her glass. "And I apologize. Nothing's gone quite as I planned."

"Planned?" He tried to make sense of that statement as he filled their glasses. "What sort of plan did you have?"

"Maybe I should lay all my cards on the table and be done with it."

That got his full attention. Quickly tucking the shaker back in the carrier, he faced her, all his senses alert. "Please do."

"I intended to give you a chance to rest up first, but here we are drinking martinis and having a conversation about my future. I didn't expect that. It's thrown me off."

"Go on." His drink forgotten, he gazed at her with new understanding. She hadn't survived on her own all these years without being resourceful. Geraldine's death had created a problem for her, and she'd obviously come up with a scheme to solve it. Apparently the scheme involved him.

She clutched her martini glass in both hands as she focused those green eyes on him with the intensity of twin lasers. "I have a proposition for you."

For one wild moment he thought she might mean a sexual proposition, and his pulse leaped. But she had an air of innocence about her that didn't jibe with that scenario. "I suspected as much."

"Instead of selling Whittier House and Le Floret, I think you should turn it into a premiere Were vacation spot."

He was aghast. "And have strangers running all over the island?" The minute the words were out of his mouth, he realized how idiotic they sounded. He planned to sell to strangers, and they could allow anyone they chose to run all over it.

"See, I knew it! This place is special to you!"

"Of course it is." He took a gulp of his martini. "But I have to put sentimentality aside, because selling is the only reasonable course of action."

"Not necessarily." She took a careful sip of her drink and glanced up at him. "I've worked in hotels all my life. Not to brag on myself, but I've learned every aspect of the business, and I'm good at it. I started out cleaning rooms, but then I moved up into management. I understand basic bookkeeping and I know how to turn a profit."

"You want to make Whittier House into a hotel?" He couldn't imagine such a thing. "But it's filled with valuable antiques and tapestries. Strangers could ruin —"

"Were you planning to take those things back to Scotland?"

She had him there. He sighed and shook his head. "MacDowell House is already stuffed with antiques. I'd love to convince my mother and father to sell at least half of them so we could walk through rooms without bumping into things."

"So whether these stay with the house or not, they'd be sold?"

He swallowed another mouthful of his drink. "Yes." And the thought of selling Aunt Geraldine's antiques tore at his heart, but turning the place into a hotel didn't make him very happy, either.

"It would be an exclusive inn," Luna said. "It would be for Were guests only. And even for them, booking a room would require references. I'd make sure the guests behaved themselves."

He gazed at her and tried to imagine how a sweet creature with a voice that sounded like warm honey could possibly control a pack of rowdy Weres. But he'd already gotten into trouble suggesting that she wasn't capable of taking care of herself, so he said nothing.

"You don't believe I could keep the peace, right?"

He couldn't help smiling at a mental picture of her standing in the middle of the drawing room cradling a shotgun as she demanded proper behavior from her guests. "I don't know. Could you?"

"Absolutely. I would set the tone right from the start. Coming to Whittier House would be a privilege, not a chance to act up."

"A privilege they'd pay for?"

"Of course, and pay handsomely, too." Matching his smile, she lifted her glass to her lips and drank.

He loved looking at her mouth. Her pink lipstick had left a print on her glass, and he found that sexy. "I must be getting peshed on gin, because I'm starting to consider this daft concept of yours."

Luna's gaze softened. "Geraldine sometimes said she was peshed. Or blootered."

He waited for a pang of longing to subside before he spoke again. "I wish I'd given myself the chance to get peshed with Geraldine." He polished off the last of his martini. "And speaking of the old girl, we have a job to do."

Pushing the base of her half-full martini glass into the sand, Luna stood. "I'm ready."

"So am I." Colin secured his glass in the sand, too, although he didn't have to worry if it tipped over because it was empty. He'd also eaten both olives.

He thought Geraldine would have relished the idea of having her ashes scattered by a couple of slightly peshed Weres. There was a little more martini mix in the shaker, and once they'd dealt with the ashes, Colin planned to suggest they drain the shaker's contents.

He crouched down next to the simple urns, each with

a Scottish thistle pattern embossed on one side. "Her instructions said to dump hers in with his, but I don't know which is which."

"His is the bronze finish and hers is the silver. She told me she'd picked them out years ago."

"Then here goes." He took the top off each urn and picked up the silver one. As part of a large clan, he'd taken part in many such ceremonies, and he knew some of the ash would be powdery enough to fly around if he didn't move slowly. So he stood up to pour, leaned over and emptied the silver urn gradually into the bronze one.

"You look like you're a pro at dealing with ashes." Her voice was subdued.

"It's part of a pack leader's job to know how." He finished pouring, set the silver urn in the sand, and replaced the top on the bronze one. When he picked it up, he discovered that the combined ashes plus the weight of the urn made for a hefty burden. He'd never dealt with two sets of ashes at once.

"So we scatter them now?"

"Not yet." Colin braced his bare feet in the sand. "She wants them shaken, not stirred."

"You're kidding."

"No, lass, I'm not." He held the urn like a giant cocktail shaker.

She clapped a hand over her mouth and her green eyes sparkled with suppressed laughter.

Looking at her, he couldn't help grinning. "I can see this won't be a particularly solemn occasion."

She took her hand away from her mouth to reveal her smile. "Geraldine wouldn't want solemn."

"You're right. I certainly hope I can do this without falling down, though. Celebration is one thing. Slapstick comedy is another." He began to shake the urn. It wasn't easy, especially considering the two martinis he'd con-

sumed on an empty stomach. He staggered once, bringing a gasp of alarm from Luna.

"Don't panic." He regained his balance. "I've got it."

"You've probably shaken them enough. She wouldn't
want you to rupture a disc."

"That would be unfortunate." He paused to catch his
breath. "All right, then. Time to scatter."

"Where, exactly?"

"She didn't get that specific. Just in the sand. Is the
tide coming in or going out?"

"Let me think for a minute." She paused. "It's coming
in."

"Then if we go down near the waterline, the waves
will eventually cover the ashes and gradually draw them
out to sea. I think Geraldine would have liked that idea."

"So do I, but as she's not here to offer advice, we have
to use our best judgment."

"Right. Near the waterline it is, then." Colin hoisted
the urn to his shoulder as he started toward the water.
He'd never thought of this as a physically taxing ceremony, but he was working up a sweat.

It was a wee crescent beach, not even half a mile from
one rocky promontory to the other. Colin made for the
north tip, figuring he would need the entire length in order to empty the urn. A breeze off the water meant he'd
need to face the shore as he moved along or risk being
covered in ashes.

When he reached the farthest end of the beach, he set
the urn in the damp sand and caught his breath.

Luna came up beside him. "Are we going to scoop out
handfuls?" She didn't sound eager to do that.

"No. I'll just walk along and pour the ashes as I go."

"Should we say something, first?"

"Yes. Yes, we certainly should." It was a measure of
his exhausted and peshed state that he'd been about to

dump Geraldine and Henry on the sand without a single blessing. He glanced at Luna. "Will you take hold of my hand, then?"

"Of course." She offered her hand without hesitation. Her skin was soft, but her grip was firm.

Gratitude rushed through him for her support at such a time—but gratitude wasn't all he felt. He became aware of her in a way that wasn't appropriate during a funeral ceremony.

He glanced toward the water as they stood in silence. He should be thinking of what he was going to say, but instead he simply absorbed the wonder of her touch. The smell of salt water and sand blended with her female scent, and the combination was more intoxicating than any drink invented. He'd never realized how inherently sexy beaches were.

Perhaps he should release her hand. He did not.

Her fingers tightened around his. "May I say something first?"

"Aye." And maybe then he'd be in better command of himself.

She drew in a breath and spoke in a steady voice. "Geraldine, thank you for being a friend and mentor to this wandering Were. I will never forget your kindness. Rest in peace with your beloved Henry."

"Beautiful, lass." He glanced at her. "Well done."

She met his gaze, and her eyes were moist. "Your turn," she said softly.

"I'm lucky to have you with me for this, Luna."

"Bless your heart. I feel lucky to be here. Now, say your piece. She would want some Scottish parts in there, I think."

He nodded. "I've been thinking about that." Turning back to the shimmering water, he kept a firm grip on Luna's hand. He wanted to do a proper job, and holding on to her helped him focus.

"Maybe a bit like this." He cleared his throat. "Geraldine and Henry, we come to this wee beach you loved so well to honor the beauty in thy character, the harmony in thy home, and the love in thy hearts."

"Very nice."

He squeezed her hand. "Not done yet."

"Oh, sorry."

"And may thy martinis in the afterlife be shaken, and not stirred. Blessed be." From the corner of his eye he saw her smile. "Okay, then?"

"Yes."

Reluctantly he let go of her hand. "Then it's time I start the pouring." He knew it would be an aerobic task, so he unzipped his sweatshirt and pulled it off, sighing in relief as cool air penetrated his sweat-dampened T-shirt.

"Too warm?"

He caught her quick glance of appraisal, even though she immediately looked away again. "I didn't realize it would be such a physical job." So she was aware of him in that way, too.

He'd file the information away for later. Now was not the time to be getting romantic notions. "Could you please hang on to this for me?" He held the sweatshirt toward her.

"Be happy to." She folded the sweatshirt over her arm.

"You might want to stand back." Facing away from the water, he picked up the urn. "Some of the ashes will probably blow toward you."

"Then I'll walk along ahead of you and pick up anything that might be a tripping hazard, like pieces of driftwood."

"Brilliant." He hadn't thought of that. He'd be concentrating on pouring ashes, and not watching for obstacles in his path. Tripping could have unfortunate consequences for everyone, including the deceased. "Then let's get started." He started to tip the urn.

"Wait."

"Wait?" He paused in midtip.

"We should sing as we go along. And I know just the song. 'Amazing Grace.' "

"You're right again, lass. Geraldine loved that song, especially played on the pipes. If I'd been thinking, I would have brought along a portable player of some kind."

"But we can sing."

"Aye."

Luna positioned herself about three steps in front of his planned path. "We'll start on three. One, two, three." She began to sing. Off-key.

Colin joined in with gusto in hopes that his voice would coax hers into some sort of compliance. But no. She sang with greater enthusiasm, to be sure, but not greater tunefulness.

Ah, well. It was the thought that counted. Pouring ashes and singing along with Luna's tone-deaf rendition of "Amazing Grace," he realized that Geraldine would have loved this scene. She wouldn't have cared whether the tune was performed well. She would have been delighted that it was performed at all, and with love, at that.

Gauging how much to pour as they moved down the beach took most of his concentration, but he was aware of Luna clearing his path of debris. Miraculously, everything came out even—the length of beach, the amount of ashes, and the last words of the song.

The sun had not set, but it hung low on the horizon and had begun to turn a rich shade of gold. A pair of gulls wheeled overhead, their cries mingling with the soft lap of the waves moving steadily up the beach.

Colin emptied the urn and set it on the sand with a sigh of accomplishment. He'd done it. No, *they* had done it. The ceremony wouldn't have been as perfectly imperfect without Luna.

She stood close beside him because they'd run out of beach. Tipping her face upward to gaze at him, she smiled with obvious pleasure and satisfaction. Her face reflected the radiance of the sun, and Colin couldn't imagine anyone looking more beautiful than she did at this moment.

"Thank you," he murmured. And then, because it seemed like the right thing to do, he leaned down and kissed her full on the mouth.

He'd probably expected, on some level, that she'd kiss him back. She didn't. How embarrassing was that? Yet she'd shown interest in him, or maybe he'd been mistaken, leaped to conclusions. He felt like an ass.

Pulling away, he felt heat spreading from his neck up to his cheeks. "My apologies. I shouldn't have done that."

She looked dazed. "Don't apologize. I liked it."

"You *liked* it?"

"Yes." She reached up and touched her mouth with her fingertips. "I was hoping it might last a little longer."

"But . . . you weren't kissing me back."

It was her turn to blush. "I suppose not, but you see, I don't have much . . . That is, I'm not very . . ."

He stared at her in confusion. If he didn't know better, he'd think she was completely inexperienced. Yet she'd been on her own for years, and she appeared to be in her mid-twenties. Sexuality was celebrated in the Were culture, and although choosing a mate for life might be delayed, sexual satisfaction was not.

Her blush deepened and she lowered her gaze. "Never mind. I'm sure you're famished after all that effort. We should eat." She turned and started back up to their driftwood bench.

"Wait a minute." He laid a gentle hand on her arm. "What's going on here, Luna?"

She glanced back at him. "Something that shouldn't be going on. You have a lovely mouth, and I was curious, but kissing someone I hope to do business with isn't a very bright idea, especially when I'm no good at it."

"How can you be no good at it? Haven't you ever . . ." He saw the answer in her eyes. "But I don't understand. You're beautiful."

"That's nice to hear."

"Surely you've had Weres who were interested in you."

She shrugged. "I don't know. I've never encouraged that kind of thing. I never . . . trusted anyone enough."

Although he still had trouble imagining that she was virginal at this stage in her life, his gut told him that no one could fake the kind of reaction she'd had to his kiss. "Does that mean that you trusted me a little, since you allowed me to kiss you?" He would hardly call it a kiss, but she might think it was, given her apparent innocence.

"I suppose I would tend to trust someone Geraldine trusted, but that doesn't mean we should be kissing." She gently pulled away from his grasp. "Come along, Colin. If you're not starving, I am."

Fascinated by this unexpected revelation, he followed her back to their temporary picnic site. He was still attracted to her, and she was attracted to him, although she might not realize how much if she'd never allowed herself to feel passion.

The last time he'd been with a virgin, he'd been a fumbling fool, only somewhat more knowledgeable than the female Were he'd had sex with. They'd made a hash of it. But that had been more than fifteen years ago.

He couldn't imagine that someone as full of life as Luna clearly was could be happy embracing celibacy. Judging from her response to him, her virginal state was a source of embarrassment to her.

If she'd allow him to, he could help her over that hurdle. In fact, the more he thought about it, the more he believed it was the gentlemanly thing to do.

Chapter 5

Thoroughly put out with herself, Luna concentrated on organizing their food. She still had Colin's sweatshirt, and she draped it carefully over a branch of the giant driftwood. Then she began randomly pulling out the food that Janet had packed for them.

Using every available flat place on the wood, she laid out plates, napkins, forks, and wrapped sandwiches. All the while she silently cursed her gigantic stupidity. Her stupidity was so big it would reach to the moon and back, with stupidity left over.

Apparently cotton was stuffed in her skull where her brains were supposed to be. Otherwise she had no explanation for why she'd stood there like a complete idiot and let Colin kiss her. Even a clueless virgin could guess what he'd had in mind when he'd leaned toward her with that soft expression in his dreamy blue eyes.

But had she ducked away? No, she had not! She'd let it happen, and then had been so amazed at the gentle contact with his mouth that she'd reacted like . . . Well, she hadn't reacted at *all*, had she? When he'd pressed forward, she could have pressed back and pretended to know what she was doing. She'd seen it a million times in movies.

"I think we should finish up the martinis," Colin said as he came up beside her. "Would you like some more?"

"No, thank you." Getting drunk would put the finishing touch on her imbecilic image. Instead of dazzling him with her business savvy, she'd paraded her lack of sexual experience in front of him.

From what she'd observed, males tended to fixate on that kind of information. Instead of thinking of her as a competent person in charge of a business venture, he'd think of her as a virgin waiting for Prince Charming to show up.

Way to go, Luna!

"Mind if I have one of those sandwiches?" He crouched beside her, his martini in one hand.

The tantalizing scent of him stalled her thought process for a second. Then she realized she was blocking access to the food she'd piled on the driftwood.

She stood, careful not to bump into him, and moved away. "Please, help yourself. As you can see, everything's there. There's a container of potato salad still in the basket, and a spoon." She should have fixed him a plate, but her hands were shaking so much that she might have dumped his meal in the sand.

Worst of all, no matter how foolish she'd been, she wanted him to kiss her again. His warmth called to her, blotting out her usually excellent sense of self-preservation. His kiss was so very different from her first one, and she couldn't stop thinking about the velvet press of his lips, the sweet scent of his breath, the careful restraint she sensed in that light, butterfly touch.

Setting his glass in the sand, he loaded a plate, stood, and offered it to her. "Take this one. I can fix another for myself."

"You take that, please. You're the guest. I'll fix one for myself."

"All right, if you say so." Carrying his food and martini, he returned to the level spot on the driftwood where he'd sat originally.

Luna grabbed a plate, plopped a sandwich on it, and ignored the potato salad. All the food would taste like sawdust, anyway, as she contemplated her self-imposed downfall. Reclaiming her spot on the driftwood, she unwrapped her sandwich and took a bite.

"This plan you have to turn Whittier House into an inn. Have you mentioned it to the rest of the staff?"

She finished chewing her bite of sandwich and swallowed before answering, which gave her time to develop extreme paranoia about why he was asking. "Everyone knows except Hector."

"And what do they think of it?"

She gazed at him and could sense nothing but a sincere desire to explore the subject. Maybe she hadn't ruined her chances, after all, which would be a miracle. "They liked the idea, but I would expect you to interview each of them about it. That's only right."

"An inn would be more work than providing for one eccentric older woman."

Luna nodded. "We've talked about that. There would be more work, but Dulcie and Sybil would make tips over and above their normal salary, and Janet could hire some help in the kitchen, which would give her more time to create signature dishes." And watch her flatscreen TV, but Luna wasn't going to mention that.

"Mm." Colin took a mouthful of potato salad. When he'd eaten that, he laid down his fork. "I can see how Janet would be a draw. This food is very good, and it's only picnic fare."

"Janet takes pride in her work." Luna warmed to her

subject. She happened to think the staff at Whittier House was top-notch. "It doesn't matter to her if she's fixing a sandwich or a seven-course dinner; she always makes everything special."

"I admire that." He dug his fork into the potato salad again and paused. "Why haven't you told Hector about your plan?"

"I'm afraid he would hate it. He loves the seclusion of this island. Creating an inn for Weres would change that. And . . ." She hesitated to say the rest, but surely Colin would pick up on it eventually, if he hadn't already. "I don't think Hector likes me very much."

"He's wary of you."

She blinked in surprise. "Excuse me?"

"He thinks you're hiding something."

A shiver of alarm traveled up her spine. "Does he?"

"That's what he told me this afternoon. Is he right?"

She could deny it, but if they had even the slightest chance of being business partners, telling flat-out lies wasn't a great idea. "Is there any of the martini mix left in the shaker?"

The corners of his mouth tilted up. "A wee bit."

She picked up her glass from the sand and held it out. "Fill me up, Scottie."

Colin groaned. "Do you have any idea how long my countrymen have had to deal with jokes about *Star Trek* Scottie?"

"A long time?"

"It's been an eternity."

"Then I promise never to make another *beam me up* joke in your presence, Your . . . How am I supposed to refer to you, anyway?"

"I told you." He emptied the martini shaker into her glass. "Colin is fine."

"Yes, but if we're going to capitalize on your Scottish

heritage and the obvious Scottish ambiance of Whittier House, then I will be billing this place as the exclusive vacation spot owned by His Supreme High Lairdness, or something to that effect."

The corners of his eyes crinkled with amusement. "That's not quite correct."

"Then what is correct?"

"Colin MacDowell, Laird of Glenbarra."

"That's it? No more flourishes?" She liked this change of subject, which directed the conversation away from her secrets and put the focus on Colin.

"You could add *The Most Honored* in front of my name, although I shudder every time I hear that. Too stuffy."

"But it would suggest elegance, which is what I'd be going for."

"Then be sure to spell *honour* with a *u*, which is how we do it in Scotland."

"That's a great idea." She shouldn't start counting her chickens about this inn project, but she couldn't seem to help it. "I should adopt Scottish spellings for anything printed in connection with the inn. It helps set the tone I was mentioning to you earlier."

"Right." He tackled his food again. "The tone that keeps guests from breaking up the furniture."

"They won't do that, I promise. I'm very protective of the beautiful things in that house. They meant a lot to Geraldine, and I would want to preserve them for her sake. And for yours, of course."

"I believe you." He put down his fork. "I also believe in Hector's instincts. What aren't you telling me, Luna?"

Anxiety turned her stomach into a rock tumbler. He'd circled back to the topic, after all. "Everyone has secrets."

"I suppose so. Apart from me, that is. My life is an

open book. I could probably do with a few more secrets. Maybe I should borrow some of yours."

"I doubt my secrets would work for you." No one would look at Colin and peg him for a virgin.

"I can't help thinking your secrets have something to do with your being celibate all these years."

There was no help for it. She'd have to give him another piece of the puzzle and hope it didn't cause more problems for her. "It does, in a way. When I said I'd been on my own a long time, that's because I literally had no home."

"There were no packs to take you in?"

She drank more of her martini, seeking courage. "My father, Byron Reynaud, was connected to the Trevelyan pack, but my parents split up before I was born."

"Split up?" He frowned. "I don't understand how that could happen if your mother was pregnant with you."

"She didn't want to stay here with my father. Pregnancy doesn't mean you have to be chained to someone for life." Now she wished fervently that her mother hadn't bolted. Maybe both her mother and father would be alive today if Sophie had stayed in Seattle.

"But a Were male can't impregnate a female unless she's pledged to be his mate for life."

"Really? Are you sure about that?"

"Of course I'm sure. We're all taught that when we go through puberty. It's one of the basic pieces of information that we—" He paused to gaze at her. "You weren't taught anything, were you?"

"Not exactly."

"Don't tell me you went through your first change alone."

She nodded. "I thought I was dying."

"That's terrible! No Were should have to go through that by themselves. Where was your mother?"

"She died when I was eight."

"Oh, Luna." His blue eyes filled with compassion.

Luna couldn't decide whether this new information about being mated was good news or bad. On the one hand, it meant her parents were destined for each other, which made her feel special as the child of that union. On the other hand, it meant her mother had abandoned her mate.

"So your mother left Seattle?"

Luna took a deep breath. "That's right. She caught a train. My father raced to the train station to try and stop her from leaving, but he had a car accident on the way . . . and died."

"God."

"I didn't find out about that until I came up here and asked if anyone knew Byron Reynaud."

He groaned in dismay. "I'm sorry, Luna."

"So am I. I never knew him, but when I came to Seattle I'd counted on finding him more than I'd realized." She stared out toward the water. "I'm sure my mother never heard what happened to him. She didn't give any indication that he was dead, only that she'd loved him, but she didn't belong here." Luna hadn't understood that us a child, but she got it now. Her mother wouldn't have fit into the Were world.

"What about her pack?"

She didn't have one. She was human. And that was the one secret Luna planned to keep forever. She'd never heard of anyone else being half-Were. What if they treated her like a freak? Being exposed as half-Were might destroy any chance she had of being accepted anywhere.

"Never mind," Colin said. "I can imagine what happened. She'd gone against the natural order by leaving her mate, so she wasn't welcome in her own pack, either." He shook his head. "What a tragedy. For her, for your father, and mostly for you."

Luna said nothing. By not contradicting him, she was guilty of a lie of omission, but considering the stakes, she felt justified. If Colin could leave it at that, she'd be extremely relieved.

"But you're using the name Reynaud," he said. "Hasn't anyone suspected that you're Byron Reynaud's daughter?"

"In the first place, I don't think anyone knew my mother was pregnant except maybe my father, and he died when she left. In the second place, when I first arrived in Seattle and contacted pack members, I told them that I was a distant cousin of Byron's and I'd been told to look him up if I came to town."

"Turns out you were right to be cautious." He set his plate aside. "But what about Byron's parents? You could have grandparents in the area."

"I do." She'd made a few more discreet inquiries about Byron's family and had discovered that Edwina and Jacques Reynaud, who lived in a wealthy neighborhood in Seattle, were her father's parents.

He cradled his martini glass between his large hands. "I'm not the one to say, but it's possible they would welcome you. It's not your fault that your mother left and caused so much pain. You're the child of their lost son, their only tie to him."

"They also could shun me as the daughter of the one who caused his death." And if they knew that their son had been involved with a human, they would know that Luna was a half-blood Were. She couldn't risk that getting out.

"It's true they might reject you." His blue gaze remained steady. "As I said, it's not my place to advise you on that. But if it were me, I'd want to know I had a granddaughter."

"I can't assume they're as kindhearted and trustworthy as you."

He smiled. "Was that a compliment?"

"Yes, Colin MacDowell, Laird of Glenbarra, it was."

"I'm not sure I deserve it."

"Why not?"

"Because I've been sitting here wanting to kiss you again."

Heat flashed through her, the kind of moist, insistent heat that she now recognized as sexual longing. "I don't think that's a good idea."

"Probably not, but I'm peshed enough not to care. You don't have to worry that I'll go beyond a simple kiss. The martinis and jet lag are catching up with me, and I doubt I could make a proper job of seducing you."

Which was exactly what she wanted him to do. She'd never thought she'd take such a chance, but she trusted Colin as she hadn't trusted any male before. She didn't know why, but she wanted him in a way she hadn't allowed herself to want anyone. Surrendering would be so easy.

If he was willing, and she thought he might be, he could teach her about Were sexuality. She could finally ask the questions that had simmered in her subconscious for years. Did Weres have sex in human form, wolf form, or both? Was there a mating ritual? Did wolves bite each other when they had sex? She knew nothing, and she hadn't worked up the courage to ask anyone.

But expecting Colin to be her tutor had a big problem attached. She also wanted him to be her boss, and having sex with a prospective boss, no matter how much Janet had encouraged her to gain leverage that way, seemed unethical.

Colin set down his empty martini glass and stood. "I suppose you're worried about being unprofessional."

She glanced up at him. The setting sun surrounded him with a golden aura and cast his face in shadow, making him look mysterious and virile. Her heart raced in anticipation, even as she opened her mouth to refuse his request. "I really don't—"

"One kiss." He walked over and crouched in front of her, his arms balanced on his knees. "I promise that it will have no effect one way or the other on your proposal. That's a separate matter, one I will give consideration to tomorrow, when I've had sleep and a chance to think about it."

This close, she could see small golden flecks in the intense blue of his eyes. "Do I have your word on that?"

His voice grew endearingly solemn. "You have the word of a MacDowell."

"Oh, well, then, if I have the word of a MacDowell, what could go wrong?"

"Nothing, lass." Putting one hand on her knee, he cupped the back of her head with the other and leaned toward her. "It's only a wee kiss, and the previous one could use some improvement, don't you think?" His eyes drifted closed.

"I wouldn't know. Counting yours, I've only had two in my entire life."

His eyes snapped open and he nearly toppled over as he drew back. *"Two?"* He regained his balance.

"That's all."

He frowned. "Who was the other chap?"

"A stranger. He was staying at the hotel where I worked and caught me in the hallway. It was disgusting, and I got away from him as quick as I could."

"Kneed him in the privates, then?" Colin sounded hopeful.

"No. I squirmed and fought until he let me go."

"Pity. That sort could use a well-placed knee."

"I'll remember that."

"Just so we're clear, lass. I'm not that sort." He leaned toward her again.

"Never thought you were."

"You can close your eyes now."

"Oh." She'd been so fascinated by his mouth descending on hers that she hadn't wanted to miss a thing. But she'd seen screen kisses and knew eyes were usually closed. Dutifully she closed hers.

"Better." His breath touched her face.

She breathed in, relishing the heady scent of him—a combination of musk, martini, and an intoxicating aroma that she suspected was exclusive to Colin MacDowell, Laird of Glenbarra.

"When I kiss you, give me some resistance."

"You want me to resist?" That made no sense.

"No, don't resist *me*." His lips brushed hers once, twice. "But when I apply pressure, you apply some, too."

Her heart was pounding so fast with excitement that she wondered if she'd pass out. He wouldn't get any resistance, then, so she'd have to remain conscious. She gulped for air.

"Don't be nervous."

"Easy for you to say. You've done this thousands of times."

He chuckled. "Hardly." He nibbled at her lower lip. "You have such a wonderful mouth."

"Thank you kindly."

"No, I must thank you for indulging me. Here comes the kiss."

She held her breath. "Ready."

"Don't hold your breath. You'll faint."

"This is more complicated than I realized." She let out her breath. "It looks so easy in the movies."

"It is easy, once you get the hang of it. Just relax, and

when I make contact, give me something back." His mouth settled over hers.

At first she froze, unable to think, unable to respond at all.

His warm lips moved gently against hers. Tentatively she matched his movements.

"Yes," he murmured against her mouth. "Like that."

Made bolder by his praise, she put more energy into making contact. And then, as if ancient wisdom had finally bubbled up within her, she knew what to do. Grasping his head in both hands, she angled her head and took full possession of his mouth.

His low moan of delight told her that she'd figured out this kissing business. His fingers tightened against her scalp and his breathing quickened. She'd succeeded in exciting him, and triumph bloomed in her heart.

Then, when she was congratulating herself on the success of this kiss, he lifted his head just enough to end it.

Her pride plummeted. "Did I do something wrong?"

"Nay. You're doing everything right. But if you would open your mouth a wee bit . . ."

"You want to put your tongue in my—"

"Desperately."

"Okay." When he resumed kissing her, she slackened her jaw. Surely this would be gross, but she would endure it because Colin wanted to . . . Oh, my. Oh, *my*.

Now the moan belonged to her as she gave herself up to the decadent sensation of Colin's tongue stroking the inside of her mouth. Innocent though she was, she understood that this was what sex with him would be like, and she wanted it. The wanting came in a tidal wave that swept aside every thought except one.

Wrenching her mouth from his, she cupped his face, gripping him tightly as her gaze bored into his. "Have sex with me, Colin. Right now."

"That's not wise."

"I don't care what's wise! I want to know what it's—"

"Not now." He gasped for breath. "Not yet." As his breathing steadied, he massaged her back in a slow, easy motion.

"But I want to!" She'd lost all shame. He'd reduced her to raw, primitive need.

"Give yourself time, lass. If it is to happen between us, I want to be rested. You deserve more than I'm prepared to give you tonight."

She threw back her head and groaned in frustration. "You *had* to go and kiss me!"

"Yes." He drew her head forward until she was forced to look at him. "I couldn't let you think that what happened down by the water was a true kiss. I wanted you to know what a real kiss is all about."

"And as a result, I'm hot and frustrated. Happy now?"

"Aye. We all need to go through these stages, and you have some catching up to do." He brushed his mouth over hers one last time and stood. "It's getting dark. And I need to go to bed before I collapse."

She drew a long, trembling breath. "Right." She'd conveniently forgotten that he must be exhausted. But that was partly his fault. He'd started it by wanting to kiss her again.

He held out his hand to help her up. "Let's go back. We both could use a breather."

"I guess so." But she knew what would happen once her rational brain took over. She'd chicken out. If he gave her a chance to think things over, as he was determined to do, she'd never go through with it.

If they'd had sex tonight, she could have blamed her behavior on the charged atmosphere of the occasion. By tomorrow, she'd remember all the reasons why having sex with him was a really bad idea, beginning with the most important one—their potential business relationship.

Tonight could have been her initiation into the wonders of carnal knowledge by someone who seemed to know his way around the subject. Apparently he thought postponing the event would make it better. She wasn't going to tell him now, but postponing it meant that it wasn't going to happen at all.

Chapter 6

Colin's exhaustion was real enough, but that wasn't his only reason for calling a halt. He had some decisions to make regarding Luna, including the business matter of her inn project, and the personal matter of wanting her with the heat of a thousand suns. Decisions on both questions should be made only after due consideration and not on the spur of the moment.

This lusty attraction had scrambled his wits, which wasn't a common problem for him. He would like to blame it on jet lag, but he feared it had to do with the beautiful Were herself. After he staggered to bed, and just before he fell into a dreamless sleep, he vowed to avoid being alone with her again until he'd sorted out his feelings.

Fortunately, he had limited time to be tempted by that deadly combination of innocence and passionate response that had nearly undone him at twilight on Happy Hour Beach. He slept until nearly noon. He barely had time to shower, dress in a cotton long-sleeved shirt and slacks, and grab a quick snack before the real estate agent, Regis Trevelyan, arrived by motor launch. Colin spent the afternoon showing Regis, a graying Were with a slight paunch, around the estate. Late in the afternoon, Colin invited him to stay for dinner.

He asked Luna to join them, and she agreed, but he noticed the rigid set of her jaw every time she looked at Regis. Maybe she thought that Colin had invited him to dinner because they'd signed a contract to list the property. The opposite was true. He'd invited Regis to dinner because the poor chap wouldn't get the business, after all, and Colin wanted to offer him dinner as a small consolation.

The dining room had never looked better, and Colin gave Luna and her hard-working staff credit for that. Beeswax tapers cast a mellow glow over the dark paneled walls, and flowers graced the center of the table and the sideboards, as well. Luna had pinned her hair up in that sexy, mysterious way known only to women, and had worn a simple ivory dress that outlined her body so deliciously that she was driving him slowly insane.

But that was his personal problem. Even with that distraction to deal with, he could see that she was an excellent hostess. In her hands, Whittier House would flourish as an inn for Weres. He still had to mull over the particulars, but he was increasingly inclined to consider her plan. He'd never really wanted to sell Geraldine's house, anyway.

"Amazing job on the salmon," Regis said as Sybil cleared the dinner plates.

"Thank you. I'll tell the chef." Sybil beamed at him and continued to gather the empty dishes. She wore a white blouse and navy slacks, which might have been her attempt at a uniform.

Colin liked the comfortable informality of the staff's clothing, which hadn't changed since the summers he'd spent here years ago. But if Luna intended to *set the tone* as she'd put it, the staff might have to wear something more formal. "The salmon was great, Sybil," he said. "Please thank Janet for producing it on short notice."

Sybil nodded. "I will." She glanced over at Regis. "In case you're wondering, tonight's meal was a special request of the laird."

Regis chuckled. "Knocks me out, these fancy foreign titles." He turned to Colin. "What does a laird do, anyway?"

"It's not that much different from being the pack alpha," Colin said. "We're the guardians of a certain area and those who live within its boundaries. In my case, I combine both roles, as my father did before me."

Regis drank the last of his wine, an excellent white from the Whittier House cellars. "And the last thing you need is another responsibility on the far side of the world, right?"

"I thought so, and that's why I scheduled this appointment with you."

"And I'm honored that you did." Regis was practically licking his chops. The commission on the sale of Le Floret and the castle on it would bring him a year's worth of income.

"But Luna has presented me with a most intriguing proposition," Colin glanced at her and savored the surprise and pleasure in her green eyes. "She's suggested turning Whittier House into an exclusive Were resort. I'm seriously considering the possibility."

Regis looked as if he'd bit into a lemon. "Risky business, the hospitality industry. Fortunes have been lost trying to gauge the tastes of the fickle public."

"But this is a specialty area," Luna said. "Not many places cater specifically to Weres. Whittier House is already set up for that, including the need for open spaces, specially designed exits and entrances, and the most important aspect of all: seclusion."

Regis gazed at her with new respect. "You have a point, and Weres do tend to have money to spend on luxury accommodations. I know of one large hotel that caters to Weres. It's near Denver, in Estes Park."

"I've heard of that one," Colin said. "A large Were conference is scheduled there, but I've forgotten when."

"Sometime in the next six to eight months, I think," Regis said. "But back to your venture. Do you really want the headache of operating a business from your estate in Glenbarra? Why not just sell and be rid of the responsibility?"

Luna clutched her napkin and leaned forward. Candlelight danced in her glossy dark hair. "Or postpone that decision until the market for such properties is more lucrative. And in the meantime, create a guaranteed revenue stream."

Regis glanced over at her. "And you would run the facility?"

"I hope to, yes."

"And the chef stays?"

Luna nodded. "She's a key factor in whether this would work."

"I agree." Regis settled back in his chair and patted his mouth with his napkin. "I hate the idea of losing the business, but if you two follow through with this plan, I'll book a couple of rooms. My wife and my in-laws would love it here."

Colin's gaze met Luna's for one brief moment. She glowed with excitement, and his heart lurched. From what she'd told him the night before, she'd struggled for every bit of security in her life. Running this inn would mean the world to her.

He understood the drawbacks of owning a business so far away from his home base. He'd have to trust her implicitly. Despite sophisticated means of communication, he still couldn't supervise the operation adequately from Scotland.

But, the devil take it, he wanted to do this. His reasons were complicated and he wasn't sure he'd examined all his motives as thoroughly as he should. Some of them might be less than noble.

He wanted Luna, more so with every passing moment in her presence. She would be grateful to him if he gave her the job of running the inn. But he didn't believe in that kind of coercion on the part of males over females.

Besides, she could have scruples against becoming his lover if he confirmed that he would also be her boss. Damnation, he knew she'd have scruples. She'd said as much last night on the beach. But she'd also agreed to kiss him.

One thing he knew for certain. If he rejected her plan to turn Whittier House into a luxury vacation spot for Weres, he would have no reason to ever see her again once he left for Scotland. If he agreed to go along with her plan, they would have to work together to make it happen.

He'd known her for a mere twenty-four hours, and many of those hours he'd been asleep in his old bedroom. But they'd also comforted and supported each other during the scattering of Geraldine and Henry's ashes. A Were's true colors tended to shine through in moments like that, and Luna had provided the kind of calm strength that had kept Colin steady and focused.

She was special, and despite being a wee bit jet-lagged even now, he had the good sense to recognize how amazing she was. Whether they became lovers or decided it was too risky under the circumstances, she deserved a chance to create a haven for herself and other Weres on Le Floret.

*   *   *

Luna barely tasted dessert, and that was saying some-thing, because Janet had made her favorite, a rich cheese-cake laced with chocolate. But who cared about food when a person's dreams were about to come true? She kept sneaking glances at Colin, who seemed to be enjoy-ing his dessert and coffee just fine.

As for Regis, he asked for seconds as he praised Ja-net's cooking to the skies. When he was offered an after-dinner liqueur, he accepted that, too, plus a refill. Luna thought he'd never leave.

If Colin really meant what he'd said—and he struck her as a man of his word—then they had plans to make, timetables to create, menus to plan, rates to discuss. She had considered all of that. An Excel file on her computer held every idea she had brainstormed since she'd hatched this concept.

That had been a mere five days ago. She vividly re-membered walking the beach in total despair at the thought of being forced to leave Whittier House. Out of pure desperation, she'd come up with the idea of an inn exclusively for Weres.

She'd thought it was highly original, but after going online, she'd discovered a Were retreat in Colorado, the same one Regis had mentioned tonight. That seemed to be the only one, though, which meant the market was wide-open in Washington State. She wanted to run across the beach, fling out her arms, and shout with joy. This would work!

Instead she had to sit at this elegant table and listen to Regis discuss his golf swing. Luna knew as much about golf as she did about the mating habits of a duck-billed platypus, and a conversation about the sex life of a platypus had a lot more going for it, in her opinion.

But Regis wouldn't be the only dull guest she'd ever have to entertain once the inn opened for business, so she did her best to look fascinated. Colin knew something about golf, so he held up his end of the conversation admirably. She hadn't realized that Scotland was the birthplace of the game, but Regis seemed thrilled to talk with someone who had actually played the St. Andrews course.

Darkness had fallen by the time Regis finally summoned his private motor launch from Friday Harbor, the nearest marina to Le Floret.

"I'll walk you down to the dock, Regis." Colin left his chair and came around to help Luna out of hers. "Do you want to come with us?"

Not when she was dying to relay the good news about Whittier House to Janet, who would still be in the kitchen finishing her cleanup duties. "Thanks, but I need to check with Janet and make sure the dishwasher's running okay. It was acting up this morning, and if it still is, I'll call a repairman first thing in the morning."

"Be sure and give her my compliments again, and put me down for your opening weekend," Regis said.

"I'll do that." *Opening weekend!* She wanted to spin in place at the prospect. "Assuming Colin doesn't reconsider his decision." *Testing, testing.*

"I can't imagine why I would." Colin glanced at her. "But we have several details to go over."

She laced her fingers together to keep from clapping like a four-year-old who'd been promised ice cream. "Yes, we do, and I have a prioritized list, along with any ideas that have come to me. It's all stored on my computer." Difficult though it was, she forced herself to be sensible. "It's late, though. We can check that out tomorrow."

His blue eyes flashed with amusement. "I'm surprised you want to put it off that long."

"Not for my sake, but you're still recovering from your trip."

"I'm recovered enough to look at your information.

After you check on the dishwasher, fire up your computer. I'll be back in a few minutes."

"Perfect." She couldn't have kept the smile off her face if she'd been paid to do it. "My office is the one that used to be Henry's."

"I figured that out when I took Regis on a tour today."

"It's an elegant estate." Regis glanced around the dining room one last time. "I predict this inn will be extremely successful."

Luna started to say that she hoped so, but decided that response was too meek. "Thank you. I'm positive it will be."

Regis still couldn't seem to drag himself away. As he chatted about the tapestries and the paneling, Luna reminded herself that a guest's reluctance to leave was a good sign, but she wanted Regis gone so she could celebrate with Janet.

Finally Colin managed to edge Regis to the dining room door. Once they'd stepped into the hall, Luna turned and hurried through the door into the kitchen where Janet was wiping down the counters.

Janet glanced at Luna and stopped wiping. "He's going for the inn concept?"

Luna kept her voice down because she was afraid Colin and Regis were still in the house. "It looks like he will. But don't start shouting or anything. I think they're still in the hallway."

Janet pulled her cell phone from her apron pocket and punched in a number. "Dulce? Get your ass down here. And bring Sybil. We have news."

Returning to the door into the dining room, Luna opened it a crack and heard the solid thud of the front door closing. "They're gone."

"So what's the story? He's not listing the place with Regis?"

"Nope!" Luna couldn't keep the triumph out of her voice. "He told Regis that he liked my idea and wouldn't be putting the place up for sale, at least not at this point."

"Hallelujah!" Janet twirled her dishcloth over her head as she danced around the kitchen singing an old Lionel Richie party song.

Luna joined in, singing and gyrating past the stainless-steel, professional-grade appliances that Geraldine had bought years ago. Even though she hadn't cooked, she'd wanted her staff to have the best.

A piercing whistle from Dulcie ended the dancing. Wearing a gold silk camisole and matching cropped pants, she strolled through the doorway of the servants' wing. "What's all the fuss?"

Janet put her hand to her ample chest and gasped for breath. "Our Luna's done it! She's convinced His Laird-ness to turn Whittier House into an inn!"

"Woo-hoo!" Sybil, clad as usual in flannel, followed Dulcie into the kitchen. "Break out the cooking wine, Janet!"

"Way to go, girlfriend." Dulcie smiled at Luna as she walked over and gave her a high-five. "How did you do it?"

"I'm . . . I'm not sure." She hoped their second kiss hadn't been a factor. Colin had promised that wouldn't make a difference one way or the other. "It may be a simple matter of him not wanting to sell for sentimental reasons and now he has a good alternative."

Dulcie gave her a knowing look. "*Or* he figured out if he wants to get cozy with you, he has to let you manipulate his assets."

"That's funny," Sybil said. "You're good, Dulce."

"I try."

"But knowing Luna," Sybil added, "I don't think she has that kind of maneuver in mind."

"I absolutely do not," Luna said.

"Still, Dulcie could be right about Colin's motives." Sybil glanced at Luna. "Dulcie often is right about matters concerning the male of the species."

"I don't care why he's doing it." Janet pulled four juice glasses out of a cupboard, grabbed a bottle from the immense stainless refrigerator, and poured them each a glass. "The main thing is we all have jobs, and we can stay here and work together." She passed out the glasses as they created a circle. "To the Whittier House Inn."

"Here, here!" Dulcie tapped her glass against each of the others'. "And to Luna, who saved our collective asses."

Praise from a member of what had become Luna's substitute family was heady stuff. Flushed with a sense of camaraderie and success, she took a hefty swallow of wine. She was surprised by how smooth it was. "Pretty good for cooking wine."

"It's not cooking wine," Janet said. "Geraldine gave me this bottle for Christmas."

"Oh!" Sybil immediately put her glass back on the counter. "You shouldn't be giving it to us. It's special."

"That's exactly why I'm giving it to you. I opened it the day after she died, but I didn't make much of a dent, as you can see. Didn't have the heart for it. So drink up. She would have loved knowing we used her gift to celebrate the start of a new venture that keeps us all together."

"She definitely would have approved of the inn concept," Dulcie said.

"I hope so." Luna sipped her wine. "I've worried about that. Geraldine loved her privacy. Would she hate the thought of inviting a bunch of strangers into this house?"

Dulcie shook her head. "I think it wasn't so much privacy she loved, as independence from any particular pack. We'll still have that, plus the house stays in the family, and we all continue caring for it the way we've done all these years."

"I agree." Sybil retrieved her glass. "To Geraldine."

"To Geraldine!" they all chorused, clicking their glasses together.

Luna glanced at her watch. "This has been great, but I should get back to my office. Colin's meeting me there to go over a few things. I plan to show him my projections."

"I'm sure he's dying to see your *projections*." Dulcie wiggled her eyebrows as she stared at Luna's chest.

"Stop it, Dulce." Luna frowned in disapproval. "This is strictly business."

"Odd time to be doing business." Janet winked at her.

Luna felt the heat rising to her cheeks. "His body clock's all messed up. I've never flown internationally, but I've heard that you get your nights and days confused."

"You don't have to make up cover stories for us." Dulcie adjusted the strap on her camisole. "Personally, I'm all for whatever makes the laird happy. I wouldn't mind taking on that assignment, but Janet and Sybil have convinced me that you're the Were for the job."

"Nothing's going on between us." Luna eliminated the kiss from consideration, because Colin had said— he'd said, *damn it*—that a kiss wouldn't affect his decision one way or the other. She'd hold him to that, too.

Dulcie obviously wasn't buying her protestations. "Just tell me one thing." She leaned closer. "Did his decision to keep Whittier House involve a blow job?"

"Not to my knowledge," said a very male, very laird-like voice from the doorway that led into the dining room. "But then, I've had a horrible case of jet lag, so maybe I missed that part."

Chapter 7

As all four female Weres stared at Colin, he realized that Dulcie's question about oral sex wasn't far off the mark. He'd approved the inn plan partly because he hoped he and Luna would get to know each other better, perhaps even become lovers. After seeing Regis off, he'd been ridiculously eager to get back to her, and when she wasn't in her office, he'd tracked her down here.

Apparently Luna's coconspirators supported using sexual favors to gain the outcome they desired. He wondered if the others had any idea they'd put their money on an untried virgin. But from Dulcie's comment, he gathered that Luna had not confessed her situation to anyone until she'd told him about it the night before.

Dulcie, who didn't seem to mind being caught wearing silk nightwear, was the first to address the awkward situation. "Please excuse us, Colin, sir, Your Royal Laird of Glenbuggy."

"Glenbarra." He cleared his throat to disguise a laugh. "And I'm afraid the word *royal* isn't part of my title."

"Of course not." Sybil, looking somewhat grannylike

in her flannel gown, leaped into the fray. "I'm sure Dulcie knew that." She glared at her fellow housemaid.

"I knew that." Dulcie braved it out with a wink. "Just teasin' ya."

"Exactly." Janet smiled brightly. "You know how it is. Females get bawdy when we think no males are around. We meant no disrespect to you, someone we admire, or Luna, someone we both admire and love."

Then Luna, her cheeks rosy and her chin lifted, faced him. "I take full responsibility for any distress this gathering or our remarks have caused you."

"It's fine. I'm not—"

"I should have gone straight to my office as promised, but instead I came back here to share the good news, which probably wasn't my place." She plowed on, clearly needing to explain. "But in my excitement, I didn't think of that. Having the chance to stay on Le Floret and be a part of Whittier House means the world to us."

Colin's heart squeezed, because he knew how sincere that speech was. "I can see why it would. This island is special."

"Oh, and the wine is Janet's," Luna continued. "None of us would take what's not ours to take."

"I'm sure you wouldn't." He surveyed the group with satisfaction. A core staff of dedicated and loyal individuals would serve Luna well in the months ahead. "The fact that you're pulling together to create a future for yourselves is impressive. That kind of initiative speaks well for how Geraldine ran the household, and how Luna has run it under Geraldine's supervision."

"Thank you," Luna said.

"I'd like to add one cautionary statement, if I may."

She nodded. "Of course."

He glanced down at the tile floor while he fought to control his grin. When he looked up again, his expression was completely bland. "A blow job is a powerful weapon. It should be used wisely."

Dulcie giggled, but the rest of them, including Luna, looked thunderstruck.

He gazed at Luna as if nothing unusual had been said. "Ready to discuss those projections now?"

"Certainly." She squared her shoulders and set her glass on the counter. Back straight and color high, she ignored Dulcie's smile as she marched out of the kitchen.

He followed. Luna was obviously still embarrassed, so he decided not to attempt conversation until they'd reached the room that had once been Henry's hidey-hole. Colin had fond memories of the office and its book-shelf-lined walls. During his summers here, he'd been allowed free access to any volume on the shelves.

Tiffany lamps, connected to a timer that kept them on from early morning to midnight, saturated the room with jewel-toned light. The interior space had no windows, so the lamps were a necessity. Henry had said the absence of daylight helped protect the books, many of which were rare. But Colin had always thought the room satis-fied Henry's wolflike desire for a cave.

"I'm so sorry." Luna turned to him the moment they were both inside the office. "That was unforgiveable, and it never would have happened if I'd come straight here instead of going back to the kitchen to . . ."

"To let your friends know that they would still have a job?" Colin finished for her. "That was a kind and gener-ous impulse, Luna. You don't need to apologize for it."

"But announcing it should have been your privilege, not mine." Her hair gleamed dark and rich in the lamp-light. "I'm sorry I jumped the gun."

He longed to touch her. His desire for her was a slow, steady ache, one he could resist for now, but not forever. The more time they spent together, the more insistent that desire became. "I honestly don't mind that you told them. It's not a secret."

She looked relieved. "But Dulcie's remark was uncalled for. It sounded like the four of us have schemed to get our way by using me as bait. I would never agree to such a thing."

"Give me some credit for being a better judge of character than that, lass." He gazed at her. "Do you even know what Dulcie was talking about?"

Her cheeks turned pink. "Sort of. I'm sure you do."

"Aye." His body tightened as he thought of what such an activity would be like with Luna, who would be experiencing it for the first time. She might be hesitant at first, but with her passionate nature, she'd be a fast learner. He took a steadying breath. "Do they know that you're a—"

"No," she said quickly, "and I'd appreciate it if we could keep that between us. If they found out, they'd pester me with a million questions."

He fought the urge to step closer. "I have questions, too."

"Does it matter so much?" Her gaze was wary. "Why is being a virgin so all-fired important?"

"It's . . . just so unusual for a Were." He massaged the back of his neck while he considered the best way to discuss this volatile topic. "To start with, sexuality is a significant part of Were culture."

"It's a significant part of human culture, too, but that doesn't mean everyone is doing it."

Colin was beginning to understand just how little she knew about her own species. "That's one of many differences between Weres and humans. Teen Weres usually are encouraged to explore their sexuality. Pregnancy isn't an issue, and Weres are naturally resistant to disease. Sex is a skill we're expected to master and enjoy along with all our other studies."

"Oh." Although she was blushing furiously, she held his gaze. "So most teen Weres have sex, then?"

"Nearly all."

"Well, that explains why Dulcie, Janet, and Sybil are always teasing me about not having sex. But they're not having it, either!"

"No, but I'm sure that they did when they were younger, and if the opportunity presents itself, they will again. Not every Were has nonstop sexual encounters their entire life. If they find a mate and that Were dies, the survivor may choose celibacy to honor their lost mate."

She seemed to consider that for a moment. "I wonder if that's what happened to Hector."

"Possibly. I never asked."

"That would explain why he lives like such a hermit on the island."

"And that's fine for Hector, but it seems like such a waste for someone who's never . . ."

"Does my virginity really bother you, then?"

"It bothers me that you're not enjoying yourself as you could be. I hate to think of you missing out on something beautiful, especially when you obviously have a very passionate nature."

"Especially when you could be enjoying yourself, too," she said with a teasing smile. She might be innocent, but she was aware of her sexual power.

He took a deep breath to steady himself. "You tempt me greatly, Luna, and I'll admit that your lack of experience presents an extra challenge to my ego."

"You sound a little desperate." She stood bathed in rainbow light from the Tiffany lamps, her green eyes luminous.

"You have no idea how desperate I am. Fortunately for both of us, I've been well schooled in self-control."

She swallowed. "I shouldn't have told you."

"But you did. Why do you suppose that is?"

"Stupidity?"

He shook his head. "You're not stupid, and you have strong self-protective instincts. Try again."

"Because I know I'm missing something, and I want to know what it is."

A weaker man might have taken that as a cue to pull her into his arms. Colin blessed the training he'd had as the future laird and pack alpha, because he sensed it was too soon. "I'd be happy to show you what you're missing. Delighted, in fact." Now, there was the understatement of the century. Imagining how he would instruct her made him tremble.

She clasped her hands tightly in front of her in a clearly protective stance. "We're in business together. What if sex ruins everything between us, even the business arrangement?"

"I swear to you as a MacDowell that I wouldn't allow that." His heart beat faster as he realized that she was considering it. But he had to move slowly. "Nothing personal between us will change my decision that Whittier House will become an inn under your supervision. It's a brilliant idea, and you're the right person for the job."

"That's good to hear." She relaxed slightly.

"If I had any doubt about your ability to deal with guests, you passed the test tonight when you didn't go facedown in your plate while Regis carried on about his golf."

A smile tilted the corners of her full mouth. "I considered poking out my eardrums with my shrimp cocktail fork."

"Be grateful you weren't the one showing him around the estate all afternoon." Colin welcomed a chance to talk about something else and dispel some of the tension between them. After all, he wasn't about to seduce her here. But in the back of his mind, he was already considering his next move.

"Surely he didn't talk about golf then, too."

"Not the whole time." Colin grimaced as he thought back over his long afternoon with Regis. "First he spent a couple of hours bragging about his business success. I can't imagine how he makes any money at all when he's such a crashing bore."

"Does he have a corner on the Were market here in the Seattle area?"

"I suppose he might, but still."

"Maybe he has a whole bunch of smart agents working for him, and he has no contact with clients anymore. But he couldn't resist getting a peek at this island, so he assigned himself to come out here."

Colin nodded. "I'm sure this island has been a tantalizing mystery for almost fifty years, and that should work to your advantage. Initially, curiosity will bring guests."

"And then word will spread about the wonderful food and the charming setting, and we'll be booked up months, maybe even years, in advance." She spread her arms wide. "We'll be a smashing success."

She seemed more relaxed now, and he enjoyed watching her green eyes light up when she talked about this project. He'd gone from hating the idea yesterday to loving it today. But he needed to clarify a few things before lust short-circuited his brain. "I have some questions."

"I should hope so."

"Will you make any areas off-limits to the guests?"

"Definitely. The staff's quarters will be private, of course, and the kitchen." She paused. "I've been sleeping in a bedroom across from Geraldine's because she wanted me nearby, but I'll move down to a spare room in the staff area to free up the space."

"I suppose you'll be needing my bedroom, too." He didn't want to give it up, but that room would be popular with its access to the tower above, and Whittier House was now an inn, not a family home.

"That's up to you. We should designate a room that's yours, though, for when you're visiting."

"No, you should use all available space. On the rare occasions I'm here, you can stick me anywhere." Everything coming out of his mouth was perfectly logical, but his heart wasn't buying a word of it.

She seemed to sense his ambivalence. "We can decide that for sure later on."

"All right." He left the subject with relief. "Are you planning to make Henry's library available to guests?"

"No, I'm not. This room will be my office and guests won't be allowed in here, but they should have books available. I was thinking Geraldine's sitting room might make a nice library."

"And it has a wet bar. I assume you're planning to schedule happy hour every evening?"

"I think Geraldine would haunt me if I didn't."

That made him smile. "Aye, she would, at that."

"Picture me registering guests and saying, *Drinks will be served at six in the library*. It has a nice ring to it."

"I agree." Her sweet scent beckoned to him, and he realized he'd unconsciously moved closer. "You're going to be a natural at this, Luna." Guests, especially male guests, would be drawn to her, too. Sooner or later an eligible Were would express interest. Colin didn't fancy that concept at all.

"I hope so. It feels right. Anyway, the sitting room already has bookshelves. It just needs more books. I could browse the used shops in Seattle, and pick up a few board games while I'm at it."

"That sounds like fun." He had a sudden, appealing

image of strolling around musty old bookstores with Luna and stealing a kiss in a narrow and secluded aisle. "Maybe we could do that before I leave."

"And when are you leaving? I don't remember a time being set."

He sighed. "I won't be here long, I'm afraid. A week is all I've allowed myself. My father's health isn't great, and my brother, Duncan, is something of a loose cannon."

"Then we need to prioritize."

He knew what would rise to the top of his priority list, but he didn't say that. Later.

She surveyed the shelves in Henry's office. "These books all belong to you now. I suppose it would make sense to sell some of the more valuable ones instead of just letting them sit here." She didn't sound particularly enthusiastic about it.

"I'd rather not sell any."

Her smile was warm with approval. "I'm glad. These books have become special to me. I look up from my desk and there they are, lined up in colorful rows, waiting for me to choose one. I'd hate to see any of them leave. And old books smell so good!"

"Yes, they do." He'd never met anyone who'd mentioned that, but it was one of his favorite scents. From now on he'd also associate it with Luna. "I used to spend hours in here. Henry let me read anything, even if it was a first edition worth a great deal of money."

"Geraldine said he was generous." She laughed. "Well, obviously he was if he built her a *castle*."

"But I've always wondered why he made it so big, with so many bedrooms."

Luna cocked her head. "She never told you?"

"No, and I didn't think to ask until now, when it's too late."

"Well, she told me, one night during happy hour down on the beach. I suppose I can say, now that she's gone."

Colin found himself feeling jealous of the closeness Luna had enjoyed with Geraldine, but he could have had that, too, if he'd made more of an effort. "You don't have to, if you'd rather not."

"I don't think she'd mind. But first of all I have to ask, were Henry and Geraldine considered truly mated?"

"I'm certain of it." Colin had fond memories of watching them hold hands and steal an occasional kiss when they thought he wasn't paying attention.

"Then I don't understand, because they tried and tried to have children and couldn't. Why not?"

"Being truly mated doesn't guarantee pregnancy. But you can't have a pregnancy unless that condition is met." He thought about all the bedrooms in Whittier House. "I can't believe they planned to have enough children to fill the place."

"No, but they wanted a bunch. They added the extra space so that any who chose to stay on the island could do so, even after they mated. I think Henry and Geraldine secretly wanted to start their own pack."

"So they wanted children, after all." Colin had convinced himself that children hadn't been important to Geraldine, but now he could see why his visits had meant so much to her. "I've been a sorry excuse for a nephew, that's for bloody sure."

Luna rested her hand lightly on his arm. "Don't blame yourself. She wouldn't want that."

Her touch, even though it was muted by the sleeve of his dress shirt, jolted him out of his guilty reverie and tossed him right back into a hot cauldron of lust. He looked into her eyes, and he must have transmitted every bit of that surge of lust with one glance, because she jerked her hand away as if she'd laid it on a hot stove. Yet she held his gaze.

"Do I scare you?" he asked.

"Some."

"I don't mean to."

"I know. It's me. I hadn't spent much time alone with a male Were until you arrived."

"Are you ready to call it a night?" He fought the strong urge to reach out and stroke her cheek as he would a frightened child, except she was not a child, and once he started touching her, he wasn't sure how easily he'd be able to stop. He clenched both hands into fists and wondered if he should make a move. Probably not.

She moistened her lips. "So you don't want to go over my income projections?"

That Southern drawl of hers just might be his undoing. It slid over him like warm honey, and he longed to hear how sweet and seductive that voice would become once he'd introduced her to the wonders of mutual satisfaction. His groin tightened, warning him that there were limits to his self-control.

"Let's do that tomorrow."

"Okay." Her eyes searched his, as if uncertain how the dance should go. "Then I'll say good night." She turned toward the door.

He didn't want her to go, but he didn't have any reason to ask her to stay that didn't involve stripping naked. He didn't think she was ready for that. Of course, he couldn't be sure what she was ready for, because he hadn't dealt with a virgin in years, and he was out of practice.

Then he had an inspiration. "I'm going to set up my telescope on the roof. Do you like stargazing?" After he said it, he groaned inwardly. What an obvious ploy to get a woman alone in the dark.

She turned back to him, her face alight. "I've never tried it, but sure. Geraldine told me how much you used to enjoy it."

"Then let's do that." At first he was astonished that she didn't laugh at his clumsy attempt to coax her into an area that contained a bed. Then he realized that she wasn't sophisticated enough to laugh at what would have been obvious to any other female Were.

"I'll go change into jeans and a sweatshirt and come to your room. See you soon." She hurried out of the library and headed toward the back stairs that were a shortcut to the corridor where she currently had a room.

Colin followed her out and walked toward the entry hall and the main staircase leading to his wing. As he climbed the stairs, he told himself not to expect the stargazing plan to pave the way for sex. It might, though, and if it did, he'd make sure the experience was all it should be.

After years of celibacy, Luna deserved excellence, and providing that was his responsibility. He felt the weight of it crushing some of his anticipation. Then again, as a virgin, she'd have no basis of comparison. She wouldn't know if he was great, adequate, or dismal.

The weight lifted and his anticipation returned. He took the rest of the stairs two at a time.

Chapter 8

Luna wasn't sure what she wanted to happen tonight, but she was thrilled for an excuse to stay with Colin a little longer. Being with him created a buzz of excitement deep inside her body, and for the first time in her life she didn't try to tamp down that delicious vibration.

She slipped out of her ivory dress, one she'd carefully chosen for tonight's dinner because she felt more sophisticated when she wore it. Geraldine had taken her to Seattle one memorable day many months ago, and had insisted on buying her clothes she never could have afforded on her own. After protesting that she couldn't accept, Luna had relented when Geraldine admitted she'd always wanted a daughter to shop for.

The ivory dress had been Geraldine's favorite. As Luna hung it in the closet, she had a strange thought. Could Geraldine have left Whittier House to Colin in hopes that he and Luna were destined to be mated? Surely not. Geraldine knew that Luna had found security on Le Floret, and Colin had obligations in Scotland.

So perhaps Geraldine hadn't meant them to be bonded for life, but she *might* have thought Colin would be the perfect Were to teach Luna about sex. Although Luna had never spoken of such things with Geraldine, anyone with Geraldine's powers of observation would have guessed that Luna was lacking in her knowledge of males.

But it was self-centered and ridiculous to think that Geraldine had willed her entire estate to Colin for Luna's sake. Wishful thinking, too. She'd spent her life dreaming that someone, somewhere, would fill the void left by her mother. Geraldine had done that for a brief time, but imagining that Geraldine had organized her will to create a meeting between Colin and Luna was not realistic.

Pulling on her jeans and a dark green sweatshirt, Luna shoved her feet into a pair of loafers and left her room. Across the hall, the door to Geraldine's old room was closed. Luna felt a pang as she imagined cleaning it out and making it ready for paying guests. But it was a wonderful room with a balcony and a view of the water, so leaving it as a shrine to Geraldine was not a sound business decision.

Luna was determined to make sound business decisions and justify Colin's faith in her. But the rest of this particular night wasn't about business. Whether Geraldine had envisioned a relationship between Colin and Luna or not, she'd set the wheels in motion for them to meet. Luna couldn't shake the feeling that Geraldine would have wanted them to be friends, at the very least.

Luna hadn't had many friends in her life. As she took the long walk from her bedroom to Colin's, she went over the short list. First was Cecily, a girl she'd met as a child in New Orleans. Luna had abandoned any hope of staying friends with Cecily after the first shift happened. As a runaway teen, she'd had superficial connections with people and Weres, but nothing lasting.

Coming to Le Floret a year ago had changed her life. Geraldine had welcomed her with open arms, and that had been enough of an endorsement for Janet, Sybil, and Dulcie to draw her into their tight circle. Now Luna counted all of them as dear friends.

Hector was the only Were on the island who hadn't totally accepted her. She would have to deal with that now that they were all staying on the island.

She didn't have to think about Hector tonight, however. Tonight she would stargaze with Colin MacDowell, Laird of Glenbarra. His door was open, but she knocked on the door frame anyway, because she felt odd simply wandering in. She didn't see him anywhere in the astronomy-themed room.

She'd been here once, when Geraldine had taken her on a tour of Whittier House and had spent a great deal of time pointing out the details of this room. Luna had wondered why this paragon Geraldine obviously adored hadn't come back to visit, but Geraldine had explained that he'd become responsible for the entire MacDowell pack and couldn't get away. She'd seemed at peace with his absence, although a little wistful that she hadn't seen him in fifteen years.

Hinges creaked, and Colin's denim-covered legs emerged from the trapdoor at the top of the metal spiral staircase leading to the tower above.

"I'm here," she called out.

"Good." His accent made it sound like *gud*. "The scope is ready." He started down the stairs, his gym shoes creating a dull chime as they hit each step. He'd obviously changed clothes, too, and had on his Space Needle hooded sweatshirt from the night before.

The first time she'd stepped into this room, she hadn't paid much attention to the bed other than to notice that the bedspread and curtains matched. But with Colin ac-

tually present in the room, the decor became less important and the bed took on more significance.

Luna had seen enough movies and read enough
books to know that sex could take place anywhere, but
beds were the most common location for humans or
those in human form. After years spent working in hotels, Luna easily identified this one as a queen size, which
was plenty big enough for two.

"My aunt probably told you that she was responsible
for my love of astronomy," Colin said.

Luna's attention, previously riveted to the bed, snapped
abruptly back to him. "She did." His chocolate and caramel hair had been tossed by the night breeze, and his blue
eyes glowed with anticipation. Maybe the prospect of
stargazing was responsible for that glow, but Luna thought
she might have something to do with it, too.

Colin glanced around the room. "She told me to aim
for the stars."

"She said that to me, too."

"And you've done that. You're determined to take
what you have, which is a foothold on this island, and
turn it into something that will benefit you and many
others."

She'd come up with her plan for primarily selfish reasons, and his praise made her uncomfortable. "It's a matter of survival," she said quietly.

"I understand, but I think it's more than that. You
have vision, Luna. I'm not sure I can say the same."

"But it's easier for me. I have only myself to think
about. From what Geraldine said, y'all have to consider
the needs of your entire pack. That takes a different kind
of vision."

He smiled. "You are entirely too good for my ego.
Shall we go up?"

The effect of that bright, genuine, and damn sexy smile

was instantaneous and devastating. She couldn't breathe, couldn't think or even manage to make herself walk toward the spiral staircase. She stared at him while a voice inside her head shouted, *Take me! Take me now!*

"Luna?" He peered at her. "Are you all right?"

With a quick shake of her head, she cleared the lust from her brain. She'd been right to avoid sexual entanglement in the past if it turned her into a deaf-mute with a one-track mind.

But now, with Colin, she'd let down her guard. "I'm fine." She held her breath as she walked past him because his musky scent was liable to draw her into another catatonic state. She didn't want him to think that she was so easily distracted or he might reconsider his decision to put her in charge of Whittier House.

Somehow she made it up the metal staircase without tripping or falling backward into his arms. She considered that maneuver, because she desperately wanted him to wrap those strong arms around her and give her another kiss. The very thought of it created squiggles in her belly and a moistness between her legs.

So this was what arousal was all about. If she turned her passion loose, would it flatten her and everything in its path? She had no way of knowing.

But Colin radiated a strength and steadiness that she believed she could count on. He wasn't that much older than she was in terms of years, but he was vastly more experienced in the ways of the world, and the way of Weres in sexual situations.

Plus Geraldine had loved him. That more than anything had convinced her that she could safely let herself go. Maybe rationalization came into play, because she wanted to surrender and didn't care to consider potential drawbacks. But whether her trust was well placed or not, she'd never know unless she took a chance.

Grabbing handholds on the roof outside the trapdoor, she pulled herself through the opening and crawled rather ungracefully onto the flat roof, which was surrounded by the gap-toothed parapet of the tower. Once out, she stood and took a deep breath of cool night air scented with the tang of salt.

The whisper of waves stroking soft sand drifted up from the beach, and a three-quarter moon cast a silver path across the dark water. Tipping back her head, she gazed at stars flung like powdered sugar over the night sky.

"Incredible, isn't it?"

At the sound of his low voice with its soft Scottish burr coming from less than three feet away, she tingled all over. "Yes."

"Ever been up here before?"

"No." She lowered her gaze before she grew dizzy. "I have a touch of acrophobia."

"You should've told me, lass. I wouldn't have asked you to climb up here if I'd known that."

"No problem." She glanced over at him. "Having someone with me makes a difference. And now that I know the parapets are waist high, that helps, too. Standing on the ground, it's impossible to tell how high they are. If they'd only been a foot or two, I'd be hyperventilating right now." As it was, she still felt slightly breathless, mostly because he appeared mysteriously sexy in the moonlight.

She had the urge to know how he looked as a wolf, although she wasn't about to ask him to shift for her benefit. But if she allowed him to teach her about Were sex, then logically they'd need to try it as wolves in order to make her education complete. Thinking of that made her shiver with pleasure.

He moved closer. "Cold?"

"Not really. I only—"

"If you are, I brought up a quilt from my bedroom."

"Oh?" The word came out high pitched—almost, but not quite, a squeak.

He chuckled. "Don't worry, lass. I'm not going to pounce on you."

If only you would and make the decision for me. "I'm sure you aren't the pouncing type."

His smile flashed in the silvery light from the moon. "What type do you think I am, then?"

"The gentle, persuasive type." And that worked for her, too, especially if he'd start persuading sometime soon. She did sort of want to look through the telescope, but she really, really wanted him to kiss her.

"My brother, Duncan, would disagree with your assessment. He says I'm dictatorial and demanding. Oh, and old-fashioned, as well. Mustn't forget that bit."

"Why?" She wondered if this was a side of Colin she should know about if he was going to be her boss.

"I believe in heeding the lessons from the past, and he doesn't." His tone was light, but an undercurrent of anger filtered through.

"I've never been part of a family, but isn't that the way the oldest and youngest tend to roll?"

"Roll?" He seemed confused.

"It's an expression over here that means how someone operates in the world."

"Ah." He sighed. "Then disregarding the past is how Duncan rolls."

"And instead, you treasure it."

"Aye, and respect it."

"I'm glad, because if you didn't, you'd probably be selling Whittier House to the highest bidder."

"True." He rubbed his knuckles against his chin in what seemed like an unconscious gesture. "About that, I know it's not practical, but I'd like to make my old bedroom off-limits to guests."

"I was hoping you would." When he was gone, she'd take comfort in knowing he had a designated space here at Whittier House, and that he wasn't quite as transient as he claimed.

"Gives me a place for my telescope," he said with a grin.

"Exactly."

"Come on over here and take a look." He walked toward the tripod he'd placed near the parapet. "I've focused it on Saturn. It's the most dramatic one. Just look into that eyepiece there."

"Okay." She found his enthusiasm endearing. Crossing to the telescope, she leaned over and peered through the lens. Her breath caught at the image, which was so clear it could have been a poster of the ringed planet. "I see it! I don't know what I expected, but this is amazing!"

"My aunt provided me with a really fine telescope." His hand came to rest on her shoulder. "I didn't realize how expensive it was until I bought myself one in Scotland."

She felt the warmth of his touch down to her toes, and suddenly the image of Saturn didn't interest her at all. That was a shame, because it really was exciting to be gazing out into space at a planet so far away from her. But his hand on her shoulder was a million times more exciting. And a million times closer than Saturn.

Still, she didn't have the heart to tell him that she'd lost interest in his carefully focused view of Saturn, one he'd set up especially for her. So she kept staring at it while she tried to remember the last thing he'd said.

Oh, yes. He'd bought himself a telescope over in Scotland. "Are there places to stargaze in Scotland?" Her voice sounded a little quivery, but maybe he wouldn't notice.

"Aye. Galloway Forest is a premier spot." He massaged her shoulder in a slow, circular motion.

Her body began to hum, but for all she knew, he wasn't even aware of what he was doing. He was, after all, crazy about this astronomy stuff and might have forgotten all about her sexual education.

Trying to be delicate about it, she cleared the huskiness from her throat. "Lots of stars?"

"At least seven thousand." He continued his absentminded caress.

"That's quite a few." Her heart pounded so loud that she thought he might be able to hear it. The image in the telescope lens grew wobbly because she couldn't concentrate on it properly.

He kneaded her shoulder now, and his fingertips pressed a little deeper than before. "In comparison, if you're in Edinburg, you might see about five hundred stars. This island is excellent for stargazing, but Galloway Forest is even better."

She was ready to melt into a puddle at his feet. She could barely think, let alone speak, but she managed a breathless comment. "How lucky for you."

"Yes."

And then she heard it—a hitch in his breathing. Either he was getting carried away by the thought of all those stars in the heavens, or he was getting carried away by something closer to home. She held her breath and listened to make sure what she'd heard wasn't the sound of waves on the beach.

Nope, it was Colin, and he was breathing *much* faster. Something was affecting him. The more she thought about it, the more she concluded that it wasn't his enthusiasm for astronomy that had him going like that.

She swallowed. In for a penny, in for a pound. "Uh, Colin?"

He took his hand away. "What?"

She hadn't wanted him to stop touching her. In fact, she wished he'd bring *both* hands into play. She lifted her head and turned to look at him. Sure enough, the rapid rise and fall of his chest told her that she'd been right. "Seeing Saturn was amazing, but I—"

"You want to see something different."

"Well, the thing is . . ." What could she say? That she felt a desperate need for something, and although she didn't know quite what that was for sure, she thought he might have a clue?

"How about Jupiter?" He stepped toward the telescope and leaned over it. "I can probably pull in—"

"I'd love to see Jupiter, but not right this minute." She paused and gulped in air.

"Mars, then. You'll like Mars." His back was to her as he began adjusting the telescope.

Not having to face him gave her courage, and she realized if she didn't say it now, the buildup to what she wanted could take the whole blessed night. "Colin, I want you to . . . to . . . for the love of God, just . . . just *pounce*!"

Chapter 9

Colin froze and every circuit in his brain seemed to short out. Slowly he straightened and turned toward her. "You *want* that?"

"Desperately."

With a groan of relief, he pulled her into his arms and captured the mouth that had been driving him bollocking crazy. Ah, *yes*. Only two kisses ago she hadn't the foggiest notion of how to do this, but as he'd predicted, she was a fast learner.

As she opened her mouth to allow his tongue inside, he tried to remember that she was a virgin. But she wasn't kissing like one at the moment. From the way she writhed against him, rubbing her hot body over his crotch, he almost wondered if she'd made up that story.

If so, he'd know soon enough, because he wasn't going for the civilized approach of guiding her down the steps to a proper bed. If she wanted him to pounce, then pounce he would. She might think of him as gentle and persuasive, but under that domesticated exterior lay a wild, Scottish heart. His ancestors had defended their land to the death, either as naked, blue-faced warriors wielding claymores, or snarling wolves in powerful packs that yielded to no one.

Luna, a maddening combination of innocence and bravado, brought out his primitive instincts. He would be her first lover, and no matter how many she had after he was gone, she would remember him. Fierce, triumphant heat bloomed in his chest and surged to his groin.

He undressed her with a quick efficiency that left her gasping. Then he asked her to spread out the quilt while he rid himself of his clothes. She was quick about it. Once he'd tossed the last thing aside, he glanced down to find her stretched out and waiting for him.

Now there was a visual—white skin gilded with moonlight against a navy quilt that created a perfect background for her hourglass figure. He'd never viewed more lovely breasts or more graceful thighs. The dark triangle tucked between them made his cock jerk with impatience.

Her eyes widened as she looked him up and down, and her gaze lingered on the length and rigidity of his penis. Her throat moved in a convulsive swallow.

A virgin. He tried to clear the red haze from his fevered brain. She'd asked him to pounce. Apparently she'd relished the deep, demanding kisses and the urgency with which he'd pulled off her clothes, because he could read eagerness in her expression. But if he took her now without any preparation, that would be brutish.

Kneeling beside her on the quilt, he leaned down, cupped her face in his palm, and kissed her with tenderness instead of lust. She moaned softly against his mouth. That pleading moan threatened to destroy his hard-won control, but he kept his kiss gentle as he began to caress her full breasts.

Then he stilled. She'd taken hold of his cock.

Lifting his head, he gazed down at her. His voice was

thick with restrained passion. "Virgins don't usually do that."

Her voice was equally thick. "Why not?" She curled her fingers around his penis and squeezed. Not too hard, not too soft. Just right.

And just right to make him come if she didn't let go. "They're generally too shy."

"Probably because they're young," she said in a throaty voice. "I've had years to think about this."

She was out to kill him. He was sure of it. "Have you imagined what it will be like when someone slides his cock deep inside you, thereby ending your virginal status?"

"Of course I have." Keeping her fingers curled, she stroked upward and explored the tip with her thumb. Naturally she found the moist result of her efforts and spread that moisture around.

He gritted his teeth against the climax that threatened. "Would you like to experience that and lose your virginity?" he said in a strained voice.

"Boy, howdy, would I ever."

"Then you need to let go of me, or I'll come now. Do you understand about climaxes?"

"Females can have several, but males get one and then they have to . . . to . . ."

"Reload. And no telling how long that would take." Although with her around, he suspected it wouldn't be long.

"I thought I might be bothering you. Bless your heart, there's a vein standing out in your temple."

"I'm not surprised."

"I want to learn how to give a blow job."

Yes, she was definitely out to kill him. "Not now," he muttered as he recited football stats in his head.

She let go of him with obvious reluctance.

He'd wanted to take his time with this, but he could still feel the imprint of her soft fingers on his cock. And while technically a Were of his experience should be in complete control of his climax, he hadn't had sex for several months and wasn't in the best shape for a prolonged seduction.

In other words, if he didn't take care of this deflowering soon, he might deliver a less-than-stellar performance. He'd tried to convince himself that she wouldn't know the difference. However, if he didn't give her a climax this first time, he thought she *would* know the difference. Even virgins knew they were supposed to get an orgasm out of the deal.

So he changed his tactics and his position. When he put one knee between her thighs, she spread them obligingly. He took a deep breath, hoping it would steady him.

Instead he inhaled her delicious scent, which created a greater problem. As a normal male Were, he wanted to bury his nose and mouth between her thighs and taste her. He *needed* to do that. It was hardwired to a Were's sexual response, a way of knowing the female that couldn't be duplicated.

But he wasn't sure he could indulge that urge without bringing his climax perilously close. Ah, bloody hell. He'd chance it. The risk was worth the prize. Stretching his legs out behind him, he levered himself downward toward her fragrant center.

"What are you doing?"

He glanced up. She'd propped herself on her elbows and was staring at him, awaiting his answer. His lust-filled brain couldn't seem to form a coherent explanation. Maybe if he just did it, she'd instinctively understand. He lowered his head.

"Wait."

He looked up again, but his mind was occupied with

the prospect of feasting on her nectar and he had to wrench it back to the point where it would understand the spoken word.

And she definitely had words to speak. "Unless your tongue's longer than I thought, I won't get deflowered that way."

His jaw muscles tightened against the desire to scoot back up and take her in one swift thrust, just to shut her up. She was the most maddening female, but she also didn't know what she was talking about, and he had to make allowances for her total lack of experience.

He strove for patience. "You want me to teach you about sex, I believe."

"I also want to lose my virginity, and I only know of one way to do that. Well, I suppose I could have used a vibrator years ago, but that seemed like cheating."

"Have you ever had a climax?"

"That seemed like cheating, too," she said softly.

"Then just stop talking, lass, because I'm about to give you your first climax, and this is definitely not cheating."

All her life, whenever she got nervous or scared, Luna had battled her fears by taking control of the situation. She wanted to do that now. His kisses had made her forget everything except his mouth, his hands, and his very large penis. She wasn't used to losing herself in the moment, and she was afraid.

Panic must have shown on her face, because his expression gentled. "I promise you'll like it," he murmured.

"Will you stop if I say so?"

"Of course." He smiled. "But I don't think you'll want me to stop."

"All right, then. Go ahead." She sounded ungracious, but when she was frightened, her manners went out the window.

"Lie back."

"No, I want to watch."

"Suit yourself." With his forearms braced on either side of her hips, he lowered his head, and his warm breath touched the hot, slick place he was about to invade.

She shuddered but resisted the urge to close her eyes. She'd never had a male's head between her legs before, and she wanted to keep an eye on him, just in case he—*Oh*. His tongue made contact with a spot that had been throbbing quite a bit since the moment he'd touched her shoulder.

Although she'd heard the clinical name for that sensitive part of her body, she'd always considered it her sacred center. She'd known instinctively that tiny spot held immense power, the power to undo her. Now Colin was circling it with his tongue, and it seemed as if each rotation tightened a coiled spring deep inside her.

The tension built, and her thighs began to quiver. Yet all he was using was the tip of his tongue to go round and round, and sometimes he'd bear down, just a little, and the pressure increased, building higher, making her heart race. Could she be dying? She couldn't take this!

"Stop!"

He went completely still. Then he slowly lifted his head to gaze at her. His eyes caught the moonlight, and they were glittering and dark, not the laughing eyes she remembered from their first meeting.

Although he'd stopped, the throbbing continued. It spread through her body, heating her veins and making her tremble with a combination of excitement and dread. She held her breath, waiting for what would happen next. Would she explode?

Apparently not. The pressure lessened slowly, and gradually the throbbing became bearable. It was going away. And she discovered, to her embarrassment, that she didn't want it to go away. Crazy as it was, she wanted to feel that tension again.

Now she knew that she truly was safe with him, because when she'd told him to stop, he had. Perhaps other males wouldn't have, but he did. If she flew apart because of what he was doing to her, he'd help put her back together.

Dragging air into her lungs, she met his gaze. "I panicked."

"I could tell."

"I won't panic the next time."

His eyebrows rose. "The next time? You want me to start again?"

Her heart beat faster as she imagined him using the tip of his tongue to make her feel the way she had only minutes ago. "Yes, please."

He hesitated for a moment, as if wondering whether he should risk it.

"I'll go through with it this time," she said.

"Aye, but will you crush my head like a grape between your thighs when you come?" He gave her a half smile to show he was teasing.

"I'm not that strong, but if you're worried, grab hold of me."

"I might, at that." Adjusting his position, he slipped his hands under her thighs and gripped her tightly with his long fingers. Then he urged her to spread wider for him.

She had better trust him, because she'd only felt this vulnerable once before, during her first shift. That's when she understood why she'd panicked. "Can a climax bring on a shift?" Although she was used to shifting, she wasn't sure how she'd react to an unexpected one.

"No, it cannot make you shift."

"You're sure?"

"Sure as my name is Colin MacDowell. All you'll feel is pleasure. Relax and let it happen." Leaning down, he blew gently.

Warm air on moist skin had an electrifying effect, and she gasped.

"Good?"

"I don't know. Do it again." He did, and she felt the spring begin to tighten. "Yes, good."

He laughed softly, which sent more warmth to caress that significant area that both intrigued and frightened her. She waited for the first touch of his tongue, but instead, he gave her a deep, highly personal kiss in her sacred center.

She sucked in a breath, shocked by the intimacy of it, but she'd promised to see this through. And she would. Oh, yes, she most certainly would. Only a fool would stop someone from doing *this*. As he settled in, pleasure flowed over her like hot fudge sauce.

Insistent pressure, more familiar to her now, built quickly. Yet her body felt languid and heavy. She discovered that closing her eyes allowed her to focus all her attention on the sensations provided by Colin's mouth and tongue. Finally, she lay back on the quilt in total surrender and allowed him to plunder at will.

He intensified his assault. Soon he had her moaning and thrashing about. She clutched a section of the quilt in each fist and lifted her hips to demand more, and yet more, not knowing what lay ahead, yet yearning for it, all the same.

Her climax came in a rush that knocked the breath from her. She cried out in surprise and wonder at the sheer majesty of it. Waves of delight lifted and carried her to shore, where she rolled like a seashell in the surf.

All the while Colin held her, anchoring her to reality so that she wouldn't panic. As the tremors gradually subsided, she let go of the wads of quilt in each fist and reached down to circle his wrists with her fingers.

Placing kisses over her damp inner thighs, he slipped his wrists free, laced his fingers through hers, and drew her arms up over her head as he rose over her. "Open your eyes."

She'd forgotten they were closed. Allowing them to flutter open, she looked up and there he was, his massive chest heaving, his expression intent. Her throat felt tight with emotion, so she settled for mouthing the words *thank you*.

"You're most welcome, lass." There was nothing relaxed about Colin. He was taut as a bow. "And now comes the next part. Are you ready for it?"

She nodded. She was so ready. Giving her virginity to Colin made sense.

"You're very wet, but this still might hurt a bit."

"Do it."

He probed with the tip of his penis, and she was glad she'd been bold enough to fondle him. Now she knew what a penis felt like, or at least what his felt like. She wasn't being invaded by some unknown object. She'd stroked this penis, and besides, it belonged to Colin, who had provided the first orgasm of her life. She would honor him forever because of that.

He entered her slowly, and she discovered that she really, really liked this feeling of Colin's penis inside her. The walls of her vagina contracted around him, and the pressure of another orgasm began to build. What an excellent idea sex was.

Then he stopped moving forward, and his chest heaved. He muttered something that sounded Scottish, and his tone suggested it was a swear word.

"What's wrong?" Even in the shadowy light, she could see that his brow was furrowed with concern.

"I don't want to hurt you."

"You're not hurting me."

His voice rasped in the cool night air. "But I will if I keep going."

"It's the hymen problem." She'd read enough to know about that pesky issue with being a virgin. "Break it."

"You're sure?"

"I'm a twenty-seven-year-old Were virgin. It's time."

"I suppose that's true. And to tell the truth, I'm not sure what I'd do if you denied me."

She'd been so wrapped up in her own first experience with sexuality that she'd lost sight of how he must be suffering. The books said postponing a climax could literally be painful.

She rubbed his back. "Bless your heart, do you have blue balls?"

With something between a chuckle and a groan, he surged forward, destroying her virginity with one firm thrust. So it was over.

And it hurt like hell. She hadn't been prepared for that, and she yelped.

"Sorry." He held still for a moment.

"Don't be." The pain was already less, and she arched upward, even though it cost her. "You deserve something out of this."

"Don't worry about that. I will come." He sounded slightly out of breath. "I might not even have to move to do it."

"Move." She wiggled against him. "I'll be fine."

"Oh, lass." With another heartfelt groan, he drew back and rocked forward again.

She'd expected more pain, but instead the easy thrust felt good. "Nice. Do that some more."

"You're humoring me."

"No, it actually felt good. Maybe virgins need this to get broken in."

"I wouldn't know." He held her gaze as he initiated a slow, easy stroke. "I'm no expert on virgins."

Her pulse rate picked up as she caught his rhythm and began to move with him. "I'm guessing you're an expert on sexual satisfaction, though."

He shook his head. "But I can tell you this, my lovely Luna." He increased the pace. "You're a natural."

Rising to meet him thrust for thrust and glorying in the fiery connection between them, she thought he might be right. Her second climax seemed even more beautiful than her first, because they'd created it together with the fusion of their bodies.

Even more joyous, Colin quickly followed. He gasped her name once, and then shuddered in reaction as he emptied himself into her willing body. She held him close and murmured her gratitude for all he'd given her tonight. She didn't have enough experience to judge fairly, but she couldn't help wondering how the joining of two Weres could be any better than this.

Chapter 10

The cool, damp air soon prompted Colin to move the party inside. As much as he loved stargazing, he preferred to gaze at Luna, and he could do that far better in the comfort of his bedroom. She helped him pack up the telescope and then she descended the steps wrapped in the quilt. He followed with the telescope in its box, and a bundle containing their clothes.

On the way down, he reminded himself that this was her first time and once was enough for her tonight. He might crave another round or two, or three, but then she'd be sore tomorrow. He wanted her to remember pleasure, not pain, so she'd ask for more.

When he reached the bottom step and looked for her, she was standing by the dimmer switch, still wrapped in the quilt.

"I wanted to make sure you were safely down before I did this." She reduced the light from the bedside lamps, and the constellations in the drapes and bedspread began to glow.

"Geraldine must have showed you how that worked."

"She did. We came up here at night so I could get the

full effect. I thought it was lovely." She unwound the quilt and laid it on a nearby chair.

Even in the faint light, she was spectacular. "Not as lovely as you." A new surge of desire added a rasp to his voice. He dropped the clothes to the floor. There were other ways to pleasure each other, ways that wouldn't cause her discomfort. His cock stiffened.

"You seem to have reloaded." She walked toward him with confidence, as if she belonged here among the glowing constellations. Of course she did. Her name was Luna, after all.

Premonition ran a finger up his spine, and he trembled. Until now, he'd missed the connection. Her name was Luna, and he was fascinated by the night sky. A true Scotsman never discounted such things.

But a wise Scotsman wouldn't mention it, in case this bonny lass might think he was daft and run in the opposite direction. He preferred having her move toward him, her breasts swaying gently with each step, her eyes alight, her mouth curved in a saucy smile.

She stopped when she was inches away, and predictably, grasped the handle he'd so conveniently provided. "Now, where were we?"

"I've been thinking." That was a lie. He couldn't think at all when she was fondling his wee man.

"Thinking?" She cupped his balls with her free hand.

He groaned. "Virgins don't usually do that, either."

"I'm not a virgin anymore."

"But you were twenty minutes ago." His breath caught as she began a slow massage. "That's hardly enough time to learn how to treat a chap's family jewels."

"As I said, I've had years to think about this. I've also done some reading and watched a few X-rated movies. I just never had someone to practice on."

He gulped in air. "That makes me one lucky bastard."

"Which is better for a blow job, sitting down or standing up? I've seen it both ways."

His laugh had a strangled quality because he really couldn't breathe properly while she played with him as if she'd discovered a new squeeze toy. "I think . . . I'd better sit on the bed." Before he fell down. The pleasure was that intense, partly because he knew she'd never touched anyone else this way.

"Then back up a couple of steps and you're there."

"You're not going to let go, are you?"

"Nope. I'm having too much fun." She kept a firm hold on him as he retreated to the bed.

When he lowered himself to the mattress, she dropped to her knees and gazed up at him. "Tell me if I'm doing this right, okay?"

He nodded, but wondered if he'd be too overcome by the experience to say a word.

"Here goes." Holding his cock in her fist, she slid her mouth over the tip and began to suck gently.

His eyes rolled back in his head. He prayed to all the gods he knew that he would conduct himself in a way that wouldn't shock her. "You . . . can take more in."

Obligingly, she did that. Holding her lips tight, she moved slowly up and down.

Meanwhile he went back to his football stats to keep from coming immediately. He had no idea if she was prepared for what would happen. He should warn her . . .

Then she flattened her tongue against the front ridge of his penis and put added pressure there. Where in bloody hell had she learned to do *that*? He groaned and tried to remember where he'd left off on the stats. His brain whirled and he began to shake. He was going to warn her about . . . what?

Oh, yes. "When I . . . when I come . . ."

Clutching the base of his cock, she gradually slid her

mouth upward. When she lifted her head, she wrapped both hands around his shaft and held him the way a rock star cradled a microphone. "When you come . . . what?" Her voice was low and sexy.

He glanced down and noticed her nipples had tightened into tiny buds of desire, which meant this exercise was good for her, too. He was glad of that. It meant she might want to do it again, but only if he made sure there were no surprises.

He combed his fingers through her hair and cupped the back of her head as he gazed into her eyes. "You don't have to swallow."

"Bless your heart," she said softly as she continued to caress him. "Thinking of me."

"I won't be offended."

"But the thing is, I want to swallow."

His heartbeat roared in his ears. "You might not like—"

"The taste?" Leaning down again, she licked a droplet from the tip of his penis before glancing up at him again. "It seems I do."

"Ah. Well, then." If ever a male Were heard sweeter words than that from a female, he couldn't imagine what they might be.

"You look happy."

"If I were any happier, I'd levitate."

"Good. Any suggestions for how I can improve?"

He shook his head.

"Then I'll continue on." With a little smile, she returned to her task.

Now that he'd warned her, he ditched the football stats, pressed his fingers into her scalp, and abandoned himself to her hands, her mouth, and her wicked tongue. Considering this was her first attempt at oral sex, he wanted to be around as she gained experience.

But his lust-saturated brain was incapable of following that thought to its logical conclusion. Soon, as she licked, nibbled, and sucked until he was delirious, he couldn't think at all. He came in a glorious rush, and she drank all he had to offer as he bellowed his satisfaction.

Afterward, he flopped back on the bed, dazed by the wonder of Luna Reynaud.

She climbed up on the bed beside him and they both scooted around until they were lying lengthwise on the bedspread. He considered trying to get under the covers and decided it took too much effort.

She nestled close, her arm wrapped around his chest. "I learned something from that experience," she murmured.

So had he. She was his perfect sexual partner. The significance of that would have to be dealt with later, but the truth of it was burned into his brain. Somehow he had to figure out a way to be with her, despite all the obstacles.

But for now, she'd made a comment and probably expected a response. He struggled to speak and had to make a couple of tries before managing a weary, "Oh?"

"But we can take care of the situation later, when you're recovered."

"Mm."

She massaged his chest. "See, it turns out, blow jobs make me hot."

"Mm." That information came as no surprise to him, and after he had a chance to catch his breath, he'd make sure she found her happy place again.

"But I can wait."

"Five minutes," he murmured. Already life had begun to flow back into his body and very soon he'd be ready to make love to her again, but gently. Very, very gently.

*   *   *

Luna was proud of herself. Judging from Colin's noisy reaction, he'd had a good time just now. She'd delivered her first blow job, and it had been a success.

She hadn't realized that doing that for Colin would make her want to have sex with him again, though. She'd read enough to know she could give herself a climax, and that was an option now that she wasn't worried about how orgasms would affect a female werewolf. Maybe eventually, after Colin went back to Scotland, she'd resort to that method.

But when he was lying right next to her, she couldn't see the point in giving herself an orgasm. That wouldn't be nearly as much fun as if she waited for him to reload and slide right into her. Thinking of that made her ache with longing. Once the dam had been breached, so to speak, she couldn't seem to stop the flood of desire.

Slowly she stroked his chest. The soft, springy hair, caramel and chocolate mixed together, swirled around his nipples and then made a little path leading directly to his penis. Following the path, she touched him there and smiled when she was rewarded with a little twitch of a response.

Perhaps she could help him reload. She ran a fingernail gently up the underside of his shaft, where the intriguing ridge seemed especially sensitive.

"I won't be using that on you again tonight, lass," he murmured.

"No more reloading?" She tried not to sound too disappointed.

"Oh, you could bring me back to attention, but it will do no good. I'm not about to make you sore and have you regret the fun you had."

"I won't ever regret tonight." Not even after he was gone. She understood that this couldn't be the love of her life, because he would return to Scotland. Last time he'd left, he hadn't come back for fifteen years.

Because she had no idea how often she'd see him after this visit, she'd make sure not to become attached. Considering how wonderful he'd been so far, she might have a slight problem with that, but she was used to distancing herself when necessary.

In the meantime, she would be greedy and take whatever he was willing to give. A little soreness wouldn't bother her. She continued to caress him, with gratifying results.

Then he reached down and grabbed her wrist. His hold was easy, but unbreakable, as if she were wearing silk handcuffs. Then he captured her other wrist, as if ensuring she wouldn't try using that hand instead.

"I'll take my chances with the soreness." She realized struggling would do no good, but perhaps she could coax him with words. "I want to feel you inside me again, Colin. That was lovely, and once you go back to Scotland, I won't have— Oh!" She cried out as he neatly flipped her to her back, moving with surprising agility considering how lethargic he'd seemed moments ago.

He loomed over her, his expression resolute, as he held her arms at her sides. "I'll not deliberately chafe someone who's only recently discovered sex. You wouldn't thank me for it in the morning."

"Yes, I would. I'll thank you right now, in fact, in advance. Just one more time. That's all I'm asking." Something hard pressing against her thigh told her she was making progress with her plea.

"No."

"Yes." She wiggled so that she brushed against his erect cock. "Once more. Just one more—"

He silenced her with a kiss, a thoroughly Colin sort of kiss, that left her gasping and writhing in frustration. Then he moved downward, still holding her prisoner, and used that talented mouth and tongue on each of her breasts.

"This isn't helping! It's making everything worse!"

"Patience." He released her left wrist, but shifted his hips away so his cock was out of reach. Then he stroked his hand down over her stomach and slid one finger into the very spot where she wanted his beautiful, thick penis to go.

Admittedly his caress felt good, and her breathing quickened. But it wasn't enough to take away the throbbing need inside her. "More," she wailed.

"Two, then." He gently inserted his middle finger.

She started to protest, but when he curved both fingers and began to stroke a special place that she hadn't even realized existed until now, she thought better of complaining. Maybe she should be quiet and see how this turned out.

He dropped a soft kiss on her mouth. "Better?"

"It's okay." In fact, it was more than okay, but she didn't want to give up on having her ultimate reward.

"Just okay?" He rubbed that special spot a little faster.

"Uh . . . I can't talk now." But she could pant, which she did, and moan, which she also did. Her orgasm built deep within her, urgent and forceful. When he settled his thumb on her sacred point and pressed down, she arched off the bed as her world erupted. She wouldn't have been surprised to see confetti raining down on them. It was that good.

"I think you liked that," he said with a smile in his voice.

She looked into his eyes. Although she loved the glow-in-the-dark bedspread and drapes, the lack of light meant she couldn't admire how blue his eyes were. "It was all right."

"Liar." He lifted his forefinger, the same one he'd recently used to thrust her into a vortex of pleasure, and brushed it across her upper lip. He left a trail of dampness and the sweet scent of satisfaction. "There's your proof."

She breathed in the aroma of her arousal. "Careful, or I'll beg you to do it again."

"Even though it was only *all right*?"

"That's better than nothing." Then she laughed and cupped the back of his head to pull him down until their lips nearly touched. "It was fabulous. But if you want to change your mind and avail yourself of my body, I'd love that, too."

"I won't." He ran his tongue over her lower lip. "But you're not easy to resist, lass. I should probably send you back to your own room for whatever's left of this night."

"I'll bet there's not much left at all. It was already late when we went up to the roof." She didn't want to leave him. Every stolen moment seemed precious. "What if we took a dawn stroll on the beach? I think we could sneak back to the house before anyone noticed."

"I'd like that." He leaned his forehead against hers. "You're good company, Luna."

"I like it when you say my name."

He raised his head to gaze at her. "Why is that?"

"I mean, it's different to be called *lass*, and I like that, too, because it reminds me of Geraldine. But using my actual name seems more personal, as if you're with me, specifically, and not just any female Were."

"I am with you specifically. I could never think of you as some generic female Were, if that's what you're saying."

"Oh, I don't know about that, considering the many lovers you've had. I could get lost in the crowd." She kept her tone light, but as the words tumbled out, she realized they came from her heart. Even if he left and never came back to Le Floret, she wanted to know that he wouldn't forget her.

He cradled her cheek in his hand. "In the first place, I haven't had so many lovers as that, and in the second place, you would never get lost among them. I will remember you, Luna Reynaud, for as long as I have breath in my body."

Her heart did a funny little flip. "You will?"

"You have my word as a MacDowell." He leaned down to kiss her, but as their lips met, bagpipes began playing from somewhere in the bedroom. He muttered something against her mouth that once again sounded like a Scottish swearword, and levered himself off the bed.

"What is it?"

"My family. It's morning there, and they didn't stop to think I might be sleeping. But they also don't call unless it's an emergency." He walked to the dresser and picked up his cell phone.

Luna didn't want to eavesdrop, so she decided this might be a good time to grab her clothes and slip into the adjoining bathroom. The moment had been interrupted, but she would never forget what he'd told her. *I will remember you as long as I have breath in my body.*

Scots were known for being poetic souls, and she could see why. He'd dazzled her with that statement, and then he'd sworn on his family name, which made the declaration even more moving and romantic. Such things could turn a female Were's head.

She dressed quickly, grateful that jeans and a sweatshirt was a forgiving ensemble that looked fine even after being wadded up and tossed on the floor. She could hear Colin's voice through the bathroom door. Although she couldn't make out what he was saying, she knew he was upset.

What a shame that his family had to call right now. She wasn't sure he'd want to go for a walk on the beach, after all. And if they did go, the mood between them wouldn't be so relaxed and happy, judging from the tone of his conversation.

Moments later, he rapped softly on the door. "It's okay, Luna. You can come out."

She opened the door. Colin was busy putting on his clothes, but his movements were jerky and his jaw was rigid with obvious displeasure. "I didn't want to intrude on your conversation," she said.

"That was kind of you." He sat on the edge of the bed to put on his gym shoes. "Still want to take that walk on the beach?"

"If you do."

"I might not be fit company, but some exercise sounds good. I considered shifting and going for a run, but it's getting light out and fishing boats could happen along. I can take a run after dinner when it's dark." He tied the laces on his shoes and glanced up. "Would you like to do that with me?"

"I . . . yes."

"You don't have to."

"I want to. That would be good, just the two of us. I'm always shy about being around other wolves because I'm not sure I'll do what's right since I've never belonged to a pack."

"We could talk about that. Maybe I can help."

"Colin, that would be wonderful."

"That's decided, then." He stood. "Are you sure you want to go with me now, though? I'll probably rant about my brother, Duncan."

"I'll be glad to listen."

"Thanks."

They slipped out of the house as quietly as possible and didn't speak again until they'd reached the sand. Gray light tinged the horizon, making it just possible to distinguish between sky and sea. The waves slid onto the shore with a soft hiss, then pulled back, dragging small rocks and shells into the water.

Colin didn't spare the scenery more than a glance before setting off for the far point of the small crescent beach. "It may take several trips across this stretch before I work out my frustration," he said.

"I don't mind." She lengthened her stride to keep up with him.

"So here's the problem." He shoved his hands into the pockets of his sweatshirt. "My brother, in spite of all my arguments to the contrary, continues to insist there's nothing wrong with Weres and humans mating. In fact, he'd like to promote that ridiculous idea!"

"I see." A tiny squiggle of dread invaded Luna's contentment.

"Not surprisingly, he's become serious about a woman from Glasgow, which is why my mother called. She's concerned that he might consider taking this woman as his mate. He's hinted that he's in love with her."

Luna wished she could transport herself backward in time, to that cozy moment before the sound of bagpipes had intruded on their shared happiness. Knowing what she knew now, she would have slipped out of bed, stolen the phone, and dropped it in the toilet.

Colin didn't seem to notice that she'd gone silent as he continued with his rant. "As I'm sure you'll agree, Weres mating with humans is wrong on so many levels. I can't speak for this country, but in Europe, humans used to *hunt* us. If they discovered we still exist, I believe they'd hunt us again!"

"Perhaps." Her stomach churned as she realized what she would have to do.

"There's no doubt in my mind. But aside from that, mating with humans means never knowing if the offspring will be human or Were, which is not smart. And even if the offspring turn out to be Were, they have human genes, too, which means they could still produce human offspring themselves. It creates all sorts of problems. But my pigheaded brother thinks—"

"Colin." She stopped and waited for him to turn around. Her heart beat a rapid tattoo as she considered the risk, but she had to tell him. She wouldn't build her new life on a lie.

He faced her. "What is it? Do you need to go back?"

"No. There's something you need to know about me."

"All right." His voice became very quiet, as if he had already guessed that he wouldn't want to hear what she had to say.

"My mother was human."

Chapter 11

Colin required several long seconds to digest this information. During that time he tried to quiet the screaming voices in his head that cried out in protest at the unfairness of it all. Luna was perfect. *Perfect.* Except, not really, not according to his exacting standards.

"I understand this probably changes everything," she said. "You may not want a half-breed running the inn. But I am right for the job, and no one here knows about my mother. I'd planned to keep it that way, in case . . . in case someone else might feel the way you do."

Colin scrubbed a hand over his face. Now everything she'd told him made sense. Her mother had run away because she didn't want to be part of a werewolf pack. She wouldn't have told Luna that she might inherit the ability to shift, because there was a fifty percent chance she wouldn't. Then her mother had died before Luna reached puberty, and Luna had gone through her first shift with no support at all.

"That's why you went through your first shift alone."

She waved her hand dismissively. "Yes, but that doesn't matter now."

"It does." He walked toward her, his heart aching for the young girl who hadn't known what was happening to her. "Of course it does." He took her by the shoulders. "I'm so sorry."

When she lifted her face to his, a mask of indifference covered the open delight he was used to seeing there. "It's not your problem."

"And it shouldn't have been yours, either." He wanted her to tell him about that first shift, because he sensed she'd never been able to unburden herself to anyone. He was the only person in the world who knew she was a half-breed. No wonder she'd decided not to contact her grandparents.

"Look, the primary issue here is whether I still have a job running the inn. If I don't, then maybe I can train Sybil to do it. Janet's needed back in the kitchen, and Dulcie's a little too focused on the male of the species, but I think Sybil might—"

"I don't want Sybil." He released her, because he realized she wouldn't confide in him, not after the way he'd talked about humans mating with Weres. And he still believed it was a mistake. Luna was proof of the heartbreak it could bring.

"Then let me find someone else, do some interviewing. Just don't throw out the idea of the inn because I'm not right for the job. Sybil, Dulcie, and Janet deserve a chance to stay on and make a go of this."

"I gave you my word that you could run the inn."

She swallowed. "That was before I told you I'm a half-breed."

He looked into green eyes that had been full of joy not long ago, and now were as cold and hard as a piece of jade. "You're still the same talented and capable Were who impressed me before. I have no doubt that you'll do an excellent job. I want you to stay."

Her shoulders sagged in relief. "Thank you."

"No, I need to thank you. If you hadn't come up with this alternative, I would have listed the property with that dullard Regis and lost any right to come back here. All those cherished memories would have been stripped away."

She nodded. "I'm glad that didn't happen."

"And I would have missed spending last night with you."

Her gaze snapped to his. "Under the circumstances, you should forget about that."

"I've already given you my word that I'll never forget."

She stared at him, and gradually her mask slipped back into place. "I release you from that pledge, Colin. I'm sure my secret is safe, because it wouldn't help business to reveal it. If you will excuse me, I have work to do." Turning, she marched back toward the steps, her back straight and her head high.

At the steps, she glanced back at him. "I'll print out the spreadsheet for those financial projections and leave it under your bedroom door."

"Luna, don't put this kind of distance between us. I was your friend before, and I want to keep that friendship. I care about you." He cared more than he was willing to admit, even to himself. But he'd held his beliefs too long and too passionately to just toss them aside. He hoped she understood that.

She stood gazing at the sand beneath her feet for several seconds. When her response finally came, it was so low that he had to strain to hear it over the sound of the waves.

She didn't raise her head, didn't look at him. "Is it the sex? Is that what you want?"

"Bloody hell! No, it's not the sex!"

She lifted her gaze to his. "That's good, because it won't ever happen again." Breaking eye contact, she turned and went up the steps.

He watched her until she was out of sight. He fought the urge to throw back his head and howl.

Luna ate breakfast at her desk while she cleaned up the spreadsheet that compared similar inns in the area with Whittier House—number of rooms, room rate, and amenities. She'd used her hotel experience to project the costs of food and beverages per person and built that into the room rate. They'd have to serve three meals a day because nothing else was available without leaving the island.

She buried herself in the work she loved, the work that would give her a haven away from a world that wouldn't welcome her if her heritage became known. Maybe other Weres didn't share Colin's prejudices, but she'd never had the courage to broach the subject for fear something she said would give her away.

She fussed with the spreadsheet for too long, but she wanted it to be beyond reproach. Besides, as long as she worked in her office with the door closed, she could avoid Colin. Sometime before noon she ventured out, the spreadsheet in a manila envelope with his name on it.

On the way up the stairs to the second floor, she had to pass Dulcie, who was polishing the wooden banisters on either side of the marble staircase.

"There you are!" Dulcie put down her cloth and bottle of lemon oil. "I've been dying to find out how everything went last night. Did huddling over those projections turn into anything exciting?"

Luna took a deep breath. "No." She wasn't a good liar, and she felt the heat rush to her cheeks.

"Aw, that's okay, honey." Dulcie patted her arm. "Don't be embarrassed. I probably shouldn't have asked, but you know we all want you to find a hunky Were who can give you some action. We, um, took bets on whether Colin would be the lucky one."

"Bets?" Luna was scandalized.

Dulcie tugged at the hem of her rhinestone-studded shirt and had the good grace to look a little uncomfortable. "Well, we saw the way he looked at you, and after you left the kitchen last night, we finished off the wine, which led to a little friendly wager. Innocent fun."

Despite being scandalized, Luna was intrigued. No one had ever paid enough attention to her activities to place a wager on the outcome. "How did you bet?"

"I put my money on you two doing the nasty last night. Janet thought it would take longer, and Sybil's convinced you're a virgin and nothing will happen because you won't take that kind of chance with your new boss."

"Hm." Luna glanced away, not wanting Dulcie to read anything from her expression.

"You did it, didn't you?"

"No." She looked Dulcie straight in the eye and reminded herself of Colin's rigid belief system. "Sybil's right. I wouldn't risk my future like that."

Apparently she was convincing, because Dulcie sighed. "If you say so. I've already lost then, but Janet's holding the money until Colin goes back to Scotland, because she and Sybil still have a bet."

"How much money are we talking about?" She hoped it wasn't a small fortune, but after a couple of glasses of wine, the Weres might have become reckless.

"Twenty bucks each. An amount we can afford to lose, which obviously I will. Damn. I thought Colin was more assertive than that."

"Is somebody accusing me of not being assertive?"

Luna glanced up and wished she hadn't stopped to talk with Dulcie. Now she was trapped. Colin stood at the top of the stairs looking as gorgeous as ever. No one should be that handsome. Despite the fact that his prejudice against half-bloods should have killed her desire, she still craved his body.

He'd obviously showered and changed clothes since this morning. He wore khaki slacks and a crisp white dress shirt open at the neck. Plus he smelled like heaven on earth, a combination of natural musk and cologne that he'd probably brought from Scotland. She didn't know what the scent of heather was like, but logically Colin would bring the aroma of Scotland with him.

She held out the manila envelope. "You saved me a trip. I was coming up to slip this under your door."

He came down the steps with an easy stride that seemed to say he hadn't a care in the world. But his blue eyes searched her expression, and lines of weariness bracketed his mouth.

"Thanks for putting this together." He took the envelope. "Actually, I was coming to find you. Yesterday we talked about taking a trip into Seattle to look for books, and I've arranged for the helicopter to pick us up. Can you be ready in the next hour?"

"Well, no." She hadn't expected him to take charge like this, and she scrambled for a reasonable excuse. "Janet and I need to start planning menus that are in line with my cost projections, and this afternoon is the best—"

"Janet can adjust," Dulcie said. "You two go on. Have fun. You haven't had a trip to Seattle in months, Luna. You deserve it."

Surely she could get out of this tangled web. "It's a nice thought, but I imagine Colin would like to get the inn up and running as soon as possible. Considering all that has to be done in preparation for opening weekend, I shouldn't take the time. We need to see about advertising, and all the rooms will have to be evaluated in terms of linens, and I also think we should consider installing a hot tub." She glanced at Colin, a plea in her eyes. "I couldn't possibly get away."

He ignored that plea. "Sure you can. We'll price hot tubs while we're in Seattle, maybe even buy one. I agree it's a great idea. So is the library we talked about, and it needs books, unless you plan to empty Henry's collection."

Dulcie waved her polishing cloth in Luna's direction. "Don't look a gift horse in the mouth. Let His Lairdness of Glenbilbo take you hot tub shopping." She waggled her eyebrows. "Could we set aside a few hours for staff use of the hot tub?"

"Of course." Colin gave her his high-wattage smile. "I believe in keeping the staff happy." He glanced over at Luna. "Meet you at the helipad in forty-five minutes. I'll ask Janet to pack us a lunch to eat on the way." He continued on down the stairs.

Dulcie flapped her hand in front of her face. "Whew, that Were is *hot.*"

"If you like the type." Luna struggled for nonchalance and was afraid she failed miserably.

"What are you talking about? He's a stud! Every female in the world would like his type, Were or human. What's the matter with you?"

"I just don't think it's a good idea to mix business with pleasure." The hypocrisy of that statement made her tummy hurt, but she was battling for her very existence and compromises had to be made.

Dulcie rolled her eyes. "I can see that Sybil has this one in the bag. I knew you were a straight arrow, but I didn't think you were quite this straight. But here's a tip.

Don't piss off the boss. Even if you don't want to play footsie with him, when he invites you to Seattle to shop for books and hot tubs, you go to Seattle and shop for books and hot tubs."

"You have a point." Luna hadn't figured that Colin would pull rank on her, but he had, and in front of Dulcie, which had worked out well for him. She couldn't refuse to go without seeming to sabotage the entire operation. And that she definitely didn't want to do.

"You bet your sweet ass I have a point. Power to the sisterhood, girlfriend! We're counting on you to keep that Were happy." Dulcie glanced at Luna's sweatshirt and jeans, which she'd been wearing since last night. "I suggest you clean up a little bit, too. I hate to say it, but your hair's a hot mess."

Luna instinctively touched her hair and realized she hadn't done a thing with it since rolling around in Colin's bed, followed by walking along a misty, wind-blown beach. She hadn't bothered to look in a mirror, but had headed straight to the office and barricaded herself in there to work on the spreadsheets. She probably looked deranged.

That wasn't far off. The past couple of days had taken their toll on her, and she only hoped she could hold on to her sanity until Colin boarded a plane and headed back to his native land. She wanted nothing more than to be left alone.

No, that wasn't true, either. There were moments when she wanted nothing more than to strip naked and welcome Colin into her outstretched arms. But she throttled those urges every time they arose. Colin disapproved of her ancestry, which meant she needed to stay out of his bed or risk further heartbreak. If sex was the only thing that would keep him happy, then they'd all get kicked out of Whittier House.

But she could be reasonably accommodating, so she

showered, washed her hair, and dressed in a flowered summery frock, another of Geraldine's gifts to her. Of course, Geraldine hadn't known about Luna's unorthodox background, either, but Luna hoped that Geraldine wouldn't have cared. She'd defied the MacDowell clan to mate with a foreigner from Vancouver.

Still, that wasn't the same as being descended from a human mother and a Were father. Luna hadn't chosen that for herself, and sadly, she could understand Colin's objections to mingling the two species. The impetuous mating between her mother and father had caused her plenty of anguish.

Yet now she lived in a castle with other friendly Weres. Assuming Colin didn't go back on his word, she had a chance to make a nice living for herself and her new friends. She didn't think he would go back on his word, but refusing a simple request to accompany him to Seattle wasn't very smart.

She strapped on a pair of sandals, grabbed a straw purse and her sunglasses, and walked out the door to the helipad. This was a simple request, wasn't it? She could manage to browse through a few bookstores and check on hot tubs without turning the day into a complicated dance.

Colin stood beside the helicopter, his hair tousled by the wind from the chopper blades, his Wayfarers making him look like a flyboy, himself. A paper bag dangled loosely from his long fingers.

Giving the two men a wave, she ducked under the swirling blades and joined them next to the cockpit. "Hi, Knox." She'd become friends with the pilot through the many times he'd taken Geraldine on shopping trips, but he'd earned her total respect the night he'd flown in the medical team. Despite being a Trevelyan, the pack Geraldine and Henry had ignored, he'd grieved right along with Luna as Geraldine had lost her fight for life.

"Beautiful day for a trip to the city!" Knox shouted above the noise of the rotor. "I'll put Colin in back and you next to me, like we did the time Geraldine took you shopping."

Luna nodded. The seating arrangement had been Geraldine's idea, because she'd wanted Luna to have the full experience of flying over the sparkling water and into the city. Despite Luna's mild acrophobia, she wasn't bothered by riding in a helicopter, possibly because she was strapped in and someone else was in charge of getting them safely back to ground level.

Trevelyan Enterprises had its own helipad at the top of one of Seattle's office buildings. It was an elegant and quick way into the heart of the Emerald City, and Luna had enjoyed her trip with Geraldine.

Colin glanced at her, but she couldn't read his expression behind his dark glasses. "You look great," he said in a voice barely loud enough to carry over the roar of the helicopter.

"Thanks." She turned away, determined to block out his considerable charm. He might not disapprove of her, but he disapproved of what she represented, and that left her emotionally vulnerable. From now on, every interaction between them would be strictly business.

Chapter 12

Colin climbed into the helicopter. The picture Luna had made as she walked toward the helipad in that flowery dress and big dark glasses, her glossy hair shining in the sun, would join all the other images etched permanently in his memory. Her beauty made his heart ache with longing for the uncomplicated connection they'd had the night before.

He'd arranged for the helicopter in hopes he'd be able to coax her aboard. If she'd refused to come, he would have gone alone. He had more than books and hot tubs on his mind. He wanted to meet Luna's grandparents. He wouldn't give her away, but he wanted to assess whether they might be a support system for her.

Perhaps she would never confide in him again after the things he'd said this morning, but she carried a heavy burden knowing she was half-Were. If her grandparents were compassionate and trustworthy, they might become the family she'd never had.

He'd already done some research online using the netbook he'd brought with him and a secure site dedicated to Weres. The site had been live for only a few months, so Luna might not know about it. But her grandparents obviously did.

Edwina and Jacques Reynaud used the site to promote their new venture, the Byron Reynaud Foundation, which benefitted orphaned or displaced Weres. Judging from the information Colin found, the Reynauds were kind and generous souls who'd decided to devote their golden years to doing good works. They didn't seem like the sort to reject a granddaughter who provided the only connection to their beloved son.

Colin wasn't sure how Luna would react when he told her how he'd spent his morning. But she needed to know what he'd been up to, and a trip to Seattle would give them plenty of time to discuss it. If all went well, they might chance a visit to the Reynauds, although Luna might choose not to identify herself as their granddaughter.

But first he'd needed to get Luna to Seattle. Barging into her office with the suggestion hadn't seemed right, and then fortune had smiled on him. With less than an hour before takeoff, he'd met her on the stairway and coerced her into coming along. Having Dulcie there to support his plan had been a bonus.

Luna hadn't wanted to go, which didn't surprise him. But he was willing to manipulate the situation to get her into the chopper and on her way to Seattle. He'd insulted her background and caused her pain when he'd wanted to give her joy.

She was right to ignore him now. But he fervently hoped that eventually she might get to know her grandparents. Helping her connect with her family again might make up for the fact that he'd unwittingly forced her to reveal her secret.

He passed out the lunch, sandwiches all around and those silly little juice boxes Americans were so fond of.

The helicopter ride was as noisy this morning as it had been the last time he'd flown over Puget Sound. He sat back and tried not to be bothered by the easy interaction between Knox and Luna.

Knox took pains to give her a good show, pointing out sights and angling the chopper so she could see more easily. When they flew over a pod of orcas, Luna pressed her nose to the window until they were out of sight, and then gave Knox a dazzling smile and a thumbs-up.

Colin ground his teeth together, not happy with being odd man out even if he deserved it. She used to smile at him like that, but thanks to the phone call and what came afterward, she'd stopped smiling when she looked at him. God, how he missed her smile.

He tried to convince himself a friendship between Knox and Luna was a good thing. Now that Colin had removed Luna's fear of sex, she was free to explore that side of her nature, and she should after being celibate for so long. He'd been lucky to be her first lover, but he didn't expect to be her last.

Knox Trevelyan seemed like a considerate, intelligent sort, someone who would appreciate Luna's finer qualities. Once the inn opened for business, Knox would probably fly guests over on a regular basis. He might even park the chopper on the helipad and stay the night.

Colin's jaw tightened. Yes, it would be extremely noble of him to give his blessing to a sexual relationship between Knox and Luna. But he wasn't that noble. Fortunately he'd be in Scotland and wouldn't know what was going on. He suspected they would gravitate toward each other, though, and his imagination would torture him with images of Knox and Luna together.

By the time Knox landed the helicopter on the roof of the Trevelyan Enterprises building in downtown Seattle, Colin was in a mood. He had no bloody right to be in a mood, either. He had no claim on Luna and would never have one.

But no matter how many times he told himself that, whenever he looked at her, something primitive inside him howled *mine*. Well, too bad. He was a civilized Were, one who wasn't ruled by his primitive instincts, thank God. If he were, he would have mated with Luna last night.

He went very still, mesmerized by that unacceptable thought. It had hovered, unacknowledged, in the back of his mind ever since he'd met her. He'd agreed that she could run the inn, but some part of him had known that he had other plans for her.

Those plans hadn't risen to a conscious level because his pack would object to an American Were with no pack affiliation. He would have had to win them over gradually, but he could have done it. Now, however . . . now he was caught in a trap of his own making.

Taking Luna as his mate would contradict his belief that the races shouldn't mix. Because she had human blood, she could potentially bear human children, although the chances were lower than with a human-Were mating. Still, the possibility was there. Unfortunately, knowing that didn't stop him from wanting her with a desperation that he'd never felt with another female Were.

"Colin?" Knox poked his head in through the passenger door of the chopper. "You coming out?"

That's when he realized the rotors were quiet and both Luna and Knox stood outside the helicopter, waiting for him to climb down. He wondered how long he'd been sitting there looking totally daft.

"Sorry." He extricated his sizable body from the small space. "I was thinking about something and lost track of where I was."

"Obviously." Knox laughed. "You were gone, man. Completely checked out. I admire that kind of concentration, though." He held out his hand. "Have a great time in the city."

"Thanks." Colin shook Knox's hand and resisted the urge to apply a little more pressure as a warning that he was a Were to be reckoned with. How juvenile was that?

"Still planning to head back around midnight?"

"Midnight?" Luna shoved her glasses to the top of her head and stared at him. "I can't stay until midnight, Colin. I have several things to—"

"Humor me." He smiled at her, knowing she wouldn't smile back at him the way she had with that cheeky bastard Knox. "I haven't had dinner at the top of the Space Needle since Geraldine brought me here as a teenager. I made reservations for nine, so we could watch the sunset and see the lights come on. It's spectacular."

Her eyes narrowed. Twelve hours ago she would have greeted that story with a soft gaze filled with understanding. Well, that wouldn't be happening anymore. Clearly she suspected him of being devious, which was right on the mark.

"You'll love the view from the Space Needle, Luna," Knox said. "As long as you're here, you should see it, and the real show doesn't happen until after dark."

She turned to Knox, and all the concern Colin used to enjoy was focused on the pilot. "Bless your heart for thinking of me, Knox. But then you'll be up until the wee hours of the morning. That seems very selfish of us." She flicked a glance at Colin that plainly said it was selfish of *him*.

"Hey, Colin pays me well for it, and besides, I get a kick out of night flying. You go enjoy the Space Needle. And then I'll show you some pretty night views on the way home."

Colin wondered if it was too late to request a different pilot—a graying, paunchy pilot.

"All right, Knox." Luna favored him with another warm smile. "You've convinced me. Take care." She pulled her dark glasses over her eyes before turning to Colin. "Shall we go?"

"Yes." Colin felt a stabbing pain in his right temple.

"That vein in your temple is standing out again," Luna murmured conversationally as they walked toward the rooftop doorway leading down into the building.

Colin noticed that he no longer rated a *bless your heart*, either. "I'm not surprised."

Luna had never been wooed before, and she couldn't imagine why it was happening now, except that Colin must have liked the sex and wanted more of it. He might think a romantic dinner at the top of the Space Needle would do the trick, but she was determined not to climb back into bed with him. He could fly her to Paris for dinner, and she still wouldn't get naked with Colin Mac-Dowell.

But she couldn't afford to tick him off, either. He'd promised that their personal relationship would have nothing to do with their business relationship, and so far he'd kept his word. But Dulcie was right. Playing along, at least when it came to the business side of their relationship, was the best plan.

"Let's visit a hot tub showroom first," Colin said as they rode an elevator down to the lobby of the Trevelyan Enterprises building. He'd tucked his Wayfarers into an inner pocket of his designer sport coat. "We'll need to drive a ways, because I checked and there aren't any in the heart of the city."

"I wondered about that." She'd wondered a lot of things about this apparently impromptu trip. "Are you going to drive?" She was pretty sure Scottish people used the wrong side of the road, which could make for some tense moments if Colin planned to take the wheel.

He glanced at her. "Worried that I'll get us both killed?"

"A little."

"Well, you can relax. I've arranged for a driver."

"When? I didn't mention the hot tub until an hour before we left Whittier House."

"I contacted George Trevelyan right after I talked to you. He gave me the name of a good dealer and offered the loan of a car."

"Oh." Luna had always suspected there were advantages to being well connected in the Were world. She'd never had that going for her, not even with Geraldine, who'd been a maverick. Geraldine had never traded on her status as a MacDowell once she left Scotland and had seemed proud of the fact.

Luna thought of something else. "Was it difficult to get a reservation at the restaurant on short notice?"

"George took care of that, too. He made sure we had a table."

"That George is a handy Were to have around."

"Yes, he is." Colin gazed at the numbers flashing by on the elevator and consulted his watch. "We're right on time."

Apparently it was an express elevator, because they were in the sparkling marble and gold lobby before Luna had a chance to ask any more questions.

Colin put a hand to the small of her back, a subtle gesture to guide her toward the revolving doors leading to the street. She moved out of reach and walked a little faster. His touch still had the power to affect her, damn it.

So did those electric blue eyes. When he'd mentioned

wanting to eat at the top of the Space Needle for old time's sake, he'd managed to tug at her heartstrings for a split second. She'd quickly squashed that reaction. This entire trip had ulterior motive written all over it.

Stepping quickly into one wedge of the revolving door, she made her way out to the sidewalk. A white stretch limo sat at the curb, engine idling. Surely Colin hadn't hired a limo to take them hot tub shopping.

He joined her on the sidewalk, and immediately the driver climbed out and opened the passenger door.

Luna glanced back at him. "Seriously?"

"It's what George had available. All the town cars were in service."

"I hope you realize that pulling up to a hot tub store in a limo will ruin any chance of getting a bargain."

Colin smiled. "You've obviously forgotten that I'm a Scot. We always get a bargain."

Now, that was funny. She had to clamp her lips together to keep from laughing.

"It wouldn't kill you to smile, Luna."

Instead of answering, she ducked into the limo. Too bad she liked Colin so much. Well, she liked him a lot except when he talked about the dangers of Weres and humans mating. But when he graced her with that amazing smile—the one that made her heart race and her body tremble—then she absolutely hated him for being so tempting.

She'd never ridden in a limo before, and when confronted with something that resembled a living room sectional, she couldn't figure out where to sit. The back seemed safest, because at least she'd be facing forward like in a normal car. She eased down on the black leather and gave an inadvertent hum of pleasure.

How embarrassing. She didn't want Colin to know that she liked the luxury ride that he was providing, or

George Trevelyan was providing because he and Colin
had some sort of alpha-male mutual back-scratching
thing. But she had to admit this was the nicest upholstery
her tush had ever enjoyed.

She held her straw purse on her lap, because clutching
it gave her something to hold on to in this cavernous
space that held a scent of oiled leather and a light perfume that might be an air freshener. The driver seemed
miles away.

Colin sat right next to her, of course, bringing with
him his maddeningly sexy scent. She could have predicted that he'd plop down right where she was, his thigh
touching her thigh.

She wasn't about to put up with that. The brush of his
pants leg against her dress was far too erotic to go on for
even one minute. She moved a few inches to the right,
and he didn't follow. His pride probably wouldn't allow
him to chase her around the black leather.

If things had remained the same as they once were
between her and Colin, she would have joked with him
that until now, she'd also been a limo virgin. But she
wasn't in a joking mood, so she didn't say anything and
pretended she'd been chauffeured like this dozens of
times.

The limo pulled out so smoothly that it took her a
second to realize they were in traffic. "Don't you have to
tell him where to go?"

"George told him. George also alerted the sales staff
that we were coming, and told them to give us their best
price."

"That George. What a guy."

Colin glanced at her. "He asked if we'd come up to his
office after we finish with the hot tub shopping. You
should probably meet him. He'd be a valuable contact to
have."

"I suppose he would." Colin was right. Geraldine might have prided herself on being totally self-sufficient, but Luna couldn't afford to operate that way if she expected to make a success of Whittier House. "Then we should go to his office, and thank him for the limo while we're at it."

"I'm sure he'd appreciate that."

"It's the polite thing to do." She gazed out the window at the bustling city and was swamped with memories of having to survive in such an environment on her own. Le Floret suited her so much better, and she hoped never to have to go back to the life she'd had before moving to the island.

"There's something I want to talk to you about."

She turned back to him, all her senses on high alert. "What's that?"

"Have you heard about a secure Web site called Lupe?"

She shook her head. "From the name, I'm guessing it's for Weres."

"Yes. It was activated a few months ago. My brother, who keeps up with such things, told me about it."

She relaxed her guard. So this was about business. "If it would be a good place to advertise the inn, then I'll check into it. I hadn't heard of it, so I appreciate the tip."

"It would be a good place to advertise, but that's not why I mentioned it. I found something on there this morning that I thought you'd want to know about. Have you heard of the Byron Reynaud Foundation?"

She drew in a sharp breath. Hearing her father's name was always a shock to her system. "No, I haven't. What ... what is it?"

"An organization to benefit orphaned and misplaced Weres. It's funded and supervised by your grandparents."

"Oh." She put a hand to her heart, as if she could

soothe its frantic pounding. "That's . . . that's . . . good, I guess." And what about her? She was an orphaned and misplaced Were, and their granddaughter. But she couldn't go to them for support, because if she told them Sophie was her mother, they would know she was a half-breed.

After taking a steadying breath, she met his gaze. "Thank you for telling me. I appreciate knowing." Even if it did her no good. Then she had another thought. "If this foundation becomes well-known, then so will the name Reynaud."

"Perhaps."

"I should be prepared with an answer if someone asks if I'm related, since I live in the area. I don't want to stammer and look as if I'm lying."

"True."

As the implications became clear, she groaned. "My name will become more well-known as the manager of the Whittier House Inn, especially if it's as successful as I plan for it to be, so it could work the other way, too. Weres could ask my grandparents if they're related to *me*."

"I suppose, but I was thinking that—"

"This is not good, Colin." She kept her voice low so the chauffeur couldn't hear. "The whole story could come out, which could be bad for business, not to mention embarrassing for you. I need to change my last name."

"Or you could consider meeting your grandparents and getting everything out in the open, so it won't have the power to sabotage you later."

She stared at him in astonishment. "No, I could not. No telling how they'd react if they find out they're related to a half-breed. After your rant this morning, I'm more determined than ever to protect my secret."

He flinched. "Point taken. But, Luna, you're their granddaughter, the only link to their dead son. I know telling them is risky, but . . . your mother and father are gone. Wouldn't it be comforting to have family again?"

His tone of voice was what clued her in. She stopped focusing on the problem and looked more closely at those beautiful eyes. Sure enough, they were filled with sympathy . . . and a certain amount of guilt.

She had a flash of insight. "I don't think you stumbled upon the Byron Reynaud Foundation by accident."

"No. I went looking for information about your grandparents."

"Why?"

"I think you need them, Luna."

Irritation simmered beneath the surface, but she forced herself to speak calmly. They were in a limo, after all. "Whether I need them or don't need them is none of your business, Colin. I'm grateful for the information, so I won't be caught unaware. The best course of action would be to change my name, so this will never become a problem."

"It's not going to be a problem."

"Of course it is. There's the potential for Weres to learn I'm a half-breed and shun me. Whittier House could lose business because of it. I could become a liability instead of an asset."

"Give Weres some credit, Luna. They won't blame you for something that wasn't your fault."

"Don't you?" She put all the hurt from this morning into that one question.

"No! That's what I've been trying to say ever since this blew up. Your parents' choices wouldn't have been my choices, but that doesn't change the fact that you're wonderful, no matter who your mother and father were.

I didn't tell you about your grandparents because I was afraid it might hurt business at some time in the future. I told you because I want the best for you."

She gazed at him and tried to make sense of it all. He still wanted her to manage the inn, despite her heritage, and she was extremely grateful for that. He probably also wanted her back in his bed, despite her heritage. But it would be no more than a fling.

Considering the way he felt about human-Were unions, the Much Honoured Colin MacDowell, Laird of Glenbarra, would certainly seek a full-blooded Were as his mate. That female Were probably would have to be born and bred in the Highlands, too, and hail from a respectable pack with a coat of arms and such other trappings as they had over in Scotland.

But Luna had known from the beginning that Colin couldn't be more than a passing lover in the night. And, she had to admit that was more than she'd had before he'd arrived on the scene, relieved her of the burden of her virginity, and taught her that she wouldn't shift or explode during an orgasm.

Colin definitely had some pluses on his side. If he had a strong prejudice against Weres mating with humans, that really had nothing to do with her, or their extremely temporary relationship. He was an outstanding lover, or so she supposed, having so little experience in the matter.

By denying him sex, she was also denying herself. Her mother would have said that was cutting off her nose to spite her face. She'd just discovered that orgasms were extremely pleasurable. Why not take advantage of what this virile Were had to offer, on her terms?

Colin cleared his throat. "So?"

She looked into those damnably attractive blue eyes.

"I'll think about the whole grandparent angle. No promises, but I'll give it some thought."

"Good."

"And much as I'd love to have Knox point out the wonders of flying over the Sound at night, I'd rather not go back at midnight."

Colin sighed. "All right. I'll cancel the restaurant reservations and call Knox. What time would you like to leave?"

She had a hard time controlling her smile, but she wanted to shock him. He deserved to be shocked, and a smile might tip him off that something unexpected was coming. "How about late tomorrow morning?"

She couldn't deny it was satisfying to see his jaw drop.

Chapter 13

Luna had rendered him speechless, and that didn't happen often to Colin MacDowell, pack alpha and Laird of Glenbarra. When he finally spoke, it was with a disconcerting stammer. "T-tomorrow?"

"Unless you have plans." Triumph danced in her green eyes. She'd gained the upper hand, and she knew it.

"No, I just . . ."

"Didn't come prepared. Neither did I. No extra clothes. Although for some of the time, we won't need any."

He couldn't believe she'd said that. He assumed the limo driver was discreet, although he'd have to count on Knox's discretion, too, because once he called Knox, the helicopter pilot would know . . . Bloody hell, the entire staff at Whittier House would know, too! Not a soul would believe he and Luna had spent the night in separate hotel rooms.

He swallowed. "I assume you've thought this through?"

"As a matter of fact, I have. When we get back to the city for our book shopping, we can stop by a department store and pick up a few things. I'll be happy with some jeans, a blouse, and a change of underwear. I can still wear my sandals, and I can go without makeup for a day. I have lipstick in my purse."

"That's not what I meant."

"Are you worried about toiletries? If we're staying in a luxury hotel, which seems to be the way you roll, then it should have everything else—shampoo, toothpaste, things like that." She shrugged. "Easy."

"I'm not worried about any of that." For a chance to spend the whole night with her, he'd sacrifice any number of grooming essentials. "I'm thinking of . . ." It sounded old-fashioned, but he'd say it anyway. "Your reputation."

"My *reputation*?" She placed a hand dramatically on her chest. "This can only improve it. Everyone thinks of me as a shy and boring virgin, and now they'll know I've finally taken the leap, and with a fine specimen, too."

"Thanks for that, but I wouldn't say that I'm such a fine—"

"Don't be modest. Every female at Whittier House is in agreement on that score. You're gorgeous. Fact is, you should be worrying about your reputation."

"I should?"

"Important laird, pack alpha, consorting with the help, a female Were who doesn't even belong to a pack and has a very murky history. How will that play in Glenbarra?"

"So long as I'm not mated, and it's consensual, nobody cares."

"In that case, I need to get while the getting's good, before Colin MacDowell is all mated up with a bonny lass and a pack of wee MacDowells."

"You sound mighty cheerful about that prospect."

"Why shouldn't I be? Isn't that what you want?"

It wasn't a question he cared to answer at the moment, because with Luna sitting inches away, her scent teasing him as much as her saucy words and outrageous suggestion to chuck everything and openly spend the night together, he couldn't seem to think about anything else, and certainly not about a life without her in it.

Moving closer, he slid his hand under her silky hair to cup the back of her neck. "Right now, all I want to do is kiss you."

"Right here in the limo?"

"No, right here on the mouth." Leaning forward, he made good on that statement, and he couldn't remember a sweeter kiss than this one, because he'd given up all hope of ever doing it again.

He kissed her with gratitude for her plump lips that tasted like raspberries, and for her nimble tongue that gave him such pleasure during this kiss, and would, if he was very lucky, give him pleasure elsewhere on his body later tonight. That prospect made his cock swell in anticipation. Reluctantly he concluded that unless he planned to take her here in the back of the limo in broad daylight, thus providing a peep show for the driver in his rearview mirror, he'd better stop kissing her.

He pulled back, and was gratified to notice that her pupils were huge and her breathing as jerky as his. "I don't mind if the world knows we're lovers," he said in a low voice. "But I'm not willing to put on a public demonstration to prove it."

"Are we in public? I totally forgot."

He smiled. "What a nice compliment. As I said, you're very good for my ego."

"No matter what our differences may be, Colin, you're the best kisser I've ever known."

"And my competition is who? The cretin who backed you up against a wall without asking and stuck his tongue down your throat? Face it, Luna, you don't know if I can kiss worth a damn. I'm just better than the Neanderthal who grabbed you years ago."

"I may not have kissed very many males in my life, but when someone can make me dizzy with only the pressure of his mouth, then I'll bet he's a good kisser." She leaned toward him and lowered her voice. "And besides being dizzy, my panties are wet."

Colin groaned softly. "You shouldn't have told me that."

"I'm only trying to prove my point," she murmured.

"Yes, but . . ." He put his mouth close to her ear. "We just pulled into the parking lot of the hot tub dealership, and I'm not sure I can get out of the car."

Her glance flicked to his lap and her smile was pure female. "Want to carry my purse?"

"No, lass, I do not." He closed his eyes and ran through a few football stats to get his penis under control. By the time he opened his eyes again, the limo driver was leaning in through the passenger door, staring at him.

"Motion sickness," Colin said. "I'm fine now."

"Yes, sir." The driver ducked his head, but not before Colin saw his knowing grin.

No matter. Colin was Luna Reynaud's lover and didn't care who knew it, including—no, *especially*—Knox Trevelyan.

Luna was so glad she'd decided to put aside her misgivings and enjoy being Colin's temporary lover. Shopping for a hot tub was way more fun when she could subtly taunt him with how they could make use of it. They actually might do those things, too, because the salesman promised delivery by motor launch the following afternoon. She and Colin chose an above-ground model, so it could be installed in a few hours.

While the salesman drew up the paperwork, Colin

pulled Luna aside. "You're a devil. You do know that, right?"

"Me?" She batted her eyelashes at him. "I simply wanted to make sure the benches would be the right height and the jets were positioned well. And we needed a demonstration of the pulsing action. That's very important."

"I'm sure it is for what you have in mind. You don't play fair, Luna Reynaud."

"Poor Colin. Bless your heart, that vein popped out on your temple when our salesman was explaining the pulsing action."

"I hope you realize that we're obliged to test that hot tub tomorrow night. I wouldn't feel right letting a guest use it until we're . . . completely satisfied."

"As they say down in the French Quarter, *touché.*" Now she was the one feeling hot and bothered as she imagined them both naked in the hot tub.

He'd agreed with her that it should be positioned beyond the croquet area on the edge of the bluff. Anyone sitting in it would have a view of the sea but be screened from the house by a row of tall hedges. Yet when she envisioned enjoying the tub with Colin, she wondered if they'd even care about the view. They'd have to make sure they tested it long after everyone else went to bed.

Colin signed the papers and wrote a check out of Geraldine's retirement account. She'd made him the beneficiary of that, too. If he'd sold the island and everything on it, he would have ended up with a sizable amount of money. Instead he was spending money to make Whittier House more attractive to guests.

Luna thought about that as they climbed inside the limo. "I'll make this venture profitable," she said. "In the long run, you'll make more money this way than by selling."

He reached over and took her hand. "Don't worry." He stroked her palm with his thumb. "I won't regret hanging on to the place."

"I hope not." The languid movement of his thumb reminded her of how he'd caressed her so intimately the last time they'd made love, when he refused to risk chafing her. She dropped her voice to a murmur. "I'm not sore, by the way."

His thumb stopped in midmotion. "You have the damnedest timing. Just when I was beginning to establish some control, you wreck it."

"I thought you'd want to know before we . . . do anything."

"Oh, I do want to know. Believe me. It's been on my mind ever since you mentioned staying overnight in Seattle." He squeezed her hand and released it. "Which reminds me that I need to call Knox and let him know our change of plans."

"You sound quite pleased about that."

"I am." He pulled his cell phone from an inside pocket of his jacket and punched in a number. "It will give me great pleasure to inform Knox that you and I will be spending the night together."

"Hey." She poked him in the ribs. "You're not allowed to be possessive." He had no right to lay a claim considering everything, but knowing he wanted to was gratifying.

"I know I shouldn't feel that way," he said softly. "But I can't seem to help— Knox? Colin here. Listen, we've decided to stay over. Could you meet us at the helipad around . . ." He glanced over at Luna and lifted his eyebrows.

"Noon."

"Around noon," Colin said. "You can? Thanks. See you then." He disconnected the phone and tucked it inside his jacket. Then he settled back with what could only be described as a triumphant smile and recaptured Luna's hand.

"I have no sexual interest in Knox," she said. "I probably shouldn't tell you that, because it's sort of fun to watch the Laird of Glenbarra get jealous."

"I'm not jealous."

"Ha."

"I'm not. I was, back when you were making eyes at Knox and he was showing off with his helicopter skills, but I'm—"

"He was *not* showing off. He knows I love orcas and when he spotted a pod of them he simply made sure I got a good view."

"Because he wants your body."

"You don't know that."

"Yes, I do, lass. Male Weres know these things about other male Weres. Knox has noticed you. You're beautiful, funny, and smart. Any male with half a brain would want you."

Warmth spread through her. Other females might be used to hearing this kind of thing, but she'd spent a lifetime avoiding such conversations. She drank in his compliments. But that didn't mean she had an interest in Knox.

She liked him as a friend, and she valued the way he'd tried to save Geraldine, but she'd never reacted to him the way she had to Colin. From the moment Colin had walked into the entryway of Whittier House, she'd been entranced by him. She knew he wasn't a real possibility in the long run, but for the next few days, he was all hers.

And if he thought he had a rival in Knox Trevelyan, maybe she should keep her mouth shut and pretend that was the case. She didn't know much about male-female relationships, but instinctively she understood the advantages of being desired by more than one eligible Were. With Knox potentially hovering in the background, Colin would try harder to please her. That could be good.

"Are you still up for a meeting with George Trevelyan?" Colin asked as they neared the business district.

"Yes." She extracted her hand from his grip. "But I need to repair my lipstick. Someone kissed it all off."

"Does it have a raspberry flavor, or is that just you?"

She glanced at him. "What if I said my mouth tastes naturally of raspberries?"

"I'd believe you. It's not a stretch to think you're delicious all over."

She wiggled happily in her seat as she imagined him enjoying every inch of her in their shared hotel room. "I'm really starting to enjoy this whole sexual thing. I wish I'd learned about it sooner." Opening her purse, she located her lipstick and a small mirror.

"Selfishly, I'm glad you didn't."

She paused in the act of putting on her lipstick as she debated telling him the absolute truth. But he had been the first to give her an orgasm, so maybe he deserved the truth. "I think holding off was a good thing for me. You were the one I needed to learn from."

"I'm flattered. But the way things are going, the student is liable to outpace the teacher."

She shook her head. "There's so much I don't know, especially about . . . how it works when we shift."

"I'm sure you can imagine."

Her cheeks grew hot. In spite of all they'd shared, some subjects still made her feel shy. She was gaining confidence in human form, but as a Were, she felt inexperienced and tentative. "I can imagine, but I could be wrong."

"Tomorrow night, after we test out the hot tub," he murmured for her ears alone, "we'll shift together and go for a run. Once we're in the forest, I'll . . . I'll show you what happens between two Weres."

Her heart pounded so loud she wondered if the chauffeur could hear it. "I'd like that." She didn't dare put on her lipstick now or she'd smear it all over her face because her hands were shaking.

"You will like it," he said gently. "The other is good, but making love as Weres adds a whole other dimension. It is, of course, how Weres bond when they mate, but of course we won't be doing that."

"Of course not," she said quickly. Still, she was curious about how a mating ritual was different from simply having Were sex. "I may never take part in that kind of bonding, but what happens, exactly?"

"I've never done it, either, obviously, but as teens we all learned what takes place, so we'd be ready. The actual sex is the same, but the two Weres circle each other beforehand while they pledge their eternal faithfulness."

A lump lodged in her throat. "That sounds wonderful." And she wanted such a bonding, but she could only think of one Were who would fill the bill. Maybe that was due to her lack of experience.

"When Weres are truly mates, perhaps even soul mates, it is wonderful, or so I've heard. Hey, you'd better fix your lipstick. We're almost there."

She'd been so wrapped up in the idea of mating Weres that she'd lost track of her original intention. Turning the base of the tube, she held the mirror in front of her mouth and outlined her top lip while doing her best to keep her hand steady.

"It's the lipstick," Colin said. "It smells like raspberries."

"You found me out." She moved to her bottom lip.

Colin put his head close to hers. "I think I could come just watching you do that."

Hot desire shot through her veins, but she pretended

to be unaffected by his comment. "Then you are easily stimulated."

"By you, apparently. This isn't the first time I've watched someone put on lipstick, but it's the first time it's given me an erection. I can't stop thinking about you kneeling in front of me, with your mouth on my—"

"Stop it, or we'll both be in trouble."

"I think we already are."

She would agree with that. Although her inexperience meant she couldn't judge whether the passion between them was off the charts, he'd admitted that the simple act of watching her apply lipstick was enough to set him off. That sounded like a strong attraction to her.

The limo eased to a stop at the curb. Luna glanced out and couldn't understand why they were facing the same way they had when they'd left. "Why aren't we across the street from the office building?"

"He took a different route so he could deposit us right here and we wouldn't have to cross traffic."

Luna blinked. "Now that's what I call service."

"Knox told me that George runs a tight ship. Guess he was right."

"Wait. Did you call to see if he's in?"

"No, but I will once we're on the sidewalk."

The chauffeur helped Luna out first, and she thanked him for driving them around as Colin climbed from the limo and pulled his cell phone from his jacket pocket.

Moments later he appeared at her elbow. "We're all set with George." Then he put some bills in the chauffeur's hand. "I appreciate your fine service," he said.

"You're welcome." The chauffeur's eyes lit up at the sight of the money.

"And your discretion," Colin added.

"Absolutely, sir. Will you be needing a limo any more during your stay in Seattle?"

Colin glanced at Luna. "If we decide to pay a visit to your grandparents tomorrow, then—"

"We'll take a regular taxi," Luna said. "I refuse to drive up to their house in a white stretch limo."

"All right." Colin turned back to the chauffeur. "Then I guess we won't be needing you again. Thanks for everything."

"Yes, sir." With a smile, the chauffeur returned to his limo.

Taking Luna's hand, Colin started toward the imposing entrance to the building. "While I was talking to George, I asked him to book us a room at his favorite hotel in the city."

"Why did you do that?"

"Because if I hadn't, he'd take one look at you and wonder what I was waiting for. As I said, single Weres are expected to enjoy their sexuality."

"Then I guess it's a good thing I suggested spending the night."

"Yes." He glanced down at her and his eyes glowed with blue fire. "It's a very good thing."

Chapter 14

Colin had communicated with George Trevelyan several times through both e-mail and phone conversations, but this was their first face-to-face meeting. After the glittering lobby, Colin had expected more of the same in George's office, but the alpha Were surprised him.

The room had a rustic feel, as if they'd stepped into a lodge built by one of the Pacific Northwest tribes. An intricately carved totem pole stood in a corner to the right of George's desk. Not surprisingly, it contained a stylized wolf's head at the top. Other pieces of Native American art decorated the walls, and many of those depicted wolves as part of the design.

The wall to their left held no hanging art, but instead featured a mural with Mount Rainier in the background and a pack of wolves in the foreground. A casual visitor would call this a flight of fancy. Officially, no wolf packs lived west of the Cascade Mountains. Floor-to-ceiling windows behind George's desk offered a view of the distant peak depicted in the mural.

George himself looked like a rugged outdoorsman more than the CEO of Trevelyan Enterprises. Because it was a regular work day, Colin assumed that George always dressed casually. He wore jeans and a green flannel shirt open at the neck, as if he might head out for a hike at any minute. At fifty-something, he was fit, with only touches of gray in his dark hair. Colin hoped to look that good in twenty years.

George stood and came around the massive desk to greet them. He took Luna's hand first and focused all his attention on her. "Luna Reynaud. It's a pleasure to meet you."

Colin was glad George was mated and nearly twice Luna's age, because if he hadn't been, Colin would have bristled at the warmth of George's greeting. He seemed ready to eat Luna up with a spoon.

George continued to hold her hand as he piled on the charm. "My aunt Edwina married a Reynaud. You're not related by any chance, are you?"

So George's aunt was Luna's grandmother. That made Luna related to George. Colin sucked in a breath and cursed himself for not digging a little deeper. Worse yet, he was the idiot who'd pushed Luna into coming up here to meet George. Without realizing it, he'd thrown her into the deep end of the pool, and he had no idea if she would sink or swim.

Then, to his relief, she came up with a brilliant response. "I'm not really sure, but I've been meaning to check into that." She sounded completely at ease.

"Please do." George released her hand. "Edwina and Jacques haven't had an easy time of it. Their only child, my cousin Byron, was killed in his early twenties many years ago. They've carried on bravely since then, but I'm sure they'd welcome more family connections."

"Then I'll definitely follow up."

Colin noticed the faint tremor in her voice, but he'd

come to know her well in the short time they'd been together. George probably wouldn't hear it.

Next George held out his hand to Colin. "We meet at
last, MacDowell! I've promised myself I'd come over
there and play golf the way it was meant to be played,
but I haven't made it yet."

"When you do, I'll be happy to swing a club with you."

"I'll make it one day." George shook a finger in warning. "But I'm a lousy golfer, so you may not want to admit you know me." He swept a hand toward two cushy
leather armchairs in front of his desk. "Sit down, please.
I want to hear all about the plans for Whittier House."

Luna sat, but Colin chose to perch on the wide arm of
the other chair. It was a Were thing. George had leaned
a hip against the front edge of his desk in a very casual
way.

But the stance was far from casual. If Colin sat down
in the squashy chair, he would no longer be able to look
George in the eye. He might be younger than George,
and he might not command George's great wealth, but
his title equaled George's. The Laird of Glenbarra would
never put himself in an inferior position to another alpha.

Luna, of course, was oblivious to all this jockeying.
She immediately began describing her vision for the inn,
and Colin listened with pride. It was a terrific concept, so
terrific that he almost wished he'd thought of it himself.

George looked impressed. "When I first talked to Colin, he seemed hell-bent on selling the place, but this is a
far better idea. I can understand why he went for it."

Colin thought there might be a double meaning there.
George could see that Luna was a charmer, and he also
knew, following the request for a hotel room, that Colin
was sleeping with her. But Colin's relationship with Luna

didn't take anything away from the brilliance of her business plan.

"Weres don't have many resorts strictly dedicated to them," Colin said. "The island is perfect—isolated with woods to roam in, yet with all kinds of amenities for those seeking luxury. Luna and I just bought a hot tub for the premises, at her suggestion. We plan to have a well-stocked library, a complimentary cocktail hour every evening, and croquet tournaments."

He'd thrown that last bit in, and Luna looked somewhat startled to hear it. But she wanted to keep the croquet playing field, and tournaments sounded like a crowd pleaser.

"Sounds terrific. I'd like to buy in," George said.

Colin winced. He should have anticipated this, and he hadn't. "That's a great offer, and I'll keep it in mind. But we're going to go it alone, at least initially." Now that Whittier House belonged to him, he wanted to keep it that way. It was his project, his and Luna's.

But he couldn't predict the future, and alienating someone like George was never good business. "But if I change my mind about that, you'll be the first person I call."

"Make sure I am. And I'd like to be on the guest list for the opening weekend, as well. I already told Suzanne what was happening out there, and she's wild to finally get the chance to see the island and the castle Henry built for Geraldine. She thinks it's a romantic story."

"So do I," Luna said. "In fact, I'd like to bill Whittier House as a romantic getaway, if Colin is willing to use that as a marketing hook."

"Absolutely." Colin turned to George. "As you can see, Luna has good instincts."

"And a great Southern accent," George added with a benevolent smile. "Where's your family from, Luna?"

Once again, Colin held his breath, not having any idea how Luna would handle such questions. He knew they were loaded, but George might not. Or maybe he did.

George was nobody's fool, and once he'd heard about the inn concept, he'd obviously thought of investment opportunities. Following that, he would have done a background check on both Colin and Luna. He would have run into some dead ends with Luna. Colin had done a similar search this morning and had netted very little.

"I grew up in New Orleans for the most part," she said. "But my parents didn't like to stay in one place, so we didn't belong to one particular pack. I regret that now."

Colin admired how she told the truth, but it was only true when interpreted a certain way. Her parents literally hadn't stayed in one place together. Her mother had moved to New Orleans, and her father had stayed in Seattle, in a matter of speaking. His ashes were scattered somewhere, and that was another thing Luna deserved to know about. A connection with her grandparents would be so rewarding if it worked out.

"A nomadic Were family." George sounded intrigued. "Did you inherit that tendency?"

"For a time," Luna said, "when I was younger. But once I took the job with Geraldine, I found my home. I have no desire to live anywhere else."

Colin had known she felt that way from the beginning, yet to hear her say it drove another nail in the coffin of his fantasy that somehow, someway, they could end up together in Scotland. The idea made no sense, yet he wasn't sure how he'd live out the rest of his days without her.

"That's good to hear," George said. "I'm all in favor of having a Were destination resort here in the Seattle area. I believe those Colorado Weres have the only one so far, and they're raking in the profits. That proves there's a market for it. Let me know if there's anything I can do to help get this off the ground." He pushed away from his desk.

Colin read that as a signal that the visit was over. Standing, he offered a hand to Luna. She accepted it, because the chair was extremely deep. Colin hated to think of how he would have lost status if he'd sat in the other one. He doubted George had expected him to.

"I appreciate your enthusiasm," Luna said as she shook George's hand. "It's important to have friends in the community when you're launching a new business."

"I have a feeling you'll be very successful." George released her hand and glanced over at Colin. "The reservation's made, by the way, and the room's paid for, with my compliments."

Colin frowned. "You didn't have to do that."

"Just promise you'll get me a tee time at St. Andrews when I show up there, and we'll call it even."

"I'll do that." Colin shook George's hand, and the interview was over.

When they were in the elevator headed back down to the lobby, Luna sagged against the mirrored elevator wall. "That was challenging."

Colin put an arm around her shoulders and hugged her close. "You were amazing."

She glanced up at him, a gleam of suspicion in her eyes. "Did you know my grandmother was his aunt?"

"I didn't, and I apologize for that. Please believe that if I'd known I would have warned you."

"If I'd known, I wouldn't have gone up there."

"But you did, and you impressed him. He'll support your business, and that kind of support could make a big difference."

She sighed. "Until he finds out that I'm the illegitimate child of his late cousin Byron." Her eyes widened. "I think that means I'm related to George Trevelyan!"

"I wondered when you'd figure that out."

She closed her eyes. "All I ever wanted was to hide out on that island. And that's looking increasingly impossible. I've known since I arrived in Seattle that I'm technically a part of the Trevelyan pack, but I'd hoped to keep that very quiet. Now there's no way I can."

Leaning down, he dropped a kiss on the top of her head. "Have you ever thought that maybe you weren't meant to hide out somewhere? That you were meant for something more grand than living like a hermit on Le Floret?"

"You make it sound like some kind of destiny or something."

"Maybe it is, Luna." He thought about the premonition he'd had when he'd realized that her name blended perfectly with his cherished love of the heavens. "Maybe it is."

Luna's mood improved once she and Colin left the Trevelyan Enterprises building. She had to make a decision about whether or not to visit her grandparents, but she didn't have to make it now. Instead she and Colin could explore Seattle, and the city in June was a magical place, especially for lovers. Much as she'd adored Geraldine, Colin was a more exciting companion.

He insisted on going into an upscale department store to buy the clothes they'd need for the following day. He bought sensible things, a change of underwear and a cotton shirt, but he nagged her mercilessly until she ended up with a pair of designer jeans and a ridiculously expensive silk blouse that matched her eyes. Or so Colin said when she walked out of the dressing room wearing it.

He took part in choosing her underwear, too, and so naturally it was black lace. "Why do males have this thing about black lace?" she asked him after they left the lingerie department, each with their purchases in a snazzy bag with handles.

"Conditioning, I suppose." He laced his fingers through hers as they strolled along the sidewalk toward Pike's Place Market, where they planned to browse through some bookshops. "Black is the color of night, of mystery, of the forbidden."

She laughed and swung her shopping bag back and forth, feeling carefree and slightly decadent. "I don't remember forbidding anything to you. I've pretty much given the Laird of Glenbarra carte blanche."

"And I hope you know that I don't take that lightly, especially considering . . ."

"I know. And I appreciate it." Her heart softened. Colin had his flaws, but at his core he was inherently decent.

"You'd have every right to forbid me everything, and yet, generous female that you are, you haven't."

"Don't give me too much credit. I'm getting something out of the arrangement, too."

"I hope so." He lifted her hand and dropped a gentle kiss on the inside of her wrist.

She shivered in delight. The Laird of Glenbarra did have a boatload of charm. "You've fascinated me since the moment you walked through the door of Whittier House."

"And I was fascinated with you from the beginning, too. You were the prettiest Were I'd ever seen, and your laughter was balm to my soul."

"I'm glad." She was so unused to getting compliments from male Weres that each one Colin gave her seemed like a glittering jewel presented in a velvet box.

They reached the market, a covered row of shops and

stalls selling everything under the sun, it seemed. Fish, vegetables, flowers, New Age products, antiques, crafts— Luna was on sensory overload. And somewhere in this visual kaleidoscope was a bookstore. Colin had looked it up.

"What was everyone laughing about that morning, anyway?" he asked. "I meant to ask you that before."

"It was . . ." She was embarrassed to think how stupid that conversation had been, but at the time, they'd all been so tense that everything had seemed funny. "It was nothing."

"Ah, come on, Luna." He squeezed her hand. "Let me in on the joke."

"It won't be funny anymore, but all right. We were confused about Scottish titles and thought a laird might logically have a lairdess, which somebody mispronounced as lard-ass, and Janet started prancing around with her bottom stuck out." She snuck a glance at him. "See? Not funny."

He grinned. "Oh, it's funny, especially when I visualize Janet putting on a demonstration. If the question ever comes up again, the proper term is *lady*, not *lairdess*."

"Well, that's easy enough to remember." She, for one, would never forget it. Knowing the title his mate would hold made it very clear to her that he would move on, and she would not move on with him. Her happy mood dimmed a fraction. She might be his lover now, but she would never be his lady. And despite understanding completely why that was so, she couldn't help being sad about that.

"Luna?"

She looked at him and forced herself to smile. "What?"

"I just wondered. You were quiet all of a sudden."

She grabbed the first evasive comment that came to mind. "I was just thinking about something."

"Must have been a serious subject."

"Sorry. Didn't mean to be a Debbie Downer."

"A *who*?"

"American slang. It means someone who looks on the negative side of everything and ruins the mood." She brought up a topic that she knew interested him. "Here's a thought. What if Edwina and Jacques Reynaud come here to shop?" She could let him assume she'd been dwelling on a potential visit to her grandparents. She would never *ever* admit that she fantasized about being his mate. It wouldn't work, and she should just quit torturing herself about it.

"They might shop here," he said. "It's obviously a popular place."

"They could even be here now. We could walk right past them and I'd never know."

"I have a picture of their house on my phone."

"Really? Can I see it?" She was legitimately interested in that. With Colin here to give her courage, she might even decide to go see them tomorrow. Maybe it was time to slay this dragon once and for all.

"Of course. I wasn't sure if you'd want to." He reached inside his jacket for his phone.

"Wait. Don't take out your phone in the middle of this crowd. We need to keep moving or we'll get trampled to death. I can look at it once we're in the bookstore."

"Fair enough. And speaking of the bookstore, there it is." He pointed to their right and they ducked inside.

Luna took a deep breath. "Ah. Love that smell."

"Then maybe I'll buy a really old, tattered book and rub it all over myself tonight."

She laughed and glanced around to see if anyone had heard that remark. Nobody seemed to be paying any attention. The clerks were busy ringing up purchases and the browsers all had that dreamy expression found on the faces of true book lovers surrounded by the objects of their affection.

She leaned close to Colin. "I seem to remember you also love the smell of old books."

"I do." He gazed down at her, amusement in his blue eyes. "I'd suggest scattering pages all over the bed so we can roll around in them, but that would require destroying a book, and I'm not sure I can do that."

"I couldn't, either, but it's fun to think about. Like a copy of *Lady Chatterley's Lover*. We could stop every once in a while and read a page for inspiration."

"I can't speak for you, but I don't seem to require more inspiration in your presence. In fact, if we stand here talking about this much longer, I'll have to browse the shelves holding a shopping bag in front of my crotch."

"Don't blame me, Your Lairdness. I'm not the one who started this conversation by mentioning that I might rub book pages all over my naked body."

"I didn't use the word *naked*."

"No, but it was implied, and I have reactions, too, for your information."

"You do?" He let go of her hand and wrapped his long fingers around her upper arm. "Then come with me, little girl. I have some books I want to show you."

She allowed herself to be pulled up and down the aisles until he found one that was deserted. Then he set down his shopping bag and pulled her into his arms. "I wanted to do this when we were in Henry's library together, but I didn't, so I'm making up for it now." Lowering his head, he kissed her with such focus and intensity that her shopping bag slid from her limp fingers and hit the floor with a soft thump. She didn't bother to pick it up.

Chapter 15

Colin kissed Luna until he realized he'd slid the strap of her sundress over her shoulder. Quickly releasing her, he repositioned the strap. "Sorry." He cleared his throat. "Between you and the smell of old books, I lost all sense of propriety."

She swayed a little, and her eyes were dark and slightly unfocused. She licked her lips. "Me, too."

"On top of that, I've smeared your lipstick." Reaching into his back pocket, he pulled out a handkerchief. "Here."

She waved it away. "If I get dark pink lipstick on that white handkerchief, it will never come out."

"Then I'll keep it as a souvenir." He cupped the back of her head. "Here, I'll do it. Hold still." He carefully wiped her mouth. "You'll have to start over, I'm afraid."

Gradually, her dazed expression was replaced with a mischievous smile. "I'm not the only one wearing raspberry lipstick."

"Oh." He hadn't thought of that, but then, he wasn't in the habit of kissing females in the middle of bookstores, or in any public place, for that matter. He'd never been overcome by the need to kiss someone *immediately* until he'd met Luna.

"Allow me." Taking the handkerchief from him, she reached up and dabbed at his mouth. "You have such a sensuous lower lip."

"I'll bet you say that to all the chaps."

"I've never said it to anyone before."

"I know. I was teasing you again, and I shouldn't do that." He caught her hand in both of his and kissed her fingertips. "Knowing I'm your first lover is an endless source of pride and joy to me. You've given me a priceless gift, Luna."

"No less than you gave to me. I feel as if I'm . . . how would I describe it? Something was missing in my life, and I knew that, but I didn't understand how different I would feel now that I'm . . ." She blew out a breath. "Like I said, I'm not sure how to describe it."

He kept holding her hand because he couldn't seem to stop touching her. "Complete?"

She nodded. "Yes, complete. I feel complete now, as if I know what the world is about. I'm so grateful, Colin."

He was mesmerized by the warmth in her eyes. "Maybe we should skip buying the books and check into the hotel. We can order books online."

She smiled. "That's no fun."

"But we could have a whole lot of fun in that hotel room. I like books, but not enough to give up a chance to—"

She laid a finger over his mouth. "We're here now. We might as well pick up some books." Removing her finger, she chucked him under the chin. "We don't have to stay long, but we should do it."

"And then we can go back to the hotel?"

"Yes."

"Excellent." He picked up his shopping bag and looped the handles over his forearm. "This will take me about five minutes. I'll take this one, and this one, and—"

"Colin! You're not even looking at them! What on earth have you got there?"

"I don't know. I liked the red leather cover." He glanced at the spine of the book in his hand. "*The Mating Habits of Crustaceans*."

"We don't need that book. Or—" She peered at the spines of his other choices. "*Fun with Chemistry* or *The Secret Life of Snails*. Put them back."

"I don't know. That last one sounds kind of sexy. Maybe they dress up in black lingerie."

"Now you're being silly." She glanced around. "No wonder! We're standing smack in the middle of the science section. Let's move to the fiction aisle."

"Wait." He spied a book on a top shelf and pulled it down. "I've never been able to find this one. I even did a rare book search with no luck. And here it is." He held the book up so she could see.

Her expression softened. "I didn't think about you finding astronomy books here."

Colin looked at his treasure. "Lowell's theories on Mars have been disproven, but I wanted to have this anyway." He glanced at the price written on the inside cover. "As I thought, they don't know how much this book is worth. It should go for several hundred dollars."

"So you found a bargain!"

He laughed. "Every Scotsman's dream. Okay, now we can go to the fiction section. I've found my treasure." Those words taunted him as he followed Luna over to the well-populated fiction aisle.

He'd found his treasure, all right, and it wasn't this book. He could take that home and place it on a shelf in the library at Glenbarra. But the real treasure, the lover he'd waited a lifetime to find, would not be coming home with him.

He wouldn't let thoughts like that ruin his time with her, though. He wasn't about to be—what name had she used? Oh, yes. Debbie Downer. He refused to be her twin brother, Donny Downer. So he'd enjoy the devil out of watching Luna choose her books.

She chortled with glee each time she found one for the growing collection in his arms. "You should choose some," she said after she'd stacked up enough hardbacks to reach almost to his chin. "I can hold those."

Considering the weight, he doubted it, but it was sweet of her to offer. "You go ahead and pick them out. I'll be the muscle of the operation."

"Are they getting too heavy?"

He wouldn't admit it if they were. "I'm fine, but I suppose we have to consider the weight limit of the helicopter." He had no idea what that was, but he was ready to finish up here and whisk her away to their hotel.

"All right." She held up a tattered paperback copy of *Lady Chatterley*. "This will be the last one."

He smiled at her choice. "I should have known you'd track that down, although it doesn't look to be in very good shape."

"Oh, it's not." She leaned close. "It's already falling apart."

"Really?"

"It's marked way down because the glue isn't holding. A few good shakes and pages will go everywhere." She winked at him.

"I see. Then maybe we need to get it back to the hotel room before something happens."

"Good plan. Let's check out." She walked ahead of him with a decided sway to her hips.

He couldn't remember her walking like that before.

Unless he was mistaken, his former virgin was turning into a vixen. And he was all for it.

Setting the books on the counter, he handed her his shopping bag from their clothes expedition, took out his wallet, and extracted several bills. "This should cover the books. I'll be right back."

She looked surprised, but he dashed out of the bookstore before she could ask any questions. He'd noticed the way she'd gazed longingly at the flower stalls, and this was the kind of day that called for a romantic gesture.

When he returned, he found her standing just inside the door of the bookstore, a sturdy double bag of books and the two shopping bags at her feet. When she saw the bouquet in his hand, her eyes widened and she covered her mouth.

He held out the flowers. "For you, m'lady."

She took the bouquet hesitantly, glancing from the multicolored gerbera daisies to his face. Then she looked at the flowers again, almost as if she couldn't quite believe he'd done such a thing. He'd hoped she might smile.

Instead, tears welled in her eyes.

He panicked. "You don't like them? Are they the wrong kind? Tell me what you like, and I'll get those instead. I just wanted to—"

"I *love* them." She launched herself into his arms, grabbed him around the neck, and kissed him, even as tears dribbled down her cheeks and flavored the kiss with salt.

Cupping her face in both hands he brushed at the tears with his thumbs. He still wasn't sure if he'd done something good or something bad by giving her the flowers, but her kiss seemed to be saying he'd done something good.

Finally she drew back. "No one's ever given me flowers before." Her voice was thick with emotion. "We've had bouquets of flowers from the garden all around Whittier House, but that's not the same as having someone buy them just for m-me. I'm a—" She paused to sniff. "A flower virgin, too."

"I thought maybe I'd made a mistake."

She shook her head violently. "It was *wonderful* of you to surprise me with these. They're such happy flowers, and all different colors. We need to hurry to the hotel so we can put them in some water. What about a vase? We don't want them to die, and I'm not sure a water glass will work."

"We'll ask room service to send something up." He looked into her eyes, needing reassurance that she really was happy about his attempt to be romantic.

"Honestly, Colin, I love them."

He took a shaky breath. "All right. You had me worried there, but if you say so, then . . . all right." He leaned down and picked up the weighty sack of books and both shopping bags. "Let's get a cab."

All the way to the hotel, Luna kept looking at her flowers. She really did love them, and they were so much more imaginative than roses. Every time she thought of Colin rushing out to buy flowers for her, she choked up.

But that wasn't the only reason. When he'd presented them, he'd said *m'lady*. If he hadn't recently told her what his mate would be called, she wouldn't have thought anything about it. But he had just told her, and yet she imagined his choice of words had been unconscious. He couldn't know that being addressed like that taunted her with what she'd never have.

Consequently, she'd become a blubbering idiot, for which she was embarrassed. She wasn't a crier, had never been one, so far as she could remember. She'd shed tears over Geraldine, and that was to be expected. But she wasn't the type to tear up over a bouquet of flowers and a misplaced endearment.

She couldn't blame it on stress, because she'd had far more stress than this in her twenty-seven years of life. So she'd blame it on lack of sleep. One thing she wouldn't blame it on—falling in love with Colin MacDowell. That would be the stupidest thing she could possibly do.

"Did you still want to see the picture of your grand-parents' house?"

She'd forgotten all about that. Sharing a kiss with Colin in a deserted aisle of a bookstore could do that to her. Being alone with him in a hotel room would likely have the same effect. "I'd like to see it," she said.

Taking out his phone, he pushed a few buttons and handed it to her. "There it is."

"Wow." The stately two-story was white with hunter-green shutters. "It looks like a mansion."

"They've done well, but they're turning the whole thing into offices for the foundation and temporary housing for homeless Weres, so they won't be living there much longer. That was all on the foundation Web site."

"Any pictures of them?"

"There might have been a couple of small ones, but I don't know how well they'll show up on a tiny screen. Want me to try?"

"Sure." She gave him the phone, although it might not matter whether she could see the pictures or not. She'd nearly made up her mind to meet them tomorrow, so she'd get an up close and personal view then.

"This is the best I can do. I've magnified it as much as I can." He passed over the phone again.

Luna already knew from pictures of her mother that she looked almost exactly like Sophie, so she didn't ex-pect to see much family resemblance in the two seventy-something people gazing back at her from the small image in the phone. So she was surprised when she felt the shock of instant recognition.

Edwina's chin was like hers, rounded and yet firm and strong-looking. As for Jacques, his ears were small and close to his head, exactly like Luna's. Sophie's had stuck out a little bit, which was why she'd always worn her hair long.

The light on the screen faded, and Luna punched a button to bring it back. She couldn't stop looking at those two people. Their blood ran in her veins.

"Can you see it well enough?" Colin leaned closer and started to take the phone. "Maybe I can —"

She maintained her grip on the phone. "I can see it fine." The picture was a posed studio shot, and so she couldn't get a real sense of what they were like because they seemed a little stiff. But they were both smiling, and they had wonderful smiles, although that part wasn't familiar. Luna's smile was pure Sophie.

Edwina's hair was a combination of blond and silver that looked natural. Jacques had a receding hairline, and what was left of his hair was quite gray. He had the kindest eyes and a bushy mustache.

"I think I would like them," she said softly.

"Everything about them seems positive."

"I know." She finally lifted her gaze from the screen. "But I can't forget that their son died because of my mother's behavior."

"But he was your father, too. And that was more than twenty-seven years ago," Colin said. "They've had twenty-seven years to come to grips with what happened."

"Or twenty-seven years to grow more bitter about losing their only child."

Colin sighed. "I won't tell you that's impossible, but if they were bitter, why would they start this foundation? I think there's a better chance that they would embrace you as their granddaughter."

"I want to see them, but I want to go with a cover story. Will you help me with that?"

"I'll do whatever you need."

That was all she had to hear. "What if we call on them to suggest using the opening weekend of Whittier House as a benefit for their foundation?"

Colin stared at her. "That's bloody brilliant, lass!"

"It is? Don't forget it will reduce our profit that weekend."

"I may be a Scot but I'm not stupid. Tying in with a charitable cause will mean cross-promotion, both for them and for us. Guests are able to say they were at the opening of Whittier House Inn, and they contributed to the Byron Reynaud Foundation at the same time."

"I mostly wanted an excuse to see them other than announcing I'm their long-lost granddaughter."

He frowned, clearly disappointed. "So you're not going to tell them that?"

"Not yet. Maybe not ever."

"But . . . what about your name?"

She'd been wrestling with that problem, the only real glitch in her scheme. "We may be able to gloss over that. For one thing, I've always thought the MacDowell name should be on all the literature about the inn. Your title will impress everyone."

"But won't they expect me to be around all the time if my name's on the brochure?"

"I'll say you jet back and forth between your two homes. That will sound worldly and extravagant. We'll put a welcome letter from you in each room, and, I know! We'll put a portrait of you, wearing a kilt and whatever else goes with that, in some prominent place."

Colin groaned. "I really hate that plan."

"Do you have a kilt?"

"Not with me."

"But you do have one. And that other thing, the pouch deal."

"A sporran. Aye, I have that, and the proper cap, the whole outfit."

She grinned at him. "When you talk about it, your brogue gets stronger. Maybe in addition to the portrait, we should have a video of—"

"No, by God. I'll not be making a video as the Laird of Glenbarra, strutting around in his plaid."

"Aw, Colin. It would be so *great*. We could have it on a continuous loop in the library!"

"You're having me on, aren't you?"

She reached over and stroked his cheek. "A little. You were so horrified at the idea of a video. But I really want to play up the laird angle and minimize my role. I'm just Luna Thisbe, the one who runs the office."

"Who?"

"Thisbe is my middle name. My mother got it from a story about two ill-fated lovers."

"I know the story."

"I've always hated that middle name. As if Luna isn't unusual enough, she saddled me with Thisbe, too. But it works as a last name if I want to cloak myself for now. I can even tell the staff I'm dropping Reynaud so people don't get confused and think I'm part of the foundation."

Colin gave her a wry smile. "It would be so much simpler if you just told them."

"Too risky. I realize eventually the word may get out and I'll have to deal with that, but if we have Whittier House off and running by then, it may not matter who I am, especially if you're the visible part of the operation."

"You do know I won't be particularly visible at all, don't you?"

"I know." He wasn't even gone yet and she was already imagining how desperately she'd miss him. Enough. She'd already had one bout of tears today, and that was one too many. "But you could be, if you'd make that video!"

Chapter 16

Colin wasn't about to push Luna to reveal her identity to her grandparents. His instinct was always to face problems squarely and then take whatever came of that, but it wasn't his fight. She had to decide, and for all he knew, she was right to postpone the confrontation.

But if her grandmother was George Trevelyan's aunt, the fat would hit the fire eventually. Colin didn't like surprises, and he didn't think Luna's grandparents would appreciate stumbling upon the information sometime in the future. Besides that, Luna would have to live with a sword hanging over her head, knowing the moment of truth could come at any time.

But for now, he was happy to be out of the cab, through the hotel registration process, and stepping into yet another express elevator with her, this time headed for the penthouse of a hotel owned by Trevelyan Enterprises. He should have guessed that George would reserve the penthouse for them. Yes, it was a generous gesture, but it was also a display of wealth and power. As a pack alpha, Colin knew all about that.

"I felt a little funny checking in with only two shopping bags full of clothes, a bouquet of flowers, and a double grocery bag full of old books," Luna said as the elevator started its smooth glide upward. "Especially when they gave us the key to the penthouse. That George is something else."

"He's an alpha Were, is what he is. Someday he'll call in his favors," Colin said. "It would be rude to reject his generosity, and his help has been invaluable. But there'll be a price, and I can't believe a round of golf at St. Andrews will settle the bill."

"Are you worried about it?"

"No, but I'll stay alert."

She lifted her chin. "Then I'll stay alert, too. I'm learning something about pack politics. You're the first pack alpha I ever met, and George is the second. Is that a representative sample?"

He couldn't help smiling. She was the most entertaining female he'd ever come across, Were or human. "I couldn't say. But there is often a similarity in how we operate. For example, those two big cushy chairs in George's office are designed to put the visitor at a disadvantage."

"I did feel sort of small and short when I sank into one." Her eyebrows lifted. "So *that's* why you didn't sit down."

"George didn't sit down, either, but even if he'd gone back to his desk chair, he still would have had the superior position because the desk chair would have kept him at a higher level than the other two chairs."

"Fascinating. If I ever go in that office again, I'll perch on the arm, too. There's no reason I have to sink down into that chair and be swallowed up like quicksand."

"True, but you're not an alpha, so you don't have to worry so much about it."

"I don't like the idea of being intimidated, though. And can't females be alphas if they want?"

He blinked. "Well, yes, they can. There are several females who run their packs. Recently Nadia Henderson took over the reins of the Chicago pack. But . . ." He paused, realizing that what he'd been about to say might not be true anymore.

"But a half-breed can't be an alpha?"

He took a deep breath. "That used to be true, but two alpha males from the Wallace pack in New York have taken human mates. Logically, one of their offspring might end up leading the pack someday." That sobering thought hadn't occurred to him until now.

"Really?" She gazed at him as the floor numbers flashed by on the display. "I'm guessing you're not totally on board with that program."

"It worries me. So much could go wrong."

She nodded. "I suppose so. But thanks for telling me about the Wallaces. Now I feel less freakish."

Guilt assailed him. "Luna, you're not—"

"You're right. I'm not at all freakish. That's a bad choice of words. But I have felt unusual, and it helps to know that I'm not the only half-breed. There's so much I don't know about the Were world, and I've been afraid to ask and expose my ignorance."

"You can ask me anything."

Her eyes sparkled with mischief. "Anything?"

"Whatever you have a question about."

"Then I have a question that I could only ask a male, and you're elected. What's your favorite female body part?"

As he started to answer, the elevator slid to a stop, and a mellow chime sounded as the doors rolled open with the barest of whispers.

"You're not saved by the bell, either, Your Much Honoured Sirness."

"I don't need to be." He picked up the bag of books,

supporting it from underneath because it was threatening to rip. "Can you get the other bags?"

"Sure." She picked both up in one hand and kept her grip on the flowers with the other.

He tilted his head toward the open elevator doors. "After you."

She went out, but turned back to him. "So what's your favorite female body part?"

He stepped into the foyer. He could hardly wait until she turned around and saw the view they had, but she seemed intent on this question of hers. "My favorite body part, particularly in your case, is your . . ."

"My what?" Her eyes lit up with anticipation.

"Your mind," he said.

The merriment in her expression changed, and her face glowed with obvious pleasure. "That's not what I thought you'd say, but it's a great answer."

"What did you think I'd say?"

Smiling, she shook her head. "I'm not telling. We can talk about it when we're naked."

That was all it took for him to decide to set the books down right there, in the foyer. Time to get on with the festivities. "I'm looking forward to that, but first, you need to see something." Stepping toward her, he grasped her shoulders and turned her gently around.

She gasped and dropped her bags to the floor, although he noticed that she still maintained a death grip on those flowers. He wondered if she'd crushed the stems by now. With an arm around her shoulders, he guided her toward the floor-to-ceiling windows.

The drapes were open to the view of the sparkling blue Sound, but more drapes ringed the entire curved boundary of the living room. Colin suspected that windows circled the entire top floor and provided a three-hundred-and-sixty-degree panorama. He was eager to find out, because he thought their plans for the evening were about to change.

Luna resisted him as he urged her toward the view. "Don't forget I have a touch of acrophobia."

"What about the helicopter? You seemed fine during the flight." With Knox in charge. The green monster reared its ugly head again.

"For some reason, that doesn't bother me, maybe because I'm strapped in. Here I'm free to fall out."

"No, you're not." He tightened his grip. "I've got you."

She relaxed slightly. "Okay. Just don't let go."

"I won't."

"Do I have your word as a MacDowell?"

"You do."

"Then let's see this view that George gave us." The tension left her body and she walked easily toward the tall windows.

Her trust humbled him. She had put all her faith in him, and not only to keep her from falling from a great height to the pavement below. She'd trusted him with her body, and on some level, with her heart.

He couldn't shake the feeling that she'd given it and wouldn't ever take it back. Luna Thisbe, indeed. He didn't want her name to seal her fate, but all the signs pointed to that very thing.

As Luna approached the window with Colin's strong arm securely around her shoulders, her heart raced, but with exhilaration instead of fear. She'd secretly been a little nervous about going up in the Space Needle because she'd seen pictures of the observation platform, and it looked something like this, with people standing right next to the abyss.

Yet here she was, gazing out across the Sound from such a height that the boats looked like toys in the water, and because Colin held her close to his side, she was not afraid. "It really is spectacular," she said.

"George is showing off, but I don't care. I have a suggestion, though."

"You want to moon passing airliners?"

He laughed. "No, but go ahead if you want."

"I suppose they wouldn't be close enough. The passengers would have to use binoculars to see us."

"The truth is, nobody can see us up here, unless maybe from a passing helicopter, but even that's not likely. I think we could run around naked up here without a soul noticing."

She glanced up at him. "I sense this has something to do with your suggested change in plans."

"Aye. But I need to know if your heart's set on eating at the top of the Space Needle."

"I doubt we could do that naked."

His lips twitched. "That would be frowned upon."

She scanned the horizon and pointed off to their left. "Isn't that it, right over there?"

"Yes."

"It is somewhat taller than we are. And you did say that alpha males like to seek high ground."

"I did say that. But this is very high ground right here, and more than that, it's exclusive high ground, which counts for a lot in an alpha's world."

"I see." She enjoyed listening to him make his case, even though she'd already chosen.

"But if you really want to see the *most* spectacular view in Seattle, we should go to the Space Needle."

"You're quite sure we can't eat there naked."

He glanced down at her with a smile. "No, we cannot. No shoes, no shirt, no pants, no underwear, no service."

"How restrictive!"

He nodded. "Quite restrictive."

"Then I'm thinking, who needs it?"

"See that, lass? My favorite part of your body just made me a very happy Were. But if I'm going to cancel our restaurant reservations, I'll need to let go of you to do it."

"I feel like I'm riding a bike with training wheels on, but let's find out whether I panic when you let go."

He gradually released her. "How's that?"

"So far so good."

"How about I take those flowers?"

"Oh." She glanced down at them and realized she'd been holding them very tightly. "I think I choked them to death."

"Look on the bright side. If I cut off the mangled part of the stem, they'll now fit in a water glass."

"And judging from this place, the glasses will be Waterford, so I suppose all is well."

"It is, Luna. It definitely is. If you think you'll be fine here, I'll make the call and organize your flowers. Otherwise I can guide you back to the sofa."

"Now, that's ridiculous." She flapped her hand at him. "Go. Make your call. Fix the flowers."

"I will." As he stepped back and consulted his phone, she began edging to her left, crablike. She'd never stayed in a penthouse before. She'd cleaned plenty of them, but she'd managed to do that without standing right next to the windows that always seemed oversized in a penthouse. She supposed that was the idea.

Eventually she reached the spot where the drapes were still drawn. But, being a clever female, she'd already figured out that the drapes disguised what was essentially a goldfish bowl of a suite. Walls divided up the circle into wedge-shaped pieces, but the edge of the bowl was all glass.

Without Colin here to steady her, she would have

hated it, but he coaxed her to stretch, to push her boundaries. Grabbing hold of the rod hanging at the edge of the drapes, she began to pull as she sidestepped along. If she kept looking out instead of down, that helped. Fools who didn't mind leaning against windows would have a view of the street below, but Luna saw no percentage in that. Gazing out, however, made her feel like a hawk in flight, and that was a sensation worth having.

"How's it going?" Colin came up beside her. He'd taken off his sport coat and rolled back the sleeves of his shirt. He looked . . . totally hot.

"It's going good." She gave him a tentative smile. "If I can stay in this room for three or four weeks, I'll probably cure myself of acrophobia."

"Was your mother bothered by it?"

"No, although New Orleans isn't known for its skyscrapers. But I used to panic if she took me out on a balcony in the French Quarter."

"Considering that, you're doing very well." He glanced behind him. "I don't know if you noticed the wet bar, but there's champagne chilling in a bucket and a plate of strawberries and finger sandwiches. Someone must have whisked it up here while we were checking in."

She clutched the drapes. "Do you want some?"

"I do. I feel like celebrating."

"What?"

"Not what. Who. I want to celebrate Luna Reynaud."

"Luna Thisbe." Although she corrected him, she was thrilled by his extravagant comment. No one had ever suggested celebrating *her.*

"You can be Luna Thisbe tomorrow if you insist upon it, but tonight, be Luna Reynaud, the Were who convinced me to hang on to a piece of my past." He held out his hand.

"All right." She placed her hand in his strong, warm grip, and he drew her away from the window into a somewhat cozy area that contained a curved sectional covered in ivory leather. A wet bar had been placed behind it, and she saw the champagne bucket and food he'd mentioned.

Nothing in this penthouse could truly be called cozy, though. Even with the drapes closed, she would still know that the fishbowl was just behind the curtain.

But Colin had shortened the stems on her daisies, put them in a whisky glass, and set the glass on a black granite coffee table tucked into the curve of the sectional. The daisies brought warmth and hominess to what was otherwise a rather intimidating space.

"Sit right there." Colin pointed to a spot on the sectional. "I'll bring you champagne and something to nibble on."

"What if I want to nibble on you?"

He laughed. "That can be arranged."

Settling onto the ivory leather, Luna took off her sandals and slid them under the coffee table. The chocolate brown carpet under her bare feet was thicker and softer than any she'd stepped on. She might never be in a place like this again, so she might as well make the most of it.

Colin walked around the end of the sectional and deposited the food plate on the coffee table before handing her a flute of champagne with the bubbles rising merrily to the top.

"That just looks like a party."

"George didn't spare any expense. This is top-of-the-line bubbly."

"I can see what you mean about him showing off. What do you suppose he wants?"

"He told us." Colin came back with his own glass and

sat down next to her. "He wants in on Whittier House. I think he would have liked to establish a Were resort himself, and you beat him to it."

"I got ahead of a pack alpha?"

"You did." Colin raised his glass. "To Luna Reynaud."

"I don't think I can drink to myself."

"Yes, you can. We're all alone in this insanely expensive penthouse, so we can do whatever we bloody well feel like."

She laughed. "I like your attitude, Your Lairdness."

"If you don't stop calling me that, I'll start thinking that's right. So are we drinking to you?"

"We are." She touched her glass to his. "To Luna Reynaud, who dreamed up a concept that's the envy of a pack alpha who's richer than God." She took a sip of her champagne. "That even tastes rich."

"Trust me, it's as rich as it tastes."

She took another sip. "I could get used to this."

"Don't. That's what he wants. I'm sure this is all an elaborate bribe to convince me to let him have a share of the action."

"But why? He obviously has more money than he'll ever need, so why mess around with a little inn on a remote island? It wouldn't be worth his time."

"He can't stand the fact that someone's launching an interesting and potentially successful business in his own backyard and he's not part of it." Colin picked up the plate of food and held it out. "You'll like this, too, but don't get used to it."

"Should we pack up our things and take a cab to the nearest cheap sleep?"

"That would be a deliberate slap in the face. We stay the night, enjoy ourselves . . ." He paused to wiggle his eyebrows at her. "And thank him profusely for his hospitality. But when he asks again to have a share in Whittier House, we tell him no."

"And then what?" Luna bit into a strawberry. "Oh, my God, this strawberry is so sweet it should be illegal."

"That's because George gets the best. And he can see that Whittier House is going to be the first, and no doubt the best, Were retreat in the Pacific Northwest."

Luna wasn't sure she liked the idea of going head-to-head with the likes of George Trevelyan. "You didn't answer my question. What happens when he asks again, after treating us to this posh penthouse, and he still gets the cold shoulder?"

He gazed at her. "I don't know. I guess that's why I'd like you to clear things with your grandparents soon. I don't want George to insert himself into that situation."

Luna's tummy began to hurt, so she drank more champagne, which helped. "This isn't a game."

"It is to George."

She gazed at him. "Not to me."

Chapter 17

Colin debated, once again, whether he dared extend his stay so he'd be around to deal with George's manipulations. But when he'd used his phone to cancel the reservations at the Space Needle, he'd seen a text message from Duncan, who wanted him to call as soon as he could. Duncan was about to do something rash. Colin could feel it.

A phone call probably wouldn't stop him, either. But it might delay whatever daft thing Duncan planned to do concerning his girlfriend, Molly. Colin was torn between the beautiful woman sitting next to him sipping champagne, and his obligation to keep his family from descending into chaos.

To further complicate matters, his father was extremely conservative in addition to being in ill health. The last time Colin had talked with his mother, she'd hinted that if Duncan went through with his threat to mate with a human, it might send his father into cardiac arrest.

The text message from Duncan weighed on Colin's mind. Maybe it wouldn't be so terrible if he made a quick call while Luna sipped champagne and ate gourmet finger sandwiches and strawberries that had been handpicked by cherubs singing the "Hallelujah Chorus." Luxury had its uses.

"I hate to do this," he said. "But I had a message from home, and I think it might be a good idea if I checked in."

"Go right ahead." Luna gestured with her champagne glass. "I know you have a crisis going on over there."

He grimaced. "Right. That's why you were treated to my unpleasant rant this morning."

"I'm over that, Colin. You have your reasons, good ones I'm sure, for thinking the way you do, and it has nothing to do with me. It's not as if what we're sharing now is a long-term thing."

Hearing her talk so casually about their relationship, when her eyes told a different story, left a bitter taste in his mouth. Yet she was right. Come to think of it, she had a more sensible attitude than he did. She knew exactly where they stood, while he was still trying to bargain with Fate to change the status quo.

"Let me give you a wee bit more champagne before I go."

"That's fine. It's very good champagne." She smiled at him as he refilled her glass. "But I promise not to get used to it. Tomorrow I'll go back to the usual rotgut."

She had a gift for making him laugh, and he was going to miss that along with every other wonderful thing about Luna. If he were more evolved, he'd be able to enjoy the present moment with her and not anticipate the eventual heartbreak when they parted. Apparently he wasn't that evolved, because thoughts of leaving her polluted every blessed moment of being with her. Bloody hell.

He added more champagne to his own glass before

carrying it and his phone to the master bedroom. As he waited for the call to go through, he pulled back the drapes and discovered Seattle spread beneath him. In a couple of hours, when it grew dark and the lights came on, it would be quite a view, nearly as good as the Space Needle.

Duncan answered on the second ring. Colin had forgotten to estimate the time change and belatedly realized it must be about two in the morning in Scotland. "Sorry. Did I wake you?"

"No, brother mine, you did not." The sound of rustling sheets and the murmurings of a female voice filtered through the phone line. "But you did interrupt me."

"Oh." Bollocks. He'd called when his brother was having sex with the very woman everyone was so concerned about.

"Can't be helped now," Duncan said. "Let me head on into the other room so Molly doesn't have to be bored with our conversation."

"Make very sure she can't hear it." Colin took a good long sip of his champagne. The last thing he needed was for the woman to overhear a mention of werewolves.

"Don't worry."

Colin couldn't help but worry. He didn't see any way this was going to go well, and he resented being forced to abandon Luna while he counseled his little brother on a proper course of action.

It didn't escape him that Luna was no more suitable for him than Molly was for Duncan, but at least Colin hadn't proposed mating with her. His heart might yearn for that, but it would be madness. She wouldn't agree to it, anyway, considering how attached she was to Whittier House.

"All right," Duncan said in a weary tone. "Here's the situation. Molly expects me to marry her, which in her world is the way these things go. Ring, church, honey-moon."

"I'm aware of the rituals."

"I can do all those things, even if they're not part of our belief system, but it's time for me to tell her who the hell I am and find out how she feels about that. I just wanted to warn you before I told her."

Colin's chest tightened. "Do you have any idea how she'll take that news?"

"She loves me. I think she'll accept it."

"That's not good enough, Dunc." Colin felt a head-ache coming on. If Luna were here, she'd probably men-tion that the vein in his temple had popped out again. "Don't tell her yet. If she doesn't react well, you'll put all Weres in danger. And think of her welfare. She might have to be sequestered if she's a security risk."

"She'll be fine, Colin. It's time for Weres to start the gradual process of intermingling. Past time. I need to tell her. Even if she reconsiders and decides not to stay with me, she's not the kind of person who would call out the mob with the pitchforks. She's very tolerant. I know she'd help us to be accepted."

Colin set his champagne glass on the bedside table so he could massage his forehead. "You're talking about a cultural shift. We're not ready for that yet. We may never be ready."

"It starts one person at a time."

"Do you love her? Are you sure without a shadow of a doubt that she's destined to be your mate?"

"I love her, but this mating business is old-fashioned hocus-pocus. I love her for being the nonjudgmental, generous person she is, and she's a perfect candidate to start moving Scottish Weres out of the Dark Ages."

Colin groaned. "You don't mate with someone be-cause she'll be a good ambassador for Scottish Weres.

You mate with her because she completes you, because she's the female you're destined to be with for the rest of your life."

Duncan snorted. "Hey, what's with the lecture on destiny and endless love all of a sudden, big brother? You don't talk about your plans much, but whenever you do, I get the impression you'll choose the most suitable Were, almost as if you're hiring someone for a job."

Colin had begun pacing during the phone call, but the accuracy of that statement stopped him in his tracks. "I might have said something like that in the past, but . . . it's not the ideal."

"You sure fooled me. I thought you were all about sensible matches."

"I was, but coming back here and being reminded of what Aunt Geraldine and Uncle Henry had together has given me a lot to think about."

"I'm dying to hear the results of all that intense brainstorming."

Colin grimaced, knowing he was still mentally tied in knots over the question. "I hope to fall madly in love with someone who's also a suitable mate."

Duncan laughed. "Good luck with that, old chap."

"Yes, well, we're talking about you, now, aren't we? Choosing a mate could be the single most important decision you make, Duncan, whether she's Were or human. Promise me you won't say anything to her until I meet her."

"I don't know if I can wait that long. When are you coming back? She's going on vacation in a couple of weeks, and I'd like to get this settled before she leaves."

Colin took a deep breath and reminded himself that his brother still had some maturing to do. Impatience was part of his makeup, and his zeal for changing the status quo was making him think he should mate with someone who *might* understand when he revealed that he was a shape-shifter. Colin didn't like those odds, but no doubt Duncan found them to be an exciting challenge.

"I'll get home as soon as I can," he said. "In the next few days, if possible. I'll definitely beat that vacation deadline of hers. Just give me the courtesy of meeting her, of talking with her. If she's going to be a permanent part of our family, I'd like at least that much consideration."

"Because you're the big, bad alpha?"

"No, because I'm your only brother, and I love you."

That produced a moment of silence on the other end. "All right," Duncan said at last. "I'll hold off until you get back here and can meet her. Once you do, you'll understand."

"That would be good. I very much want to understand. I'll let you return to her now."

"Thanks." Duncan paused again. "I have to say, I guess you have been thinking, because you sound different."

"I do? How?"

"I don't know exactly. But it's as if you're listening to me for a change. I expected you to yell at me, but you . . . you didn't. If you had yelled, I probably would have told you to sod off and I would have told Molly everything tonight. But . . . I'll wait."

"Thanks, Duncan. See you soon."

"You, too."

Colin blew out a breath as he turned off the phone, tucked it in his slacks pocket, and picked up his champagne. Close call. Sadly, Duncan's description of his former attitude toward the mating process was dead-on.

And it had been dead wrong. He could no longer settle for mere affection from a mate who was suitable.

He needed passion as part of the bargain. Luna had shown him that. She might not be his destiny, but she was his equal in passion and fire.

As he sipped his champagne, he thought about her and whether she and Duncan would get along. He almost wished they would have a chance to meet, because instinctively he knew they'd be friends. That idea didn't bother him in the same way he'd been bothered by Knox Trevelyan's attentions to Luna.

For all Duncan's impetuous behavior, he would never make a move on a female Colin wanted. At bottom, Duncan was a good-hearted chap with a zest for life, but that enthusiasm got him into more trouble than any Were Colin knew. Consequently he'd been a bloody pain in the ass.

Although Duncan was only four years younger than Colin, some days it had seemed like ten. But they'd had good times, too, some moments when Duncan had made him laugh until his ribs ached.

Now Colin was needed back at Glenbarra to talk Duncan down off the ledge. That meant his days with Luna were nearly at an end. With that in mind, he started to leave the bedroom, but then decided to take a quick look around first.

A glance into the bathroom revealed a promising Jacuzzi tub placed next to a window. If the view wouldn't make Luna dizzy, they could have a good time in there. After today's hot-tub shopping, he knew that she had an imagination when it came to benches and jets.

The bedroom also looked promising. The raised platform bed was at least king-sized, maybe even custom-made to be larger. It was covered with various shapes and sizes of pillows, all snowy white.

The bed had been designed as a playground, and Colin hoped they'd use it that way. A chest sat at the end of it, and when Colin pushed a button, the top slid back and a flat-screen monitor rose from its depths.

"Planning to catch a reality show or two?"

He turned toward the doorway.

Luna rested a shoulder against the door frame, her half-full champagne flute dangling between two fingers. "Or maybe your taste runs more toward X-rated videos," she said. "I'm sure those are available."

"I'm sure they are." Holding her gaze, he pushed the button again and the flat screen whirred back down into its cabinet. "I don't need them." As if to prove that point, his groin stirred. He deposited his glass on the top of the cabinet.

"I didn't hear your voice anymore, so I decided to wander in and find out if you're okay." Pushing away from the door frame, she moved into the room.

He crossed to meet her and slid one hand around her waist and the other beneath her hair to cup the back of her neck. "You have a caring nature, Luna Reynaud, to ask about my problems at home." He began a gentle massage, taking pleasure in the feel of her silky skin under his fingertips.

Her green eyes darkened in response to the simple caress. "I don't have a sister or brother, but it must be distressing to have issues and be so far away." Resting her palm on his chest, she reached up with her champagne flute and rubbed the cool glass against his temple. "I'll bet that pesky vein popped out again."

"I'm sure it did, but it's better now."

"Here I was out there relaxing like a princess, and you were in here arguing with your brother."

"It wasn't so bad."

She stopped rubbing his temple and brought the flute

down to his mouth. "Have some more of this stuff. It's very tasty and will wash away all your cares." She tipped the glass.

He swallowed the fizzy champagne and smiled at her as she lowered the glass. "You're fussing over me."

"I am. Is that okay?"

"If feels wonderful, lass. I can't remember the last time someone fussed over me."

"Everyone needs it once in a while, especially a big strong laird who takes all the responsibility for his pack on his very broad shoulders."

"You make me sound like a hero, and I'm not."

"You are a hero to me. And probably to Duncan, too, when he stops to admit it."

Colin nestled her closer. "I don't know about that, but he complimented me on listening to him for a change. I have you to thank for that."

"Me? Why?"

He savored the way she settled against him so trustingly. "You've challenged my assumptions and poked holes in my belief system. Before I met you, my world was divided into black and white, Weres and humans."

"And now?"

"That kind of sharp division doesn't exist for me anymore. It can't, because it would put me on one side and you on the other. I couldn't live without us being . . . friends." What a ridiculously inadequate word that was.

"Neither could I." Her gaze searched his. "Does that mean you won't object if Duncan mates with a human?"

"I'll still object if he's only doing it to make a statement, and judging from what he's said, I think that's his main motivation."

"Will he go ahead anyway?"

"I hope to talk him out of it, but . . . I have to do it in person."

A stricken look flashed briefly in her eyes and was gone, replaced by acceptance. "That makes perfect sense. In person is always better."

"Unfortunately, I'll need to leave very soon, perhaps in a couple of days if I can arrange it."

"Right." She nodded, as if the matter was not up for debate.

"He's agreed to hold off telling her he's Were until I've met her. Once I've seen them together, I'll have a much better idea of whether they're meant to be mated. No one should choose a mate, whether she's Were or human, to prove a point."

"No, I suppose not." She gazed up at him, her green eyes giving nothing away. "Why should they choose one, then?"

His heart contracted. She would have to ask the hard question. But he owed her his best answer, culled from his most recent thinking. "Because they've found someone they can't live without." He was very much afraid he'd done exactly that.

"But what if the other someone doesn't feel the same?"

Ah, the cold slap of reality. If she'd begun to guess his feelings, she was reminding him that both parties had to be fully committed. "Then perhaps they're not destined to be mates," he said.

"Perhaps not." She took a deep breath. Then she gave him a bright smile. "Well, enough deep philosophy! I see you discovered the flat screen that we're not going to make use of. What else do we need to explore before we continue with our decadent evening?"

She was obviously ready to change the subject and the mood, and he admired her resilience. She could very well be more resilient than he was. "There's a Jacuzzi in the bathroom," he said.

"Is that right?"

"It's next to a window, though, so that could prove to be a problem for you."

She lifted her glass. "All I need is you and more champagne."

"That I can provide." For now, at least. Maybe before he left he'd order a case of that bubbly for her. It was a poor substitute for being there personally, but it might help.

Chapter 18

While Colin turned on the tap to fill the black Jacuzzi with water, Luna went to fetch the rest of the champagne and the plate of food. On a hunch, she opened a small refrigerator under the wet bar and discovered a second bottle of the same pricey stuff. That could come in handy as she adjusted to the fact that Colin was leaving.

He didn't seem particularly happy about it, either, but that wouldn't keep him here. He wasn't essential to the development of the business, but he was essential to the running of his pack in Scotland. He'd only agreed to her plan of opening an inn because he trusted her to manage it without him.

She'd known all that, but had hoped for more time with him. She wasn't going to get it, and expensive champagne would help blunt her disappointment. She clutched the nearly empty bottle plus the unopened one against her stomach while carrying the plate of food in her free hand.

"Look what I found," she announced as she walked into the bathroom.

"Nice." Colin came over to relieve her of the bottles.

He emptied the last of the old bottle into his glass, briskly opened the new bottle of champagne as if he'd been doing it for years and neatly filled her glass without spilling a drop. He handed her the glass. "Maybe we should order some more food, too, so we don't get completely peshed."

"And what's wrong with that, my Much Honoured Laird of Glenbarra? What better time to get peshed than in a complimentary penthouse with complimentary high-end bubbly?"

He flashed her a grin. "You have a point. We'll worry about food later."

Luna raised her glass. "To George Trevelyan."

"To good old George." Colin touched his glass to hers. "Don't let him intimidate you, lass."

"I won't, but if he tries, will you come over here and kick his butt?" Colin's slight hesitation told her all she needed to know. "I'm kidding. I can handle George just fine."

"Of course you can."

She longed to ask him when he would come back, but she might not like the answer. If she ran the inn as efficiently as he expected her to, he wouldn't need to come back at all. She took another swallow of champagne and set her glass on the black marble counter. Time to get this party started.

Standing in the middle of the bathroom, she glanced at Colin. "Ever watched a striptease?"

His eyebrows lifted. "Can't say that I have. Have you?"

The champagne fizzed through her veins, making her feel sexy and bold. "Only in movies, but I know the general idea. I think I should perform one for you."

Colin turned off the faucet and sat on the edge of the tub, his champagne glass in hand. "I wouldn't object."

"Didn't think so. I'll provide my own music." She

vaguely remembered a tune that she'd heard and she began to hum it.

Colin's lips twitched as if he were trying very hard not to smile. " 'The Stripper.' Good choice."

"So you recognize it? I'm not such a great singer."

"In my book, you're a very fine singer."

"Now, that's a lie, but I'm good enough for this, anyway." She kept humming as she began to swivel her hips and ease her sundress strap down over her shoulder. Then with a wink, she pulled it back into place and started on the other strap.

"Tease."

"That's the idea." She rolled her shoulder and gave him a melting look as she eased the second strap down and continued to hum. This time she managed to get the strap all the way off, although it might not have been the smoothest move in the world.

She had more trouble with the second strap and had to stop humming while she struggled with it.

"Want any help?"

"Nope." She got the strap off and held out both arms as she began to shimmy. That much she did know how to do. "Ba-dum-dum-*dum*, ba-dum-dum-*dum*, ba-dum-dum-*dum*."

He grinned at her, his blue eyes sparkling.

"Don't give me that Chesire-cat smile. It makes me laugh and I can't concentrate."

"Right." He covered his mouth, but the crinkles around his eyes gave him away.

Humming louder and with more emphasis, she began a bump and grind as she slowly peeled her dress down. It had a built-in bra, which made the striptease easier, but it wouldn't last nearly as long. So she took her time about peeling the dress down to her waist.

Colin, she noted with satisfaction, wasn't grinning anymore, and his eyes weren't crinkled up with laughter, either. The sight of her girls was getting him hot, judging from the way he focused on them.

She wished she had a couple of tassels, but that wouldn't do much good unless she could twirl them, and she figured that took practice. As a substitute, she cupped her breasts in both hands as she continued to hum and dance for him. He was a very easy audience to please. He never took his eyes off her.

For her next maneuver, she turned her back to him and waggled her bottom from side to side in time with her humming as she gradually pulled up her skirt, then slowly, very slowly, pulled down her panties. She couldn't see his face, but she could hear him breathing. He was becoming a desperate Were.

Once she'd worked her panties down over her bare feet, she turned, keeping her toe hooked through one leg opening. Then, with a well-timed *ba-dum*, she kicked the panties right at him. To his credit, he caught them before they sailed into the Jacuzzi. She almost forgot to hum as he raised them to his nose and inhaled.

Funny how the striptease seemed to be getting her hot, too. She'd intended to make this last awhile, but every time she looked at Colin, the front of his slacks stuck out a little more, and she was starting to ache like nobody's business.

Still, she wanted to end this performance with a flourish, so she forced herself to ease her dress down inch by torturous inch. She kept humming and creating circles with her hips. When she paused right before exposing her pièce de résistance, Colin groaned. Now, that was gratifying.

With one final shove, she pushed the dress all the way

down. Humming at full volume, she grabbed it from the floor and twirled it over her head to loud applause and whistles from the audience of one.

She stood there flushed and panting, and highly aroused. "You liked it?"

"I'll show you how much I liked it." He stood and tore off his clothes. "Sorry, but I'm not taking time for a strip-tease. This is a straight strip, without the tease."

She watched him with hungry eyes. "Works for me." She'd never tire of this view of Colin MacDowell, naked, his muscled chest gleaming with moisture, and his glorious penis fully erect.

He held out a hand. "Come with me, you naughty wench. You've put me in a fine state, as you can see. Time for you to do something about it."

She loved how his brogue thickened right along with his cock when he was really excited. "I would be honored to do something about it." She put her hand in his. "What did you have in mind?"

"I crave having you sit on my lap, if you know what I mean."

"Not exactly, but I'm sure I've probably seen it done in the movies."

"Oh, I'm sure you have, at that. The idea is I'll sit on the bench there, and you'll sit astride, a knee on either side of my hips."

She glanced up at him. "Sounds like fun."

"I guarantee it. And the warm water will soothe your parts."

That made her smile. "My parts?"

"I still want to take good care with you, lass. You're a beginner yet. Though I wouldn't know it to watch you stripping off your panties and tossing them in my face."

"I thought that was a nice touch." And she wouldn't

let him treat her like a beginner much longer, either. He was going home soon. She could worry about being sore after he left.

"I'll help you in." He steadied her as she climbed into the roomy tub.

"And here I thought my first hot tub experience would be on Le Floret." Jets pulsed, sending warm water swirling above her knees.

"In my opinion, it will be. A Jacuzzi in a bathroom doesn't qualify as a hot tub, which I think of as being outdoors."

"Outdoors, and with room for more than two." She thought about the hot tub that would be delivered tomorrow. Tomorrow night could be Colin's last one on the island. She pushed the thought from her mind as he stepped in beside her.

"While this Jacuzzi is perfect for two." He kept hold of her hand and moaned softly as he eased down on the built-in bench on the far side. "As if I need more stimulation." He tugged on her hand. "Climb aboard, while there's still a pole to steady you."

"Something tells me Colin MacDowell never discharges before he's ready." But she followed his suggestion and placed a knee on either side of his hips. "Guide me into the dock, Captain."

"I will." He spanned her waist with his big hands and positioned her above his cock.

The warm water felt wonderful pulsing against her *parts*, as he'd called them, but his thick penis sliding in felt much better. This time, there would be no barrier, no flash of pain. Just pleasure.

So much pleasure. She gripped his shoulders as he drew her down, down, until he was deep inside her. She clenched her muscles, wanting to hold him there forever, and felt his cock twitch in response. But even more amazing, her womb reacted, too. She felt the first twinge of an orgasm.

She clenched again and felt another twinge, this one stronger than the first. She lifted her gaze to his. "What's going on?"

Heat burned in his blue eyes, but his lips curved in a smile. "You have power, too," he murmured. "When you tighten around me like that, it's good for both of us. And you'll come faster."

"I think . . ." She trembled as she clenched again and the response was a swift tug at her womb. "I think I could stay still and make myself come."

"Do you want to?"

"No." She held his gaze. "I want to feel your penis moving inside me. That's more exciting."

"I'm glad. But this time, the moving is up to you. You'll have to work a little bit, if you don't mind."

"So I move and you stay still?"

"Not totally still. I won't be able to help myself once you start. But the major up and down is your department."

"Ah." Her breathing quickened as she contemplated the maneuver. "I will be in control."

"Aye."

"I like that."

He laughed softly. "After watching your striptease, I thought you might."

"Let me know if I'm doing it right." Looking into his eyes, she braced her hands on his broad shoulders and rose up on her knees, going slowly so she didn't lose him. "How's that?"

His jaw tightened. "Maddening."

"Is that a good maddening or a bad maddening?"

"Both. Drawing out the suspense is making my heart pound like a bass drum, but what I really want is for you to go . . . faster."

She sank down onto him and rose up again. "Like that?"

"Faster than that."

She noticed that the vein was standing out on his temple again. "Colin, do you want me to ride you like you're a bucking bronco? Is that what you're trying to tell me?"

His answer came through clenched teeth. "Yes."

"What if I rise up too far and miss? What if I break your lovely cock?"

"I won't let that happen."

"All right, then." Clutching his shoulders, she began to pump vigorously up and down, and sure enough, his firm grip on her waist kept her from disconnecting and causing a painful disaster.

And what a wonderful rhythm it was, full of life and wild passion. The water frothed and churned madly around them and splashed out of the tub. The jets were total overkill.

Thank goodness he had a good hold on her, because she discovered the fast pace worked for her, too. Before long she approached the point when she would soon fly off in all directions.

She thought he deserved fair warning. She gulped in air. "Colin . . . I'm going to . . . come . . . any second."

His grip tightened. "Do it."

"But you . . ."

"I'm there, lass. Waiting for you."

She had no idea how he managed to hold off his climax in the middle of this frenzied coupling, but she didn't have time to think about it as strong contractions surged through her, interrupting her rhythm and wringing wild cries from her throat.

Colin took over the reins, keeping them in sync, urging her up and down as he bellowed in triumph with his own release. Then it was over except for the panting, and the water still sloshing back and forth in the tub and dribbling over the sides onto the floor.

Luna lifted her head and grinned at him. "That was outstanding."

"Not bad."

She splashed water in his face. "You mean for a beginner?"

He wiped the drops from his face with one large hand and laughed. "Well, there was that dodgy bit in the beginning, when I thought for sure you were going to turn this into a water ballet, but things improved after that."

"You just wait. Next time it's going to be like the Kentucky Derby."

"I look forward to it." Cupping his hand, he filled it with water and dribbled it over her breasts. "You are so incredibly beautiful, Luna."

She started to tease him about saying that to all the female Weres, but then she realized it might be true. "In some ways I'm glad that I'm a beginner, but in other ways, I wonder if I'm not as exciting as I could be because I'm so new at having sex."

He stopped dribbling water and cradled her face in both hands as he focused his earnest gaze on hers. "Luna, I was teasing you. I didn't mean to imply that you aren't exciting. You are without a doubt the most exciting female I've ever been with."

"That can't be right. I don't know what I'm doing."

"You know more than you think you do, but even your inexperience makes you fascinating to me."

"That's one thing I've got going for me, then. I have to be the most inexperienced twenty-seven-year-old

Were on the planet." And she couldn't help wondering whether having more seductive moves would lure him into coming back to the island, at least once in a while.

"And I'm the lucky male who reaps the rewards of that. You're not jaded. Everything is new and wonderful for you. Do you realize what a gift that is to your partner?"

"Then you're not just humoring me?"

"Good God, no. Normally I'm really good at delaying my orgasms, but you're so sexy I have quite a struggle holding off."

"I did want to ask about how that's done."

"I can't speak for other males, but I go over football stats in my head."

"During sex with me you're thinking about *football*?"

"Not American football," he said. "Our football. In other words, soccer."

"But that's outrageous! You're supposed to be thinking about me!"

He gave her a wry smile. "I do most of the time, but toward the end, if I thought about you, and your luscious body, and what you're doing to me, I'd go off like a rocket, and I like to wait . . . for you."

"Oh." She was somewhat mollified that he was forced to use football stats because she was more than he could handle. "That's okay, then."

"Luna, I cherish every minute I get to be with you, even the times I have to resort to football stats." He stroked his thumbs over her cheeks. "If I could stay another month, I'd do it. But I can't. I'll find it very difficult to leave you."

"Will you ever come back?"

"Of course I will. I can't promise when that will be, but . . . you'll probably have taken another lover by then."

"No, I won't." She might have been smarter to keep her mouth shut about that, but the response popped out before she had time to think.

He looked into her eyes for a long time. Then he swallowed. "As much as it kills me to say this, you probably should take another lover. You have a passionate nature, and you've said yourself that you feel more complete now that you've discovered how wonderful sex can be."

"Would me taking another lover make you feel better, then?"

"Yes." He squeezed his eyes shut and opened them again, misery shining there. "No, damn it, I hate the thought of you being with anyone else, but *yes*, I want you to be happy, and find someone who can do for you what I can't. So the answer is yes, I'd feel better if you took another lover."

She smiled, the pain in her heart eased by that muddled answer. "I don't think so. And that's what I wanted to hear."

Chapter 19

Bollocks. Luna had asked Colin the right question, and he'd cocked up his answer so thoroughly he wouldn't ever forgive himself. A litany of colorful curses marched through his brain as he and Luna mopped up the mess they'd made in the bathroom with several of the fluffy towels hanging from decorative hooks.

He was a selfish sod to have told her that he'd hate knowing she had another lover. And yet, when he'd given his first answer, she'd looked devastated by it. Unable to bear her tragic expression, he'd reassured her by telling her the truth. But what was the truth, really?

If he cared about her, then logically he'd want her to live a full life, complete with sex and maybe, eventually, a devoted mate. He definitely wouldn't want her to pine away for him as she went back to her celibate existence on the island. Well, a part of him did want that, the selfish sod part.

"We soaked the sandwiches." Luna held out the plate for his inspection. "Maybe we should order some dinner, after all."

"George would expect us to if he discovered we'd

cancelled the restaurant reservations. Since he made them in the first place, someone might have already double-checked with him on that. He's a powerful figure in Seattle, and I'm sure restaurants have instructions to treat him well."

"So if I understand this right, we need to order an expensive meal from room service, or George will be offended."

Colin nodded. "That sums it up."

"Then I'll take this back to the wet bar and find a room service menu."

"He may not expect us to order off the menu."

Luna turned at the door. She wore naked well. Her body was taut where it needed to be and filled out in all the places that gave a male pleasure. Colin could look at her all day and all night without tiring of the view.

She shifted the plate of soggy food to her other hand. "If we don't order off the menu, how do we order?"

"We dream up what we want, call room service, and ask them to fix it for us. In fact, it should be something that's specifically *not* on the menu."

Luna shook her head. "Alpha Weres are just plain crazy."

"That may be true, but remember our goal. We need to show George Trevelyan that we're not peasants who can be toyed with."

"But I am a peasant."

"No, you're not. Your grandmother is George's aunt, which puts her in the same league as Sinclair Trevelyan, who was the alpha before he passed on the title to George. Your connections are as powerful as his. Had your father lived, he might even have challenged George for his position."

"Let's see if I have this straight. We need the menu so we can make sure we order *off* the menu. Is that right?"

"Aye."

Shaking her head, she left the bathroom. "Alphas," she muttered on her way out.

In principle, Colin agreed that the posturing was ridiculous, but those who ignored the unwritten rules often found themselves outmaneuvered. Wolves had a hierarchy, and pack members understood and respected that. Luna hadn't grown up that way, so she didn't get it.

That was another reason to establish her connection with her grandparents. That would establish her standing in the pack, and her grandparents could teach her the rules, especially as they applied to the Trevelyan pack. All that would provide a certain amount of protection.

The decision to open a Were-specific inn had become far more complicated than he liked, but he wasn't about to back down from it now. Honoring his promise to Luna was the main reason, but now they were in a pissing contest with George, and Colin wasn't about to lose that, either.

George didn't just want to buy in, and Colin knew it. He wanted a controlling interest. He would get that over Colin's dead body. Colin hadn't realized the scope of George's ambition until today's visit to his office.

That was partly because of his inexperience in the alpha role compared with George's. But Colin didn't plan to use George as a role model, other than taking note of the older Were's obvious physical fitness. George had aged far better than Colin's father.

But Colin had no desire to become a tycoon like George, who obviously relished his role as Seattle's premiere mover and shaker. Colin smiled. There wasn't a whole lot of moving and shaking going on in Glenbarra. He'd leave that to the wealthier Weres in Edinburgh and Glasgow.

Tossing the towels in a corner of the bathroom, Colin walked into the bedroom as Luna returned carrying a menu and her battered copy of *Lady Chatterley*. He smiled. "Planning to do some reading?"

She sashayed over to him. "Only if we feel the need."

He liked the confident way she moved, and he knew part of that was a certainty that he felt possessive about her. It was a double-edged sword, but he couldn't take back what he'd said. She'd never believe him.

After handing him the menu, she opened the paperback in her hand and stroked the open pages over her breasts. *"Eau de Literature,"* she said with a very cute French accent that she'd probably picked up in the New Orleans French Quarter.

He couldn't let that pass. Tossing the menu on the bed, he cupped her breasts, buried his nose between them, and inhaled noisily. She did smell good, but he wasn't sure if it was old book or aroused Luna that had his cock stirring again.

Luna started laughing, which made her breasts jiggle against his face. No red-blooded male of his acquaintance would be able to feel all that sweetness moving against him and not want to taste, so before he knew it, he was nuzzling and nibbling.

Her sigh of pleasure was all he needed to guide her toward the bed and tumble with her onto the snowy comforter. There he began to enjoy her breasts in earnest now that he didn't have to lean down to reach them. When he took her nipple in his mouth, she arched upward. She was learning fast.

He meant to fondle her, kiss her all over, and perhaps give her a nice orgasm in the process. But damn if he didn't soon find his cock buried to the hilt.

Gazing down at her, he apologized. "I didn't mean to do this."

Her mouth curved up. "It seems your wee man has a mind of his own."

"And when he's in charge of things, I have no mind at all. But you must tell me if this hurts." He eased out and back in again. His breath hissed out at the splendor of it.

"Am I hurting you?"

"No. That was pure delight you heard. But I asked you first. Did that hurt?"

She grasped his buttocks. "No, and you'll have to stop treating me like a china doll, Colin. I'm a full-fledged sexual being now, and I want everything I can get." Lifting up both legs, she wrapped them around his waist and pulled him in tight. "Like that, Your Lairdness."

The pleasure was so intense it brought a low growl from deep in his throat. "You test me, lass."

"I mean to. I want the full treatment. And forget about the football stats. Just go for it."

As if he could help himself. She'd mastered the art of clenching her muscles to massage his cock, and that alone would have roused him to action, without her taunts. But the combination was irresistible. His thrusts grew in speed and intensity, and she rose to meet him each and every time.

"Yes," she murmured. "That's what I want, Colin. Yes!"

He forgot that she'd been a virgin a mere twenty-four hours ago. He forgot to be careful, to go slow, to make sure she was all right. Her panting cries drove him on. He tried to wait for her, but an orgasm roared through him without warning, and as he plunged forward, shuddering in reaction, she came, her spasms milking even more pleasure from his trembling body.

When it was over, he rolled to his side, bringing her with him. He might have used her unmercifully to satisfy his lust, but he wouldn't crush her afterward. A part of his fevered brain was still working.

As sanity returned, he drew back and gently combed the hair from her eyes. "That was wrong."

"No, that was *right*." She took a long, shaky breath. "At last you loved me without holding back. I needed to know what that was like, Colin."

"If I hurt you, I—"

"I'm not hurt, not in the least. I feel glorious." She narrowed her eyes. "Were there football stats involved?"

"No." He caressed her smooth hip. "I wanted you too much. I wanted to come inside you, and I didn't care about anything else. That's not the sign of a considerate lover."

"It's the sign of a lover who's abandoned himself to the glory of it all. That's what I wanted, at least once. Even if it never happens again, I had that mad, impetuous . . ." She leaned over and whispered a four-letter word in his ear.

He laughed. "Aye. You did get that, all right. And I have to admit the smell of old books could have been part of it. You might want to consider a sideline, creating a special perfume for guests who share our strange obsession."

"It's an idea. Unique."

"And now, my sweet temptress, we really should order up dinner."

"All right." She glanced down at their entwined bodies. "But are we going to answer the door like this?"

"That would be awkward. I've never tried to walk with my cock buried in someone's—"

"I meant *naked*." She pinched his bottom.

"Oh, well, probably not. We'll put on the bathrobes. A suite like this always has bathrobes."

"True." She drew in a breath. "Hold on, brilliant idea coming. Whittier House needs bathrobes!"

"Absolutely. Fluffy, white terry cloth bathrobes."

"With *Whittier House* embroidered on the pocket, and . . . we need an emblem of some kind."

"Crossed thistles. List the bathrobes for sale in the brochure, in case someone wants to take one home, and you can explain there about crossed thistles being a mainstay of Scottish lore."

"Colin, the inn is going to be so wonderful."

He looked into her eyes, alight with the excitement of the venture. "It is."

"Can you come back for opening weekend?"

His heart twisted. So many duties awaited him at Glenbarra. She had no idea how many. "I don't know, Luna. But I'll try."

She nodded, and seemed willing to drop the subject. He was relieved to let it drop, because he didn't want her to get her hopes up only to have them dashed if he couldn't make it. When he changed the subject to ordering dinner, she participated with enthusiasm.

He suggested haggis, but since neither of them would eat it after it arrived, they nixed the idea as being too wasteful. Finally they settled on fried peanut butter and banana sandwiches because it was so ridiculous that it might look new and trendy. Plus it would serve as both dinner and dessert.

"Order six," Luna said when Colin picked up the phone on the bedside table. "I'm hungry."

"Then I'll order ten, because I'm starving to death."

"You should have said something!"

"While you're rubbing *Eau de Literature* on your plump breasts and inviting me to roll around with you on that big bed? I'm not a fool, Luna. Priorities."

"Well, the good thing about fried peanut butter sandwiches is that they'll be ready quick."

"What kind of bread?"

"Plain old white. Wait, they'll probably have to send out for it. Take whatever they have. We could carry this so far that we faint from lack of food."

"Let's see what they have to say for themselves." Colin thoroughly enjoyed the reaction he got from the room service operator when he made the request. He hung up and glanced over at Luna. "We're causing a mild panic, but they understand we're very hungry and will have something up to us in fifteen minutes."

Luna climbed out of bed. "Then maybe we should locate those bathrobes."

"I'll go. You can stay the way you are. It suits you." He hated to see such a lovely sight hidden away in a bulky terry robe.

"Do you realize I have never been naked in front of another person? That I remember, anyway. I'm sure I was naked in front of my mother when I was little, but once I was at the age when I understood we should wear clothes, I was fanatic about it."

He gazed at her. "Thank you for trusting me enough to be naked with me."

"You seem to enjoy it so much, I don't have the heart to cover up."

"I do enjoy it. That's why I'm going to put on the robe and you're going to stay here, adorning the big bed."

"That's something else that always scared me about shifting, and why I haven't done much of it, once I learned to control it. You have to be naked to start with, or you rip your clothes, and I never had clothes to spare. And then you have to run the risk of being naked again to shift back."

"Aye." He wished she'd brought this up after their dinner had been delivered so that he wasn't listening for a knock on the door with one ear. "So you haven't shifted much?"

She shook her head. "It scares me. I don't know what to do once I become a werewolf. Sometimes I've gone into the woods, and it's freeing to run, but . . . I've been alone. It's not really so great to run through the woods alone. Maybe a male feels differently, but I was always a little afraid."

"You were right to be cautious." He couldn't imagine being a young female Were trying to figure things out on her own. "You didn't have a pack to protect you."

"I realized early on that was a disadvantage, but I didn't know how to hook up with a pack." She shrugged. "I didn't know much of anything, except what I could find in books and on the Internet, and those aren't particularly reliable resources."

"No. They're liable to scare you more than help you."

She nodded. "That's what happened. I became scared and nervous about my Were heritage. I was hoping maybe my father would help me, but . . ."

He cursed the family issues that pulled him home. There was so much more he could share with Luna, so much more she needed to know. He'd do the best he could, but he was afraid if he delayed his trip too long, Duncan would grow impatient and tell Molly everything.

"What about Geraldine and the staff at Whittier House?" he asked. "They all seem supportive."

"They are, but after Henry died, Geraldine lost all interest in shifting. You can probably understand."

Colin sighed. "I can. The three of us used to go for night runs, but Henry was the leader on those trips. Geraldine was bloody independent in her human body, but she let Henry be in charge when they shifted. I'm sure she missed him terribly."

"She did. I got the impression that when Henry was alive, the staff would sometimes be invited on the nightly runs, too. But when Geraldine gave it up, the staff didn't feel right going without her. Dulcie suggested it a few times since I've been there, but she didn't get any takers."

Colin began to get a picture, and it was heartbreaking.

Not only had Luna denied her sexual side, she'd also denied her wolf nature. "How long has it been since you shifted?"

She glanced away, as if trying to remember.

"That long?"

"I'm afraid so. I'll bet it's been at least two years."

"Do you want to try it tonight? With me?"

She stared at him. "In this penthouse?"

"Why not? You can shift, get used to the sensation for an hour or so, and then shift back if you decide it's time to use the Jacuzzi again or read some *Lady Chatterley.*"

A knock sounded at the outside door.

"That'll be our fried peanut butter and banana sandwiches." Colin opened a closet and pulled out the hotel bathrobe he knew would be in there. "Think about my suggestion. I'll be here to help. I won't let anything happen to you."

"I know." She gazed at him. "You're a blessing, Colin MacDowell."

And a curse, he thought as he went to answer the door.

Chapter 20

Luna thought about Colin's suggestion as they ate fried peanut butter and banana sandwiches on the floor in the living room next to the window. Gazing out at the lights of the harbor, she felt only a squiggle of uneasiness, even though they sat right beside the glass.

Colin had helped her to grow in so many ways. He'd encouraged her to find her sexual self, and she realized that her werewolf self, while technically functioning, was dormant. Without a pack, without encouragement from other Weres, she'd allowed that side of her to languish.

She'd paid a price for that, too. Sometimes she'd have the overwhelming urge to shift, and repressing it cost her in lost sleep and a troubled mind. But if she didn't feel safe to embrace her other side, then she wasn't going to risk it. Colin created a safety net, one that would be available for only a short time.

Licking her fingers, she glanced at the empty plate of sandwiches. "What did you think?"

He laughed. "I was hungry enough to eat anything, probably even haggis."

"These take some getting used to. My mother used to fix them for me."

"In that case, lass, I'm glad you ordered them. It's good to remember those things, and I got to try something unusual. But my next dinner will include a rare steak. It's more suited to a werewolf's constitution."

"I totally understand." She admired him for eating the sandwiches without complaint. "And I'll join you in that steak dinner."

"Excellent." He gazed at her, an unspoken question in his eyes.

She knew without asking that he was waiting for her decision. Her heart rate picked up. "You'll shift too, right?"

"I will, after you do. I've had a lot of practice, so I'm reasonably quick."

"I've had very little practice, and so I'm excruciatingly slow." She made a face. "You will get sick of waiting for me to manage it."

"I won't."

"Also, I don't think it's a very attractive process."

He smiled. "It's like birth, Luna. That's a wee bit weird, too, but we celebrate it every time it happens. Shifting should be like that for us. A rebirth."

"I hadn't thought of it that way. It's always been awkward and . . . shameful."

"Ah, no. Never shameful. It's a gift to be able to shift into a completely different sort of being, with totally different abilities, yet have our mind retain both sets of experiences. Have you experienced telepathy?"

"Like when I can hear thoughts from other Weres? Only a couple of times, by accident. Shifting alone doesn't lend itself to that."

"Mm." His tone was rich with sympathetic understanding. "You'd love that part, if you get a chance to do it with someone you know, like me. Are you willing to try?"

She wiped her hands on a cloth napkin and put it on her empty plate. "Yes, I am." She glanced around the living room. They'd left most of the lights off so they could enjoy the sparkling view below.

She spotted a dark corner. "I'd like a little privacy. You may think it's like birth and needs to be celebrated, and someday maybe I'll have that attitude, but I don't yet."

"Whatever makes you feel comfortable." He gathered the dishes from their meal. "I'll put these on the bar and sit here waiting for you. Have you ever watched someone else shift?"

"No." Her heart raced at the thought, which was both scary and fascinating.

"Would you like to watch me do it?"

She hesitated. "If you don't mind."

"I'd be honored if I'm the first Were you've ever seen shift. As a teenager, we were always watching each other. It was like a game, so I'm not shy about it. But if you didn't grow up like that, it might take you some time to lose that shyness."

"I can't even begin to say how much I envy your upbringing. Envy is a terrible emotion, but I'm feeling it now. I want the childhood you had."

"But the childhood you had created the amazing and talented Were that you are." He stood and offered her his hand.

She allowed him to help her up and draw her into his arms. There was nothing sexual in his embrace, and for that she was grateful. She wrapped her arms around his solid warmth and held on.

Apparently he understood that if he distracted her in a sexual way, she would never go through with her shift. She needed a friend more than she needed a lover.

He held her close, his cheek resting on top of her head. "You can do this, Luna. You're braver than anyone I know."

"You help me find my courage."

"Aye, but it's there waiting when you look." He hugged her tight and released her. "Go on with you, now."

With one last glance at him, she started toward the dark corner. The she turned back. "As I said, I could be very slow."

He smiled. "Take your time. I don't have any pressing appointments."

She turned away quickly so he wouldn't see her eyes fill up. He was everything she'd never realized she wanted. She was grateful that fate, and perhaps Geraldine, had brought him into her life. If he left and never came back, she would be heartbroken. But she'd rather be heartbroken than to never have known him at all.

Making her way into the dark corner, she stretched out on the carpet. This was the most luxurious surface she'd ever used for shifting, that was for sure. She'd shifted on threadbare carpets, on dirty floors, on the cold ground. This would be a treat.

But it wouldn't be easy. Lying there with her eyes closed, she conjured up the images that she'd learned would initiate her shift. She imagined deep, cool woods. Her feet, now paws, scattered leaves as she raced through the darkness, and her vision became tuned to the night and the creatures dwelling there.

The images wouldn't hold. Her concentration was affected by her surroundings, and the male Were sitting on the floor only twenty feet away. He wasn't looking at her, but he was thinking about her. She knew that even though she couldn't yet read his mind.

She covered her face with her hands and strained to

focus. It had never occurred to her that by not using her gift she might lose it. What if she could no longer shift? Then she'd lose that special link with Colin.

Colin. She imagined him as a magnificent wolf, his coat burnished with starlight. She envisioned the varied colors of chocolate brown and caramel in his ruff. He would be powerfully built, with massive shoulders and a wide, intelligent head. She wanted to know Colin as a wolf, and unless she could shift, she never would.

His eyes would be the same clear blue, but they would be wolf's eyes as they gazed silently into hers. With a shiver of awareness, she pictured herself as a wolf, looking into Colin's wolf eyes. And she felt the beginning of her shift.

No wonder she'd thought that an orgasm might trigger this process. The stretching, aching pressure was different, but similar. It built in the way that a climax built, except that at the end of sex, she was the same as before.

Not so with shifting. Her muscles contracted, although there was no pain as there had been with her first shift. Her skin began to itch as hair grew where before she'd had only milky-white skin.

Her vision changed, giving her a different view of the darkened room. Furniture loomed larger, and scents grew sharper. What had seemed familiar became foreign, because it was an environment for humans, not for a wild creature of the forest.

And then, as if a final switch had been thrown, she became a wolf. Energy flowed through her, giving her a heady feeling of grace and power. Rising to her feet, she padded over to where Colin sat immobile, as if mesmerized by the lights beyond the window.

At her approach, he turned his head. His breath caught. "My God, you're beautiful. I knew you would be, but my imagination didn't do you justice."

Those were words of praise she'd never heard before, words she'd craved without realizing it. Her wolf form was pleasing to him. That meant more than he could know.

He smiled. "It didn't take so very long, either."

It hadn't, and she wondered if he'd beamed his thoughts toward her, boosting her ability. With Colin, she would believe anything was possible.

"Now it's my turn." He stretched out on his side and closed his eyes. His muscles relaxed, and he exhaled in a long, heartfelt sigh of total surrender.

He likes this, she realized. For him it was a privilege to shift, not an embarrassing compulsion to be avoided if possible. She had so much to learn.

Although she'd been afraid the transformation would repel her, she watched in complete fascination. As his shift began, he seemed to glow from within. Maybe she did, too. She had no way of knowing.

The glow suffused his entire body as the transformation proceeded far more quickly than hers. But as he'd said, he'd had a lot of practice. In less than a minute, he rose from the carpet and stood before her.

He was huge, much bigger than any common wolf, with a powerful chest that indicated he could run for miles without tiring. His chocolate and caramel coat gleamed with good health and his blue eyes flashed with intelligence. He was as awe inspiring as she'd imagined he would be.

Walking toward her, he touched his nose to hers. *Welcome to our world, Luna.*

She felt his words stream through her mind, and she responded, dazed by the wonder of being able to communicate with him like this. *It's beautiful. You're beautiful.*

He snorted. *Would you be willing to say I'm handsome, instead?*

She looked into his eyes and saw the twinkle there.
This wolf truly was Colin, her Colin. She'd had so little
experience interacting with other Weres that she could
easily forget that he was the same Were she'd known in
human form.

With an elaborate bow, she sent out another thought.
*You are extremely handsome, Your Much Honoured
Laird of Glenbarra.*

Saucy wench! He leaped upon her, bowling her over,
and they wrestled on the soft carpet, nipping playfully at
each other.

But gradually she felt a change in the mood. He licked
her face more than he nipped at it, and when he pinned
her to the carpet, she became aware of the heat radiating
from his powerful body. His scent changed from earthy
to a more tantalizing aroma, one she found irresistible.

The ache that began deep in her womb was familiar.
She wanted him, wanted this wolf in the same way she'd
wanted him in human form. She whined and licked his
face.

His voice, rolling through her mind, held a note of
urgency . . . and warning. *We must be careful, lass. Keep
your mind free of any thoughts of commitment, of perma-
nence, or —*

Or we will be mated? She shot the words back at him.
See that you do the same! Bonding takes two.

*Aye. I want you very much. And you deserve to know
the joy of coming together as wolves. Just . . . be careful.*

She gazed into his wolf's eyes, her heart thudding rap-
idly. *I will be.* Then, acting on an instinct she didn't know
she possessed, she turned, presenting him with her hind-
quarters.

With a low growl, he mounted her.

Wonder surged through her veins at the intensity of
that moment when he entered her. Sex with him in hu-

man form had been incredible, but this . . . this touched her in a deeper, more primitive way, as if he claimed her with each powerful thrust.

But he was not claiming her. And she would not claim him. She forced those dangerous thoughts from her mind and concentrated instead on the pleasure. It rose within her, a fountain of hot passion. The sensuous slide of his penis gave her reason enough to join with this virile wolf.

His wolf self was as accomplished as his human self. He seemed to know exactly what she needed, and as the pressure built, he pumped faster, and faster yet. Her climax rocketed through her with a force that made her stagger.

He growled again, pushed home once more, and slumped against her, his massive body shuddering as he poured his hot seed into her. Amazingly, his weight did not topple her. She trembled in the aftermath of their joining, but her legs remained strong.

Now she understood why he'd warned her. Having sex as humans was an added bonus, but this . . . this was the truest connection a male and a female Were could have. And if she yearned for that bonding he'd tried so hard to avoid tonight, she'd have to get over it.

With regret a heavy weight on his heart, Colin eased away from Luna. He'd fought hard not to bond with her and hoped he'd succeeded, but the fight had seemed wrong. Avoiding that ultimate connection went against everything he felt for her.

But it was for the best. At least he hoped so. His judgment didn't feel particularly reliable at the moment. Once he returned to Glenbarra, he'd be able to think more clearly, and no doubt he'd see that they must always remain . . . friends.

Walking up beside her, he licked her face. *Are you all right, lass?*

Her green eyes held a curious mixture of joy and sorrow. *Yes. Very much so. I liked that, Colin.*

So did I. You were wonderful. And you've worn me out. He hated admitting that, but weariness settled over him, and he would need sleep soon. Considering what they'd been through in the past forty-eight hours, she must be as exhausted as he was.

We both need sleep. But we should shift first.

All right. He understood her reluctance to go to sleep in wolf form. She wasn't used to being that vulnerable, and although he thought they were perfectly safe up here, he wouldn't try to talk her out of it.

She gazed at him intently. *When you shifted, your body glowed.*

Aye. That's the way of it.

And when you shift back?

The same.

She blinked, as if not quite believing it. *Do I glow, too?*

You do. He was amazed that she didn't know that, but why would she? She'd never had anyone guide her through the process. *But if you doubt it, you can go first and I'll confirm that you glow.*

I would like that, Colin. She settled down on the carpet and rolled to her side. Then she closed her eyes and heaved a sigh.

He wondered if she had the energy to shift back, or if she'd fall asleep like that. If she did, he'd simply curl up beside her. They could always shift in the morning.

But she wasn't asleep. Her luxurious dark coat grew luminescent, and the process began. He watched over her tenderly.

She was so delicate, and yet so strong. He'd never met

such a combination of feminine sweetness and iron will. He'd heard of steel magnolias, women raised in the American South, and perhaps that described her nature as much as anything.

She was quicker at shifting this time, and soon she lay before him in human form, white skinned and blushing under his scrutiny.

"Did I glow? Oh, wait, I forgot. You can't speak." She sat up and made a flapping motion with both hands. "Go ahead and shift."

She was a bossy wee thing when she chose to be, and he found that endearing, too. Like an obedient dog, he dropped down beside her, rolled to his side, and began his shift. He did it very quickly because if he stayed in that position too long, he'd nod off. If she was in human form, he wanted to be, too.

Once he accomplished that, he sat up and gazed at her. "Yes, you glowed. It was magical."

She clapped her hands together. "Magical. I don't have to worry about being ugly when I shift! It's magical."

"And so are you." He stood and held out both hands. "Come with me. We're going to bed, and we're only going to sleep in that bed."

She grasped his hands and allowed him to pull her to her feet. "Amen to that." But she glanced up at him, a twinkle in her eye. "But come morning, all bets are off."

He laughed and walked with her hand in hand back to their oversized bed. They turned off all the lights, leaving the room bathed in an amber sparkle from the city spread below the window.

"It's too bad we're both so tired." She stood next to the window and looked out. "It would be lovely to have sex right here, with the lights shining on us."

"No more acrophobia?"

"A little." She glanced over at him. "But that would make it all the more exciting, to be sort of scared and aroused at the same time."

"Dear God, I've created a monster. Now you'll turn into a thrill seeker." His cock twitched. "Do you want to do that? I could probably manage one more—"

"No, I don't want to." She smiled and walked over to the bed. "Well, I do, but I'm ready to fall asleep standing up. Let's go to bed."

"You talked me into it." They settled naturally into a sleeping position as if they'd been sharing a bed for years. She turned her back to him and he curved his body against hers, spoon fashion, with his arm tucked around her waist.

She sighed with obvious contentment. "This is nice. I feel as if I could sleep for a week."

"Me, too." But they couldn't even sleep in tomorrow. In the morning they had to be up and moving if they hoped to pay a visit to her grandparents. How interesting that her grandmother had turned out to be George Trevelyan's aunt— His eyes snapped open.

Bloody hell. He'd been an idiot. Being sleep deprived and lust filled was no excuse for not anticipating George's next move. George had casually mentioned that Luna should check out whether she was related to Edwina and Jacques Reynaud. But as Edwina's doting nephew, George wouldn't wait for her to do that, would he?

George would want to be on top of things, especially now that he had his eye on Luna's project. By now he would have contacted his aunt about her. No doubt he'd mention that she had a Southern accent and a mysterious past, but had apparently started life in New Orleans. He might even describe what she looked like and approximately how old he thought she was.

Unless Edwina and Jacques had known nothing about

Sophie, the woman their son had loved—highly unlikely—
they would now suspect who Luna was. Her plan of
cloaking herself for the first meeting was already com-
promised.

He could wake her and tell her that, except that
seemed pointless. Whatever happened tomorrow, she'd
need sleep in order to face it. And so would he. But no
matter how this played out, he would not allow George,
or the Reynauds, for that matter, to hurt her.

Chapter 21

Luna woke up to sunlight streaming in the open window and Colin singing some Scottish ditty in the shower. Taking a deep breath, she caught a whiff of warm cinnamon buns, along with the distinctive scent of bacon. Sitting up, she noticed a cart had been wheeled into the room while she slept.

A couple of dining chairs had been placed at either end of it, and two covered plates obviously contained their breakfast. Two carafes held coffee, tea, or both. She wouldn't put it past Colin to have ordered both coffee and tea so that he'd covered all the bases.

The single red rose in a bud vase had probably been a flourish added by the hotel staff and not Colin. No matter. He'd already won her over on that score with the bouquet of daisies from the Pike Place Market.

Luna stretched her arms over her head. She could get used to waking up like this—rested, pampered, and happy to be sharing the space with a hunky Scot.

Once he turned off the water, she called out to him. "Your breakfast is getting cold! Come and eat!" Climbing out of bed, she thought about getting a robe out of the closet and decided against it. If she could shift in front of Colin, then she could certainly eat breakfast naked in front of him.

He walked in from the bathroom still toweling off that gorgeous body.

She looked him up and down as she sashayed closer. "If you want, I can finish the job with my tongue." She took great satisfaction in watching his reaction, especially the one south of the Mason-Dixon Line.

He grinned at her. "I thought you were worried about our breakfast getting cold."

"I am. I just said that because I wanted to see what would happen."

He gestured toward his crotch.

"I already noticed." And the harder he became, the wetter she got.

"You're quite the tease, aren't you, now?" Stepping toward her, he looped the towel around her waist and dragged her against him. "I'll teach you to taunt my wee man and get him agitated."

"I'm *so* frightened."

His laughing blue gaze roamed over her. "I can see that. Your nipples are scared stiff." Dropping the towel, he spanned her waist with both hands, lifted her up, and spun her toward the nearest wall. With arms braced on either side of her head, he caged her there. "Now what have you got to say for yourself?"

Lifting her chin, she gave him a wicked smile and took hold of his cock. "Think you can manhandle me?"

"I do." He grasped her wrist and easily removed her hand. "And I will. I hope you like cold eggs, lass, because your breakfast is about to be delayed."

"Oh, no." Flushed and giggling, she pushed against his muscled chest. "Anything but that."

"Too late for pleading." Cupping her bottom in both

hands, he lifted her up against the wall, probed once, and shot the bolt home.

She gasped with delight. "Well done."

He dragged in air. "You could help, you know, if you'd wrap your lovely legs around my arse."

She complied, and she also braced her hands on his shoulders for better balance. "I love it when you talk Scottish."

"Ah, do ye now? But ye like action better than speech, I ken." With that he began to drive into her with sure, masterful strokes.

"Aye," she said with a strangled moan. "Aye, I do."

He plunged into her until she was cross-eyed with pleasure, yet begging for more.

"I'll give ye more, ye sexy wench." He boosted her up the wall so that he was pushing up and in.

The different angle stimulated a whole different set of nerve endings. "Ohhhh." She began to pant.

"Like that, do ye?" He increased the pace.

"Yes, *yes*!" She exploded, coming with a joyous shout of release as he continued to pound into her.

"Again!"

She gulped for air. "Again?"

"Oh, yes." His breathing was ragged. "You can." He thrust upward and rhythmically squeezed her bottom with his long, talented fingers.

She came again, crying and whimpering with the beauty of it, whispering her gratitude as she convulsed around the sure strokes of his thick penis.

Then, and only then, did he surge forward, quivering in the grip of his own orgasm. Breathing hard, he leaned his forehead against hers. "Incredible."

"I . . . I didn't know I could . . ."

"I did." There was a smile in his voice. "Oh, I did. You just needed a little rest, is all."

*   *   *

Colin happily ate a cold breakfast, but he wasn't happy at all knowing he had to deliver the insight that had come to him right before he'd fallen asleep. He waited until Luna finished eating. He would much rather have said nothing and kept the mellow mood they'd established.

More than mellow, actually. On some level, if he could shut out the problems with his family and whatever Luna would face with the Reynauds, he'd never felt more at peace in his life. With Luna he felt at home and settled in a way he never had with anyone else.

He hated like the devil to shatter that feeling, both for his sake and hers. But she needed to hear his conclusions.

She was understandably distressed. "So my grandparents may already know who I am?"

"It's quite possible." He took another swallow of his tea. Thanks to the carafe, it was still hot. "But maybe not. It depends on whether George did what I would expect of him, and how much Edwina and Jacques knew about your mother."

"I have no idea. She told me the bare minimum about my father, obviously leaving out the most important fact, and she never mentioned his parents." She brightened. "Maybe she never met them. Maybe, because she was human, he kept her a big, dark secret."

"Even if he tried to, you said that some Weres you talked to mentioned that he died going after a woman. His parents found that out, I'm sure."

"Probably, but if they never saw her . . ." She continued to look hopeful that her plan would work.

"Do you resemble her?"

"Yes. I have her picture in my room at Whittier House. I look a *lot* like her."

"In a way, that's better than if you looked like their son. They'd pick up on that immediately."

Luna glanced at the clock on the bedside table. "It's almost nine. What should we do?"

"Get dressed."

"Well, duh."

He couldn't help laughing. "I'm serious. Until you put some clothes on, you're a walking temptation to forget all about this and take you back to bed."

Her green eyes grew serious. "Maybe we should forget all about this. We don't have to hook up with the Byron Reynaud Foundation. They may suspect something, but if I never go knocking on their door, they might not find out for a long time, if ever. They're old, right?"

"Not that old." He shook his head. "If you're imagining you can wait them out, keep this under the rug until they die off, then—"

"Not exactly! Well, sort of, but I don't want anything to happen to them. It's just that . . . I'm scared."

"I know," he said gently. "But think of all the scary things you've conquered recently. Taking a risk and meeting them is just one more. What's the worst that could happen?"

She took a shaky breath. "The worst that could happen is that the two living relatives who would understand my Were nature could be forever lost to me if they reject me and say nasty things about my mother. If I never go to them, then I can hang on to my fantasy that they would have loved me if given the chance." She shrugged. "Maybe that makes no sense."

"It makes sense. But it's the coward's way out, and you've proven to me time and again that you are no coward."

She met his gaze. "Damn your hide, Colin MacDowell," she said softly. "You expect so much of me."

"Because I know you can do it."

A smile tipped the corners of her mouth. "Sort of like having two climaxes in a row?"

"Don't you dare start talking about sex."

"Who knows? Maybe, with the right circumstances, I could have three in a row."

With a groan, Colin left his chair and grabbed his phone from the bedside table. He'd keyed in the number for the Byron Reynaud Foundation yesterday, and he clicked on it now.

"Want to have phone sex?" She left her chair and came over to stand beside him. "Go into the living room and I'll call your phone from the one on the nightstand."

"This is for your own good, Luna." He put the phone to his ear and willed his erection to subside. He couldn't make her go to see her grandparents, but he could set it up for her and give her the option of going or not.

"I have a bad feeling about this."

"Trust me."

"That's what they all say." She looked worried.

A receptionist named Angela answered the phone. "Yes, Angela, this is Colin MacDowell, Laird of Glenbarra."

"Show-off," Luna muttered.

Colin ignored her. "I now own Whittier House in the San Juan Islands, and I plan to convert it to an inn. I'd like to make an appointment this morning for me and my associate, Luna Reynaud, to meet with Mr. and Mrs. Reynaud about having a benefit for their foundation on our opening weekend."

"Luna *Thisbe*."

Colin turned his back on her while the receptionist put him on hold and quickly returned with a suggested time. "Yes, eleven would be fine. See you then." He disconnected the phone.

Luna regarded him with a dark expression. "Now you've gone and done it. And you used my real name."

"George Trevelyan knows your real name, so you might as well give up that idea." He gazed at her and waited to see what she would do. "You don't have to go. If it's really that frightening, I can call back and cancel the appointment. But if I'm right about George and his strategic nature, you'll have to face them, perhaps sooner rather than later."

"And if I do it later, you won't be here."

"Probably not."

She swallowed. "Then I want to go this morning, with you."

"That's my girl."

"But if they're mean, then—"

"If they're even slightly mean, or the least bit rude, we'll leave. I won't let them tear you to shreds, Luna. That's why I want to go with you, to be your backup."

"What if it turns into a scandal and affects business at the inn before we even open?"

"I'm not a shrewd businessman like George, but I have paid some attention, because lairds are expected to do that. I've noticed that scandal doesn't usually hurt business. If anything, it helps."

"Oh, great!" Luna rolled her eyes. "Are you hoping for a scandal, then?"

"Of course not." He set his phone on the nightstand and took her by the shoulders. As he did so, he told himself to resist the soft temptation of her skin beneath his fingers. "I want this meeting to go well, for your sake and theirs. But if it doesn't, don't worry about the inn. If I ever doubted it would be a huge success, George's interest tells me we'll have a booming business in no time at all."

She held his gaze for several long seconds. "Then I guess we'd better get dressed, Your Much Honoured Laird of Glenbarra."

He smiled, and because he couldn't deprive himself completely, he gave her a quick, hard kiss before he let her go.

"You're sure you don't want to try the phone sex thing?"

He shook his head. "We can do better than that once we get back to the island, lass." He was already anticipating the night ahead, and he refused to think about the possibility that it might be their last.

"Can I see their picture again?" Luna spent the cab ride to her grandparents' house alternately checking her lipstick in a small mirror she kept in her purse and asking Colin for his phone so she could look at the picture of Edwina and Jacques Reynaud one more time. He always handed it over with a patient smile.

He kept his arm loosely around her shoulders during the ride. A couple of times she started to tell him how much that meant to her, but she was afraid she might get choked up if she started talking about . . . anything, really, but feelings in particular. So she squeezed his thigh and hoped he knew that his presence was the single most important part of the trip.

The house looked even more imposing than it had in the picture. It was on the right side of the street, and Luna had chosen to sit on the right side of the cab, so she had a fine view as the cab pulled up to the curb.

On a street filled with lovely big homes, all with groomed lawns and lavish flower beds, the Reynaud mansion was perhaps the most impressive. The paint seemed whiter, the drapes in the windows more elegant, the flower beds more carefully tended, the lawn more manicured.

Sidewalks flanked the street, along with several large shade trees. Their roots had buckled the sidewalk in places, which spoke of the age of the trees and the neighborhood, but other than the cracked sidewalk, nothing was out of place.

The homes suggested wealth without trumpeting it. If the owners drove Bentleys and Ferraris, they were tucked away in garages. No children played in any of the front yards and no dogs gamboling about fetching sticks. A couple of sleekly dressed runners jogging by on the sidewalk were the only people Luna could see.

She stared out the cab window and tried in vain to slow her racing heart. A little cottage would have been easier to deal with, although the people inside were the scariest part. Maybe the size of the house was unimportant. Geraldine had lived in a very large castle, and she'd been a sweetheart.

Luna glanced at Colin. "I know it will be expensive, but I'd like to have the cab wait for us, in case we need to make a quick getaway."

"I can wait," the driver said, looking back at them from the rearview mirror. "Long as you don't mind the meter going all that time."

"We don't mind," Colin said.

"Then I'll just pull up under that tree and read my newspaper."

Luna swallowed. "Then we might as well go in, I guess."

Colin was out of the cab in a flash. "Let me get your door."

His gallantry touched her. Yet this was the same Were who had backed her up against the wall less than three hours ago. She'd loved that, too. Whether he was treating her like royalty or coaxing her into a lusty round of sex, she felt like the luckiest female in the world to be near him.

She took his hand as he helped her out of the cab. "Keep holding on to me," she said.

"You're sure? I said we were business associates."

She laced her fingers through his as they started up a flagstone walkway. Ahead of them, a balcony on the second floor shaded the carved entry door. "If George has blabbed to them, he's probably told them we're more than associates."

"True." He gave her fingers a quick squeeze. "That blouse looks great on you."

"So you said when we bought it yesterday."

"But not because it matches your eyes."

"It doesn't match my eyes?" She knew he was making conversation to distract her, and she appreciated that.

"Oh, it does match your eyes, but that wasn't the main reason I like it."

"What was the reason, then?"

"When you tuck it into your jeans, your tits look amazing."

"Colin!" She laughed, and that was probably what he'd hoped for.

As he reached for the doorbell, the large door swung open before he could push the button. Edwina and Jacques Reynaud were framed in the doorway. Edwina, dressed in a pale blue lightweight suit, her hair perfectly styled, stood in front. Jacques, wearing a short-sleeved shirt and looking considerably more casual, hovered behind her.

Edwina stared at Luna. Slowly her mouth opened, but nothing came out. She seemed dazed and disoriented, and her hand went to her heart. Finally she spoke. "Sophie?"

Luna squeezed Colin's hand so hard she felt him wince. "No, Mrs. Reynaud. I'm her daughter."

Chapter 22

So they did know. Colin balanced on the balls of his feet, even though there would be no physical fight involving these two seventy-something Weres. But he wouldn't mind fighting someone, if he only knew who deserved the blame for this cock-up.

He'd like to make George the culprit, but from the way Edwina had looked at Luna, there was no villain. Edwina would have recognized Luna as the reincarnation of Sophie no matter when and where they'd met. George might have planted the idea, but this mess had been created more than twenty-seven years ago.

Edwina's face nearly matched the white exterior of her house, and she looked a little unsteady on her feet.

Colin stepped forward, drawing Luna with him, and cupped his free hand under Edwina's elbow. "Maybe it would be best if we could all sit down," he murmured.

"Yes," Edwina said faintly. "Yes, it would."

Jacques stumbled backward, and Colin hoped he wouldn't have to hold him up, too, because he was running out of hands. He'd promised Luna he'd keep his connection with her, and she'd maintained a death grip on him that might leave a mark.

Fortunately Jacques got his feet under him and led the way down a hallway with floorboards so highly polished that Colin worried about everyone's footing. The hall was wide enough for him to walk between the two female Weres. With one hand locked through Luna's fingers, and the other supporting a wobbly Edwina, Colin felt like the conduit between two sparking batteries. Either one could short out at any second.

Now that Jacques was moving, he looked taller and more in command. His stride was firm, his shoulders back. Once, when he ran a hand over his thinning hair, Colin detected a slight tremble, but that was to be expected. These two Weres had just met their dead son's child, one they'd had no idea existed before.

Jacques reached the end of the hall and turned left into a sunroom furnished in cheerful yellow and white. Colin thought it was a fine place to settle these jumpy people and bring peace to all concerned. He hoped it worked out that way.

"You three sit there." Jacques waved them to a plump couch as if he assumed they'd all stay connected like Tinkertoys. "I'll tell Bethany to bring us . . ." He paused and peered at them through his bifocals. "What would you all like?"

"Vodka," Edwina said.

Jacques blinked. "Vodka?"

She waved a hand at him. "You know. Screwdrivers. Vodka and orange juice. Have Bethany mix up a big batch."

"But, dearest, it's eleven in the morning." Jacques gave her a tentative smile.

"I don't give a good goddamn what time it is, Jacques!

Byron's daughter just arrived! That calls for something stronger than iced tea, don't you think?"

Colin glanced over at Luna and she widened her eyes at him as if to ask, *What the hell?* He gave a little shrug. For now, he'd be the filling in the sandwich. He prayed he wouldn't have to be the referee.

Edwina leaned forward, so Colin leaned back, allowing her to look at her granddaughter.

"Luna, is it?"

Luna edged forward a little and peered around Colin at her grandmother. "Luna Thisbe Reynaud. Although they never married, my mother took Byron's name. She told me he was my father. But that's . . . that's all she told me."

"She didn't say he was Were?" Edwina flung the question as an accusation.

Luna tensed. "Why would she? She didn't know which I would be, Were or human."

"And which are you?" Edwina's voice shook.

"I'm Were," Luna said quietly. "But I'm a half-breed."

Edwina sank back against the cushions. "Byron's child," she muttered, almost as if speaking to herself. "Byron's child." Then she popped back up to stare at Luna. "Change places with this fellow so I can have a better look at you."

Colin glanced at Luna, who nodded. He stood, and she scooted over next to Edwina. When he sat down again, Luna reached for his other hand. He offered it freely. She could mangle that one, too, if she needed to.

Edwina adjusted her position, turning her body slightly so she could study Luna. "You have his chin, which was like mine. Pull back your hair."

Colin expected Luna to start objecting to this series of commands, but she pulled her hair back as instructed.

"You have his ears, too." Edwina's voice caught. "He had the most beautiful ears, just like Jacques."

Jacques bustled back into the room. "What's this about my ears?"

"Luna has Byron's ears, which are your ears, too," Edwina said.

Jacques edged closer and crouched down to gaze at Luna. "Huh. So she does." He looked Luna up and down, but then his attention returned to her feet. "And Byron's toes."

"Toes?" Luna lifted her feet off the floor. The sandals she wore displayed toes painted with pink nail polish.

Edwina leaned over to examine Luna's toes. "You are so right, Jacques! Her second toe is bigger than her first toe, like mine, and like Byron had." She pulled off one of her low-heeled shoes. "Damn. I'm wearing panty hose. You can't see as well, but my second toe is longer, Luna, just like yours. You'll have to take my word for it."

"I believe y'all," Luna said.

"Did you hear that, Jacques? She talks just like Sophie did. I swear it's like Sophie walked in here, except for the ears, and the chin, and the toes."

Whatever Colin had expected out of this meeting, it hadn't been a comparison of ears and chins and toes. He'd prepared for wailing and gnashing of teeth, icy coldness, cutting remarks. Not a discussion of body parts.

Bethany, a plump redhead, arrived with a tray of drinks and a pitcher for refilling once the first round was gone. "Good morning, everyone. I understand we have an honored visitor." She picked up two goblets and handed one to Edwina and one to Luna. "Welcome, Luna Reynaud."

"Thank you."

"What an exciting day." Bethany took the second pair of goblets and gave the first one to Colin. "Isn't it amazing?"

"Yes, it is," Colin said. And surprisingly calm, all things considered.

"I can't believe our granddaughter is sitting here," Jacques said in a bewildered voice as he accepted a goblet from Bethany.

"Risen from the dead." Edwina took a hefty swallow of her screwdriver.

"No, dearest, that's not quite true," Jacques said. "She was always *alive*. We just didn't *know* about her. That's a big difference."

Edwina flapped her hand dismissively. "Whatever. The question is, where is this Sophie person?"

Colin winced, expecting a heated response from Luna. He'd guessed wrong, though.

Her voice was gentle as she turned to her grandmother. "She died when I was eight, Mrs. Reynaud. But I can tell y'all without a shadow of a doubt that she was true to your son."

"I didn't know she was pregnant, so I didn't realize they'd mated," Edwina said. "But now . . . now it's obvious they did."

"Yes." Luna's voice was husky. "They were truly mated."

"Yet she left."

"She was human, Mrs. Reynaud, in every sense of that word. She told me she didn't belong here, so I guess she couldn't accept living in a community of Weres. But she was in love with Byron Reynaud, her mate, to the end."

Colin squeezed Luna's hand. *Nicely done, lass.* He wished they could communicate telepathically, but he thought she got the message.

"Well." Edwina patted the arm of the sofa and stared off into space. "Well."

No one said anything for a while, as if each of them wanted to give Edwina a chance to collect herself.

Finally she cleared her throat and raised her glass. "To the startling discovery of our granddaughter, Luna Thisbe Reynaud, although I can't say I approve of that middle name. We might have to do something about that. Anyway, cheers."

"Cheers," everyone chorused, and took a sip from their goblets.

Following the toast, Edwina leaned forward to scrutinize Colin. "And what have you to do with all this? Our secretary said you were a laird of something or other. Glenbugle or some such."

"Glenbarra. A small village north of Glasgow."

"Never heard of it, but that doesn't matter. George called this morning, but I confess once he started talking about Luna and how she might be Byron's daughter, I lost track of everything else. So why are you here?"

"I'm Geraldine and Harry Whittier's nephew. She left Whittier House to me."

"Oh!" Edwina put a hand to her chest and almost spilled her drink. "That's where Byron used to work as a teenager. He *loved* it out there. He didn't see much of the Whittiers, but he was very close to the groundskeeper. If memory serves, his name was Hector."

"Hector's still the groundskeeper," Colin said. "At least for now. Luna and I plan to open the house as an exclusive inn for Weres, and I'm not sure how Hector will adapt to that. He likes a more secluded environment."

Edwina nodded. "That's because he never got over losing his mate, Althea. I knew Althea better than I knew Hector. We were in school together. When Byron started working out there, I told him about Althea dying soon after she and Hector were mated, and how Hector became something of a hermit. Byron treated everyone with compassion, but he gave extra consideration to Hector." Edwina took another long swallow of her screwdriver. "God, I still miss that son of mine so much."

Jacques came over to lay a hand on her shoulder. "We all do, Ed."

She glanced up at him. "Not *all*, Jacques. This laird never laid eyes on Byron, and obviously Luna didn't have the chance to know her father." She turned to Luna. "But you would have loved him."

"I'm sure." Luna sounded very subdued, and she'd barely touched her drink. "I wonder if Hector remembers him. He didn't react to my last name at all."

"That was a long time ago. Although it hurts to think that anyone would forget Byron, Hector might have by now. Or maybe he'd recall the first name but not the last. He's had lots of teenagers working for him over the years. I'm sure they run together after a while."

Jacques looked more animated than he had since they arrived. "We should talk to him and show him a picture. I'd love to pay a visit to that island. Byron said he felt more at home there than anywhere."

Luna glanced up eagerly. "He did?"

"Oh, yes, and it made perfect sense. He was never a city boy. He loved the woods, and the sea. Watching a pod of orcas play along the shore was his idea of heaven."

Luna made a small sound deep in her throat, one that Colin didn't think anyone noticed but him. But he could imagine the intensity of her reaction to all of this. She might look like Sophie, but in so many ways, she was her father's daughter.

He sensed that she was on emotional overload. The Reynauds had been different than he'd expected, but welcoming in their own way. It was more than he could have hoped for. Yet Luna might need time to process what she'd discovered so far.

He turned to Edwina. "Thank you for agreeing to meet

with us, but we have a helicopter to catch, and I'll be leaving for Scotland tomorrow, so there are plenty of loose ends to tie up before then. We should probably get going."

Next to him, Luna sagged in relief. He'd made the right call.

Jacques frowned. "But there was something about a benefit for the foundation, wasn't there?"

"Yes." Luna straightened. "I'm managing the inn, because Colin will be in Scotland a good bit of the time. I considered setting up opening weekend as a benefit for the Byron Reynaud Foundation, if you would agree."

Jacques nodded enthusiastically. "I think that's a very—"

"Problematic idea," Edwina finished for him. "It's not your fault, Luna, but some of the older Weres in the Trevelyan pack remember the circumstances of Byron's death. If they discover Sophie was pregnant when she left, well, they might not be ... *happy* ... to support her daughter's enterprise."

That was Colin's cue to get Luna the hell out of there before things got ugly. He stood and drew her up with him. "Maybe involving the foundation isn't such a wonderful idea. As owner of the inn, I won't advocate anything that would make my manager uncomfortable."

"We need to talk about this some more," Jacques said. "Let us digest everything. Take stock, as it were."

"And talk to George," Edwina added. "He's been one of our chief advisers for the foundation. I'm sure he'll have some good advice."

Now Colin knew they really needed to leave. "We'll be in touch," he said. "Luna, the cab is waiting."

Edwina stood. "Before you go, Luna, let me take another good look at you. Turn loose of this Colin person for one minute. I swear you two act the way Sophie and Byron did, like you can't bear to be parted."

Luna released his hand as if his touch had burned her. "Colin is only a friend, Mrs. Reynaud. I was nervous about coming here and he's been a steadying influence."

Edwina looked from Colin to Luna and back at Colin again. "If you say so. That's not what I see, and I haven't lived on this earth for seventy-six years without learning a thing or two about mutual attraction."

Colin's gut clenched. He hoped Edwina was wrong about the depth of their involvement, both for Luna's sake and his own.

Edwina took Luna by the shoulders and gazed intently into her eyes. "You are a Reynaud." She gave Luna a quick, awkward hug. "So you must stop calling me *Mrs. Reynaud* and call me *Grandmother*. Now, go before I start blubbering like a fool."

"Same for me." Jacques hurried over and gave Luna a pat on the back. "I mean, don't call me *Grandmother*, but call me *Grandpa*. I rather like the sound of *Grandpa*."

"Okay, I'll do that." Luna's voice was suspiciously thick.

"We'll see you again," Jacques said.

"Yes." She gave a short cough. "Yes, you will."

"Thanks for everything," Colin said as he recaptured Luna's hand. To hell with what Edwina might think of him doing that. He needed to guide her out of there before she broke down. She would hate that. The hallway seemed endless, but at last they were in the open air.

"Oh, Colin." She put a hand to her mouth and her green eyes filled with tears.

"Come on." He slid has arm around her waist. "Let's get in the cab."

"I don't . . . I don't know if I'm up to this. It's so emotional!"

He urged her toward the cab, where the driver had the back door open and the motor running. "I know. But it wasn't bad for a first meeting."

"No." She was quivering. "I guess not."

"George may complicate things."

"Yes."

"Bloody hell, I wish I didn't have to leave."

"So do I." She wrapped her arm around his waist and hugged him back before she climbed into the cab. "So do I."

Once they were safely inside the cab and on their way, Colin called Knox and told him they'd be a little late. Luna couldn't imagine what she'd do without Colin to handle the details right now. Her mind was reeling with discussions of ears, toes, chins, and whether or not her newly discovered grandparents would support her in the long run. The jury was still out on that one.

Colin disconnected his call to Knox and put his arm around her again. "Look at it this way. They didn't reject you."

"No, and they didn't trash my mother. The closest Edwina came was when she called her *this Sophie person.*"

"I think that's her way. She called me *this Colin person.*"

Luna rested her head on his shoulder and relished the solid feel of him. "They were blindsided by this. I've had years to imagine what it would be like to meet my grandparents, and they didn't know I existed."

"I think they're going to come to love the idea of having a granddaughter with Byron's chin, ears, and toes."

She sighed. "This is going to sound dopey, but I adored that part. Nobody's ever looked at me and said *you have his ears*! It made me feel connected in a way I haven't been since my mother died."

"What about your other grandmother?"

"She never carried on like that. I was illegitimate in her eyes, and that's all she saw. I can only imagine how she would have reacted if she'd learned how truly different I am."

With a murmur of sympathy, Colin reached over and stroked her hair.

Luna sighed. "She's lost to me and I'm lost to her."

"But these two we just met," he said as he continued to stroke her hair. "They have possibilities."

"But will they become a tool of the manipulative George?"

Colin hesitated.

"Give it to me straight, please. I'll have to handle this after you're gone."

"I'm afraid he's going to try. If Edwina thinks he's some kind of business guru, and he tells her you need him on this project, she'll push for you to involve him in some way."

"And if I resist, that will be a bone of contention with my newly minted grandmother." She looked up at him. "Tell me again why you think I need family in my life?"

"It has to do with the ears and the toes."

She laughed, the first time she'd felt like doing that since before they'd stepped into her grandparents' house. "I'm going to cling to that discussion, because it was the truly real part of going there."

"There were other real parts. Like when you told Edwina that your mother had been true to your father."

"Yes." Luna snuggled closer. "That got to her, and I'm glad, because it's true. All the discussions you and I have had about those who are truly mated have convinced me that my parents were. But going to live in that world was too frightening for my mother." She paused. "Or maybe it was the scary prospect of having Edwina as a mother-in-law."

"Personally, I think Edwina has a soft, squishy center that she does her best to hide. I'll bet you'll discover

she's more of a pushover than you think the next time
you visit."

Luna shuddered. "I'm not sure how soon I'll be up for
another visit. Without you to bolster my courage, I may
put it off for a very long time."

"Don't." Colin kissed the top of her head. "They need
you and you need them. And I just had a great idea.
They're family, so why don't you dedicate Geraldine's
room as their private suite? Let them come there free of
charge, whenever they want to."

"Do I dare do that?" The idea both thrilled and terri-
fied her. But it would be something she could do for her
grandparents, and she wanted to be able to give them
something special.

"I don't see why you shouldn't," Colin said.

"It's probably the premiere room in the whole castle.
We could get a small fortune for that room."

"Money isn't everything, lass. If it pleases you to do
that for them, by all means, do. I can guarantee that Geraldine would have approved."

Turning in the seat, she lifted her face to his and
kissed him. "You're the best."

"The best what?"

She grinned. "You have too many talents to name, My
Much Honoured Laird of Glenbarra."

"You could try."

"I will, I promise. While we're sitting in that new hot
tub later tonight, I'll do my best to list every single one."

Chapter 23

Knox seemed especially cheerful when they walked out on the roof of the Trevelyan Building, ready to climb into the helicopter. Luna wasn't sure why he was being so nice considering how they'd messed with his schedule. She thanked him for being so patient with all their last-minute changes to their plans.

"No worries." Knox got them settled into the helicopter in the same order as before, with Colin in the back and Luna in the front passenger seat. He glanced over at her before putting on his headset. "My dad says you and I are practically kissing cousins. I didn't know that!"

Luna stared at him as anxiety twisted in her gut. George had been busy. "What did your father say, exactly?"

Knox gave her his typical uncomplicated grin. "That you are the newly discovered granddaughter of my great-aunt Edwina and great-uncle Jacques. My dad's really excited about this inn you're opening. He wants to keep it all in the family."

"What family?"

"The Trevelyan family, of course. You're officially part

of the pack now, and that means you get the full support of my father and his cronies. He's ready to back you a hundred percent. I think it's exciting."

With the noise of the rotors, Luna doubted that Colin heard any of that, but her stomach churned right along with the blades. George was slick, all right. He'd try to sweep her right into the Trevelyan net, and he wasn't above using her grandparents as bait.

But there was one major problem with that plan. She didn't own the inn. Colin MacDowell, Laird of Glenbarra, owned it. And he had no intention of turning control over to George and the Trevelyan pack. But as she thought of that, her blood ran cold.

George had so much power in the area that if he decided to boycott the inn because she and Colin wouldn't let him have a controlling interest, he might be able to shut them down. Eventually she hoped to draw guests from all over the country, but initially she'd depend on local traffic to keep the inn profitable. In fact, she'd planned on making local traffic her mainstay.

George could indeed ruin everything, and if he had the lust for control that Colin seemed to think he had, he might be ruthless in trying to get what he wanted. Driving Whittier House into bankruptcy would mean that he'd eventually get it, after all.

Knox, bless his heart, saw only the lovely family connection now that Luna was going to manage Whittier House. He knew that she and Colin were involved, so he might even think that made Colin an honorary member of the pack. She hated to disillusion Knox, so she said nothing.

But the flight back to Le Floret wasn't quite as fun as the flight to Seattle had been. All the way back, she was in a mental wrestling match with all the complications that had popped up. When she'd first thought of opening

Whittier House as an inn, it had seemed like such a simple plan.

Now, whether she wanted to be or not, she was enmeshed in pack politics. She thought about something Colin had said not long ago. He told her that maybe she wasn't meant to hide herself away on the island, that maybe she was meant for greater things. She hoped that didn't include taking on George Trevelyan.

The helicopter landed on the island only minutes ahead of the motor launch bringing the new hot tub and the prefabricated redwood decking that would surround it. The dealership had hired a boat big enough to accommodate a forklift, and Luna, Colin, and Hector all supervised the work crew as they brought the hot tub and the deck materials up from the dock and began installing everything on the bluff overlooking Happy Hour Beach.

Luna realized that she still hadn't told Hector about the plan for the inn, and either she or Colin needed to inform him. With a hot tub arriving, he might suspect that something was afoot. That could explain why he spent so much time grumbling during the installation.

"Plain foolishness, if you ask me," he said to no one in particular. "Who needs to climb into hot water when they're outdoors? You won't catch me in this thing."

Colin stood back to admire the way the hot tub looked with the redwood deck added. "It's supposed to be good for arthritis, Hector."

"So is using a shovel and a pair of hedge trimmers. Keeps a body nimble. Don't need a damn tub for that. And what about critters getting into it?"

"We bought a cover, too," Luna said. "In fact, it will be covered a good part of the winter. It's more for summer use."

"Then I don't see the point of it. There are plenty of

other things to do in the summer besides sit in a giant bathtub staring at each other."

Before hearing the story of Hector's lost mate, Luna might have been irritated by his rant. But now she was less so, although she thought it was a terrible shame that Hector's life had ended when his lover died and he'd chosen to nurse his misery for so long.

When the hot tub was almost installed, complete with the buried electric cable required to run power out to it, Luna decided the time had come to fill Hector in on what was about to happen at Whittier House. Yes, she could ask Colin to tell him, and Colin would do it, but she was the manager. She might as well get used to managing.

She touched Hector on the shoulder. "Could I talk to you for a minute?"

"Guess so." He looked wary.

"Let's go over to that bench and sit down. It's been a long day."

"Look, if you think I'm so old that I need a bench to hold me up, then—"

"*I* need the bench. You're free to stand." She marched over there and hoped he'd follow. She chose a spot at one end of the backless stone bench so that he had plenty of room to sit and still avoid her.

He ambled over and sat on the opposite end of the bench.

She gazed at him and tried to imagine him as a young Were in love. Nope, couldn't do it. Fifty years of unhappiness had stamped him with a face that didn't inspire her to think of gentleness and compassion. And yet he was a link to her father.

"I realize you've never warmed to me," she said.

"Don't think about you one way or another. Just do my job."

"Colin said you thought I was hiding something."

His head whipped around toward her. "That was a private discussion. He shouldn't have—"

"I *was* hiding something, Hector."

Under his bushy white eyebrows, his eyes widened. "I knew it!"

"But before I tell you my secrets—and I will tell you—I want to ask if you remember a teenager who worked for you named Byron. It would have been almost thirty years ago."

Hector rubbed a hand over his shock of white hair, displacing it even more. "Byron ... Byron ... Do you know his last name?"

"Reynaud."

He stared at her as comprehension slowly dawned. "*That's* why your name sounded so familiar! I knew I'd heard it somewhere before. Yeah, now it's coming back to me. I remember Byron Reynaud. Tall, gangly, earnest. Nice kid ..."

Luna's heart ached for the person she would never know. The next time she visited Edwina and Jacques, she'd ask to see baby pictures, sports trophies, school essays, anything they'd saved. She was suddenly hungry for any little detail.

"So he was a good worker?" she asked.

"Yes, yes, he was. Better than most. Certainly better than that stuffed shirt George Trevelyan. Can't believe how well he's done, all things considered."

"George worked for you?"

"Only for a couple of weeks, when both George and Byron were around eighteen. George wanted to be in charge, which didn't sit well with me, but that wasn't the only problem. He was always trying to outdo his cousin Byron, and when he couldn't, he'd pick fights with him. I had to let George go."

"I don't think George has changed. He's still very competitive."

"Most don't change, not really." Hector shook his head. "George was a hothead, and Byron wore his heart on his sleeve. Got killed in a car wreck on his way to stop his sweetheart from leaving town. If I remember right, she was human, so he should've just let her go."

No matter how many times she heard it, the story always broke Luna's heart all over again. "Hector, she was human. She was also my mother. Byron was my father."

He stared at her, dumbstruck. "Oh, hell. I'm sorry, Luna. I truly am. Is your mother still alive?"

"She died when I was eight."

He shook his head. "That's pitiful." Then something seemed to occur to him. "Does that mean that you're . . . you're . . .

"I'm half-Were, half-human."

He peered at her. "I've never met a mixed-breed before."

His response was so openly curious that she couldn't be offended. "Neither have I, except for me. I felt like some kind of freak, and I'd planned to keep it a secret forever."

"But you're telling *me*?" He scooted closer. "Listen, I won't say anything, but I think keeping it quiet is a good idea." He tilted his head toward where Colin supervised the cleanup of the hot tub installation. "Don't tell him I said so, but Colin is a bit prejudiced."

"I know." She glanced over at Colin, who stood with his broad back to her and his feet braced apart as he watched to make sure the job was finished correctly. His air of command was obvious even from this distance. He was the most gorgeous prejudiced Were she could imagine.

But her heart warmed toward Hector for the first

time since she'd arrived at Whittier House. She'd told him her big secret, and instead of trying to use it against her, he was willing to help her keep it. "It's kind of you to warn me."

"I wouldn't want him to give you the sack."

"I appreciate that. But Colin knows, and he's letting me stay on. In fact, he's agreed to let me manage Whittier House and run it as an inn for Weres."

Hector's mouth dropped open. "An *inn*? You mean like a *hotel*?"

"An exclusive hotel, but yes, that's the plan."

"Colin's not going to sell it?"

"Not unless the inn turns out to be a bad idea for some reason."

"I'll be damned." Hector dangled his work-roughened hands between his knees and stared at them. "Well, I knew something had to change around here, but I never figured on this." He shrugged and glanced up at her. "Guess it doesn't matter. Either way, I'm outta here."

She'd expected that reaction, but she wasn't going to quietly accept his resignation. "I wish you'd consider staying on, Hector. It's your home, and we need you here. *I* need you here."

"Nah, you don't. Get a younger man in. In fact, get a younger crew. You'll need a more organized deal than an old guy and his ragtag bunch of teenage Weres that come over every summer from Seattle."

"Speaking of that, why haven't any shown up yet? It's June. They're out of school by now."

"After Geraldine died, I put out the call that we wouldn't need them this year."

"But it's a tradition, Hector! You've been doing that for years, now."

"More than forty," he said with a touch of pride. "Taught those kids the meaning of putting in a good day's work. Taught them about respecting the earth and the creatures that live on it." He sighed. "But that wouldn't work for a fancy hotel."

"Oh, yes, it would. It's a community service." Luna had come up with yet another marketing hook. "I'll bet the kids you hired grew up and sent their kids over."

"Many did. Last summer I even had a couple of grandkids from my first batch. Three generations coming over here to earn a little spending money doing something healthy, something that works those young muscles."

"Hector." She almost reached for his hands, but decided he wouldn't welcome that kind of familiarity. "You're an institution around here. A celebrity."

A red flush rose from beneath his collar. "I wouldn't go *that* far."

"I would. Guests will come just to reminisce about the summers they spent working here. They'll want to see how the tree's grown that they planted, or whether the flower beds still curve the way they remembered, or whether you still have trouble with weeds in the croquet lawn. We have *history* here, living history. Don't leave! I don't want to lose all that!"

He looked dazed. "I never thought of it that way."

"I might not have, either, except that I visited my grandparents today."

"You did? How did that go?"

"It was ... interesting, but the minute I mentioned Whittier House, they started talking about how much Byron loved coming here to work. They wanted to know if you still worked here and they want to visit and talk about him a little bit. It would help them, I think."

Hector nodded, which Luna took as a good sign. Then he glanced at her. "You haven't had much tradition in your life, have you?"

"No, I haven't. None, really. That's probably why I recognize how important it is. And why I want to preserve it whenever I can. Please stay, Hector."

"I promise to think about it."

"Good." She was in a lot better position with Hector than she'd been before. She would keep her fingers crossed that he'd make the decision that would, she believed, make everyone happy. She wanted to say something about Althea, but hesitated, not sure how he'd take it.

But if she didn't say something now, she might never get another chance. "Edwina, my grandmother, said she knew Althea, your mate."

His head came up quickly, and his tone was almost harsh. "What did she say?"

"Only that it was very sad."

Hector blew out a breath and looked toward a point where sky and sea blended together, obscuring the horizon. "It *was* sad. And unnecessary. A simple fall, in our kitchen. Her head hit the counter just right. Massive concussion."

Luna gasped.

"She was gone." He snapped his fingers. "Just like that. It happened nearly fifty years ago, and I still remember it like it was yesterday. Nobody talks about it anymore, though, especially me." He looked at her. "That's probably a mistake, not to talk about it."

"I think it might be. Especially if you loved her very much."

"She was my true mate. I could never love anyone the way I loved Althea. Here, I'll show you something." Standing, he dug in the pocket of his work pants and pulled out a small, shiny object. "She wore this around her neck all the time. Only took it off when she shifted into Were form, but otherwise, always wore it."

Luna gazed at the tiny gold trinket made up of two entwined hearts with a small diamond in the middle. She doubted it was worth much money, but to Hector, it was priceless. "It's beautiful."

"It's always with me. That way, Althea's always with me." He tucked it carefully back in his pocket and sat down again.

Luna's throat tightened. She wanted to be loved like that. Even more specifically, she wanted to be loved like that by Colin MacDowell, Laird of Glenbarra, the Were who had stolen her heart. But it was a foolish wish that had almost no chance of coming true.

Chapter 24

Colin hoped the discussion between Luna and Hector was going well. They were still talking when the installation crew left, and before Colin could walk over to the bench, the household staff trooped out to view the new addition. Colin suspected somebody had been sneaking out periodically to report on the progress.

Dulcie came over, doing a little cha-cha step on the croquet lawn. "Party time! Oh, yeah. Time to par-tay!"

"Is it filled yet?" Sybil followed close behind Dulcie, her eyes bright but her enthusiasm held carefully in check. "I know these things take a lot of time to fill."

"It's filled," Colin said. "The chemicals are in, and the hot tub is officially open for business. They promised us a functioning hot tub by the cocktail hour, and through the wonders of prefabricated construction, they've accomplished it." He glanced at Dulcie and Sybil and smiled. "How come you aren't in your suits already?"

"Because," Dulcie said, "we happen to have manners, and we're waiting to be invited."

"Then consider yourselves invited."

"Woo-hoo!" Dulcie pumped both fists in the air.

"Come on, Sybil, let's get Janet. Oh, wait. Are we allowed to bring appetizers and a bottle of wine?"

"We shouldn't do that," Sybil said. "Hot water and alcohol don't mix."

"They do in my world," Dulcie said. "What's the verdict, Your Lairdness?"

"The water's not very hot yet. I'll turn the thermostat down if you want wine. So which will it be? Hot water or wine?"

Dulcie stuck her hand in the air. "I vote for wine. Sybil?"

"Wine, I guess. It's still warm out. We don't need the water too hot. Let's get Janet."

"Is this a private party?" Colin asked. "Or can anybody join in?"

Sybil blinked. "You want to go hot-tubbing with us?"

"Why not? Let's christen the thing. I have a couple of chores to take care of, but then I'll put on my suit and be down."

"You have a suit?"

"I always pack one when I come to Whittier House. I usually go down to Happy Hour Beach for a swim, but I think we need to try out this hot tub. I'll ask Hector and Luna on my way back to the house."

"Hector won't go for it," Dulcie said. "He doesn't do anything fun. But ask Luna. She'll want to. We'll be back in a flash."

"I'll get there as soon as I can." Colin couldn't picture this kind of informal celebration ever taking place at MacDowell House in Glenbarra. The atmosphere there was serious, deadly serious. As he walked over to the temperature control and turned it down several notches, he thought about whether Luna would like MacDowell House at all.

It was a Scottish castle, an authentic one as opposed

to the new, modernized version Henry had built for Geraldine. MacDowell House was the real deal and it had
the balky plumbing and moldy storerooms to prove it.
He loved the place, but he wasn't sure if Luna, used to
Whittier House's conveniences, would.

And then there was the issue of the general mood of
the place. His mother and father weren't party animals,
that was for sure. Duncan could be counted on to cheer
things up, though.

If Colin showed up with Luna, and Duncan invited a
lively female friend, the four of them might be able to
blow the cobwebs out of the dreary old place. That was
pure fantasy, of course. Luna wouldn't want to go in the
first place.

He needed to stop thinking about impossible dreams
and enjoy her company while he could, along with that of
her three partners in crime. Who knew? Maybe she'd
worked miracles with Hector and he'd decide to hop in, too.

Colin approached the spot where Hector and Luna
sat talking. "Hot tub's ready," he said. "Or I should say,
warm tub's ready. Dulcie and Sybil want to drink wine,
so I turned the temperature down. We're all invited to
join them. I'm going upstairs to change into my suit."

Hector stood. "Count me out. Not my thing." He
paused and studied Colin for a moment. "Luna seems to
think I should stay on, even though you're turning this
into a fancy hotel. I say I'd be out of place."

"Luna knows what she's doing," Colin said. "A smart
Were would stick around." Which didn't make Colin very
smart, now, did it?

"I told her I'd give it some thought. Well, time for me
to be off. I'll leave you all to your community bathtub."
He headed toward the small groundskeeper's cottage
he'd lived in for decades, but his step seemed lighter than
it had a day ago.

Colin took Hector's place on the stone bench. "Sounds as if you presented your case well, lass."

"I realized that he's been bringing teenagers here to work all these years, which makes him a draw for those who want to come back and reminisce about old times on Le Floret. He's up to the third generation in some families. That's loyalty."

Colin gazed at her with admiration. "Brilliant concept, Luna. And I'll bet it made him feel valued to hear you say that he was an important part of the operation."

"I think so. He told me something interesting. George Trevelyan worked out here very briefly as a teenager, and according to Hector, George always considered himself in competition with my father."

Colin digested that piece of information. "That doesn't surprise me at all. I wish . . ."

"What?"

He shook his head. "It's pointless. I just wish I could be here to see how this shakes out with your grandparents and George." He sighed. "But I can't, so I should quit brooding about it and enjoy the time I have left with you."

She reached over and squeezed his hand. "Go on and take care of your reservations, and then come down and join the party. We'll keep you occupied for the first half of the night, and I'll take it from there."

He turned his hand over and wove his fingers through hers. "That sounds promising."

"I don't intend to waste a minute of the time you have left. You can sleep on the plane."

"That's fine for me, but you have to work after I leave."

"And that's what will keep me sane," she said. "I'll be so busy, I'll barely notice you're gone."

"Really?"

"No, not really. But it's the closest thing to a strategy I've got, so I'm going with it." She slipped her hand from his and stood. "Time to get moving, Your Much Honoured Lairdness. I'll meet you back at the hot tub."

"Or we could run away together." He hadn't meant to say it, but she looked so beautiful standing in the sunlight, her eyes bright as emeralds.

She shook her head and gave him a tiny smile. "Don't be daft." Turning, she hurried toward the house.

So that was that. He'd asked her and she'd refused. Time to make those plane reservations.

Had he meant that? Luna couldn't imagine that Colin had seriously asked her to run away with him. But she couldn't get the question out of her mind as she pulled a one-piece bathing suit out of her drawer. Geraldine had talked her into this suit after meeting resistance on the purchase of a bikini.

Luna stepped into the emerald green suit, which had laces up each side. Once Luna had modeled it for Geraldine, she'd proclaimed it sexier than a bikini. Thoughts of Geraldine combined with Colin's outrageous suggestion.

What would Geraldine have done? That was easy. She would have responded, *Let's go,* instead of, *You're daft.* Geraldine had, in fact, run away with Henry, or at least stayed with him in America when the MacDowells ordered her home.

Geraldine had thrown caution to the winds, laughed at everyone's expectations, and made a life with the Were she loved. Had Henry suggested running away together in that same offhand, almost teasing way?

Luna sighed. "Geraldine, I wish you were here."

Grabbing a towel and slipping her feet into flip-flops, she hurried out of the house and over to the hot tub, where the party was already in progress.

"Hey, Luna!" Dulcie waved at her from her spot in the bubbling water. "This is awesome! You and Colin picked out a great model!"

"That's good!" She hurried across the croquet lawn. She smelled fresh lumber and a hint of pool chemicals as she climbed the sturdy steps to the deck area.

"Killer suit," Dulcie added. "Will it to me, okay?"

"Sure thing." Luna laid her towel on the decking.

Sybil lay in the water with her head propped on a towel and her eyes closed as she cradled her wineglass in both hands. "I'm in heaven," she said. "If I'm not, don't bother telling me. They should have hot tubs in heaven."

"Amen to that." Janet sat on one of the molded benches. Her lycra-covered breasts bobbed in the water as she munched on a piece of cheese. "Oh, and not to worry. Dinner's baking in the oven. There's a salad in the fridge, and dessert's in the freezer."

Luna climbed into the tub next to Janet. "I never doubted that you'd have everything under control."

"Have some wine, chica." Dulcie handed Luna a plastic glass of white. "Fortunately I found these plastic doodads in the pantry. I'm not a big rules person, but we need some for this most excellent hot tub. No glass, for one thing."

Sybil sipped her wine, her eyes still closed. "And no negative comments, ever. I'm finding my Zen."

Janet laughed. "Don't mind her. She's going all California on us. But I sort of agree with that. Geraldine would have, too."

"To Geraldine!" Dulcie lifted her glass.

"To Geraldine!" they all cried in unison.

Luna glanced around at her new friends and knew she couldn't run away with Colin and leave them in the lurch, even if he had been serious, which he probably hadn't. They also deserved to know the news about her that could break at any moment. Hector wasn't the only one who needed to hear it.

She took a fortifying gulp of her wine. "I need to tell y'all something."

"You've slept with Colin," Dulcie said. "Old news."

"That wasn't what I was going to tell you."

Sybil's eyes popped open. "He has a tiny little wiener? I don't want to hear that. I want to keep my illusions."

"No! Honestly, y'all are so fixated on sex that it's pitiful. This is important. My . . . my mother was a human."

"No way!" Dulcie stared at Luna in obvious fascination. "Girl, you know how to keep a secret!"

"Hey, hey." Janet made shushing movements at Dulcie. "This could be a painful situation for our Luna. Have a little compassion."

"I don't care if your mother was a gecko," Sybil said. "You're still tops in my book."

"A *gecko*?" Dulcie started to laugh. "Sybil is officially toasted. But I second what she said. Your parentage isn't really important, but I've never known anyone who's half-Were and half-human, so I'm just curious. Sorry if I offended."

"I'm not offended." Luna felt a rush of affection for her three friends. She would watch out for them, no matter what. "But I was worried that no one would accept me if they knew, so I've kept it to myself."

Janet poured herself more wine. "If anyone has a problem with it, tell them to come and see me. I have a drawer full of very sharp knives. And a cleaver."

"I have cleaning products that would fell an ox," Sybil said. "One blast from my spray bottle, and they'll wish they'd never been born."

"And *I* can do wicked things with a broom handle," Dulcie said. "Wait a minute. That sounded rather exciting instead of threatening. Let me rephrase that."

"Forget about the broom handle, Dulce," Janet said. "That's only going to get you into trouble. You know karate, remember?"

"Oh, right. I'm a black belt, come to think of it. And, hey, if none of this works, we'll just go all Were on who-ever threatens our Luna, right?"

"Right!" everyone shouted.

Luna didn't know whether to laugh or cry. "Thanks. You guys are terrific. I was so worried, and you don't even care."

"We care about *you*, toots," Dulcie said. "And I'm so delighted that you're not a virgin anymore."

Luna gasped. "You knew I was?"

"Oh, please." Dulcie rolled her eyes. "When it came to sex, you were dumb as a box of rocks. We all took a straw poll, and the results came out solidly in favor of virginity as the only logical explanation, because you were so smart in every other way."

Luna set her glass on the deck. "I'm so embarrassed." She allowed herself to sink down until the water covered her head.

Janet grabbed a handful of hair and pulled her back up.

"Ow." Luna rubbed her scalp.

Janet smiled at her. "Didn't want you to drown from being embarrassed. Now that we know you grew up in a somewhat wonky fashion it all makes sense."

"And now," Dulcie said, "we can tell dirty jokes and you'll actually *get* them instead of just pretending to."

Luna retrieved her wineglass and took another gulp. "I didn't know I was such a burden on y'all."

"You haven't been, sweetie," Janet said. "You've been a joy, and however you influenced His Lairdness to go along with the inn project, we're grateful."

"Here, here!" Dulcie hoisted her wineglass in the air again. "To Luna!"

"To Luna!" all three of them shouted as Luna turned pink with a combination of embarrassment and pleasure.

"Give me a glass," said a male voice. "I'll drink to that."

"Well," Dulcie said. "If it isn't the Laird of Glenbarra, the stout lad who deflowered our Luna."

Colin grinned at her. "Congratulations, Dulcie. You finally got my title right."

Luna took a deep breath and sank back under the water.

Chapter 25

Colin hesitated to intrude on the female bonding he heard going on as he approached the hot tub. But he'd promised Luna he'd show up, and he was a Were who kept his word. Fortunately he'd caught enough of the conversation to know that Luna would have a support system after he left. George Trevelyan wouldn't ride roughshod over this lot.

"This is not a bad hot tub, is it?" He climbed in on the other side of Luna and glanced down. She was still under the water. "Does she do that often?"

"I don't know," Sybil said. "This is our first time going hot-tubbing with her."

Dulcie handed him a glass of white wine. "For all we know, she's a hot tub virgin."

About that time, Luna erupted from the water, gasping for air. "Y'all are talking about me. I can feel it."

"We are," Colin said solemnly. "And the big question of the day, the one all our viewers want answered, is, are you a hot tub virgin?" He wondered if she'd remember the distinction they'd made last night between Jacuzzis and hot tubs.

"Okay," Dulcie said, pointing at Colin. "He can hang with us anytime. Am I right?"

"You are *so* right," Sybil said. "He can even bring his pet gecko, if he wants."

Janet snorted. "I don't know what it is with Sybil and the geckos all of a sudden, but it's sort of disturbing."

"So are you?" Dulcie asked Luna.

"Am I what?"

"A hot tub virgin," Janet said. "Try to keep up."

"Yes!" Luna threw her arms in the air, splashing water everywhere. "I'm a hot tub virgin! And a phone sex virgin! And a vibrator virgin!" She glanced around. "Whoops. Did I overshare?"

Dulcie was laughing so hard she almost choked. "No!" she said, gasping for breath. "Feel free to drink more wine, and tell us anything you want!"

Luna ducked under the water again and combed her hair back from her face. When she resurfaced, she looked like a mermaid as she peeked at Colin through lashes dotted with water. "We're not always like this."

"Yes, we are," Sybil said. "We're just not always this wet."

Colin smiled down at Luna. "It's great. I like it."

"See?" Dulcie stood and refilled everyone's wineglass. "He likes it. Luna, babe, I don't know what you've got going with this gorgeous Were, but he's a keeper."

"He's heading back to Scotland tomorrow," Luna said.

"He's not!" Dulcie looked horrified. "Tell me it isn't so, Laird of Glenbarra, just when I learned to say your title."

"It's true." He took another swallow of wine. "I need to straighten out a few things with my younger brother, Duncan."

Dulcie's eyes widened. "Be still my heart. You have a *brother*?"

"I do."

"Is he as good-looking as you?"

Colin smiled. "Better."

"Well, then, that settles it." Dulcie finished topping off everyone's wine. "You go right back there, and you bring him over here. If he needs straightening out, we're just the crew to handle it. Right, ladies?"

"Right!" rang a chorus of female voices.

Colin could swear Luna's was among them. He wondered how Duncan would react to this bunch. Chances were he'd fit right in. It was definitely something to think about.

"Oh. My. God." Sybil sat up and wiped a hand over her face. "Do my eyes deceive me, or is that Hector walking this way in a bathing suit? God, it looks ancient. I hope it stays on him."

Janet turned. "It is Hector," she said in a low voice. "Don't anybody say anything crazy, or you'll scare him away. We're about to make Whittier House history, so don't any of you muck it up."

"I'm sorry," Dulcie said. "But that's just not how I roll." She made a megaphone of her hands. "Hey, Hector! Get your bony ass over here! We've been waiting for you!"

"I thought so!" Hector yelled back. "How could you have a decent party without the Hector-man?"

"The *Hector-man*?" Janet looked around frantically. "Is hell freezing over? Is the world coming to an end? I can't handle the shock!"

"It's all Luna's doing." Colin leaned down to kiss her wet cheek.

"That's not true," Luna said. "It's just . . . us, all of us, working together."

"Yeah," Janet said, "but it's also you, toots. We were blessed the day you showed up. I hope you plan to stick around."

"I do."

As Colin heard the ring of certainty in her voice, it underscored her answer to the question he posed earlier, the one she'd called *daft*. No, she wouldn't run away with him. She was anchored to this place and these friends, as well she should be after all the years she'd spent as a vagabond.

Only a selfish lover would insist that she give up the first safe, secure home she'd ever known. Only someone protecting his own interests would rip her from this spot and hope that she'd flourish in an alien environment. He wanted only the best for her. And from what he could tell, the best was right here on Le Floret.

Luna had never been surrounded by so many Weres who cared about her. Laughing with them, teasing and being teased, was so new and so special. Best of all, she could share this time with Colin, who seemed to enjoy himself as much as she did.

She longed to stop time and hold them all in this moment forever. But Dulcie said she was turning into a prune, and they'd finished the wine, and Hector said he was cold, although he'd been as boisterous and crazy as the rest of them. Luna hoped this was the night he started taking some joy in life.

As they left the hot tub, they all agreed to meet in the dining room for dinner after they showered and changed. Eating together wasn't their normal routine, but it was appropriate for this special night, the last night Colin would be in residence.

Everyone pitched in to get the food on the table, and more bottles of wine were opened. As a farewell meal for the owner of Whittier House, the Much Honoured Colin MacDowell, Laird of Glenbarra, it worked.

Hector even proposed a toast to the success of the

Whittier House Inn, and Luna knew then that she'd convinced him to stay on. The inn would be a blending of the old and the new, and Luna was optimistic about its future, even with George Trevelyan hovering menacingly in the background.

They'd talked a little business during dinner, and Colin had suggested creating a walk-in freezer out of a little-used pantry. Hector thought he'd need a riding mower, and Dulcie said the vacuum cleaners should be upgraded. None of it was startling, and everyone seemed confident they could handle the new regime just fine.

They all agreed that with a concerted effort, they could open for business the first weekend in August.

"Can you be here?" Janet asked Colin.

Luna was glad Janet had asked the question instead of her.

"I don't know," Colin said. "I can certainly try."

"If not, you can always make a video to welcome the guests," Luna said.

He gave her a long-suffering glance as everyone asked about the video and he had to explain that he wasn't doing a video, come hell or high water. He'd do his best to be here in person, he said.

Luna wasn't counting on it. He'd meant to come back while Geraldine was alive, too, and the obligations in Scotland had prevented him from returning. Considering that, she wouldn't expect him at all, and would be thrilled if he happened to show up every couple of years.

Obviously, if she could wave a magic wand to stop Colin from leaving, she'd do it. But then he couldn't handle the family problems that troubled him so. He did have to leave, and she'd faced that reality. She'd spent her whole life facing tough realities and disappointments, and she was good at it.

As they all sat discussing more plans for the grand

opening, Luna thought about the good fortune that had led her here. She loved the island and the castle, but she loved these Weres far more. They were her family as much, or maybe more than her grandparents.

They accepted her for who she was. At last there were no more secrets, which meant the friendship and love would grow as they all worked together to make Whittier House a success. She was home at last.

Sybil finished off the last of her dessert and laid down her fork. "You know what we should do now? We should all go back to our rooms, shift, and go for a run in the woods. It would be like old times."

"Sybil!" Dulcie gazed at her in open admiration. "That's a brilliant idea."

"I have ideas sometimes," Sybil said. "I just don't usually mention them because I'm afraid they're stupid, but we've had such a great time, and it seems fitting on Colin's last night that we should all go for a run." She glanced around the table. "I'm faster than I look."

"I'm not," Janet said. "But I wouldn't mind working off a little of that dinner. Let's do it."

"I would love for us to go for a run," Luna said. "Thanks for suggesting it, Sybil." She made a mental note to draw Sybil out more as the weeks went by. She'd been living in Dulcie's shadow far too long.

"Does the front door still have that revolving panel in the bottom section?" Colin asked.

"Yep." Dulcie nodded. "I tested it just the other day. I've been hankering for a run, but I didn't really want to go alone."

"I would have gone," Sybil said. "I didn't know anybody else wanted to."

"I think this is a great idea," Colin said. "But I haven't run through these woods since I was seventeen. Anybody want to volunteer to take point?"

"Me," Hector said. "We'll meet down by my cottage. I go for a run nearly every night, so I know the best trails."

All heads turned toward Hector. Luna was beginning to wonder if she'd completely underestimated the grounds-keeper.

Dulcie was the first to comment, as usual. "Hector, you sly Were. I had no idea you've been gallivanting through the woods every night. Maybe sometime you'll take me along."

"I might." He gave her an assessing look. "If you think you're up to it."

"I can certainly keep up with you, you old Were."

Hector smiled. "We'll see about that, won't we?"

Luna was fascinated by the interchange. Hector seemed to have dropped ten years in the past few hours and was acting like a robust man in his early sixties. Dulcie had definitely taken note of it. Interesting.

"Let's carry the dishes to the kitchen and stick them in the dishwasher before we go," Sybil said. "Janet shouldn't have to come back to a mess."

"Good plan," Luna said.

"Excellent plan," Janet said. "Thanks, Sybil."

Sybil flushed. "You're welcome."

Luna smiled to herself. Sybil, having scored with her previous idea, had promptly lobbed in another one. No doubt about it, Sybil had promise. Maybe Luna should ask if Sybil wanted to learn how to keep the books for Whittier House.

With everyone helping, the dishes were dispensed with quickly and they each left for their respective rooms. Luna gave silent thanks that Colin had encouraged her to shift the night before in the penthouse. Otherwise she might have begged off for fear she'd keep everyone waiting. Instead she was eager to join in the fun.

Even so, she wondered if they'd all be down at the

cottage ahead of her. Once she'd shifted, she loped out of her room and started down the stairs. Colin, his chocolate and caramel coat shining in the light from the chandelier, waited for her at the bottom of the stairs.

He glanced up when she appeared. *There you are!*

I know I'm slow. Is everyone else already outside? She hated being the last one out the door. She'd have to do this more often so she got faster.

Don't worry. Janet just went through the door. You're not that slow.

She joined him at the bottom of the stairs. *Thanks to you. Thank you for last night.*

His blue eyes flashed with amusement. *Which part?*

All parts. Now, let's go! She trotted quickly toward the door and pushed her head against the bottom section. It revolved silently, giving her ample room to step through.

She turned as Colin came out the door right behind her. He barely fit, but she didn't expect her future guests to be bigger than he was, so the door should be adequate. He gave the panel a nudge, and it clicked back into place.

She stayed by his side as they loped toward Hector's cottage. *Maybe, when the inn opens, I should offer nightly guided runs.*

Colin glanced at her without breaking stride. *Led by Hector?*

If he'll do it. He's an interesting Were.

Colin snorted softly. *Dulcie seems to think so, too.*

I'll let you know what happens. She planned to keep in touch with Colin by phone and e-mail, which might be more frustrating than no contact at all, but she'd take what she could get.

I'm glad we're doing this group run. Colin's voice was clear and strong. *But when it's over, don't go in. I want time alone with you.*

She was amused by the alpha nature of that statement. He didn't ask. He announced. At times he could be open and flexible, but this wasn't one of them. He was in full wolf mode.

Because she wanted alone time as much as he did, she would agree, but she couldn't resist teasing him. *I'm at your command, Your Much Honoured Lairdness.*

He looked over at her. *Good.*

She couldn't be sure, but she thought he was smiling.

They reached Hector's stone cottage and found his small front yard dominated by the presence of three wolves. Dulcie was the trimmest of the females and her reddish coat had a slight curl to it.

Sybil remained stocky in Were form and had a glossy black coat similar to Luna's. Janet was broad of chest and her rich brown coat looked well cared for.

Hector hadn't shown up yet, and then Luna saw him coming around from the back of the cottage. She stared at the large, silver wolf as he walked with regal assurance to the front of the cottage. As a human, Hector wasn't the sort anyone would notice, but as a wolf, he was imposing.

Luna glanced over at Dulcie to see how she'd reacted to Hector's somewhat grand entrance. Dulcie seemed riveted by the sight of Hector, his head held high, as he surveyed the small pack he was about to lead through the forest.

Hector looked at each wolf in turn, as if counting noses. *We're all here.* Even his voice sounded stronger. *Follow me.*

Dulcie leaped into action and took off after Hector. Janet and Sybil followed.

Colin held back. *Go ahead of me, Luna. Hector's taken point, so I'll guard the rear.*

Luna had never run with a pack of wolves before, but Colin had, so she followed instructions and bolted into the trees after Sybil. Joy rocketed through her as her fantasy came to life. Running full out along a narrow path through the trees, she stretched her muscles and savored the freedom of using her powerful legs the way they were meant to be used. Leaves scattered beneath her paws as she ran.

Along the way she caught the scent and sounds of night creatures—the soft hoot of an owl, the scurrying feet of raccoons, the sour smell of a skunk that had crossed the path. Best of all, she wasn't alone.

Colin's voice came from behind her. *Having a good time?*

Colin, I love this. All these years, I've missed so much!

And now you can have it all.

That startled her. Did he really think he meant so little to her? *Not quite all, Colin.*

Tonight then. Tonight you can have it all.

Yes. And it would have to be enough.

Chapter 26

Colin hadn't been sure that he'd recognize the route after fifteen years, but he did. A few trees had fallen and others had grown, but Hector obviously maintained this running path along with everything else on the estate. And he'd used it, even when no one else had.

The route took them in a large circle that would end at Hector's cottage. Once around should be plenty for Janet and Sybil, but Colin fully expected Hector and Dulcie to add a second lap. Luna, who wasn't used to this, already sounded out of breath.

Yet she kept bravely on as Hector broke out of the trees and skirted a bluff on the far side of the island. Few boats came this way in daylight, and none at night. That was fortunate, because if anyone happened to spot wolves running along a bluff in the San Juan Islands, wildlife officials would seek access to the area.

But Weres had learned to be very careful. They'd successfully kept their presence a secret for centuries, which was why this new concept of mating with humans was so risky. Luna's mother had apparently kept the secret, but what if she hadn't? Colin couldn't agree with Byron Reynaud's decision to mate with a human, just as he couldn't agree with Duncan's stated desire to do it.

Although Colin might not be able to keep Duncan from making a potentially dangerous mistake, he had to try. But bloody hell, how he hated the idea of leaving Luna tomorrow morning.

She would be fine, though. After seeing how the staff had rallied around her this afternoon, he was not worried about whether she could survive without him. It wasn't Luna's mental health that concerned him now. It was his own.

Three-quarters of the way around the circle, Janet slowed to a trot.

Sybil's telepathic message floated through the cool night air. *Thank you, Janet. I was dying back here.*

Then Luna, her sides heaving, also slowed to a trot. *I like this running business, but I need to get in shape.*

Janet's trot became a walk. *We all do. Well, three of us. Dulcie's doing just fine, the show-off.*

Sybil snorted. *Showing off for Hector.*

And he's showing off for her. Janet tossed her head. *I didn't see that coming.*

Luna added to the telepathic conversation. *I think it's sweet. They could be good for each other.* She glanced back at Colin, who had slowed to a walk along with the female Weres. *Sorry, Colin. You would probably rather be running.*

I'm fine. I don't mind conserving my energy. He wondered if she'd figure out what he was conserving it for. She must have, because she looked back at him with a definite gleam in her eyes.

When they reached the end of the path, Hector and Dulcie stood waiting for them. They barely looked winded.

Dulcie faced the latecomers. *Who's up for another lap? Hector and I are going around again.*

Janet shook her head. *Not me.*

Sybil flopped to the ground. *I'm done.*

Colin decided this was the moment to break off from the group. *Luna and I are going down to Happy Hour Beach. We'll see you all in the morning.* He turned and started back to the main house.

Luna fell into step beside him immediately, but she glanced over her shoulder as she walked away. *Bye, y'all.*

Ah, he was going to miss that sweet Southern accent, although he could hear it over the phone whenever he called. But a phone call wouldn't give him what he had in mind right now. He walked faster.

Impatient, Your Lairdness?

He slowed down. *Yes, but you're tired. Sorry.*

Not that tired. She trotted ahead of him.

Got your second wind?

Could be. Race you to the bluff!

He could have outrun her, but he didn't try. Instead he loped alongside her and matched her stride. When she picked up speed, so did he. When she slowed, he slowed.

You have good rhythm. Can you dance?

Yes. He thought of the lessons he'd been forced to take as a young Were. *Can you?*

No, you'd have to teach me, like you've had to teach me most everything.

I'll teach you next time I visit.

All right.

He was glad she hadn't asked him when that would be, because he couldn't give her an answer.

They reached the stone steps leading down to the beach, and he went first, testing to make sure it wasn't too slippery for them. The steps were damp, but if he moved slowly, he kept his balance.

He turned back to her. *Watch your step.*

I'm a very careful Were. That's how I've survived this long on my own.

You're not on your own anymore.

I know. I have Janet, Sybil, Dulcie, and Hector. And maybe my grandparents.

He accepted the fact that she hadn't included him, although mentally he put himself squarely on her list. If she needed him, he would come. It might take him at least twelve hours, but he would get on the first available plane. He doubted she'd require that kind of heroic gesture, though.

He reached the bottom of the steps and gazed up as she came toward him. The scent of her was an aphrodisiac that never failed to arouse him. He'd wanted her from the moment they'd met, and his response to her had only grown stronger.

A leisurely stroll along the beach sounded like a nice prelude to Were sex. When she reached the sand, he turned to lead the way to the far corner of the crescent beach.

She obviously had a different scenario in mind. With a yelp of pure pleasure, she took off, flinging sand in his face. He spit it out and raced after her. He'd been thinking sweet and romantic. He didn't know what the bloody hell she was thinking.

The night had been calm until now, but the weather was changing. Clouds scudded across the sky, driven by a wind that whipped the waves and sent them pounding against the shore. The water was wild, and so was Luna. She splashed through the swirling water and danced with the surf.

Pausing, she lifted her head and looked over her shoulder. *Come on! Play with me!*

And then he understood. This was her way of handling their inevitable parting. She'd work off the tension she felt by cavorting in the sea.

They would come together eventually. He was confident of that. But first, they would chase away their demons by playing in the waves. He plunged toward her, but spun away at the last moment to lead her in a race across the wet sand.

She followed, and in a startling burst of speed, she passed him and jumped straight into the water. Well, if she was going to swim, so would he. The cold shocked his system, but once he started swimming, he began to warm up. Moving fast, he put himself between Luna and open water.

She swam to the end of the crescent before turning toward shore. Thrashing through the waves, she regained solid footing, and Colin followed close behind. He arrived just in time for her thorough body shake.

The shower of salt water didn't matter. He was already soaked. But he took some satisfaction in shaking next to her so that his spray covered her, as well.

She dropped into a play bow, and then raced away again. He took off after her, all the while thinking he hadn't had to work this hard to pin a female in his entire sexual history. Maybe that was the idea.

She'd been a willing partner from the first time he'd kissed her, mostly because she'd been dying of curiosity. But now she understood the process and might think he needed a challenge. He could imagine her deciding that his last episode with her shouldn't be too easy for him.

He'd been willing to play along, but by God, she'd had the upper hand long enough. He caught up with her halfway down the beach and dashed in front of her, blocking her path. She whirled and started back the other way, but he got there first.

She wouldn't win this game. He'd spent far more time as a wolf, and when he put his mind to it, he could outmaneuver any Were. The chase had accomplished one thing, however. He wanted her with a fierceness that put every other coupling to shame.

She stood panting at the edge of the water, the surf sliding up over her paws.

Holding her gaze, he advanced. *Game over, Luna.*

Maybe. Maybe not. Wheeling, she ran back into the water.

He reached her before she lost her footing and mounted her before she could dodge away. *Be still!*

Miraculously, she was.

He managed to keep his balance as the waves rolled past, surging against his groin as he sank into her. The pleasure surpassed anything he'd known, and he concentrated on that pleasure as he blocked any thought of a soul-deep connection. The possibility hovered on the edges of his consciousness, but he denied it with every frenzied movement of his hips.

When he felt her contract around him, he surrendered to a mind-shattering climax. Then it was over. The water cradled them both as he stayed buried within her and stared out at the rolling sea. They'd shared so much, including this numbing sorrow for what could not be.

There were moments, Luna realized, when silence was kinder than words. As she and Colin returned to Whittier House, neither spoke. Yet she knew he battled the same bittersweet emotion that filled her heart.

The incredible joy of their physical connection was overshadowed by the knowledge that their special time together was nearly over. She'd tried to lighten the intensity with her beach romp, and he'd obviously understood.

Her plan had even worked for a while. But then . . . passion had taken over, sending them dangerously close to a true mating. They'd fought that urge and won. Sadly, they'd won. As if they both understood the cost of that victory, they'd touched noses in the entry hall and parted.

She would see him again before he left, but this was the private farewell they would both remember. She should take comfort in knowing he was as miserable as she was, but that didn't work for her. For the first time, she began to understand why Hector had shut himself away from the world.

Luna didn't plan to do that, even if she understood the motivation. But turning herself into a recluse wouldn't benefit anyone, especially Colin. As the manager of the Whittier House Inn, she would stay visible and actively promote the business in any way she could.

Colin left the following morning in a flurry of good-byes. Luna's comments mingled with everyone else's as they all gathered in the entry hall in a tableau similar to the one when he'd arrived. But so much had changed between his arrival and departure.

Luna didn't watch the helicopter take off. She had her limits. When the sound of the rotors shook the house, she was in her office with the door closed working on spread-sheets. If she took a few seconds to bury her face in her hands and weep a little, no one had to know.

She kept herself extremely busy for the rest of the day. Colin sent her a short text message when he landed in Glasgow, but there was nothing personal in it. Luna forced herself to delete it from her phone.

After a fitful night's sleep, she was at her desk again early the next morning comparing linen prices online. The phone on her desk rang, and she debated how to answer. Should she say *Whittier House* or *Whittier House Inn* and get the ball rolling?

She settled on giving that ball a swift kick toward the goal. "Whittier House Inn. This is Luna Reynaud. How may I help you?"

"Miss Reynaud." The voice was crisp and female. "I have George Trevelyan on the line. Please hold."

Luna was taken aback. She'd never dealt with someone who employed an assistant to place phone calls, but she probably should get used to it. If Whittier House became as popular as she hoped, the rich and famous would flock to the island.

"Good morning, Luna." George's voice contained equal notes of friendly condescension and somber concern. "How are you?"

"I'm fine, George." She did her best to match his tone. "How are you?"

"As a matter of fact, I'm troubled."

"I'm sorry to hear that." She didn't rise to the bait and ask why.

"It's imperative that I meet with you ASAP. I have an unexpected opening in my schedule tomorrow. Knox can pick you up around ten and bring you to my office."

Her jaw tightened at his assumption that she'd drop everything to meet with him, but she reminded herself that was an alpha tactic. "Unfortunately, I can't get away tomorrow."

"That is unfortunate." He sighed. "Then I'll come to you. I can be there by three."

She worked to keep her breathing steady. She would not allow him to steamroll her. "I'm afraid that's not convenient, either."

He adopted a more coaxing tone. "Surely you could spend thirty minutes with me, Luna. I promise not to stay long. I just want to discuss something with you concerning your project. It's an excellent idea and I want it to succeed."

She wondered what was so urgent that he'd fly over for a thirty-minute meeting. If he was determined to meet with her, maybe she should just get it over with. "All right," she said. "I'll see you at three tomorrow."

"Good. See you then." He disconnected the call.

Luna replaced the phone in its holder. She couldn't help feeling uneasy about George inviting himself over, but he'd said he wanted the inn to succeed, so perhaps she had nothing to worry about.

Besides, he couldn't negotiate a buy-in by talking with her. Colin owned Whittier House, so if George planned to bully his way into being a partner, he'd have to deal with Colin.

She could claim one small victory in the conversation, though. George had summoned her to his office, and she'd refused to be summoned. If she had to meet with him, at least she'd be doing it on her turf, backed up by her staff. And that staff needed to be informed of George's impending visit.

After she reached everyone by cell phone, they gathered in the kitchen. Each took a stool around the center island. Even Hector showed up. Scraping the mud off his work boots, he chose a stool next to Dulcie.

Luna described the phone call and the outcome. Then she cleared her throat. "I just want to warn everyone that George Trevelyan has his eye on this place. He'd like to make it part of his empire, and both Colin and I are against it."

"I'm glad to hear that," Hector said. "If George gets his hands on Whittier House, I really will quit."

Dulcie glanced at him. "Then we just won't let that happen, will we?"

"Damn straight," Sybil added. "No way can we let some big wheeler-dealer muscle his way in. This is our project."

"Absolutely." Janet slapped a hand on the counter. "He may control half of Seattle, but he sure as hell doesn't control what happens on this island."

"No, he doesn't." Luna loved the way the staff had

assumed ownership of the inn project. They were a force to be reckoned with. "But he is powerful and he's used to getting his way."

"Are you saying we have to treat him with kid gloves?" Sybil asked.

Hector frowned. "I don't much like that idea. You have to stand up to bullies like George Trevelyan."

"I agree," Luna said. "To be honest, I'm not sure why he's coming, since I have no power to grant him a financial stake in Whittier House. Maybe he hopes to convince me I can't run the inn without his help."

"I can see him trying to undermine your confidence," Hector said. "That was the tactic he used as a teenager. I'll make sure I'm available at three tomorrow to monitor the situation."

"I dare him to find fault with Whittier House," Dulcie said. "It rocks!"

"And so do we." Sybil leaned forward. "We're all invested in this place, which is why the house is immaculate, the grounds are gorgeous, and the food is to die for."

"Speaking of food," Janet said, "I may show off a little and have my world-famous chocolate chip cookies coming out of the oven around three tomorrow."

Luna smiled with relief. Their moral support meant the world to her. "I don't know what I'd do without y'all."

"We're just grateful you came up with the idea of running Whittier House as an inn," Dulcie said. "I wasn't looking forward to taking potluck with a new owner."

Sybil nodded. "Me, either. And we're not going to let George Trevelyan screw things up. Just tell us if there's anything else we can do to help tomorrow."

"It's enough to know that you're standing by, ready to keep him from marching in here, thinking he can boss us around."

Sybil lifted her chin. "I'd like to see him try."

Luna smiled. If mild-mannered Sybil was ready to fight for Whittier House, then George Trevelyan had better watch out.

After everyone left to begin their respective tasks, Luna returned to her office. She thought about sending Colin a text message about the visit and decided against it. He'd be busy dealing with the crisis of his brother Duncan's decision to mate with a human. She couldn't go running to him every time something came up, and besides, she didn't know what George had on his mind.

She glanced at the clock and automatically added eight hours, which she'd been doing ever since Colin had left. It would be past five in the evening in Scotland. Colin would be looking forward to dinner, perhaps with his family. No, she wouldn't disturb him about this. She and the staff could handle it.

Chapter 27

"So now you've met Molly." Duncan sat across from Colin at their favorite neighborhood pub in the late afternoon as the after-work crowd began to drift in.

Duncan's dark hair was a typical tousled mess because they'd driven back to the small town of Glenbarra with the top down on his MG. But his gray eyes were more thoughtful than usual. "What did you think of her?"

"I liked her." As Colin sipped his whisky, he pictured the petite brunette who'd met them for lunch a few hours ago at a trendy spot in the heart of Glasgow. "I wanted to find something wrong with her, but I couldn't. She's all you said she was."

"Yeah, Molly is terrific." Duncan picked up his glass as if to take a drink, and then put it down again. "But as we were sitting there having a nice lunch, I started to ask myself if mating with her is what I really want."

Colin stared at him. "Pardon?"

"I know, I know. It's a total reversal for me, and usually I dig my heels in when I get an idea."

"Really? I hadn't noticed."

Duncan rolled his eyes. "As if you didn't inherit the MacDowell stubborn streak, too."

"I suppose I did." And he'd begun to question what that stubbornness was costing him. "But what's changed your mind about Molly?"

"Something you said on the phone keeps running through my mind. Remember that bit about finding someone you can't imagine living without?"

"I do." Colin took a swallow of his whisky. He hoped the liquor would blunt his longing for a certain lass he was having great difficulty living without.

"Well . . ." Duncan hesitated. "This is hard for me to admit, but as you said, this could be the most important decision I ever make. I love the *idea* of mating with Molly. I love it a lot. And I love her. But maybe not enough to take this big step."

Colin said nothing. He'd spouted off on the phone, but what did he know about such matters? He was a fine one to advise his brother, when he couldn't figure out how he wanted to live his own life.

"The thing is," Duncan continued, "I *can* imagine living without her. And I'm damn sure she can imagine living without me. She's heading off without me next week, as a matter of fact."

"Are you upset that she's going on holiday without you?"

Duncan shook his head. "Not at all, which proves my point. We have a good time when we're together, but there's no compulsion to be with each other. Do you know what I mean?"

Colin sighed. "Aye. But a compulsion to be with someone isn't much of a test, either. We can be compelled to be with the wrong person." He took another gulp of his whisky.

Duncan studied him for several seconds. "All right, big brother, who is she?"

"Who is who?"

"This wrong person you're compelled to spend time with."

Colin scowled at his brother. "I didn't say—"

"Don't even try denying it. This is me you're talking to. You've been edgy and distracted ever since I picked you up at the airport, and I blamed it on jet lag and the whole Molly problem. But it's not about me, is it? Who did you meet in America? A sexy human?"

Colin gazed into his nearly empty glass. Then he polished it off and signaled for another. By the time he'd finished his second whisky, he'd told Duncan everything except the extremely personal bits. He'd even included the tragic story of Sophie and Byron.

"Bloody hell." Duncan stared at Colin. "What are you going to do?"

"I haven't the faintest idea. Stick it out here and hope the feeling goes away, I guess."

"Doesn't sound like much fun to me."

"So far it hasn't been, but I just got back, and I mean to give myself time to accept the situation as it is."

Duncan shook his head, as if he didn't believe a word of that. "You really are a stubborn fool."

"I'm inclined to agree with you."

Draining his glass, Duncan set it on the table. "There's one part of the story I don't understand, though. Sophie and Byron must have been truly mated if Sophie got pregnant. That compulsion you keep talking about had to be at work there, right?"

"I assume so."

"So you're telling me that Sophie, who was compelled to be with Byron and pregnant with his child, ran away? Why would she do that?"

Colin shrugged. "She told Luna she didn't belong there. When Luna realized her father had been Were, she interpreted that to mean her mother hadn't wanted to live with Weres for the rest of her life, so she left."

"I don't buy it. If she was pregnant, that meant she and Byron had a true mating. There's nothing accidental or casual about that. They went through the mating ritual, and she knew if she got pregnant, her kid might be born Were. Byron obviously wanted her to stay, and she continued to love him until the day she died. That's not the mark of a quitter."

"So what happened, then?"

"I wonder . . ." Duncan rolled his empty glass between his palms. "Apparently the rest of the pack didn't know Byron had revealed himself to Sophie, or they'd have tracked her to New Orleans and brought her back to Seattle for security purposes."

"Right. I thought of that."

"But let's say one pack member somehow discovered that Sophie was in the know. If that Were objected to a human joining the pack they might have quietly convinced her that Byron's life would be miserable with a human female as his mate."

Colin allowed the idea to settle. "That's possible." Sad to say, it was the sort of interference he once would have understood, although he liked to think he would have met the problem head-on instead of taking a manipulative approach.

He still wasn't convinced that Weres and humans should mate, but a deep and abiding love . . . Nothing and no one should be allowed to sabotage that. "So you think she left for his sake?"

"That's more logical than thinking she abandoned her mate because she couldn't deal with the lifestyle. She doesn't come across as that shallow. But if someone told her that the Were she loved so desperately would be an outcast if she stayed . . ."

"She very well might leave, especially if she hadn't yet discovered she was pregnant." Reaching for his drink, Colin settled back in his chair. "That makes her decision noble instead of cowardly. Luna deserves to hear that theory and maybe check it out."

Duncan nodded. "But if I were in her shoes, once I suspected that, I'd want to move heaven and earth to uncover the bloody Were who ruined so many lives."

"I think she would, but it could be her grandmother. I don't want to suspect her, but she might have thought she was doing the right thing for her son."

Duncan gazed at him across the battered table. "In that case, you may decide to leave well enough alone."

"That's not fair to Luna, who thinks her mother abandoned her father after making a commitment for life. If she investigates and discovers differently, she shouldn't have to deal with the fallout by herself."

"I sense a trip in your future."

"Aye." Colin's smile was rueful. "I hate to wreck your love life and run off, but I'm flying back to Whittier House. I want to tell her about this in person, so I can help if she needs me." He dug in his pocket for cash to pay the bill.

"I've got it." Duncan tossed money on the table.

Colin looked up in surprise. "Thanks, Dunc. I appreciate it." He couldn't remember the last time Duncan had picked up the tab. Maybe his brother was ready to accept more responsibility, which could mean lightening Colin's load at Glenbarra.

"You're welcome. And while you're at it, you might as well thank me for giving you an excuse to go back to Washington."

Colin's denial evaporated when he realized that his brother was right. Viewed dispassionately, Duncan's theory might not warrant a trip across the ocean. It could be explained during a phone call. Luna was a strong female with a good support system. She might not need him as she investigated the possibility that her mother had been coerced into leaving.

But he couldn't view anything concerning Luna dispassionately. He might as well admit that *he* needed *her*, and that was why he was taking the next available flight to Seattle. He could hardly wait to surprise her with an unexpected visit.

"You're compelled, old chap," Duncan said. "If I were you, I'd pay attention to that."

"I will." Colin met his brother's gaze and realized that within the past hour they'd traded roles. It was a humbling thought, one of many he'd had recently. "I definitely will."

Luna had hoped Knox would come in with George, but she heard the helicopter take off again before Hector ushered George into the entryway.

Once again, George looked like an Eddie Bauer commercial in an open-necked denim shirt and khaki slacks. He stepped forward, his expression almost fatherly. "Luna. So good to see you again."

Luna drew strength from having Hector standing in the doorway. "George." She extended her hand to him but didn't echo his sentiments. "I'm sorry Knox couldn't join us."

George gave her hand a squeeze and released it. "I sent him to Friday Harbor on business. I'll call him when we've wrapped up here." He sniffed the air. "Something smells good."

"Our chef just baked cookies, and the coffee's made, if you'd both like to follow me." She started toward the hallway that led to Geraldine's sitting room.

"Both?" George sounded surprised.

Luna turned. "I thought you'd enjoy reminiscing with Hector about old times, so I invited him to join us."

George glanced at the groundskeeper. "What old times?"

"When you worked for me." Hector's tone was deceptively casual.

"Good God, are we talking about the summer after my senior year in high school? I'm sorry, Hector, but I wouldn't be a good companion for a walk down memory lane. I vaguely remember spending a couple of weeks on this island, but I don't remember you at all."

Hector seemed unfazed. "In that case, I'll just tag along for the sake of the cookies."

"I can't blame you, there, but it would be better if you enjoyed them in the kitchen with the rest of the staff. What I have to discuss with Luna is private."

Anger fizzed through Luna's veins as she faced George. "I realize that you are used to being the one in charge, but with all due respect, I'm in charge at Whittier House." She glanced at Hector. "You're welcome to have coffee with us."

"The truth is, I have some information about your mother," George said.

"My mother?" Her resistance faltered.

"That's right. It's a personal matter." He shrugged. "I'm only considering your feelings."

Luna had suspected George knew more about her parents than he'd let on. She was hungry for any insight into the past, but if George was about to reveal something embarrassing or humiliating, she'd need time to process it before sharing it with her friends. After being a lone wolf for so many years, she instinctively protected her secrets.

She exchanged a look with Hector, who excused himself, but told her he wouldn't be far away if she needed him.

Moments after they were settled in easy chairs in Geraldine's sitting room, Janet appeared bearing a silver tray with the coffee, cups, and a basket of fragrant cookies. Janet left the tray and gave Luna's shoulder a squeeze before she exited the room.

Luna imagined everyone gathered in the kitchen debating what George had to say that required a private discussion. She was pretty damn curious about that, herself. After serving the coffee, she set the basket of cookies within reach of George's chair. She'd always loved those cookies, but this afternoon they might as well be hockey pucks, because she'd lost her appetite.

"Great atmosphere." George drank some coffee and picked up a cookie. "I can see why MacDowell went for your plan."

Luna set her untouched coffee back on the antique table beside her chair. She'd chosen Geraldine's favorite seat in hopes it would give her strength. "What did you want to tell me about my mother?"

"First of all, you look so much like her that it's startling." He bit into the cookie.

"So you knew exactly who I was from the time I walked into your office, didn't you?"

He nodded as he chewed his bite of cookie. Then he swallowed. "But you didn't seem to want to acknowledge it, so I didn't push. Maybe if you'd changed your last name and disguised your looks, you might have gotten away with this."

She forced herself to take a deep breath before answering. "I'm not trying to get away with anything."

"Aren't you?" He skewered her with a glance, but then looked away again. "So, I could be wrong. Just because your mother was a gold digger doesn't mean you are, I suppose."

Her blood ran cold. "She was *not* a gold digger."

"I didn't say she was an *effective* gold digger. When she realized that Byron could be disinherited because he was involved with her, she decided to cut and run, so she lost out on the gold, after all. That doesn't change her original intent, however."

Luna's nails bit into her palms. "My mother was not after the Reynaud money. I don't know why you're making up lies about her, but—"

"I was there, Luna. I was Byron's cousin and closest friend. I can testify that's the way it was." He chose another cookie. "And here you come along, attach yourself to a wealthy old woman who conveniently dies, and now you're getting cozy with her heir. Like mother, like daughter."

Anger flowed through her like lava. "How dare you! I'm not after anyone's money!"

"Maybe not. But now that you've identified yourself as Sophie's daughter, that's the story that will circulate. Once it's out there, the Were community won't come within miles of this place. If you truly want to help Colin, you'll go back where you came from. You're nothing but an anchor around his neck."

Her chest was so tight she could barely breathe. "I know very well how that story will *circulate*. You're trying to get rid of me."

"Bright girl."

"Why?" She gripped the arms of the chair. "I'm not the one standing in the way of acquiring an interest in this place. Colin has all the control."

"Yes, but you're the driving force behind the project,

and I've seen the way he looks at you. Once you're gone, he'll lose interest and decide to sell."

"No, he won't. He loves Whittier House." But the sick feeling in the pit of her stomach told her that George was right. Colin had gone along with the inn project mostly because of her. A few years down the road, if the inn became a huge success, keeping it might be a logical business decision, but right now he was motivated primarily by his emotional ties, of which she was one.

Without her, he might choose to sell, but she couldn't let that happen. Her determination had very little to do with herself anymore. Now she would fight for the sake of Janet, Dulcie, Sybil, Hector, and even Geraldine, who would have *hated* the thought of this filthy, rotten Were getting his paws on her beloved house. And she would fight for Colin, too, who needed a connection with Whittier House whether he fully realized that or not.

The vibration of helicopter blades overhead made them both glance up.

George sighed. "Kids these days. Can't follow a simple set of instructions. Well, seeing as how Knox is here already, we might as well cut this chat short. I've said what I came to say. I'm sure you'll do the right thing."

She stood, her back straight, her gaze locked with his. "You've put me in a tight spot, but I've been in tight spots before. You can't force me to leave. I'll do everything in my power to make sure you never own Whittier House."

"Stay if you must, but you'll create huge problems for Colin if you do." He stood and reached in his shirt pocket. "I'm betting you don't really want to make his life tougher than it already is." He held out an airline ticket envelope. "I've added a little cash for the journey."

Trembling with rage, she smacked the envelope from his hand. It sailed to the floor, spilling hundred-dollar bills.

He shrugged. "I agree that cold, hard cash is a bit in-
sulting, but I'm only trying to smooth your transition. I'll
just leave all that there, in case you change your mind."

"I would rather die than accept anything from you!"

His eyebrows rose. "Seriously? You're that stupid?
You have no other options, Luna. If you don't leave of
your own free will, I'll crush you like a bug, and your
precious laird with you."

"Guess again, Trevelyan."

Luna's heart slammed into her ribs and she spun toward the doorway, certain she was hallucinating. Colin
couldn't be here. He was in Scotland, thousands of miles
away.

And yet there he stood, his furious blue gaze fastened
on George Trevelyan. For the first time since she'd met
the Seattle pack alpha, she felt a little sorry for him. But
not much.

Chapter 28

Luna hadn't called him. Colin took that information like a sucker punch to the gut. She'd planned to handle George Trevelyan on her own, without his help and support. And for that, he had only himself to blame.

Why should she call him? He'd constantly reinforced the idea that his precious obligations took precedence over her needs. He'd warned her that his life was in Scotland, not here with her.

But the moment he'd walked into the sitting room and discovered Trevelyan there, his priorities had shifted, and they were never shifting back. Luna was the center of his existence. If that interfered with his obligations, so be it.

George quickly covered his surprise with a genial smile. "I swear the world gets smaller every day, Mac-Dowell. Apparently a trip across the pond is nothing more than a long commute for you."

Colin walked into the room. "Something like that." There was so much he wanted to say to Luna, but he had to keep his attention on George. He flexed his hands, fighting the urge to take George apart physically. But breaking him mentally would be much more effective and wouldn't hurt the furniture.

"If you'd told me you were coming, I'd have sent Knox over to SeaTac."

"No worries. I managed." Colin had deliberately chosen a different air taxi service because he'd wanted to surprise Luna. He hadn't realized he'd surprise George, too. Excellent bonus. "So what's going on here? I only caught the tail end, but it sounded as if you were threatening my manager."

George adopted a regal stare. "As the Trevelyan pack alpha, it's my job to police the Seattle Were community. Luna is a disruptive influence. It's in everyone's best interest, including yours, for her to leave Seattle."

"Nice speech." Colin kept his voice and his gaze steady. "Is that the same one you gave Sophie twenty-eight years ago, or have you refined it since then?"

Luna gasped, but Colin didn't lose focus. This was a pitched battle between alphas, and maintaining eye contact was crucial. By doing that, he detected a slight flicker of an eyelid that told him George wasn't as calm as he appeared.

Yet George's reply was nonchalant. "I haven't a clue what you're talking about."

"Then let me jog your memory. Twenty-eight years ago, a beautiful human female caught the attention of two Weres—cousins, in fact. The more competitive of the two was rejected in favor of the other. Rejection didn't sit well with him. He talked the woman into leaving by claiming that if she stayed, she'd ruin her chosen sweetheart's life."

A muscle in George's cheek twitched. "Nice try, but it didn't happen like that."

"Maybe not, but Edwina and Jacques remember that you took Sophie's rejection hard. They've always wondered why Sophie left so abruptly. One minute she was nuts about their son, something that did worry them, by the way. But then, all at once, she hopped on a train."

"You're lying." All the affability left George's expression. "You haven't talked to them."

"Once I realized that it made no sense for Sophie to have left of her own accord when she was mated with Byron, I wondered who might have talked her into it. During a layover in Chicago, I phoned Edwina."

George's eyes glittered. "Edwina's losing it. You can't trust anything she says."

"Don't you say that about my grandmother!" Luna started toward him.

Colin put a restraining hand on her arm. "He knows that's not true, Luna. He's bluffing, but it won't work. Edwina and I had a long conversation, and we both agreed that if Byron had told anyone about mating with Sophie, it would have been his cousin, the Were he loved like a brother."

George's face turned gray.

"If I had any doubts about your role in this tragedy," Colin continued, "your actions today erased them."

Luna's breath hissed out. *"You."* The word was filled with equal parts of horror and loathing. Fingers curled, she lunged at George.

Colin grabbed her around the waist and held on tight. "Don't. He's not worth it."

She struggled in his grip. "But he's responsible for my father's death! He deserves to pay for that!"

"Don't you think I pay for it every day of my cursed life?" George's face twisted with agony.

"Oh, I'm so sorry for you!" Luna's breathing was ragged. "What about the price my father paid? And my mother? And my grandparents? And *me*?"

"How could I know he'd go after her? I told him she

didn't love him anymore, that she didn't want to live as a Were. Why didn't he believe me? If he'd believed me, he'd be alive!"

Heat came off Luna's body in waves. "He didn't believe you because he knew she would always love him, that they were mated for all time."

George began to shake. "I get that now, but back then, I didn't understand ... God ... the wreck ... the blood ..." Burying his face in his hands, he wept.

Colin had looked forward to this moment with relish, but now that it was here, he took no pleasure in George's complete humiliation. He just wanted the Were out of his sight. "I'll call Knox," he said. "He'll take you home."

"God, no." George's shoulders quivered. "I can't face my son right now."

Luna stepped away from Colin, and he let her go. Although she might have been ready to claw George's eyes out a moment ago, Colin didn't think she'd do it now.

She took a shaky breath. "Sit down, George," she said. "Get yourself together."

His eyes red and his face damp with tears, George located the chair he'd recently vacated and sank unsteadily into it. He glanced once at Luna and looked away. "Every time I see you, I see Sophie. That's why I wanted you gone."

Luna folded her arms. "Let's not forget the plan to buy Whittier House when my absence made Colin lose interest in the project. Don't pretend it was all about your guilt."

George coughed. "Okay, I admit that was a consideration." Reaching in his back pocket, he took out a handkerchief and began mopping his face. "But now I'm finished." His whole body sagged. "Once this gets out—"

"Maybe it doesn't have to get out," Luna said.

Colin glanced at her in surprise. "Don't forget that I've talked to Edwina."

"And how did she react?"

"She's upset." He directed his attention to George. "And she expects you to atone for what you've done, which means clearing Sophie's name and welcoming Luna fully into the Trevelyan pack. However, once she finds out that you tried to drive her granddaughter out of town . . ."

"She'll want my head on a platter," George said.

Colin nodded. "Yes, she will. And I'm prepared to hand it to her."

Luna looked at Colin. "But we don't have to tell her about this."

"Why wouldn't we? The bastard deserves whatever he gets."

"I agree, but think about it for a minute."

Finally he understood her intention. Although she'd been put through an emotional wringer, she'd kept her wits about her. She was even smarter than she was beautiful, and that was saying something. "No, I guess we don't."

George stared at both of them in amazement. "You would do that?"

"Yes," Luna said, "on the condition that you throw all your support behind the Whittier House Inn, without—"

"Done! I'll do whatever you say. I'll—"

"Wait." Luna held up her hand. "I'm not finished. Colin and I welcome your support, but there can be no more discussion of buying in. We didn't want to be part of your empire before, and now we'd rather drink battery acid than be in business with a weasel like you." She looked at Colin. "Right?"

"Damn right."

George blew out a breath and stood. "Okay." He offered his hand first to Luna, and then to Colin. "It's a deal."

Colin shared a triumphant glance with Luna. He'd never been more proud of her, or more desperately in love.

Luna held herself together until the helicopter lifted off the helipad, taking George Trevelyan back to Seattle. Wind from the whirling blades buffeted her as she stood next to Colin, who'd tucked his arm securely around her waist.

As they watched the helicopter rise up over the trees, she allowed herself to lean in to his solid warmth. "That was intense. Thanks for showing up."

He tightened his grip. "I'm the one who should be thanking you. I was willing to let Edwina and the pack take him down, but thanks to your quick thinking, we have him right where we want him—on a tight leash."

"Yes, but you handed me the leash." Glancing up at his profile, she felt her heart constrict. He meant far more to her than he should under the circumstances. "That insight about my mother was brilliant. I wish I'd thought of it."

He turned, slid both arms around her waist, and gazed into her eyes. "I can't take credit for the insight, either. My brother, Duncan, came up with it."

"Then please thank him for me. I have a much better image of my mother now." She rested her hands on his broad shoulders and looked into his face. She never grew tired of doing that. "And how is that situation with your brother, by the way?"

"He's breaking up with Molly."

"And you're happy about that, I'll bet." So Colin had efficiently subdued his brother's rebellious impulse. She felt a prick of disappointment. Colin's prejudices were still firmly in place.

"I'm happy only because she wasn't his true mate."

"You're absolutely sure she's not?"

"*He's* sure, and that's what counts."

She nodded, but she wondered if Duncan had simply caved under pressure and told his older brother what he wanted to hear. Colin could be extremely convincing, as she knew firsthand.

He started to say something, then shook his head and glanced away.

"What?"

He looked into her eyes. "I wish you'd called me when you knew George was coming. I understand why you didn't, but I still wish you'd called to let me know."

"I wasn't about to bother you when I didn't know what he wanted." This laird of Glenbarra had a lot of nerve, but then he was a pack alpha, so it probably went with the job. "Speaking of calling, I wish you'd called *me* to say you were flying back here, and I don't understand that at all. Why the hell didn't you?"

"I wanted to surprise you."

"Mission accomplished. I thought I was hallucinating. You had no reason to be here."

He pulled her closer, surrounding her with his heat, his scent, his charisma. "I had every reason to be here." His gaze searched hers. "I've been an idiot, Luna. I hope someday you'll forgive me."

"For what?" Something in his expression was different, and he'd never called himself an idiot before. That wasn't particularly lairdlike. She wondered what he was leading up to. Then a horrible possibility occurred to her. "Please tell me you didn't sell Whittier House."

"No! I wouldn't do that."

She let out a breath. "For a second there I was really scared. So what am I supposed to forgive, then?"

"My arrogance, my meddling, my stubbornness, my insufferable snobbishness."

"Oh." She paused while she debated whether to be honest or not. Honesty won out. "I have to admit you're guilty of those things, but I —"

"Just don't reject me yet." His plea was reflected in his amazing blue eyes. "I know I have flaws, but give me a chance to redeem myself."

"Who's rejecting you? You and your flaws are still welcome in my bed anytime."

He reached up and cupped her face in his hand. "And that makes me a very lucky chap, indeed." He stroked her cheek with his thumb. "But I want more than that, lass."

"More?" She blinked in confusion. "Look, I'm not into bondage."

He smiled. "Neither am I."

"Then what is it you want?"

His smile faded and his gaze intensified. "A mate, Luna."

Her body vibrated as if she'd touched a bare electrical wire. She opened her mouth to speak, but nothing came out. *A mate?* She must have misunderstood.

He took her face in both hands and looked into her eyes. "I know why you're confused. I've done a fine job of convincing you we don't belong together. So now I have to convince you that we do. Let's start with this." He lowered his mouth to hers.

As a persuasive technique, it worked like a charm. After a few seconds of the loveliest kiss he'd ever given her, she was willing to believe anything he said.

He ended the kiss slowly and raised his head. His smile was heartbreakingly tender. "I love you. And I mean to reform so that you'll love me back."

"But I already do." She clutched his shoulders and prayed this wasn't a dream, but he felt very real.

His eyes filled with joy. "I can't imagine why that's so, but I'd be a bloody fool to question it." He started to kiss her again.

"Wait! What about Scotland?"

"Scotland?"

"You're the Much Honoured Laird of Glenbarra!"

"So I am. And I may need to make regular trips there, even if Duncan takes on more responsibility for the place. But I won't ask you to leave the island. I know how much it means to you."

She wrapped her arms around his neck. "Just try leaving without me, mister."

"You'd want to go?"

"Providing you'd want me there." Belatedly she realized she might not be totally welcome.

"I do. I'll be proud to introduce you as my mate and the Lady of Glenbarra."

"But I won't be the one they would have chosen for you."

"No." His expression hopeful, he met her gaze. "At least not at first. But if you're willing to make trips over there, we could work together to open some minds, and that would be a good thing. I realize I'm asking a lot of you, but—"

"I'm up to it." As she said that, she knew it was true. She was surprised to realize she didn't need constant contact with this island. It wasn't home. Colin was. The island could serve as her base as she helped her newly tolerant mate spread even more tolerance in his homeland. "You once told me I might be destined for more than a secluded life on Le Floret."

"And so you are, my lady." His lips hovered over hers.

"My lady. I like the sound of that."

"I'm glad." He brushed her lips with his.

"Think of it. I'm going to have a Scottish title."

He lifted his head and grinned at her. "If I'd known you'd be so taken with the idea, I would have started with that instead of listing all my failings."

"What failings?"

He laughed. "Now, lass, I'm not perfect and you well know it."

"You are perfect . . . perfect for me." And to prove it, she pulled him down for the steamiest kiss in her short but extremely eventful kissing history.

Epilogue

Opening weekend at the Whittier Inn could have turned into a disaster, but Colin had agreed with Luna that they should invite all the major players, including her grandparents and as many of the Trevelyan pack as could make it, even George. On top of that, Colin had decided to go for broke and invite Duncan and their mother, Brigit.

His father was too ill to make the trip, but Duncan and their mother had arrived right on schedule, eager to meet the half-breed Were Colin had claimed as his mate. He'd told his mother everything and had let her decide how much to tell his father. He suspected she hadn't revealed much.

But none of that mattered on this bright August day as the guests gathered outside for the croquet tournament Luna had organized as an ice breaker. Colin stayed in the background, content to watch his lady shine. And shine she did, moving through the crowd in her bright flowered dress.

Guests, including his mother and brother, buzzed

around her like bees seeking nectar. Colin understood. He wanted to do the same, but he resisted the urge. Later tonight he would have his turn. He could wait.

Hector, looking sporty in a polo shirt and crisp navy slacks, sauntered over to where Colin stood. "So she talked you into wearing your kilt, I see."

"Aye." Colin didn't add that Luna could talk him into anything, anything at all. Hector probably knew that already. "Thank you for agreeing to mingle with the guests. I know it's not your favorite thing to do."

Hector chuckled. "It seems to mean a lot to her. And it's not so bad. In fact, it's good to see how some of those boys turned out."

"Hors d'oeuvres, gentlemen?" Dulcie, dressed in a sequined top and tight white pants, appeared bearing a tray of bite-sized delicacies Janet had spent the afternoon creating.

"Thanks, Dulcie." Colin picked up a still-warm pastry that oozed fragrant cheese.

Hector helped himself to a cracker with a swirled topping. "Don't mind if I do." Then he reached down with his free hand and pinched Dulcie's bottom.

"Hector, you old reprobate!" Dulcie pretended outrage, but her color was high and her eyes sparkled.

"Catch you later, Dulce." Hector winked at her.

"Only if you're fast enough, Hec." She walked away, hips swaying.

"I'll pretend I didn't see that," Colin said.

"Hell, at my age, I don't care who sees it. I'm just grateful that I still have lead in my pencil."

Colin almost choked on his cheese-filled pastry.

"Don't hurt yourself, son."

"Right." Colin swallowed the last of the pastry and wiped the moisture from his eyes.

"By the way, I'm also grateful that you and Luna

haven't instituted any rules against fraternizing among the staff members."

"Would it matter if we did?"

Hector shrugged. "Not really. We'd just get sneaky about it."

"That's what I thought."

"The dynamic around here is better, now that Dulcie and I have something going. Sexual frustration makes folks cranky. I do believe I suffered from that problem a bit, although I doubt anyone noticed."

"I doubt they did." Colin controlled the urge to laugh. The rest of the staff was overjoyed that prickly Hector had been replaced by mellow Hector. Dulcie seemed quite happy with the turn of events, too.

"It's all coming together," Hector said. "Sybil's ready to take over temporarily when you and Luna are in Scotland, and Janet gets a kick out of bossing around her new recruits in the kitchen." He paused. "Geraldine would have loved this."

Luna walked over, smiling as she approached. "What would Geraldine have loved?"

"All of it." Hector swept an arm to encompass a landscape filled with cheerful guests against a backdrop of green grass, flowers, the bright sea, and a magnificent castle. "She intended to fill this place with family, and when that didn't happen, I don't think she knew how to correct the situation." He gazed at Luna. "But you did."

Luna flushed with obvious pleasure. "Thank the Laird of Glenbarra for taking a chance on me."

Colin knew an opening when he heard one. Walking toward her, he held out his hand. "And I want to thank the Lady of Glenbarra for taking an even bigger chance . . ." He drew her close. "On me."

"Ah, go ahead and kiss her," Hector said. "It'll do you both good."

"I believe it will, at that." Leaning down, Colin savored the sweetness of Luna's mouth for as long as he dared. Then he drew back. "Later, lass."

With a knowing smile, she returned to her guests.

"See?" Hector gave him a sly wink. "Nice to know you have lead in your pencil, isn't it?"

"Yes." Colin willed his erection to subside. "Except when you're wearing a bloody kilt."

Hector's laughter was contagious, and soon Colin was laughing with him. Yes, he thought, Geraldine would have loved this. All of it.

Read on for a look at the next fun and sexy
Wild About You novel by Vicki Lewis Thompson,

WEREWOLF IN DENVER

Available in October 2012 from Signet Eclipse

WERECON 2012:
HOWLERS CHALLENGE WOOFERS

**Exclusive *Wereworld Celebrity Watch* report by
Angela Sapworthy**

(Denver) Excitement mounts on the eve of this
landmark conference, the first of its kind in werewolf history. A star-studded list of attendees from
the far reaches of the globe will gather at the elegant Stillman pack lodge in Estes Park near Denver
this weekend to debate the conference theme,
"Our Future in a Changing Environment."

As readers of *WCW* know, opinion is sharply
divided on the topic. Weres have rebounded after
being hunted nearly to extinction, but their presence as a significant economic force in the major
cities of the world remains unknown to the human community.

Extremely eligible bachelor and Scotsman
Duncan MacDowell, younger brother of Mac-

Dowell pack leader Colin MacDowell, wants that to change. Last spring he founded Werewolves Optimizing Our Future (WOOF), and his wildly popular blog, *Wolf Whistles*, champions his belief that wolves should stop hiding their shape-shifting abilities, openly partner with humans in business, and even consider interspecies mating. Obviously human females would rally to that cause if every male Were looked like Duncan MacDowell in a kilt!

But not all Weres are ready to climb onboard Duncan's bandwagon. This summer the Were blogosphere heated up as Denver-based Kate Stillman, granddaughter of pack leader Elizabeth Stillman, launched Honoring Our Werewolf Legacy (HOWL). Her well-known dating Web site, Furevermore.com, celebrates Were–Were mating as the only way to go. Kate, who claims she's never dated a human, advocates the beauty of tradition and the safety of keeping our secret secure.

But is the tide turning in Duncan's direction? This reporter recently spoke to the Wallace brothers of New York, both of whom shocked the Were community last year by taking human mates. From all indications, their human brides are blissfully happy. And why not, if they share an address with sexy wolves like Aidan and Roarke Wallace?

Despite the apparent success of what's being called the Wallace Experiment, Kate Stillman predicts that such unions spell disaster. Although Emma and Abby Wallace have proven trustworthy, Kate insists the Wallace brothers' behavior may still adversely impact the Were community.

Predictably, Duncan MacDowell calls the Wallaces heroes for bucking tradition.

For months Kate and Duncan have traded barbed comments on their blogs and via our online instant messaging system, affectionately named Sniffer. Adding fuel to the controversy, they've each published best-selling ebooks—available only through Were distribution channels, of course—defending their respective positions.

Duncan's followers (Woofers) are poised to confront Kate's supporters (Howlers) at the conference and will no doubt fill the room during the final session when Duncan and Kate face off in what promises to be a heated debate—and great fun for this reporter! Duncan's last Sniff before he left Scotland was a succinct call to arms: *Woofers, it's on #primedforaction.*

And so am I, my friends! For on-the-spot conference updates and celebrity sightings, be sure to follow me on Sniffer @newshound or #werecon2012. I'll be your eyes, ears, and nose!

To gain an advantage over Duncan MacDowell, do the unexpected, my dear. Meet his flight and disarm him with some old-fashioned Stillman hospitality.

Standing at baggage claim, Kate replayed her grandmother's words and wished she'd argued against the idea. But Grandma Elizabeth had been totally in love with the thought of Kate standing with a sign and a smile when Duncan arrived to collect his luggage. No accompanying staff, no fancy limo.

Okay, the limo wouldn't have worked now that the first snow had hit Denver. The storm had begun around noon, dashing hopes that Denver could get through the month of October without the white stuff. Judging from what had already fallen this afternoon, Kate would need the four-wheel-drive capacity of her Jeep Cherokee to navigate the winding road back to the resort.

The dicey road conditions didn't bother her. She'd been driving on ice and snow for more than ten years. But meeting Duncan MacDowell face-to-face worried her more than she cared to admit to anyone, least of all her grandmother.

Offering friendly hospitality to the Were she'd called a pig-headed radical who had his head up his ass seemed hypocritical. But treating him like a bitter enemy seemed rude. Online interactions were so much easier. Knowing that Duncan would appear in a matter of minutes had her pacing the baggage claim area.

She'd responded on Sniffer to his arrogant last statement—*Woofers, it's on #primedforaction*—with her own challenge—*Bring it, Woofers. Howlers R ready 4 U #firmlyconvinced*. Other Howlers had added equally feisty comments, which had sparked pushback from the Woofers, although nothing had come from Duncan yet.

Thinking of that, Kate checked her cell phone. Sure enough, there was another Sniff from @DuncanMac-Dowell: *Slippery landing in Denver. Can't scare a Scotsman/Woofer #Braveheart*.

Kate rolled her eyes. He was so blasted macho, it was sickening. Tucking the printed sign under one arm, she quickly typed a response. *Just don't get off the plane naked, with your face painted blue.*

The response came almost immediately: *How would you know if I did?*

She answered with a few rapid taps. *Turns out I'm your ride.*

I'm honored.

Sarcastic bastard. She started to type *It wasn't my idea*

and realized that would be ungracious. Her grandmother would disapprove. As she started a new message, she breathed in the scent of masculine Were.

Glancing up, she had no doubt she was eyeballing Duncan MacDowell, in the flesh. Judging from his purposeful stride and intent focus, he'd figured out who she was, too.

"Hello, Kate."

Hearing his rich baritone for the first time felt surreal after months of online communication. And the brogue. Damn, it was sexy as hell.

"Hello, Duncan." She kept her tone neutral but pasted on the smile her grandmother had asked of her. "Welcome to Colorado."

"Thank you." His sculpted lips curved in an ironic answering smile.

As she looked into his eyes, she was momentarily distracted by how beautiful they were—soft gray and elegantly fringed with dark lashes. She quickly reminded herself of his arrogant attitude and reckless stance regarding Were security. He was ready to risk everything for some crazy Utopian dream.

He regarded her with a heavy-lidded gaze that probably had more to do with jet lag than any attempt to be seductive. Yet it sent an unwanted quiver of sexual awareness through her system anyway.

He was taller than she'd expected. The top of her head reached only to his shoulders. And speaking of shoulders, he had broad, powerful ones, the kind that inspired confidence and marked him as a leader.

His hair was longish and his jaw darkened with new beard growth. He could have shaved on the plane if he'd been so inclined. Obviously he hadn't troubled himself.

His rumpled appearance only added to his sex appeal, as if he were silently demonstrating how he'd look after a long night of fabulous lovemaking. She'd read all the nauseating blog comments from his bevy of female admirers, so she'd expected him to be reasonably good-looking. She hadn't been prepared for gorgeous.

Not that it mattered whether he was an Adonis. His physical attributes didn't change the threat he posed to the Were way of life. If anything, they made him a more dangerous opponent.

"I can't say I expected you to meet my plane, lass," he said.

Now would be the time for her to turn on the hospitality spigot as her grandmother had suggested, but sugary words stuck in her throat. "Maybe I wanted to get a preview of what I will be dealing with this weekend."

He surveyed her with those bedroom eyes. "You do realize you're giving me a preview, as well."

"That depends on how much I allow you to see." She hadn't meant that to be a sexual comment, but it sure sounded that way once she'd said it.

His smile widened. "I'm very good at uncovering whatever interests me."

There was that sexual quiver again. She ignored it. "Considering that we're on opposite sides of this debate, I can't imagine I'd be of any interest to you."

"On the contrary. I'm sure you've heard the old saying 'Keep your friends close, and your enemies closer.'"

"I've heard it." But never spoken with a Scottish burr. "Is that why you came to pick me up?"

"No." She finally settled on the truth. "I'm here because my grandmother asked me to come. She thought the gesture would disarm you."

"Oh, it has." His gray eyes took on a wicked gleam. "It most certainly has."

"Bullshit."

He laughed. "I'm not kidding. As tired as I am, I'm easily disarmed, which might have been your grandmother's plan."

"Maybe." Kate decided the time for chit-chat was over. "Listen, we need to get your bags and leave before the snow gets any worse."

"Right." Turning, he surveyed the luggage circling the carousel. He walked over, retrieved his suitcase with athletic grace, and returned to her. "Ready."

He must have been tired, because she managed to talk him into waiting inside the building while she brought the Jeep around. Once they were on their way, he peered past the flapping windshield wipers at the snow that seemed to be flung by a giant hand. "Are you sure it's safe to drive in this? Maybe we should stop somewhere and wait it out."

"We'll be fine." She wasn't about to admit that the snowstorm had become nasty enough to intimidate even her. "I'm used to this."

"If you say so." Leaning his head against the headrest, he closed his eyes, and within seconds was asleep.

Impressed with his ability to surrender control, Kate drove slowly and kept to the plowed sections of the highway. Traffic thinned once they were outside the city limits, and she began to wonder if she'd made the right call. Hers were the only headlights taking the exit road to the resort. And she had several miles yet to go.

Turning back wasn't an option. As long as she moved slowly and didn't hit a patch of ice, they'd get there. She'd always been lucky driving on snowy roads.

But not this time. When the skid started, she did everything she'd been taught so they wouldn't flip, but nothing could have prevented them from plowing into a snow bank, nose first.

The impact woke Duncan, who sat up, startled. "What happened, lass?"

She sighed. "We're stuck."

"Can we get out?"

The wind whistled as snow swirled around the Jeep and blocked the view from all angles. Kate surveyed the situation. It wasn't good. "I don't know. Maybe not."